BIRTH OF A SON...
AND A TEXAS DYNASTY...

Ellie closed her eyes when the next contraction hit. . . .

Half Southworth and half Ewing, she thought, no more Southworths when Ellie was gone. They loved hard and they loved faithful, her Pa and Grandpa. Maybe that meant she wasn't a true Southworth, because she'd turned from one man to another so easy. Here she was a married woman. Yet pictures of her first lover kept popping through her head from time to time. It wasn't like she dwelled on Willard Barnes; she just couldn't keep him out of her memory. . . .

The young doctor and nurse were all smiles when Jock came busting up the stairs, so he knew everything was all right. The bedroom door was open a crack, and as he started for it, Granny said, "Got you a fine, strappin' boy, deserve him or not."

"Thanks, Granny," Jock said. "Oh lord, thank you all."

DALLAS

Lee Raintree

Based on a series created by
David Jacobs,
from screenplays by
**David Jacobs, Arthur Bernard Lewis,
Camille Marchetta**
and **Virginia Aldridge**

A DELL BOOK

Published by
Dell Publishing Co., Inc.
1 Dag Hammarskjold Plaza
New York, New York 10017

Dell ® TM 681510, Dell Publishing Co., Inc.

ISBN: 0-440-11752-6

Printed in the United States of America

First printing—November 1978

Sam Southworth lay dying, and it was the right day for it, dark and drear with lowering clouds and the far-off muted drumbeat of thunder.

There should be whipcrack lightning and louder crashes, Ellie thought, a more fitting tribute to her father and the life he had lived. But then there ought to be so many things—white-hot suns and sandpapering winds, and a way to show dry-mouth thirst and belly-flat hunger. But how could this mournful sky be painted with the pain and sweat, the other dyings on this land, the blood?

He turned onto his back and his eyes opened— washed-out blue eyes that had peered ten thousand miles on the watch for trouble. Beloved face, she thought, stamped with eye wrinkles from staring into blizzard and blistered suns, carved with heavy slashes of determination around the now-sunken mouth, scarred with what he'd wanted and where he had been.

"Anything I can get for you, Daddy?"

Like desert wind over coarse sand, through harsh cactus, his worn-out whisper came: "Whiskey—water."

She hurried, mingled the red-brown and clear, and lifted his head, surprised how thin his hair was at scalp lines and gouges beneath the light silver sheeting. He swallowed, and some of it dribbled from the corner of his mouth, where decades of leaked tobacco juice had left a permanent stain.

The pillow she laid him easy back on was also old, worn shredding thin, her mother's needlepoint raveling, the colors faded. Stronger now, but still no more than the rustle of dried leaves, Sam Southworth said, "Man—man never figures on it happenin' thisaway, bound to his bed."

She didn't know about that, so she waited, bent over, the pain coiled in her.

Her father said, "Ain't so bad, come down to it. Fight it all your life, but then you just get so damned run-down and wore out and hurtin' that you'd go to meet it glad-like."

"Daddy—" she whispered.

Withered and knotted upon the quilt, his blue-veined hand stirred. Ellie covered it with her own, bent her cheek to browned and puckered skin and could not keep a tear from sliding.

"Ain't no shame to cry," the voice said, a soft stirring, like leaves. "Done it once myself, when your ma passed."

The bed shivered and ancient springs rattled, and Ellie clung to his hand, thinking this was the time. Shadows lengthened in the room and she wanted to jump up and light a lamp, but she held to his hand.

And he said, "Ellie—you been a pride to me. You been son and daughter and partner to ride the river with. You been it all, gal."

She wanted to kiss his hand, but that would have bothered Sam, so she brushed her tear against it and sat back, sat up straight.

It was quiet for a long time, so long that she was afraid and leaned closer to hear the rasp of his breath. Then he said, "Now I understand some how them damned Injuns felt; best to be kilt in war than whine on outa' life."

"Y-you never whined, Daddy," she said.

"Nor begged, neither. But I'm askin' a favor now, gal."

"Anything," she said, and never meant it more.

"The ranch," he whispered, the tone and words slipping downhill together, "the land, Ellie. They want to drill holes in my land, my daddy's land. They—they want to stink up the air and spoil the water and turn the grass black. Don't—" His eyes blinked shut and opened with a struggle. "Don't let 'em do it to this land. Promise me that, daughter."

"Yes," she said, her eyes squeezed shut and a rawhide band tightened across her chest. "Yes, Daddy—I promise."

And inside, she pleaded with a God who must be listening, who must now be very near, that she might keep her word.

"Good," he muttered.

When Ellie opened her eyes again, only the flat and hollow shell of him was there.

The rest of Sam Southworth was gone.

(handwritten notes)

The Ewings

Jack Ewing	Jim Davis
Ellie E	Barbara Bel Geddes
Jo.R. E	Larry Hagman
Sue Ellen E	Linda Gray
Bobby E	Patrick Duffy
Pamila B E	Victoria Principal
Lucy E	Charlotte Tilton
Ray Crebs	Steve Kanaly
Cliff Barnes	Ken Kercheval
Liz Craig Pam Boss at the Store	Barbara Babcock

Kristen Shepard - Sue Ellens sister
      maref ~~Herasby~~

mrs Patricia Shepard - Sue Ellens mom
      Martha scott

Degger Barnes - Keenan Whynn
The part was also Played By David
wayne Keenan Replaced him

Donna Culver (Ray's girl)
      Susan Howard

alan Bean - Randalph Powell

Valene Ewing - Lucys mom
      Joan Van ark

gezry Ewing - Lucys Dad
Ted Shackolford

CHAPTER 1

Every barfly, railroad bum, and down-at-the-heels cropper for miles around was crammed into the saloon, bellying up to the bar because Digger Barnes was buying.

Jock Ewing pushed into the crowd, shoved past grinning, unshaven men who'd been given another look at the end of the rainbow. Though they stank of sweat and despair, beyond them was the perfume of raw crude staining Digger's clothes, that promised-land smell of money.

He'd watched this scene a dozen times over, and Jock was tired of it, of paying the bills. Because this nearest saloon was only the start; Digger would spread himself from here, boozing and brawling, whoring and playing poker, and leaving a trail of IOUs as wide as prints on a cattle drive. It would end somewhere between Amarillo and Abilene, with Digger Barnes in a drunk tank, all sick and sorry. But as far as Digger was concerned, why the hell not? Another well waited to be brought in, more black gold to be called forth by his magic touch.

"Yonder he comes!" Digger bellowed. "My buddy, my partner—give him room, you damned roughnecks. Make way for the Midas of Muleshoe County; rich and gettin' richer, long as ol' Digger punches holes in the right places."

He had the heft and holler to stand about nine feet tall, Jock thought; and most of it was gristle and whang leather. Stomping around on a high lonesome after he brought in a well, it seemed like Digger was yay high to a derrick, but when you looked at him frontside-to, there wasn't a loafer in the place didn't top him by a head or more.

Ignoring the glass of red whiskey sloshed at him, Jock said, "You didn't even try to cap it."

"Hell," Digger said. "I only sniff 'em out and bring 'em in. Render unto Caesar what is Caesar's—and the bullshit gang can waddle a cap on her. Ain't blowin' all that much."

"You just couldn't wait," Jock said. "Had to come hootin' into town right off."

Digger spread his feet and threw back his head like a bantam gamecock. "Goddamn! I bring us in a new well, and you start crying over spilt crude. How much is it worth, sixty, seventy cents?"

"Eighty-five a barrel," Jock said, "and as much wastin' on the ground as these bums make in a day—when they make *anything*."

"Oh shit," Digger said. "Lubricate your goozle with some of this stump whiskey and maybe you won't be so goddamn tight. Come fill the cup, for the bird of time has but a little way to flutter—or somethin' like that. What you want out of life, partner? Can't drive but one fancy car at a time; can't eat more'n one bellyful of steak at a sittin'. Guess you can put it to more'n one woman, but when you get down to the short rows, one woman's aplenty."

He nudged Jock in the ribs. "Drink up, man—you already got more money than you'll ever spend, unless you piss it away like me."

Somebody whooped and pounded Digger on the back, and he called for more liquor all around. Somebody else hammered Jock between the shoulders, and he half-turned to put cold eyes on the man until the bum eased away.

He said to Digger, "Ellie rode up, time you left."

"Sticks in your craw, don't it? Quoth the raven, Eleanor—or somethin' like that. Ellie don't fault a man for celebratin'; she knows it's natural."

Jock took a deep breath of cigar smoke, raw whis-

key, and crude. He said, "She came by to say her pa
died in his sleep. Must have been about when you hit
the pool, about time I was runnin' across the county
tryin' to buy up more leases at a reasonable price.
Ellie took her pa's death harder'n she showed."

Blinking, Digger drank from a bottle. "Kind of
figured ol' Sam Southworth to keep on till he was
older'n God. Well, I expect it'll be easier on Ellie
now. She can sell some leases and take the strain off,
and you know somethin'? I can flat out *smell* oil down
on that south forty, where the arroyo comes in from
the west—"

"Damnit," Jock said, "Sam was her daddy, and you
go on about oil when he ain't even buried."

"Listen who's talkin'," Digger said. He took another
long swallow. "*You* the one hollers about gettin' on
with business, and you know damned well Sam Southworth was a son of a bitch could give ornery lessons
to a mule. Ellie knows it too. And everybody knows
the Southfork has just been hangin' on. She needs to
pick up lease money until cows are worth somethin'
again."

Jock got tired of some alky-breath scudder leaning
against him and put an elbow into some ribs. "Sam
wouldn't have a damned thing to do with drillers;
claimed he didn't want his good land stunk up."

"Like you said." Digger grinned. "Sam's dead;
Ellie's a heap smarter."

"You don't know her at all," Jock said. "She's her
pa's girl clear through."

"*I* don't know her?" Digger laughed, head thrown
back.

Jock picked a spot on his partner's chin and damned
near punched it. "Go on, you stupid son of a bitch,"
he said. "Drink yourself rummy, fuck yourself dry,
give the cardsharps all you got, and sign more notes.
There's always another well, right?"

Jaw stuck out, Digger said, "Goddamn right, and
ain't nobody in Texas can find it better. Seek and ye
shall find, but covet not thy partner's woman—or

somethin' like that." He banged the bottle on the bar. "Look, I don't cotton to you and how you do things no more'n you like the way I swing my rope, but we need each other. Leastways, we're already partners and you can't find a better driller nowhere, so I reckon that's it."

Putting his back to Jock, Digger hammered the bar and yelled for more whiskey, more cigars, and where the hell was the action. Jock stared at the broad shoulders for a long moment, then pushed back through the crowd. Near the door, he stomped on somebody's foot, and the man said, "Hey, now—"

Jock leaned all his weight into the short left hook that knocked the man out from under his hat and hurled him into the wall. He hung there for a second, eyes glazed, then slid on down. The throb in Jock's knuckles felt good as he went outside and climbed into the muddied A-Model.

He barreled into the night, slammed and bounced with only his grip on the steering wheel holding him in the truck. Maybe Digger was right and there wasn't a better, or luckier, driller in the country. And maybe second best would do just fine.

He was headed back to the well and the mess there. The crew probably had it capped by now, right enough. Then he could go on to the Southworth place and see Ellie again, see how she was making out. Drawn by bouncing headlamps, moths suicided wet against the windshield as Jock followed the dirt track that wound back through the hills, and he wondered why the hell he'd bothered to go find Digger Barnes in the first place.

Maybe it was that hurt look on Ellie's face when she found he wasn't at the drill site, when she needed so badly to talk out her pain and uncertainty. And now he couldn't go back and tell her Digger wouldn't come; to keep from adding to her load, he'd be bound to lie.

It wasn't the lying that bothered him; lord knows he did enough of that in everyday dealings. The business called for it—you gave your word only when backed into a corner, then you kept it. Lying to Eleanor Southworth was something else. Maybe he wouldn't have to; could be she'd see through all that poetry and show-off to the hollowness Digger Barnes wrapped his shell around.

Christ, why *Ellie?* Sensible, proud woman, come down from Southworths that rode west to fight beside Sam Houston. She was a woman of the land, petite and pretty, straightbacked and determined. Beautiful, too, Ellie was, although not in the frizzy-haired, painted-up style of the day. She let her cornsilk hair hang down her back, or put it up in a bun if it got in the way of work. Maybe she touched her lips and dabbed something to her cheeks, but not the way flappers did. On Ellie it looked natural, like dew on a bluebonnet.

She was natural, damnit; not flighty nor uppity nor play-skittish as a town girl. So why Digger Barnes? She ought to see he'd never amount to anything, that somebody'd stick a knife to him in a fight, or he'd take a header off a derrick, or die squalling and slobbering drunk in a jail. What the hell could a throat-catching, special woman like Ellie Southworth care for in a mouthy little rounder like Digger?

But care she had to; Ellie wasn't the kind to go crawling into the hay barn with just any man. She was a Southworth clean to the marrow, nigh stubborn as her daddy, and she walked in a shining beauty all her own. Jock's hands tightened on the steering wheel as the A-Model hit another chuckhole. How many nights had the thought of her stripping herself down for another man knotted his belly so he couldn't sleep? Dreams of Ellie's sleek flanks and deep breasts, of her glowing power—

"Goddamn," Jock thought, "she'll have to show another kind of strength now, use up her juice on somethin' besides Digger Barnes."

These acres he was driving through right now—and thousands more out of sight, all pretty good grassland, all part of the Southfork—were too much for a woman alone to handle. There'd come a time when cows would be worth something again, but right now they were only hide price, and little enough of that. If old Sam had sold off some oil leases, instead of threatening to let daylight through any boomer who set foot on the ranch, he'd have left Ellie with more than mortgages and a fine old name. Jock grunted; the Southworth name wouldn't rattle worth a damn in a cashbox. Hard money wasn't easy to come by in 1934, even for banks.

Everywhere in the country folks were poor-mouthing and just scraping by. The Depression made the oil fields look like hog heaven, and here they came by the hungry thousands for that five dollars a day. Most never saw it, just as most never heard the rumble of oil come busting up from the ground nor saw the great black gush of it against the sky. For every producing well you hit, nine more were dry holes, dusters that could bankrupt a small company right sudden.

Jock wheeled the Ford around a brushy curve and hit the wheel with one fist. That's what made a driller like Digger Barnes so much in demand. He was damned good and damned lucky, and the combination paid off. For a little independent outfit, EB Oil was doing okay, but with as much of it due to Jock's maneuvering, lease swapping, and such, as to Digger's strikes.

More, maybe, Jock thought; Digger blew money faster than it came in, never worrying about pipe and shipping, about mud, a new donkey engine and drills, about barreling and marketing and trying like hell not to get squashed like a boll weevil by one of the big outfits. When to buy a lease and when to turn it loose quick for a profit, how to wrangle a signature out of some suspicious old bastard without throwing your shirt into the deal—these were important too.

The headlamps picked up the big house, and Jock eased off the gas, surprised he'd come here instead of the well. Cars and wagons and buggies were already pulled up around the Southworth place. There'd be plenty of neighbor women doing for Ellie's daddy, plenty to sit by her during the wake. Tomorrow, the preacher would say words over Sam in the family cemetery yonder on the little knoll, and Ellie might cry some but not make a sight of herself.

Switching off the car lamps and motor, Jock sat a spell in the dark, watching shadows cross the lighted windows of the big old house. And after Sam was put down, what? Would Ellie see it clear to lighten her load by leasing that south forty, or would she bow her neck like her pa and be-damned to stinking oil, ruining country God meant for raising cows?

He'd see that Ellie got what she needed, Jock thought, anything she wanted, as a loan or outright gift. He climbed from the truck and shook his head, knowing damned well Ellie wouldn't accept a gift like that. Drawing a deep breath of night air, he knew he was going to pay his respects, lie like a gentleman to Ellie about Digger Barnes, find sleeping room in the bunkhouse, then stand with her at the burying tomorrow. After that would be time to talk business, because she had to face up to a choice, and setting back, listening to poetry from Digger Barnes, wouldn't help her make it.

She saw him coming across the parlor, tall and browned as any cowhand, sun wrinkles already gathering at the corners of his eyes. Ellie moved slowly to meet Jock Ewing, thinking he'd never really been young, that even as a child there must have been a kind of quiet desperation to him, a drive that set him apart and turned him lonesome.

Twisting a hat in big, square hands, he looked down at her. "Couldn't find him, Ellie. Expect he'll hear the news and come runnin'."

She said, "Hit a gusher, did he? That means Digger won't hear anything but his own voice for a spell. It's his way, Jock."

"His way," he repeated, and she could sense the unsaid things moving in him, words he didn't know how to say, words she didn't want to hear right now.

"Get some coffee," she said, "or have a drink. I appreciate your trouble, and thank you for it."

His hand clamped on hers, and she felt a quick tremble move through him. She said, "I'm right proud you're here, Jock. Pa never had a son to stand with him, just me, and I reckon there's things a man's needed for."

She moved back to the circle of women, to those seamed faces of an older generation, friends of her ma and pa, those eyes more tired now, more worried because another of their own was gone. There were women her own age, too, every one of them married and mothers, or happily swelling with seed.

The whispers faded when she approached, but Ellie knew what they'd been . . . poor girl, having to stay and do for her daddy, work like a man and never had time to look for one . . . less'n you count those oil crews hanging around, and the good lord knows you can't count on *them* . . . reckon now that she's got this whole shebang to run, Ellie's going to forever stay an old maid?

If they only knew, she thought, meeting their eyes and looking sad. She *was* sad. But her pa had been dying for a long time, and she'd only been loved into a woman for a few months. If they only knew, these women already turning dumpy and smug.

Had a single one of them been loved right out in the bright sunshine, loved so deep and hard and long that the world wobbled around and you didn't give a damn if you fell off? And how many of her classmates had known the delicious frightened secrecy of a lover slipping so daringly into her bedroom, with Pa snoring only a wall away?

He knew a woman, Willard "Digger" Barnes did, knew her from nape of the neck to the soles of her feet. He knew to be gentle, to be lingering and loving when other men might go gruff and wall themselves in. And lord, couldn't he make a woman aware of every throbbing inch of her body, and so proud of its doings?

Thinking on that, Ellie went all warm and touchy, then turned some shamed to be dwelling on such happiness when her pa's body was laid out fresh in his box. Lifting her face, she looked across the room and saw Jock Ewing staring at her.

Pa must have been like Jock when he was young, she thought, and Jock would be a heap like Pa when he got older. Both of them silent and stubborn, neither of them speaking out their true feelings, afraid it would somehow make them less of a man to say: *I love you,* or *I need you.* And both men set in their ways, the kind of men who had to spit farther, jump higher, go harder than anybody else. Yet they hadn't given a damn for each other; one was cattle, the other oil, and that ran a barbed-wire fence between them, though it didn't have to be. Other big ranchers straddled the line, kept on running their cows while making money hand over fist on oil too.

Jock Ewing and her pa always walked around each other stiff-legged, like two he-dogs meeting for the first time. Maybe that was because they were so much alike.

Pa had never paid the least mind to Willard Barnes, though; it was like Willard was some heat wave rising off the desert floor, all shimmery and cool-looking as spring water, a mirage that faded quick as you got close up on it. But Pa just didn't know Willard. Ellie kept looking at Jock Ewing across the room until he flushed and turned away.

Or it could be, Pa had taken one quick look at Willard Barnes and *did* know him.

CHAPTER 2

"Your hair," Digger murmured, "has reached out and captured the sunlight, held it close and perfumed it, so the light don't ever want to go back home." He stroked her gently, slowly, his fingers walking from collarbone to breasts and around the bared, stiff nipples.

"And down here—" His hand slid tantalizingly over the flat, pale mesa of her belly.

Ellie stretched languorously and turned toward his embrace.

Digger laughed then. "You were sure spooky about doin' it the first time, right enough."

"Because it *was* my first time, with you or anybody else."

"I know that," he said. "Oh, woman, how sweeter than a serpent's tooth is the heaping of thy belly—"

She said, "You made that up. It's not in the Bible that way."

"Ough to be," Digger said, caressing her. "Song of Solomon is about the only *good* writin' in the whole book. He sure was horny, that Solomon, even though he had him a bunch of wives and concubines."

Ellie crossed her arms over her naked breasts and pressed down. "Like you."

"Never had a wife."

"Am I a concubine, or a mistress?"

Digger's arm went around her shoulders, and pulled her close to nuzzle away her modesty and find the tips of her breasts. "You're my lover, my girl, my woman. If you want to be my wife, that's okay too."

"You mean that, Willard?"

"Ummm," he said, curling his tongue around her nipple, moving his hands just so, and she was caught up in the leaping flame of being naked with him. Everything else spun out of focus, as it always did, and she went whirling into the magic place. There she was someone else, transfigured, released to spread brilliant wings and fly . . . fly. Here there was no drabness, nothing plain about her; she was beautiful because he told her so, made her so. Here she was free, unfettered by tradition and family and man's work always waiting. With Willard she was fully, wonderfully a woman, all her enraptured mind celebrating his touch.

This couldn't be wrong, couldn't be dirty, not the least tainted with any imagined sin the preacher might holler down from his tall pine pulpit. It was too wondrous, all-encompassing; if it was in any way evil she would never go to church again, but stay on the other side.

When he held her close, Willard Barnes was a giant among men; when he was away, he still towered in her memory. Never a short man to her, he was far bigger than anything life had showed Ellie as yet, and so she could forgive him his trespasses. There was so much little boy in him, needing to show off, to brag on success. And as the near-famous Digger Barnes, such hoorahs were expected of him. Ellie understood.

Her daddy wouldn't have wanted Willard at the funeral anyhow, nor anybody else smelling of oil; maybe not even the neighbors who came out of duty and for old times. A hard, taciturn man, Sam Southworth had not been given to sentiment, although there must have been some hidden behind his washed-out blue eyes and sunbaked hide. Sam had never married again after fever killed her mother, and kept his sometime whoring off at a respectable distance. He accepted Ellie as the son he never had and, once she grew out of rompers, treated her as an equal, man to man. Maybe he even loved her.

She'd miss Sam, but there was so much to do. And there was Willard Barnes to fill up any gaps left over from keeping the ranch going. Just as often, there'd be tall, kind of fumbling, Jock Ewing, toeing around on the Navajo rug and asking was there anything he could do to help, anything at all.

As for Digger, it made him feel pretty good knowing he had something Jock would swap his hide and hair for. He considered that all the way back to the rig. Jock didn't stand so goddamned tall when he bugged his eyes and let his tongue hang out over Ellie Southworth. He didn't walk so uppity, nor give orders so sassy, when she was anywhere close. It was just as well, Digger thought, because Jock just about knew the difference between a crown block and a horn socket; he was better off finagling around bankers and slick-talking ranchers out of leases. He was good at scaring up credit when money was tight, and getting the crude shipped, stuff any smart clerk could handle. But none of that was worth a hoot and holler unless the next well came in. And the biggest, the greatest, was yet to come.

Digger could just about taste that whopper, knew the gusher would be bigger than Spindletop, and when he brought it in, his name would sound clear across the land. Wherever wildcatters gathered, wherever roughnecks came together, they'd say the name of Digger Barnes with awe, mixing the truth up with tall tales until he'd be another Gib Morgan, the oilman's legend.

He grinned at the idea of that, and at the faint odor of Ellie's perfume that still clung to his skin, and set about getting the wagons loaded. By now Jock would have talked Ellie into signing all the leases they'd need to drill that south forty. Maybe, just *maybe*, that's where the *big* field would be waiting— the Big Digger, or The Barnes; he liked Big Digger better. It had more of a lasting ring to it.

The A-Model was bouncing across the field, with Jock Ewing steering it. Digger leaned against the load of pipe and waited, listening to the crew work at a balky engine, hearing pipe rattle onto a wagon bed, hearing talk and pumps but not really letting them register. Once a well was in and producing the fun was gone and it was up to others to run it. His job was hunting another, finding the dome that would make him famous; this piddling little old well was just another in a line of nothing-special producers.

The truck pulled up, dust billowing around it and taking a spell to settle, but Jock was out and slapping it off his clothes while it still billowed. "They're cuttin' off our tank cars," he said.

"How?" Digger asked. "Who?"

"Aritex," Jock said. "Don't know how we can stop the sons of bitches either. Railroad claims they got prior orders."

"Too damned big to rear up at," Digger said. "Just sell out to 'em and move on, like always. If it ain't Aritex, it'll be one of the other big outfits."

Jock pushed back his hat with a blunt thumb, exposing lighter skin where the sun hadn't reached. "Not this time. I'm pretty goddamn tired of pullin' in my horns. Been talkin' to a fella about our own refinery, about a pipeline, maybe."

"Talkin' a heap of money too. You get Ellie to sign off that south forty?"

Jock shook his head. "You'll have to make do with the Pardee leases. And Digger—we can't afford any more runnin' drunks; not until everything's paid up. Credit's stretched mighty thin as it is."

Digger yawned. "Want *me* to talk to Ellie? That arroyo looks better'n anything on the Pardee place, and it's closer to a road, do we have to ship refined oil by truck."

"I already talked to her," Jock said, frowning. "She's her pa's daughter, and there's somethin' about old Sam's will and no drillin'—"

"You ain't *me*," Digger said. "Reckon I can get about anything out of Ellie."

Jock stiffened. "The whole damned crew can hear you."

"That ain't what riles you. It's knowin' I'm right. Ellie Southworth—"

Jock hit him then, a winging, solid punch in the mouth that drove Digger stumbling backward and sat him down. The oil-well pump went *ka-chug, ka-chug* and the crew stopped moving around to look.

Coming to one knee, Digger said, "All right, all right." He came off the ground in a rush, arms spread wide and bullet head down, powerful slab of a man hurling himself at Jock.

Jock slid to one side and hooked twice, once over the eye, the other behind the ear. Digger sprawled face down and his legs twitched. He rolled over and got up, slower, more careful. Jock's stinging left hand didn't keep him off long, and he bobbed under the right to land a crunching shot to Jock's ribs, another alongside the neck. Jock staggered back into the load of pipe, caught at a joint, and stayed erect.

Digger moved toward him, hands cocked, blood leaking over his right eye. "Been comin' a long time, I reckon. Can't be but one big dog in the yard."

Slipping to his left and ducking low, Jock got away from the leap. He fisted Digger twice behind the neck before the man could turn. Digger's head rattled against the pipe and he dropped to one knee, wiping at his face. When he turned, it was with a quick savagery that surprised Jock. Digger pulled him down, and they rolled on the ground, kneeing and gouging, hammering and pounding.

Dimly, Jock could hear the well crew yelling, and he thought it strange that he didn't hurt so much. His eyes just kept going in and out of focus, and it was pretty damned hard to catch his breath. Somehow then, he pulled loose, swaying on weak legs and then he was blinking down at Digger and the pipe wrench in Digger's hand.

Wobbling a step, then another, he stomped on Digger's hand, then turned him sideways with a kick and stomped on his ribs. Digger got his head covered up by rolling into a ball, but that didn't stop Jock from trying to cave in his spine.

One of the roughnecks took hold of him and eased him back. "No sense tryin' to kill him, Mr. Ewing. You done took his measure."

"For now," the derrick man said. "Digger Barnes don't stay down."

Sucking for air, trying to hold his voice steady, Jock said, "I'll be in town. At the hotel. Anybody wants to quit with him, can come on in and draw their time tomorrow." He was beginning to hurt all over, hurt like hell, but he held stiff and straight until after he got in the truck and drove off. Then he hunched over the steering wheel and gritted his teeth. Twice before he got to town, he stopped and threw up alongside the road.

In Travis City he made it to his room and soaked in cold water, pouring it over his head until he could think pretty clear. The mirror told him he'd be a mess tomorrow, and he had a sinking feeling in his gut about Ellie Southworth. Well, the hell with it; he'd gotten something out of his system—jealousy, envy, whatever. It might be the fight had little to do with Ellie, that it had been coming to a boil for a long time.

"No, goddamnit," Jock said. "It was Ellie last month and today and it'll be Ellie tomorrow, and if she stays with Digger Barnes, if she leases *him* her land—that's up to her and I'm done with it. Meanwhile I'll just have to find me another driller."

He lay on his narrow bed and stared at the ceiling. The Pardee leases were in his own name, not the partnership's; he'd been thinking on Digger's foolishness for some time, and figured this was the best way to protect them both. Now, though, Digger could find his own way and be damned to him. Jock had paid the man's last gambling debt, his last whorehouse bill. But what would Ellie think of him? He lay sleepless a long time, listening to the town go quiet and feeling his body turn black and blue. That son of a bitch Digger had gotten in some good licks, with the wrench and without; it was lucky he hadn't caught Jock on the side the head.

What the *hell* would Ellie think? What would she do? *Reckon I can get about anything out of Ellie,* Digger had said. But if she gave him leases on land where he wanted to drill, she'd be going against her daddy's will. Jock rolled over slowly and breathed deep against the pain of a cracked rib. There wasn't a court in the state of Texas that wouldn't hold up her right to do it, though. And if she didn't do something before long, the banker would be sticking out his hand for more than she could pour in it. Be a hell of a note, was she to lose the whole Southfork because her daddy was single-minded as a terrapin heading for shade at high noon.

The next morning, half Jock's head was blue, and he could just make out a crack of light through his left eye, but his right eye was clear, and nobody in the café said a thing about his marks, to him or around him. He was being careful chewing bacon when Digger Barnes, Willie B. Jones, and Dutch Feuhauser came in. He saw that Digger looked like he'd fallen off a derrick and been waddled around in a mudhole. Through blue lips like a couple of rolled-up flapjacks, Digger said, "Come for my share of the company; men come for their time."

Sitting back and keeping the water jug close to hand, Jock wrote out checks for Willie and Dutch. "Sorry to see you go," he said.

"Where's mine?" Digger said. "I want a full bigod accountin'."

"You'll get it," Jock said, "over to the bank. Every goddamn IOU of yours I ever picked up is there; every keg of whiskey and all the breakage paid for, all the fines. Off the top of my head, I'd say you got maybe six, seven thousand dollars comin' from this partnership."

Digger slammed a fist on the table. "Chicken

scratch! Six, seven thousand dollars, after all the wells
I brought in?"

"Costs money to operate," Jock said, watching the
three men, "even without you hellin' around the country and sheddin' money like a cow pissin' on a flat
rock. Costs to buy leases, to ship, to drill, replace
equipment—every goddamn thing you never think
about. It's all there at the bank, all figured out."

Marked-up face working, Digger said, "I just bet it
is. You're screwin' me, Jock Ewing, and I ain't about
to take it."

"You can stay with the company and do your share,
and come out way ahead," Jock said, "or haul ass right
now with what you got comin'."

"You poor-mouthin' bastard," Digger said, "*I'll* do
the screwin,' not you. I'll get the leases on that Southfork land, and every time I put the meat to—"

"Shut up," Jock said, bringing up his hand from
below the table with a snub-nosed .38 in it. "Shut up,
you stubby little son of a bitch, or you'll finish talkin'
in hell. Now get out of here, all of you."

They backed a step or two, and turned for the door,
Willie B. Jones and Dutch Feuhauser hurrying, Digger
Barnes deliberately slow. Jock put the .38 back on his
lap under the napkin. After a spell, somebody across
the café said, "More coffee?" and somebody else said,
"Don't mind if I do"—quietly.

CHAPTER 3

He held her locked to him, his legs wrapped around
hers, and it was strange for Ellie to be with Willard
in her own house without worrying about her pa bust-

ing in on them. Downstairs, out of sight and mind, the Mexican servants went about their business like brown shadows.

Willard's sweat was sharper, and his lovemaking had been more anxious, more demanding, and less giving. It was as if he needed to prove something and she was there only as a convenient body. There would be times like this, she understood now, dark and somehow lonely moments when sex wasn't a shared joyousness, but a man's way of striking back at the world—this man, anyhow.

She was sorry for his terrible, swollen face and the blue-black clots along his ribs, but it wasn't the time to say so. A stifled rage still crawled inside him, writhing and impotent. Ellie tried to stroke it away, trailing her fingers down the knotted muscles of his broad back, stroking his haunches until he relaxed a little.

"I don't need him," he said. "It's the other way around. Ewing can't find oil without me; he don't have the know-how, and he sure don't have the luck. The thievin' bastard left me enough for a start, and they know I'm lucky, the bankers. They'll credit me for what else I want. If you help me first, Ellie."

She said, "You know I will."

Turned to her, arm across her belly, he said, "I can smell oil on that piece of land I showed you before, when the ground rises just so and falls just so. That means there's a big old pocket of black gold just waitin' for me to drill down to it; no more'n a thousand feet, I'd say."

Ellie wondered what had brought on the fight between her lover and big Jock Ewing; she didn't want to think it was herself. She said, "How long will it take, Willard?"

He came up on one elbow. "The drilling? Can't never say for certain; depends on how much and what kind of rock we hit, a lot of things. If you're willin' we can go into Travis City in the mornin' and make it all legal."

"No need for that," she said. "You can have whatever you want."

Tenderly, he kissed her. "I know that, darlin'. Damn! If my mouth didn't hurt, I'd kiss you all over, just for bein' so sweet and givin'. But the bank needs to see it on paper; oil leases—they're just about like money in this neck of the woods."

"Whatever you say, Willard."

Chuckling, he said, "You know what Jock Ewing told me? That you were ol' Sam Southworth all over again, and wouldn't let the Southfork get spoiled by drillers. That's *another* goddamned mistake he made, and I'm goin' to rub his nose in it. He's got so much tied up in startin' his own refinery and layin' out a pipeline, that if the Pardee field *don't* come in, he's in bad trouble."

Ellie said, "Do you hate him so much?" She thought, And do I love you so much? She was remembering her promise. But she knew the answer was yes. There was nothing she would not give Willard Barnes, did she have it to give. And the land was what she had. All she had.

Digger rolled onto his back and winced. "Never really cottoned to him. It's like he's got somethin' eating away at him, somethin' that makes him get up earlier and go to bed later'n anybody else. He ain't never goin' to get enough of anything. If he goes broke on the Pardee field, he'll be out beggin' nickels and dimes to start all over—and I sure hope he has to."

"You've been together a long time."

"Too damned long. He can go his own way, see how long he lasts. The hell with him, Ellie; forget Jock Ewing. Think about us."

"I am," she said.

"It's findin' my wife to serve papers on her," he said. "Soon's I bring in a well, I'll put men onto findin' her, I swear."

"Willard," she said, "did you ever really love her?"

He grunted and put one hand to his face. "Hell, no. I was just a horny kid and she was a hot lil' Mex knew it all, and lookin' to stay in the States. Marry in haste and repent thee forever—or somethin' like that." Then, with the grin she never could resist: "We're goin' to be different, you and me, 'cause look at what we got goin' for us at leisure—all this good country lovin'."

She went into town with him and signed the leases, stood by while Willard Barnes talked credit out of the banker, then stood by some more until he gathered a crew and ordered his equipment.

"Gonna use that Mex houseman of yours, that Manuel, to help build the derrick," he said, helping her back into the buggy. "Noticed he's passable handy with a hammer. Oh damn, honey—you go on back to the house; I got to get a mud wagon lined up. I'll catch a ride out on the pipe truck."

She smiled at him, at his eagerness and bustle, at how cheerily disorganized he was. And as she trotted the horses back out to the Southfork, she wondered if he really would get everything going. Willard didn't seem a man for details; he kept running off in too many directions at once. But that was part of what made him Willard Barnes, and Ellie was just as glad she didn't see Jock Ewing in town that day; she felt just a little uncomfortable about facing him. He must have been carrying a mean grudge for quite a spell, to stomp on Willard that way.

Clucking to the horse as the buggy rounded the last curve before the ranch house would come into view, Ellie thought again that she may have been part of the bad blood between Jock and her lover. A woman knew by the way a man looked at her, could sense the want in him, and although Jock Ewing did his best to hide it, when he was around her he gave off an aura she could recognize.

It was the same thing she's known in Willard, except Willard didn't shuffle around and back off. He came straight ahead, talking so pretty, acting so easy and knowing and gentle. But he didn't say he was married until after the first time she gave herself to him. It wouldn't have made any difference, Ellie admitted; she loved him so much by then that his wife could have been within hollering distance.

Ellie drove around back to the stables, where Manuel appeared to take the horse. She used the buggy because she liked to, and it wasn't far to town, but when Willard started spudding in the well, she'd take the Ford truck. Her pa'd been partial to the truck, because in good weather it covered more ground than his best horses could, though it had taken him a while to face up to the change.

Walking to the house, she murmured, "Takes all kinds of changes to keep goin', Pa." Bringing in a well wouldn't hurt more than a few acres; better that, than sitting and waiting forever for the beef market to jump. Maybe it wouldn't *ever* jump. And maybe this wasn't exactly what Sam would've done, but it was Ellie's way.

"*Señorita?*" asked a soft voice from the kitchen, as Ellie passed.

"*Nada*, Lupe," Ellie said. "Just talkin' to myself. Be gettin' bad as Pa was, if I'm not careful." She went through the side door and upstairs to lie across her bed, not sleepy but wishing Willard back. With her.

Funny thing, she thought, if she'd have figured it to come down to a fight between Willard and Jock Ewing, she'd have put her money on Willard.

The president of the Travis City bank made a steeple of his fingers and looked over them at Jock. "Be a big thing for this town, was it to come off."

"It has to come off, C.J.," Jock said. "It's the only thing that makes sense for us little independents. I'll refine it right here and run it out through the pipeline to the rail spur. Makes it all move quicker and cheaper. And Travis City gains by a hundred jobs—more, later on."

"I ain't arguin' you," the banker said, "but I'd as soon Aritex Company don't know you're gettin' backing from me."

Jock used the bank's money and his own money, and all he could squeeze from other independents who were running as scared as he was. He kept busy, kept moving, so that about the only time he thought of Ellie Southworth was when he dropped across the bed at night, too tired to undress. Or fell asleep at the wheel of the truck, or on a tarp at the refinery site.

Nobody ever knew where to expect him, and that was good. He came up on a pair of Aritex's hired men just as they were about to torch the toolshed as warning for men not to work for Ewing Oil. Jock's message was clearer, one everybody in that part of Texas could understand: he shot both men through the legs and left them hollering for help in the street. Then he went out and hired better men to ride shotgun on his pipeline and to watch over the spidery steelwork of the refinery as it climbed skyward, bulging and taking shape.

Aritex didn't see fit to back down right off. The company was used to having its own way, and running over anybody who happened to be standing in the road. Despite Jock's guards, some sections of the uncompleted pipeline were blown up; a well caught fire; truck tanks had sugar dropped into them.

Sheriff Marston Browne said, "Reckon you're right about who's doin' it, Jock—but knowin' ain't provin'."

"Nothing you mean to do, then?"

"You know how it is, Jock."

Jock said then, "Long as *you* know. Weather's coolin' some; might be a good time to hunt wild hogs south of the river."

Marston Browne lowered his polished boots from his desk top. "You gettin' pretty big, mister, but I don't reckon you growed big enough to tell me what to do."

"Sheriff," Jock said, "all I mean to do is go back in the hills and talk it over with the McCreadys; you know how hammer-headed that bunch can get when they're provoked. And the Jessups—them that shoots at anybody so much as leaves a footprint on their land.

Oh, yeah, and the Whitsons. Seems the last time they got riled, Travis City was some tore up, to include a couple of deputies."

Browne rubbed his chin, then got up and reached for his Stetson. "Didn't know all them folks stood with you, Jock. I expect you're right about them hogs acrost the river; they need thinnin' out, and it'll take a spell."

The next day, a string of tank cars blew up. That night, a truck convoy hauling Aritex pipe vanished; the drivers called in three days later, from another state.

A few Aritex administrative men were roughed up; others got the message and sought jobs elsewhere. Rig crews went missing or got taken down drunk, so that strings of tools were lost and accident rates climbed. When Aritex sent in new people, they arrived nervous and got shakier; it was easy for them to make costly mistakes.

Back East, the board of directors came to the conclusion that bank statements made more sense than blood feuds, and the word went out: the independents were to be allowed their nibbles at the loaf. Sheriff Marston Browne came back from his Mexico vacation and folks around Travis City figured Jock Ewing had grown tall enough to be seen clear from the county seat. Wouldn't be too long, they said, before they could make him out from Austin too.

On the Southfork, untouched by the brief war, Digger Barnes had the derrick torn down and started spudding in a new site. He'd pushed too deep on the first drilling, so damned sure that oil lay just a few feet farther down, just a few more feet. He wasn't used to dry holes; dusters were for other drillers, not for a man with a legendary nose for oil. So the pool just *had* to be down the arroyo, waiting for him. All the signs were there, pointing the way to riches, a big anticline where rock folded into a big land bump.

"It'll be bigger than anything I ever brought in for that damned Ewing," he promised Ellie. "Just you wait, girl; they think *he's* big, head of the independents and all that? When I bring in this field, all they'll be able to talk about is the Big Digger. Hundred thousand barrels a day, it'll be, just this one well—Burkburnett, Hogtown, Mexia—none of 'em will be remembered next to the Big Digger."

"You'll make it," Ellie said, and hoped so with all her heart. The bank wouldn't give Willard any more money, and the last two cattle shipments had just about paid off his crews and the Southfork hands. Beef just wasn't bringing a price, and the market didn't look any better for next year. If the coming winter was a hard one and she had to buy outside hay, and the calf crop came up short—

"Don't you fret, honey," Digger said. "Long as you're with me, I can't lose. A rosebud set with little wilful thorns . . . and sweet as Texas air can make her, she . . . or somethin' like that, accordin' to Tennyson." Then, grinning: "Soon's I get this dirt off me, I mean to get scratched by some of those little wilful thorns."

But his lovemaking had changed, even though Ellie sensed him trying to take it back to the sometimes wild, often gentle, always sweet thing they'd had before her pa's death and Willard's break with Jock Ewing. She hit the crests with him, went rioting off among the stars, but it seemed the tidal waves weren't as high and powerful, that the trips into blinding space were shorter, so that she came back to earth quicker. Maybe that happened after a while, like with old married folks getting tired of each other. But it might be Willard's worry over the dry hole—and her own about what would happen if the next was a duster, too.

Digger had been a week on the new location when a trucker brought word of the Pardee strike. "Twenty thousand barrels from the first well, they say, and three more drills a-goin'. Looks real good, but damned if Jock Ewing ain't got every square inch of land tied up for ten mile around, and can't nobody get in on the bonanza."

"By rights," Digger said, "half that strike belongs to me. I was partners with him when we bought them leases."

"Too bad you ain't still partners," the trucker said. "Ewing Oil's gettin' so fat and sassy it's just about runnin' the show."

"This strike will put Ewing in the shade," Digger said.

"Hope so," the driver said, "because I ain't carryin' no more pipe until I see some hard money."

Digger glared at the man. "You'll get paid, damn it! Go on, haul ass outa here. You're just like all the rest, suckin' up to Ewing and hopin' to ride his shirttail, but Jock Ewing ain't goin' to be nothin', you hear me —nothin'!"

"If you say so," the driver said, and gunned away the empty truck, spewing dust behind. Fine and dry, the stuff left a gritty taste in Digger's mouth.

That evening, Digger stayed late at the site, feeding in the mud himself, running a check on the sand every hour or so. There'd be shale soon, he was certain, and the porous stuff that would lie just above hard-rock that trapped the pool.

The moon came up and his crew knocked off, but Digger kept at it alone until his legs trembled with fatigue. Only then did he shut down the engine and drive back to the ranch house. He didn't go upstairs to Ellie but fell asleep on the sofa, wearing everything but his boots.

In his dreams, the Pardee field sprouted one gusher after the other, all capped quickly by Jock Ewing's use of the Christmas Tree, a gadget most wildcatters never bothered with. Black and rich, the spouts were sky-tall geysers, raining into pure gold when they hit the ground. The Pardee field, which ought to be half his. *He'd* picked it as a likely location, not Ewing. Damn, damn—the Pardee field, while the Big Digger was still just out of reach, and that bastard Ewing was laughing his ass off. Fat and sassy, Ewing Oil, slowly buying out or pushing out the smaller outfits, trying to turn into a giant like Aritex. Horseshit—Ewing had just been lucky this time. Next time around, all he'd see was a string of dry holes.

Like the Big Digger?

Digger came awake sweating, and kicked off the quilt somebody'd laid over him during the night. The thick, dusty taste was still in his throat, and coffee the Mex maid gave didn't cut it much until he poured in some whiskey.

He had a smile for Ellie when she came down to breakfast, and made little jokes about getting so old he couldn't make it up the stairs. The Mex girl, Lupe, served an omelet that had too damned many chilies in it, and he told her so. Ellie sat there at the head of the big table where her pa used to sit, looking calm and golden and pretty as all get out. For some reason, this infuriated him, but he choked down anger with the omelet and biscuits.

Then Ellie said, "If we strike oil, will Jock Ewing let us use the pipeline and refinery?"

"He's just head of the independents," Digger grated, "not God Almighty."

"Jock owns most of the stock," Ellie said, "in the refinery and pipeline both."

Digger stared at her. "Seems you know a heap about Jock and his business."

"Can't help but know," she said. "Everybody's talkin' about him and how fast he's come up."

"You ain't everybody," Digger said. "But if you mean to gossip along, make sure you tell how he did me out of my share of the Pardee field."

She looked at him. "Did he?"

CHAPTER 4

"I'm sorry," Ellie breathed. "What can I do to help?"

Digger sat naked upon the edge of the big bed, looking into the fireplace where green oak wood was banked with dry kindling to hold the fire through the night. "It's okay," he said. "It'll be all right. I just been workin' so goddamn hard and long—"

"Yes," she said. "You're tired and worried."

"Not all that worried. The pool's there; I *know* it. The bit's gone through sandstone, sedimentary rock. If we hadn't had trouble with the kelly and that old casing, I'd've brought in the well already. Damn! That sandstone has the *taste* of oil in it."

"You'll do it," Ellie said. "If anybody can do it, you can." She caressed his back, trailed fingers down to his hips.

"Keep workin' with old pipe, beat-up casing, tryin' to make do with bits that just about chewed off their teeth. Damnit—if I had half the money Ewing's rakin' in, if he'd just give me my share of the Pardee field, I wouldn't have to scuffle this way."

She placed a lingering kiss upon his backbone. "Forget the Pardee strike, Willard; it's his and he won't let go any part. It's you and me and the Big Digger field, right?"

Slowly, he began to expand under her teasing, but only so far, only so long.

"That time me and Ewing went to fist city—some of it was my fault," he said. It was a hell of a note, he thought; beautiful woman willing—no, *wanting*, and he couldn't get it going. Never happened to him before, Digger thought. Hell, any woman along the border could tell you what a man Digger Barnes was, how he was just about the horniest he-coon in all Texas and half of Mexico.

He kept talking to conceal his embarassment. "Owe you an apology over that, I reckon. Kind of bad-mouthed you to Ewing—oh, not right out by name, and not direct, but he sure as hell knew who I was talkin' about. Made him jealous and poked him madder'n I figured he could get. Still can't think what the hell he poleaxed me with; must have been a rock or somethin'. Didn't make a heap of difference, though; I was beatin' his drum with a wrench."

Ellie said, "Lie back. I don't much care if Jock Ewing is jealous or not. I'm right here with *you,* and it's where I want to be. Lie back, honey—please."

He jerked away from her. "I'm *tired,* goddamnit! Nothin' wrong with me but I'm worn out." Digger put his back to her as he stretched out, hoping she'd fall asleep. Maybe it was her waiting so patiently for him to bring in the well, or laying her in this house, where the gaunt, forbidding shadow of old Sam Southworth still lingered.

It could be caused by a whole lot of things, Digger admitted as he lay there wishing to hell she'd turn off the light. He wouldn't put it past the Mex servants to snoop and pry, and wouldn't *this* be something to put on the gossip swap in town? A man couldn't be blamed for having his mind somewhere besides between a woman's legs.

Like how damed rich Jock Ewing was getting, and the way he was buying up smaller independents one by one, gulping them down like a rattler swallows field mice. What the hell more did Jock want—to be big as Aritex, another oil giant owning land far as the eye could reach and all the men who walked it?

Digger couldn't understand ambition like that. It just didn't make sense to him. The fun wasn't in own-ing, but in finding and spending. Good lord, there were untapped wells waiting from here to yonder and back, in places nobody had even thought of yet, down in South America, across the seas in other countries. If you just latched onto everything to hand and hunkered down over it, you'd never even get to see any of those other fine places.

Digger could understand how the old-time ranchers felt, when more and more people started putting in barbed wire and cutting everything up with fences: this chunk is mine, and that one is yours. With all that great, rolling country out there, it wasn't seemly to be squabbling over one little piece or another.

Could be all of it was turning him less of a man with Ellie, because Eleanor Southworth sure as billy hell was wedded to her land and wanting him tied down to it, too. But he wasn't a substitute for her daddy and never would be. The Barneses had never owned anything but their hats, and always cropped for somebody else, until he came along. They moved here and got moved there, but it didn't take him that many years to find there just wasn't any future to looking up a mule's ass and hollering gee-haw. He took to the road and the rails and wound up in the oil fields.

The first gusher he saw come in, it was like those heroes in books finding treasure. He was always reading whenever he could get hold of a book, borrowing one when he could, stealing when he couldn't. But he learned about oil from riggers and roughnecks and derrick builders; he learned by peeping over a driller's shoulder and watching how the samples were tested, by getting the feel of land where oil lay hidden below. And bigod, he wasn't an old man when he got his own drilling job. Not with Jock Ewing; that came later, after he already had a reputation established.

He could tell by Ellie's breathing that she wasn't asleep, so he said, "You know, it didn't take me long to make it as a driller. Bet I was the youngest driller anywhere, but nobody was afraid to take a chance on me after my first two strikes. Damn—those wells came in so pretty, it was like storybooks. And I didn't have to be no college geologist to find the pools, neither."

"The storybooks," Ellie murmured, not touching him now, only the heat of her body so close that it reached out. "What kind did you read, Willard?"

"Anything; everything. Trouble was, most of them ended where the guy married the princess and got half the kingdom and lived happy ever after. I couldn't see that, so I started in on poetry."

"Couldn't see living happy every after?"

He turned onto his back and his thigh brushed hers. "Not if it meant just hangin' around and doing nothin', or whatever princes do. A man needs to see new places, find new wells. Just bein' rich would be borin'. Hell, I get tired spendin' money after a couple of weeks. Can't imagine havin' to keep on with it. Like the book says, while some coveted after money, they pierced themselves through with many sorrows—or somethin' like that."

Ellie said, "Money gets bigger when you're short of it."

Digger's jaw tightened. "I aim to see you don't get short. It won't be long now—two, three more days at the most. We'll be in hard-rock by tomorrow, the lid trapping that pool. She'll blow in soon after, the crude pushed up by gas or water—I ain't sure which yet, but I'd lean to gas."

Carefully, Ellie said, "Willard, the Southfork, the land—it's important to me. I wouldn't feel right if I had to sell even an inch of it. Southworths bled for this land, died on it; a lot of 'em are buried here, like I mean to be."

Slamming his hand against the bed, Digger said, "Damnit, I already told you—"

"If this well is dry, too," Ellie went on, "neither of us can help it. I just wanted you to know I feel about my land the way you do about your oil wells—partly the same, but partly different. The land will always be here; the oil won't."

"Oh, for chrissake, Ellie! You sound like all the busted-up, sunbaked old Texans I ever saw—land and cows, cows and land, as if there ain't anything else and never will be. Jesus, look around you. Look at Travis City and that big refinery Ewing's puttin' up; then look at the cattle market and tell me which one means something'."

"The land," she said. "The good, solid land. It lasts, it goes on. People turned nigger-rich with oil money, they don't stand any taller than they did before. Look at *them*—little bitty scrub landholders, storekeepers, even drummers who saw a chance to make a dollar on oil leases. You think that makes them good as anybody in Muleshoe County, good as folks that fought Comanches and Apaches for this land? Trash with money is still trash, Willard."

He rolled off the bed and jerked on his drawers, his shirt, and overalls. She was silent behind him, and he didn't give a damn now that he couldn't lay her. "You mean roughnecks like me," he said. "Poor damn croppers, railroad bums; anybody didn't come out here with one hand on his scalp and the other on a Winchester."

"No, I don't. I mean trash and you never were, never will be."

He jammed his feet into boots. "Goin' back to the well."

"No need to run from us, Willard. Best we say what's botherin' us."

"Somethin' botherin' *you?* Ain't much troublin' me." He wanted to turn around and slap at her, grab the goddamn bed and turn it over, throw the lamp through the window—something.

Ellie said, "Whatever happens with the well, it can be worked out, Willard. Somethin' can be worked out."

She was too good, too damned sweet, and he didn't know any poetry to fit the moment. He said, "Just let me be for a spell, woman. Don't try to ear crop me till I'm ready."

He was already in the hall when she said from

behind him, "I didn't *try* to cut you, Willard. If you're gelded, you did it to yourself."

Damn her, goddamn every shiny inch of her body and every unsuspected, hidden turning of her woman's mind. He'd show Ellie Southworth when he brought that black semen boiling out of the ground like it was roaring up from a pair of swollen balls. He'd make her wallow in it. Damn her and those bluebell eyes of hers, so innocent, yet searing as noonday August sun.

He'd get Ellie down in the warm crude and rub it into her, over her sunshine hair, so that she would stink of oil and it would be perfume. Digger Barnes would show her who carried a set of big nuts in his sack. She had no call to name him gelding just because he didn't put it to her every blessed night in the week. . . . O woman! Thou were fashioned to beguile; so have all sages said, all poets sung. . . .

And to be a burr under the saddle; a woman like Ellie now—she might as well wear big, Mexican rowel spurs when she wrapped her legs around him, because she not only meant to mark a man, but hog-tie him and keep him in the feedlot. Digger Barnes wasn't ready to stand at stud and raise up a bunch of younguns.

But as he went out into the dry coolness of the night, as he keyed the ignition on the solid-tired truck and turned on its lights, he knew damned well he wasn't about to come up on any other woman that suited him better. Maybe he could talk to her, get it settled so she'd know he meant to come back when it was time to pasture. She'd have her ranch to run, and royalty money from the well to see to; he could even spud in a couple of more holes close by to keep the Southfork solvent long as Ellie wanted to strut her stuff at bossing a ranch. But he had to breathe free. He had to.

At the Alamo Hotel, Jock Ewing licked at his long golden cigar and sat back while a waiter held a match to it. He blew out mild blue smoke and thought he could acquire a taste for these Havanas, but only after a big dinner. They didn't have the honest, satisfying bite of a quirly rolled from Bull Durham or Duke's Mixture.

He looked down the table at the pale, fat faces and thought of the power gathered here—not cheap and sweaty muscle but power stronger than steel drills and railroad engines. Yet all that strength held glasses of brandy delicately, or puffed easily on cigars. Now some of it glanced over at Jock Ewing, waiting.

"Gentlemen," he said, repeating it as the conversation diminished, "I realize as well as you that Ewing Oil is just a two-bit outfit alongside Aritex and the other big companies. But I can speak for other little independents—Domestic, Sam Houston, and the like; lumped together we have a few acres under lease. Not like Aritex's five million—"

At the other end of the table, Aritex's representative, a faded, eyeglassed little man smiled. "Closer to six million, Mr. Ewing."

"Thank you, Mr. Robinson. Thing is, part of Aritex's production is runnin' through Ewing pipe, like everybody else around here. And that's good; that's just fine. We ought to cooperate, 'cause there's enough for everybody—right now."

They caught his hesitation, and the state senator said, "You mean there's danger of a shortage, Mr. Ewing?"

"If we don't take care," Jock said. "Folks once thought the buffalo would last forever, but they didn't. That's why I'm askin' everybody here to go along with the new conservation statute and planned spacing of wells. Driving one shaft down right next to another gets more oil right now. But what about next month, next year? We have to think of the future, gentlemen."

A red-faced man leaned forward, elbows on the table. Jock ran through the file cards of memory and came up with a name: Mellin. The man said, "And keepin' down any reduction of your own production at present. How you goin' to stop them little outlaw outfits from pumpin' what they want and shippin' when they like?"

"Senator Connally here has been most helpful on that," Jock said. "His bill just passed the senate, and the Connally Hot Oil act prohibits the transportation of illegally produced oil from one state to another."

Mellin grunted. "That's all well and good, but who enforces that law? You got enough Texas Rangers ain't doin' anything else?"

Bowing to his right, Jock indicated a big-bellied man with silver hair and a pigeon-blood ruby ring about big as a real pigeon egg. "Colonel Thompson will take care of that, since he's head of the Texas Railroad Commission. Oil has to be got out by tank car, or not at all; the highways are easily blocked."

"Good enough," Mellin said around his cigar. "But some of them little outfits are sure goin' to get their backs up at you, Ewing. You been one of 'em, but now you outgrowed 'em and they won't like it."

"They have to like it," Jock said, "or haul their crude in trucks, and to some other refinery, but *in* the state."

Senator Connally laughed big and bold, his chins bobbing. "Any time you want a shot at a political office, Jock—damned if you ain't got the stomach for it."

Jock grinned at him as if at an accolade, then looked over at Aritex's field agent. "But I also got the good sense to know how easy a puffed-up horny toad can outgrow his own patch of sand. That's when somethin' bigger slips up on him, like a lazy ol' Gila monster maybe, and *zing!* There goes a horny toad got too fat and sassy and wound up a quick dinner. Thing is, that speckledy ol' Gila, he wouldn't even have noticed the horned toad if that lil' booger hadn't come hoppin' around where it didn't have no protection."

The Aritex man fiddled with his glasses, his worn-out banker's face serious. "I see you've made a study of horned toads, Mr. Ewing."

"More like I studied up on Gila monsters and rattlers, bobcats, tarantulas, and them big desert scorpions; even cactus and alkali water holes—whatever can hurt a man real quick, does he bite off more'n he can digest without lookin' careful over one shoulder."

"Quite," said Mr. Robinson, the Aritex representative.

And when they'd all shaken hands and said how smart it was for everybody to get along, instead of fighting like tomcats with their tails knotted and tossed over a clothesline; when the smoke hung blue lonesome in thick air, Jock Ewing took a bottle up to his room. Travis City was getting too small for all this, he thought, too countrified. Dallas, maybe—it had all the earmarks of a town that would grow big and important some day, and it wasn't so far a man couldn't keep in close touch with everything here.

That sickly looking Robinson bastard come all the way out from New York. Little shit looked like a hangman and probably was, but Robinson had been soothed for now. Jock didn't mean to lock horns with Aritex, or Sinclair, or the Texas Company. Or any outfit that could come down on him like a landslide if he irritated it too much. They knew he'd fight to keep his territory and were willing to let him have that much, provided he didn't get too big for his britches. People back East might not even understand a wildcatter who wouldn't stop at killing to hold his own. If the bankers and Wall Street manipulators thought on it some more, they might also realize a crazy bastard like that played by his own rules and could turn the whole thing personal.

He sipped good bourbon with his boots off and shirt open, with stockinged feet propped on the bed while he leaned back in a chair. It was good, but the night wasn't filling. There was a hole in it, and Jock looked out the hotel window toward where the Southfork lay, wrapped in darkness and sleep.

Or moving sinuously, whispering, making little squeaking noises on a bed?

No. He shook his head and took a long drink from the bottle. That hammerheaded Digger would be out yonder, breaking his crew's backs and his own heart, trying to bring in oil where there wasn't any. The Southfork leases were a loss; one duster behind, another dry hole coming up.

Jock wasn't a damned bit sorry for Digger Barnes; the mashed-down little bastard always thought he knew it all, and it was time he stepped in a gopher hole and busted his ass. But Ellie—she was something else. He knew how deep she was into the bank, how badly the last cattle shipments had gone, how many of the hands were behind on their pay. He knew a heap about Ellie Southworth's business, and was paying to learn more—the minute anything happened.

CHAPTER 5

Billygoat Smith said it first: "Let it go, Digger. It's a duster and that's the end of it."

"No damnit! Another hundred feet, maybe less—"

Walker Johnson said, "If'n we had the pipe and drills, wouldn't do no good, Digger. Look at the samples, man—through hard-rock and back to porous and nothin'."

"What the hell do you guys know?" Digger hurled the core sample off the platform. "*I'm* the witch; *I* know where oil is and where it ain't, and I say it's down there."

"Halfway to China, maybe," Billygoat said. "Look, Digger—we all knowed we was takin' our chances along with you, and it's our tough luck we don't get paid for the last two weeks. But a man's a fool that throws good time after bad, and if you wasn't so hard-headed set on bein' right, on provin' yourself to Miss Ellie—"

"Latch your mouth," Digger said fiercely, "or I'll—"

"No slight meant to her, nor you neither," Billygoat said, "so stay back from me, Digger Barnes. You'll have to whup us all."

"*All* of you? Johnson, Pastor, Kelly—all of you quittin' on me, givin' up when we're so close?"

"Only makes sense," Walker Johnson said. "They're hirin' at the Pardee field, or over to the refinery. No hard feelings, Digger. You'll do better next time."

"Fuck you," Digger said. "Fuck all you quittin' bastards. Go on—sell out to Ewing; hurry up and kiss his ass; maybe he'll throw you two bits once in a while."

Billygoat Smith shook his scarred head. "Hard times and hard luck, Digger. Was it anything else, I reckon I'd be buttin' you into the middle of next week. Let it go, man; turn this loose and take hold somewheres else."

Digger watched them gather their stuff and ride off in Walker Johnson's rattletrap A-Model. He stood alone on the platform, listening to wind whistle derisively through the derrick. The donkey engine was still, the arroyo gone silent. Everything was too damned quiet. Even at a funeral there was some kind of noise, if it was no more than a woman sniffling.

He stomped down on the green-milled boards of the platform. The sound they gave back was hollow, like dry dirt clods hitting a coffin. They were right, goddamn them, right to go off and find jobs that paid, right about this duster. Twice in a row, dry holes. The lay of the land was good, the signs all pointed to a producing well, and nothing, damnit—*nothing!*

The bank would send out to pick up anything it could get some money back on, but he wouldn't give them the truck until they ran him down and took it. The stuff would all sell to Ewing at bargain prices. Trust Jock to be sitting there like a goddamned buzzard, waiting to peck out the eyes of the Southfork corpse.

Ellie, he thought, Ellie—every dime she could raise without selling off land had gone into these dry holes. All his money, too—what little Jock Ewing had left him with. But Ellie mattered more; the ranch meant so much to her. Maybe she could cut down the herd some more and still carry enough brood stock for next year.

Shoulders drooping, he climbed down and got into the truck, but sat there without turning on the motor. He was kidding himself; the Southfork was in hock all the way. What the hell could he tell Ellie, now that the promises were all worn out and blown away like the dust from those holes?

Breaking the silence, a cricket chirped, not knowing frost would soon kill it; a bullbat loosed its deep-throated cry, searching for insects also soon gone. And what the hell did bullbats do when there were no bugs to eat? Digger could just make out the outline of the derrick. Against blackening sky, it looked more like a scaffold. It wasn't right and it wasn't fair to come this far and lose, just when it meant the most.

All those childhood nights with nothing in his belly but poke greens flavored with a little fatback; cold Oklahoma mornings when breakfast was a biscuit and flour gravy; and wrapped for school in the same stained brown bag, another biscuit with a slice of raw purple onion on it, or a hole filled with molasses and replugged. Hell, a boy had to get away from barefoot and damned near bare-assed, and the nearest escape was into pages where poor, honest knights got to ride off with the golden-haired princess.

But you couldn't eat storybooks, either, and after a spell of following that goddamned mule, a couple of years of looking over at his pa in the next field, dragging along with his head down and a permanent crook in his back, anything had to be better for young Willard Barnes.

Rising wind, colder now, mourned through the

frame of the dead derrick, and Digger saw the boxcars again, felt the icy rattle of them again. If you got caught out on a flatcar, or coal car in the winter mountains, some railyard bull rolled a stiff corpse off where it wouldn't bother anybody and he didn't have to make out a report on it.

But there were things nearly as bad as freezing on some high lonesome. There were the old jocks, meaner than the dried shit in corners of the car, and carrying single-edged razor blades worked into a stick of soft pine. They were bad on kids, raping them and sometimes keeping them for weeks, like wives. If you wouldn't drop your overalls, they'd come at you with those goddamn razor blades.

Unless you toted a knotted oak stick and busted their goddamned heads with it, and if they got under the stick, then you put it to them low and hard with a sharp penknife. One old jock son of a bitch screamed like a woman when he got cut between the legs, and squalled again when he staggered, hunched, out the boxcar door. The train was highballing downhill, Digger recollected, making up time and doing maybe sixty when the bum went out. His partner held out both hands so Digger could see they were empty, and backed clear to the other end of the car, leaving the spare bindle roll.

Digger started the truck, and flicked on its lights, but still didn't put it into gear. The motor was a pulse, a heartbeat, and it was as if by not leaving the drill site, he could somehow keep it all alive.

Pick cotton with bloody fingertips where the stiff, dry splits gouged you—two bits a hundred pounds, and damned lucky to keep up with the big, hungry nigger next row over. By the time you grew finger calluses, the cotton was gone and maybe you could bag two, three fryers from somebody's hen house to start you on the road.

To the night, to the wooden gallows whose killing noose reached more than a thousand feet underground, Digger said: "It ain't like I didn't pay my

dues. I never had money, never got enough to eat
unless I stole it. And it was like I'd been waitin' for
the oil fields all my life, or them for me. Hard work,
good work that grew me into a man and a good
driller; the *best* driller."

The motor throb, the bright wash of headlamps—
they were like tubes and wires doctors stuck into a
man to keep him going, keep him breathing when he
maybe didn't give a damn anymore. Sometimes they
didn't work; they didn't now, so Digger said amen,
and dust to dust, goddamnit. He moved the truck off
down the tire ruts until he came to what had been
a wagon road for Sam Southworth in the old days. It
was beaten smoother now by years of horses and cows
and iron-rimmed wagon wheels, Sunday-go-to-meeting
buggy wheels.

Farther on to the east, it came out on a sure-enough
road, gravel hauled in to make sure Southfork beef
could get hay trucked to them in the roughest winters.
Digger reached that road and looked left, to the little
rise where the ranch house had stood against Indians
and storms and more hard years than anybody alive
had ever seen. Faintly, he could see a light waiting
upstairs, but he didn't turn the truck that way. He
turned right and floorboarded the old White. He was
in a big hurry. He had never needed a drink more
than right now.

Ellie waited two days and nights before she started
to look for him. She went first out to the well, and
saw bank scavengers there, the crew long gone. Men
said something to her, but all she heard was the blood
in her ears. She left without answering. She didn't talk
to Manuel and Lupe at home either. When she
couldn't stand it any longer, she saddled the bay
gelding because Willard had the truck, and took out
after him.

He wasn't in Travis City, they said, and she rode
off quickly when she saw Jock Ewing coming across
the street from his new refinery. Then she legged the

bay, pointed him west, and stayed six more hours in the saddle before she came up on the cantina.

He had to be there because the truck was there, smashed up against a big rock. It was some little Mexican collection of shacks that probably didn't even have a name, but they knew enough to steal the wheels and such, to lift out the battery and suck the gas tank dry.

Ground-tying the gelding, she carried a quirt as she went into the cantina. It stank of tequila and peppers and mansweat, of sickness in a corner, cigarillos, and a cheap perfume that flared Ellie's nostrils.

He came from somewhere in the midday shadows, barman, owner, whatever, to blink rheumy eyes at her. *"Señorita?"*

"He's in the back," she said. "The short gringo?"

"Esposa?" the man asked. His bald head was splotched, suggesting there was a pinto in his background. "You are his wife?"

She went on past him, slapping the quirt against her boot, spurs jingling. Not the first door, nor the second, but he was there behind the last one, half-full bottle on the nightstand, empty ones patterning the floor. He had one bare leg across a naked Mexican girl who couldn't have been more than sixteen.

The girl sat up, tangled-hair, with pert, pointy breasts that would sag in another year or two. She was darkly pretty, sleepy, pouting. "What the hell you want, woman? You want your husband?"

Taking a long stride, Ellie flicked the quirt against Willard's buttock. He muttered and took his leg off the girl. She flicked him again, hard enough to cut.

"Sommabitch," Willard said.

The girl stared sulky at Ellie, sassy. "Can't keep him home, *gringa?* You ain't woman enough?"

Ellie cut at the girl with the quirt, deliberately missing her, making her roll off the bed and come up spitting mad. Then she fisted the red mouth, splitting rich lips with the full powered punch of an arm hardened by a lifetime of ranch work. The girl went down, unpretty with her legs bent awkwardly and looking used and raggedy sitting on the dusty dirt floor.

On the bed, Digger sat up. He blinked owl-eyed at her, his face stubbled and smeared. He'd been in a fight; there was a fresh cut in his left eyebrow, a bruise at the corner of his mouth. He rubbed at his ass. "What—I mean—who the hell—"

"You didn't have to tuck your tail between your legs," she said. "You didn't have to run off like a whipped hound."

"Ellie?" he said, rubbing his eyes, his whiskery mouth. "Ellie—you here?" His hand was shaky and uncertain, but it found the bottle of tequila. Digger Barnes took a long, life-giving drink. "You—you got no call to be in a—a place like this."

She pointed the quirt at the girl, sitting up now and holding her mouth while quiet tears streaked her olive cheeks. "You can make love to her, but not to me. Is that it?"

Digger swallowed, choked, and fought to hold the stuff down. After a second, he said, "The well's dry. It's another duster. I took all your money and poured it down a dry hole."

"So you didn't come tell me. You crawled into a bottle and crawled into a whore to hide. All right, then. My grandpa took a bullet and two arrows, and trailed the Comanches who shot him for twenty miles, to kill them. He didn't whine and crawl off. My pa lost ninety percent of the herd in a blizzard, and the rest to a grass fire the next summer; he got snakebit and tromped by a rank stud, and lost his wife to fever and never had him a man-child to help. But he didn't holler calf rope, not even on his deathbed."

It took him another drink to clear his throat, but then he brought it out loud and clear: "I ain't Sam Southworth, nor your grandpa, nor Jock Ewing, goddamnit! I'm Digger Barnes, and I *earned* the name, every letter of it." He took another swig, and quoted, "In honest truth, a name given a man is no better than a skin; what is not his own falls off and comes to nothin'. You know what that means, Miss Eleanor Southworth? Means Digger Barnes is me and I'm him, and there ain't no more and no less."

She said, "And the sadness of it is, there never will be any difference. You're right pretty, *Digger* Barnes, in your mind and how you love a woman, as well as sayin' what she needs to hear. I don't know all that much about poetry, but I learned some of the good book because I damned well had to, and there's a part that says: 'and when I was a man, I put away childish things'—*or somethin' like that.*"

Digger wiped his mouth, glanced at the crying, naked girl on the floor, at the crosspatch of empty tequila bottles and stained cornhusks from tamales and cigarette butts. He said, "Ellie, Ellie—you don't understand; you just don't know."

"Afraid I do know," she said, and wheeled out of the room. She never said good-bye, not out loud.

He didn't call after her, and the bald-headed Mexican bartender or owner or whoremaster stayed quiet in his shadows, so she marched on outside. The gelding was tired but gave her his best, until shamed, she slowed to let him catch his breath.

It wasn't the young whore; she could forgive that. It was in a man's nature to be randy as a stud horse, if the edge wasn't kept off him.

It was Willard—Digger—Barnes running off without the guts to face up to her. It was because they could have thought out something, some way, if he had to go to work for wages, and she had to let cowhands go and take up the slack herself. Maybe the bank could be put off, the herd cut, some horses sold. There were antiques in the house that would bring fair prices in Dallas, even in these hard times.

But he hadn't even tried. He just turned belly up when the second well didn't come in, and she couldn't have that in a man; she *wouldn't* have it in a horse or dog or a fighting rooster, so why in a man?

Oh, damn, but he was handsome, and he knew so much and his hands could be as soft and knowing as the searching of his mouth. It hurt like billy-be-damned to put her back to all that, knowing full well she meant to keep it all behind her, even if he were to come crawling back, sorry and ready to try things her way.

Never! Willard—and damn Digger!—Barnes wouldn't come begging to her. He wasn't tempered true in the furnace, and was likely to snap in places he ought to stand strong; he was ornery and muley-headed and kind of stupid, for all his book reading. But he wasn't one to ask pity of anybody, much less a woman.

Bobbing loose in the saddle, she let the gelding pick his way at the walk, not really paying attention. It was coming on sunset, and she'd put on the jacket she carried back of the saddle. It could be, this was *her* bullet and two arrows, but she couldn't just keep trailing like Grandpa until she found Comanche. Killing off the man who'd wounded her wouldn't help a lick, and the hurt would always be there, no matter what.

Grandpa Southworth had ridden down those warriors out of logic, not pure cussedness, because he realized the Comanche had to be shown to stay clear of the Southfork. The land was more important than the leaking of his blood, his scalp. He had sons at home to carry on, to hold and guard the land.

Sam Southworth had only a daughter, just Ellie. She had to do it all, for him, for the land—and by God, she would.

She rode into the ranch at dusk, and swung aching down from the bay gelding to hand the reins to Manuel. Walking stiffly into the house, she went straight to her pa's office and drank two big swallows of the old whiskey always kept in the bottom right drawer of the rolltop desk.

Then she went to the telephone in the parlor and asked the operator for the Alamo Hotel in Travis City. Ellie knew the woman was still on the line when she told the desk clerk she wanted to talk to Mr. John

Ewing, but it didn't bother her. The whole county would know in a matter of hours anyway.

He wasn't there, and it was just as well. Ellie left word for him, and went back into her pa's office to take another drink before climbing the stairs and shucking her clothes. Nude, she stood and watched hot water run into the cast-iron tub, wondering what she'd say to Jock Ewing, *how* she'd say it.

The hot water and steam made her head swimmy, and Ellie could taste whiskey in her throat. She soaped and rinsed and wanted to just lie back and soak until the world went away. Lupe tapped on the bathroom door, then rapped louder until Ellie answered.

"On the *teléfono*—Señor Ewing. I said you were in the bath."

Ellie swung one long leg out and reached for the towel. "And he said he is coming out here?"

Lupe made a noise through the door. "But how did you know?"

CHAPTER 6

He'd shaved earlier in the evening, before going down to supper. But Jock found himself before the mirror again, lathered up and hurrying, trying to scrape too close. Twice, he nicked himself before getting under control and settling down.

No, he decided, he didn't need another bath, and it would be a damnfool trick to make the barber open his shop just for a trim. Jock Ewing wasn't a pimpled kid in knickers, shaking in anticipation for his first date. But he felt like it, as if the juices were pumping and swelling and damned near ready to come busting out like the highest gusher there ever was.

But just because Ellie Southworth called, that didn't mean she was all ready to spread her legs for him. She was a special kind of woman, proud and made of the stuff to stand up to any hardship, and not just take it, but survive. She was early pioneer stock. Her family had had its bootheels dug in here while Texas still flew the Lone Star flag of the Republic, and Ellie had the bloodlines, the style, the core of steel.

But it was all so neatly cased in velvets and silk; high-headed as any blooded filly, she moved with that sort of fluid, almost awkward grace, easy but purposeful. To watch her trim tail undulate in faded, tight Levi's made a man sense the power latent deep inside her, like the speed of a King's Ranch quarterhorse, balanced right on the trembling edge of flashing out in a magnificent burst of speed.

It was under control, that blind, heart-busting strength, but champing at the bit, and it'd take a man with a firm hand on the reins to gentle her—firm, but giving enough so she wouldn't throw down her head and fight. Eleanor Southworth, if you compared her to bucking stock, would be sure-enough outlaw, a sunfisher turning belly up to the sun, going up in the east and coming down in the west, squealing and biting and ready to savage any rider she unseated. She'd be an unrelenting fighter every kicking, bone-jarring jump of the way, and demand respect from any bronc stomper ever saw her fire out of the chute. So it would be a heap better not to have her set her jaw and bow her neck; it's be easier all around, was she to be given her head—up to a point.

Settling the new suit coat around his shoulders, Jock pressed on the bits of toilet paper over his razor nicks. He'd pull them off before he got to the Southfork ranch house, and hope he wouldn't start leaking. He wished he'd been in the hotel when Ellie called; it might have been easier talking with her first. Now he

had to drive out and face her without really knowing
what she wanted.

He settled his Stetson on his head, took a last quick
check in the mirror and left his room. The hell he
didn't know what Ellie Southworth wanted. She
needed money, and right bigod now. He even knew
how much, to the penny. She'd wasted a good chunk
in Digger's dry holes, but that wasn't what had hurt
her most; it was the market price of beef and damned
few buying, even at that. It was a bad winter before
and a dry spring for grass and Sam Southworth's bullheaded refusal to sell off leases before anybody knew
no oil was easy found on the Southfork—at least, not
in that south forty arroyo. Dusters there didn't mean
there wasn't a field waiting to be tapped somewhere
else on those thousands of acres.

"And," he said to night bugs fluttering through the
stabbing of his car lights, "it sure don't mean that
Ellie will want anybody to try again either."

She was smart, he thought, sharp as the wind from a
norther. Else she wouldn't have called him tonight,
quick as she got back from chasing down Digger
Barnes. Sure, he knew about that. Guadalupe Lopez
had called from the cantina when Digger showed up
there, and again after Ellie stomped out. He'd heard
from Manuel at the Southfork, too, and before that,
from Billygoat Smith about the dry hole. One thing a
man in the oil business learned, and that was to keep
a close tally on everything that happened, even if it
didn't seem to concern him right off.

How did he feel about Ellie being kind of second-
hand, about her picking Digger over him in the first
place? Sort of mean and sort of sad, but mostly
damned happy that she'd come around to changing
her mind, that she hadn't just let everything slide and
run off with Digger.

There was a way of looking at Ellie and Digger—
something that would eat away at a man until he
might explode, if he kept seeing them together in his
head, picturing them naked, with her slim legs

wrapped around Digger's back like she'd lock them around a horse's barrel.

Or he could accept that she thought she loved Digger, and being the woman she was, didn't hold anything back. He could roll it all around inside his head and call himself lucky he'd be next in line. For the truth of it was, if Digger's drill sites hadn't come up empty, Jock would have had to find a way to chase him out of the county anyhow, run him off or break him or whatever it took to pry him loose from Ellie Southworth.

Because Jock Ewing *wanted* Ellie, more than money or power or the need he had to stand higher than most anybody else. He wanted her and everything she had to give—her beauty, style, and strength. He might need the Southfork for all it represented and what that would mean in the future, but mostly he hungered after Ellie herself, the woman flesh of her and the fire within.

The car bumped across cattle guards. He was moving through the tall gate of the Southfork ranch, seeing the big iron letters intertwined, a brand that rode the hips of a few thousand cattle. It had always reminded Jock of two snakes twisted together in mortal combat.

He'd been on the ranch for some miles, but this was the core of it, the big house and barns, the stalls and bunkhouses; this was the only part fenced—except in the minds of the Southworths and all their neighbors. Any landowner in the county could take you straight to any Southfork corner stake, quick as they could find their own. It was a good place, one that was part of history, and in normal times the Southfork made money. With an emergency fund for support, it would again.

Jock saw men moving in the lamp-lit bunkhouse, lanterns bobbing around the barns. They'd be readying for winter, seeing that the hay stayed dry, that grain was safely stored and firewood cut. Some of the crew, the younger men, would draw their time and move on elsewhere; some would return in the spring, when extra hands were needed. The old punchers stayed on, making repairs to harness and buildings and holding pens. They'd take turns doing a week or so in line shacks, from where they'd ride out daily to check on herd conditions in their section, do some doctoring, maybe draw bead on a wolf or traveling panther. Mostly the old hands stayed on because the ranch was home to them, although there wasn't all that much to do in winter.

Stopping the car several yards from the big house, Jock climbed out, took off his hat, wiped inside the sweatband with a bandanna, and put the Stetson firmly into place again. He walked firmly to the steps and climbed them to the porch. Wisteria vines, their leaves long shed, contorted brown lengths around unpainted supports. The house would look better done all in gleaming white, with tall, round columns reaching up to the second floor. And a white gravel drive curling around in front, with plenty of flowers and maybe a pond.

The front door swung back before Jock could put his knuckles to it. There was a Mexican maid and another one cooked for the house, he knew, but as he whipped off his hat and stepped into the lamplight of an ornate old parlor, he saw that Ellie had opened the door herself.

"I'll take your hat," she said, and he damned near dropped it, handing it to her.

She wasn't all dolled up, but somehow it would have been better if she were. The long, simple dress Ellie wore clung jealously to her legs and breasts as she moved, and looked like a nightgown so soft it would dissolve under a man's fingers. And her hair— brushed loose and clean and swinging clear down her back that way; it was harder on a man floating free so that he wanted to bury both hands in it, than if it was put up in a knot. Cream and gold and flower blue, that was Ellie, and when she turned to him from the hat rack, Jock cleared his throat. But she went by him, trailing a musky perfume that caught in his throat.

When he got that aired out, she was handing him a glass of whiskey he purely needed. Jock downed it at a gulp, and blinked at the way she matched him with her own glass.

"Guess we both needed that," she said. "Another one?"

Nodding, he followed her to the sideboard. For a man getting to be known for slick talking, he hadn't done so good here, hadn't said a damned word, in fact. So he took another drink and so did Ellie. She didn't move away from him or offer him a seat on the sofa. Ellie just stood there, close, and looked steadily at him with those blue eyes so deep he couldn't see bottom.

"I got a proposition for you, Jock Ewing," she said.

"Figured you might," he said.

She moved away then, but left a warm place in the air where she'd been. He put his empty whiskey glass on the sideboard and propped an elbow there, too. His new suit felt scratchy, his shirt collar tight.

Ellie kept her chin high and never dropped her eyes for a second, but there was a tiny movement of her bottom lip, as if she was having trouble keeping it still. She said then, "You know I've been goin' with Willard Barnes."

"Yes," Jock said.

"I'm makin' no apologies for it," she went on. "He's pretty and talks pretty and knows how to please a woman. I thought on makin' it permanent."

"But you found out he's not a permanent kind of man?"

She took a deep breath. He watched the firm pointy-tipped melon-ripe breasts rise to strain against the thin material of her dress. It was so sheer he could just about see through it. She said, "Wasn't all that easy for me to call you, Jock—nor admit I've been wrong. My pa said it was best to say things straight out, but that's pretty damned hard, too."

"Reckon I can understand that," Jock said.

Her eyes clouded up then, like pieces of summer sky with sheet lightning flickering off a piece. "You think so, do you? I don't know as anybody can know how I feel right now—like a plumb damned fool, and a two-bit whore and—and—like I'm standin' by and watchin' the auctioneer sell off my good furniture."

"None of those things," he said. "You're Eleanor Southworth, and there's only one of you in the world."

She tried on a smile that wanted to keep slipping. "You can talk pretty, too." The smile fell off. "But what I have to ask you—"

"Nothin', Ellie; let me make the offer: I'd be proud to catch up on anything the Southfork might have due at the bank, and pay me back when you get ready."

"Why'd you beat me to it?" she asked. "Why didn't you make me eat humble pie?"

"Because a woman like you, a very special woman like you, she ought never to *have* to ask for anything. And you be humble? That ain't in you, Ellie; you're too spirited for it."

She took a step closer, so that the tips of her breasts were just about touching his vest; he swore he could feel their heat burning right on through his clothes. They'd be dark pink, he thought; a pair of dark pink torches that would sear the skin. Ellie said, "I meant to make a trade."

Jock swallowed; the sweet musk of her was heady, dizzying; there was a damp shine to her red mouth. "You don't have to."

Her smile was a little pouty, a little sad, but it stayed put. "Overpriced myself all to hell, didn't I?"

His hands caught her upper arms. "Don't say that, Ellie. Just because you—"

"Bedded down with Willard Barnes every chance I got? Can you put that behind you, Jock? I don't ask you to forget, just to put it behind."

"Who the hell *is* what's-his-name?"

She came into his arms, fitting herself to his body, lifting up her mouth. Ellie's breath was like hot butterfly wings against his cheek as she murmured, "Now I want to, Jock; I really want to."

Then his mouth was on hers, and the shock of her tongue jolted him clear down to his boots. The flavor of her wasn't springtime, although there were flowers to it; Ellie tasted more like warm and rumpled beds on a long winter night, like silky-fine hair spread over both pillows and soap-smelling flesh.

When she broke the kiss, he was wobbly at the knees. He just nodded when she told him the servants were gone and it was no cowhand's business if a car parked out there overnight. She took him by the hand and they climbed the stairs together, slowly. Her thigh kept touching his, brushing across his, and before he got to the second floor, Jock quit trying to hide his hardness.

Inside, the room smelled of her. Ellie said, "No—don't turn down the lamp. I want us to know each other, Jock. I want us not to hide anything, and for certain, I want you to see what you're getting. Because I stopped acting a damned fool don't mean I stopped bein' the rest of me."

Shaking inside, he watched her slide the gown over her head and drop it. Ellie stood there with lamplight glorifying her skin and hair, caressing her skin and making mysterious shadows in the hollow places. She was more beautiful than all his dreams of her; this time she was real, all polished and excited and sure enough, her nipples were dark pink, and the deep, curly hair of her mound was a coppery shade darker than her head. She was so damned beautiful that the sight of her proud and naked hurt a man's throat and cramped his belly.

Not taking his eyes from her, Jock managed his vest and shirt, but got a leg tangled in his pants. She came over to help, and suddenly it wasn't embarrassing at all, but damned funny, and very good that they should be laughing like this together. He'd never been able to be serious and funny with a woman at the same time.

Then they were on the bed, and he was covering her too quickly, like a stud horse turned loose at his first ready mare of the season. Her slender legs came up and over him, locking him into the upreaching cup of her, so velvety smooth and without a bottom. It clung to him and drew him down and struck back at every thrust he made, pushing and pulling and gripping so hot and sweet and crazy. He shuddered to a stop, the rounded wonders of her haunches in his hands, their bellies glued together. He bucked and shuddered while the night sky loosed rainbow lightning bolts and all the hunger built up in him came together to melt his spine.

"Oh no!" she panted, flattening her breasts to him, her nipples drilling into his flesh. "Oh, no—you just *think* you're done, Jock Ewing, but you got another think comin'!"

Before he could catch his breath good, she'd rolled him over and straddled him, raking at his thighs. She bit his throat and got her mouth clamped around one of *his* nipples. It was the damnedest feeling, and when he struggled to pry her face loose, he was turned bronc and Ellie was the rider, spurring him good and gasping every time they went arching up to hit the ground together. She pounded him heavy as he'd hammered her before, and for a few, brightflash seconds it turned into a fight, a battle between rider and ridden.

But then it didn't make a damn who was what, because they were welded together, gushing together, oil and a pipeline, sky and ground and air; one of them slid into the other, through the other. The flowing satin waves of her hair tented them, covered them from the world and kept them snugly private within its perfumed netting.

Still holding him within her, Ellie eased over so they could lie side by side. His eyes were closed and she pretended hers were also, peeping through almost meshed lashes. It had been good, very good, and as the waves of their mating ebbed slowly, Ellie found time to be surprised. She'd deliberately planned this seduction, thought it out, and offered herself up on a sexual altar, to save the Southfork. She'd been ready to grit her teeth and become a great actress, to fake the ecstasy she'd known with Willard.

But she didn't have to; she'd started out uneasy and wound up going wild. Ellie pulled him closer with her leg, kept their bellies tight. Was she a whore, some kind of sick woman, that she could love one man and reach crazy heights of rapture with another? She'd only bedded down with two. Migod, she thought, *only*!

Maybe it was possible to love two men.

Or maybe she'd had this feeling for Jock Ewing all along, and blotted it out because she was ripe and ready and Willard got to her first.

Ellie pillowed his face against her breast and wondered if she could lie to herself without knowing it.

CHAPTER 7

Everything about the big house had sparkled, but the most golden thing had been Ellie herself, outglowing the lamps, the candlelit chandeliers. There'd been an orchestra brought out from Dallas, for those who didn't like to hear that Mex music all the time. And the food—Jock had to admit the party was all done proper, from the whole barbecued steer down to the Cape Jasmine flowers.

The Cape Jasmines were in tribute to his ma, those creamy white blossoms, though God knows he didn't owe her a damned thing, not even a memory. How old was he when she ran off—three, five? Old enough to retain a hazy picture of another golden woman, all soft and shimmering, a woman who laughed a kind of music. She'd always smelled of Cape Jasmine, though he hadn't known what it was until he got bigger, and had squatted under the flowering bush that night while Pa visited with the Thomases on the porch, letting the blossoms soak him in perfume.

On the way home, when he asked Pa what kind of flower that was, Pa wouldn't answer. That didn't mean too much; most times he never bothered to answer Jock. So he waited to ask the black housekeeper-cook he'd grown up knowing. "Lord," she said, "Mast' John, that's what your ma wore, but don't never tell your pa I said it." It had taken him a couple more years to find out that his ma'd just up and run off one day, leaving her baby and husband behind, leaving everything but some jewelry she'd brought as her dowry and the clothes on her back.

Jock looked at the stairs, at glasses spilled or set everywhere, stinking cigar butts, stained napkins. First thing would be to get electricity run out from Dallas; the company owed him favors for rights of way and such, and it would be a nice surprise for Ellie. He looked at the stairs again, and poured himself one more drink.

It wasn't as though they hadn't bedded down together before their wedding night, and he would be climbing up to a bride all scared and trembly. And it sure wasn't like whatever his pa and ma had. His golden woman was so eager in bed that it shook him some. Not that he didn't like it; he just caught himself wondering if a *wife* was supposed to act like that. Jock sipped bourbon; it wasn't something to walk up to other married men and ask.

"*Señor?*" The girl Lupe stood in the doorway, the other Mexes behind her, relatives hired for the party and cleanup.

"*Nada,*" he said, emptied his glass, put it down, and headed for the stairway. Some kid sniggered, and Jock felt his neck go red. All these sons of bitches *knew*. They'd gotten the word straight from Lupe and were

making jokes among themselves about the bridegroom
that wouldn't get a cherry from his new wife. Some
day he'd clean out these greasers and bring in black
help; niggers knew their place better.

Jock deliberately ignored them and took his time
going upstairs. Logically, it wasn't any more than a
horse whinnying or a bluetick hound baying at the
moon; best thing with Mexes was to ignore them, unless they didn't get out of the way. Then you just
naturally stomped over them; they weren't all that
hard to stampede.

He stood before the bedroom door long enough to
roll a quirly and thumbnail a match to it. For some
fool reason, he felt like he ought to knock. Jock
turned the knob and went on in.

Smiling, Ellie said to him, "Accordin' to the rules,
I oughtn't be wearin' white. But I *feel* like a bride,
and I've had this fancy nightgown in my hope chest
for so damned long—"

"You look beautiful in it," Jock said, and it was
true. He walked over to where she was seated on the
side of the bed and stroked the sunshine hair she'd let
down. Her fingers wandered over his shirtfront and
buttons, and they were tickly against his bare skin,
but not so much as the hotness of her breath.

He stepped back quickly and she puzzled up at him.
He said, "It ain't—"

She said, "But I want to, and we've never—"

"No, goddamnit! he said. "A *wife* don't—"and went
into the bathroom before he said too much. When he
pulled the chain, the gas pump outside kicked on, and
he thought he could make out the echo of derisive
Mex laughter.

Always before, Ellie had wanted the lamp on, but
now it was dark and he had to feel his way across to
the bed. She lay still there, breathing deeply, not
saying anything. Jock stared up into blackness and
caught the scent of Cape Jasmine. Ellie seemed a long
reach away and to be getting farther.

Had it been something like this between his own pa

and ma? She'd waited it out a long time, if so. He didn't want to be like Pa; he didn't want to look like him or act like him. All Jock had ever wanted to do was grow bigger than Leander Ewing and stomp the shit out of him.

Into the chill and apartness between them, Jock said, "I wasn't close to nobody, especially not my pa; not close like you and Sam Southworth. My old man was a wildcatter too; sometimes rich but mostly broke. Kept a house for me, though—run by this ol' colored woman. Hardly even said howdy to me when he *did* come home. It surprised the hell out of me when he got killed tryin' to dynamite a rig fire, and I found out he left me the house and some money."

Small-voiced, she asked, "Why should that surprise you?"

"Maybe I wasn't even really his son," Jock said. "My ma wore perfume like the flowers I got for you tonight. She ran off when I was little. I remember how she tried to laugh all the time, but the laughin' stopped and she'd just sit and rock me. I'd smell that perfume."

He swung his legs off the mattress and felt across the bedside table for tobacco and papers. "Jesus!" he said. "I never knew if I was pleasin' my pa or not; he never said. All I wanted to do was rub his goddamn lockjawed face in it, to whip his ass any way I could. But the son of a bitch got blowed up before I could show him I was bigger'n he ever hoped, that I'd just keep right on gettin' bigger, while losers like him chased their own tails." The match flared, outlining an old-young face beginning to turn craggy.

"Jock," she whispered, "I'm sorry."

"Me too," he answered. "Sorry I come down on you; especially this night."

Her hand eased across the sheet and found his. "It's not like a real weddin' night, is it?"

"Sure it is. It's better'n the others, because we don't have to learn each other, and because neither of us is scared."

"I'm scared, Jock—scared I won't learn you right enough to be a good wife."

He went to her, nuzzled the marvel of her hair. "You're the best wife there is; already best before the preacher said words over us."

"Oh, Jock, Jock—I will be; I promise I will be."

"Hush," he said gently. "You already promised, remember?"

And it was more than good for him, better than if she'd been a virgin. She was just as giving, but more passive; the fire was still right there, like it ought to be, only he controlled it. That was like it ought to be, too.

In the morning, he stopped at the bank first, making a transfer of funds and paying off Southfork debts. Next stop was the lawyer, where Jock had a will made out, one copy to stay there on file, one to be sent to his bank box in Dallas. That would have made him feel old and mortal, except for that part about "heirs and assigns." He and Ellie would produce good younguns; a strong stud crossed on a classic, refined mare always meant good get.

Stepping out onto the street again, he watched one of his tank trucks swing onto the refinery road and was glad he didn't recognize the driver. Not so long ago, he'd known the face of every man who worked with him, but then he'd been a two-bit independent with a partner who wasn't pitching in a full share.

Damn Digger Barnes for a heap of things, but most for shaming a good woman so. It was bad enough that talk about him and Ellie was all over the county, but for him to take an upstanding, innocent girl and teach her—

Jock clamped even teeth around a cigar end and made his way up the street to the electric office. It didn't do him any good to dwell on Digger and Ellie; the pure wonder of it was that she was his now. *His*— sweet and laughing and smelling of creamy-white flowers. He never for a second had a doubt about Ellie now, Ellie *Ewing*. When she gave her word, she stood by it. That business of Digger's—it was understood between them that Ellie wouldn't try it again, and he'd bet she never really wanted to. There was one hell of a difference between some bordertown whore and a lady of quality; for all his book reading, Digger hadn't been smart enough to know that.

Hadn't been—past tense, and that changed Jock's mood again. There'd be no more poetic bullshit, no more chasing down the man through every whorehouse and saloon in the territory, no more catching up on bills that should have been paid long ago, or never owed. Digger Barnes thought he was something special, always running off at the mouth about what a great nose for oil he had, always running off at the mouth about something, anything—even a lady.

"Mr. Ewing?"

Jock didn't know the new man at the electric company, but the man knew him, so he told him what was wanted out at the Southfork. The man went big-eyed, a hoot owl caught out in daylight.

"But Mr. Ewing, that will cost us—ah, the company—"

Flicking cigar ash on the floor, Jock said, "Sport, it'll cost your company a heap damned more if you don't get a crew on it *pronto*. I'd say first, your job; then no travelin' over a few thousand acres except on them skinny right-of-way roads—where there *are* any. Then—"

"Sir," the man said, rubbing at his eyes like he'd looked straight up at the noonday sun, "we'll get on it right away."

"Appreciate it," Jock said, and strolled across the street to have dinner in the hotel restaurant.

Thank you kindly, he said to everybody who passed by his table with a word of congratulations, and smiled widest at those who hadn't gotten an invitation. Just a year ago, he'd have probably thrown open the ranch to one and all, turned cowhands and roughnecks and railroaders loose onto more red-eye whiskey than they could handle. After the fight, his wedding reception would have been a mess. Now he'd been pickier, inviting high-up folks who could do some good, as well as the hard-nosed bunch of old-time ranch families that thought they'd squat forever on land taken away from the Indians. The thing was, they'd been in Texas so long that their kinfolks stretched to the state capital, stretched clear to Washington.

City people who thought money talks were right— up to a point. Money didn't say a damned thing a mule wanted to hear, and then about the only way to reach him was to tie a wad of banknotes under his tail and set them on fire. Stripey-backed mules didn't have a lock on being stubborn; most of the old cow families had lantern jaws and Roman noses and could land one hell of a kick, if a man didn't watch them close.

He was on probation with them; Jock knew that. Just marrying Ellie Southworth didn't automatically make him acceptable, but it would help him reach into places that had been fenced off to him before. Finishing up his steak and potatoes, Jock reached into his coat for a sack of tobacco, but brought out a fresh cigar instead. Rich looked rich and acted that way even when they weren't; that was another truth Jock had picked up along the road.

Davy Thorpe came over and asked real polite if Jock was done eating, and Jock said, "Sure, sure; set yourself down, Davy. Been meanin' to talk to you about that Dallas office buildin'."

He passed a pleasant afternoon, using the table for an office. Men showed up looking for work and he found them some, or sent them to the refinery with notes. Davy Thorpe fidgeted some, but Jock figured that would do him good. Davy was pricing that downtown building a mite high, but hanging in like a bulldog, so he'd come down later even if he had to shave his commission. Dallas was the place to be, all right; spreading out, even in the Depression. Even so, a man ought to get that building cheap. Jock figured some speculator had gone bankrupt by the time he got it done and couldn't find anybody to rent it, account of hard times. Maybe a Dallas bank wanted out from under.

Turning again to Davy Thorpe, he said, "Look here, friend; I don't *have* to be in Dallas now. Big D and me been gettin' along without each other for some time. But if you was to cut, say twenty percent—"

"Good lord, Jock! *Twenty* percent?"

"Make it eighteen and give you dickerin' room with the man you workin' for. See what he says and let me know."

Davy Thorpe wiped his forehead. "Even eighteen off—"

"Beats a busted flush," Jock said. "I don't expect there's no long line waitin' to move into that place."

On the street again, he felt pretty good, tipping his hat to the ladies, howdying men, and winking at boys. Squinting at the sun, he reckoned the time before reaching for the gold railroad watch he'd taken to carrying. One of them, Jock or the watch, was five minutes off, but there was plenty of time for a drink or two before driving back to the ranch for supper— and Ellie.

The thought of her stirred low in his belly and tightened him. A whole lot of woman, yessir, and then some. But it wouldn't do to rush home to her; some might get the idea he meant to keep an eye on her like she couldn't be trusted. He trusted Ellie all the way. Now that she'd made her pick, Jock never doubted her.

Digger Barnes, he thought, you poor, dumb bastard —you threw away the Pardee field and Ellie Southworth about the same time, and anybody in his right mind would have to think hard and long on which was worth more.

When he stepped into the saloon, beer smell closed around him, and cigar smoke; mansweat drying off and sawdust; laughter. He put a foot up on the rail and ordered bourbon.

"Well now, *Mr.* Ewing."

"Billygoat," he answered.

Billygoat Smith pushed his scarred head closer and lowered his voice. "You know, I heard you were hirin', but all your man'd give me was a job any snotnose kid could do, for kid wages. Makes me kind of sorry I kept you in on the news, up there on the Southworth place."

"The Big Digger—wasn't that what he called it? Nobody stuffed money into your pocket, Billygoat. And you're drunk, so back off and quit blowin' on me."

The man rolled his shoulders. "Guess I should of gone with Digger. But I might just wait till he comes back."

Jock didn't say anything. He pushed his glass at the bartender and nodded. Their end of the bar had gone quiet as people listened. Billygoat said: "Oh, he'll be back, right enough. Seems his partner screwed him outa some leases, or was it Digger doin' the actual screwin'?"

Drunk or sober, Billygoat was nobody's fool in a saloon fight, and he was quick. He nearly made it to Jock's face with the top of his head, but the palmed .38 slapped him alongside the temple and threw him off target. Still, his shoulder caught Jock, and they both staggered.

Jock pistol-whipped him again, slashing hard with the barrel—*whack-whack!*—a slap and a backhanded blow that opened up both Billygoat's eyebrows. He couldn't see worth a damn for the blood, and pawed out blindly. Jock hit him again, across the hands, the forearms, and got in a powerful downward lick that snapped Billygoat's collarbone.

The barman said, "For chrissake, Jock! You mean to kill him, don't do it in here."

Billygoat went to his knees, one arm dangling, the other hand wiping at his eyes. Jock knocked him flat onto his back and stood over him with the pistol.

"Jock," the barman said, whispering his name into the pulled-tight silence.

Shaking himself, Jock Ewing leveled his bloody fist with the bloody gun in it, muzzle sweeping back and forth across the watching men, the staring, frowning men. "This time," he said, voice shaking. "This is the *only* goddamn time, you all hear? I mean to *kill* the next son of a bitch lets his mouth overload his ass, and I'd just as soon kill his goddamn friends. You all hear that *real* good, because I ain't sayin' no more about it."

Using the bar towel to wipe off his hand and pistol, Jock stood there and finished his drink. Then he stepped over the man in the sawdust and went out to climb into his Ford and drive home.

CHAPTER 8

He wouldn't make it. Ellie knew that now, and had probably known it when she called him in Austin. But she couldn't fault him for going off on business; he usually was. Still, a body would think Jock Ewing ought to be home when she had his firstborn, much as he claimed to want a son.

It would be a boy. The midwife said so, and even if the young doctor and nurse sent out by the hospital smiled smart-ass at each other, old Granny Richards had birthed more babies than the two of them could tally.

Still, Ellie didn't hold to all the old ways. She let the doctor give her something in a needle and disinfect the whole room, like he was spraying for boll weevils. She insisted on having the baby at home, though. Three generations of Southworths had been born in this very bed, and Ellie wasn't about to break the chain. The baby would be half Southworth, though she couldn't do anything about the name disappearing, since her pa had been an only child and sired her the same. There were times, she thought, that the Southworths had been plain out-and-out muley-headed, not marrying again and breeding more.

The medicine made her light-headed, and she giggled, since that was some different from being stubborn. Granny Richards leaned forward. "You all right, child?"

"Doin' just fine, Granny. Better not get too close; they do say what I got is catchin'."

"Shoot," Granny snickered, "I give up on that thirty year ago. Ain't give up on men, though; just havin' trouble findin' one that's slap-dab *blind*."

"Please," the young nurse said, as starchy as her white clothes.

Ellie closed her eyes when the next contraction hit. It smarted, but no more than a mashed finger. She'd be madder'n a banty hen caught in a norther, did the nurse try and run off Granny. The old scudder probably wouldn't go, anyhow.

Half Southworth and half Ewing; no more Southworths when Ellie was gone. They loved hard and they loved faithful, her pa and grandpa. Maybe that meant she wasn't a true Southworth, because she'd turned from one man to another so easy. Here she was a married woman, yet pictures of her first lover kept popping through her head from time to time. It wasn't like she *dwelled on* Willard Barnes; she just couldn't keep him out of her memory, and it was damned peculiar she would bother about him at a time like this.

Putting hands lightly upon her swollen belly, Ellie waited for the next spasm. When it came, it wasn't much. Ellie knew a whole lot less about human babies than calves or foals. She didn't want to think about them either, about having to get a rope around a leg bent the wrong way, or go elbows-deep into the cow to try and turn a little critter set wrong.

"Goddamn," she said.

"What's that?" the young doctor asked. He'd started a moustache to make him look older, but he wouldn't have to worry over trimming it for a spell.

"Wasn't callin' on you," Ellie said, and started to drift. She wasn't studying on being guilty for Willard, no more than for what she learned from him. Some things a wife had to render unto her husband, and if Jock didn't want to know about real giving—well, that was up to him. Ellie missed being loved and giving love like that, but she got along without it. Jock Ewing was randy as any stallion and near about as strong, and if he didn't vary much she could live with that, too.

With both of them backing up some, and butting heads some, they'd done just fine for three years. He let the ranch alone, and she didn't stick her nose into the oil business. Like Willard had said once, Jock had a fever burning him, and there was no denying that, so she didn't yammer at him. It was kind of nice to have him gone so much, because when he made it home, it was as though they were new with each other every blessed time.

"That one hurt?" the nurse asked crisply.

"Not much," Ellie answered.

Granny Richards said, "Holler, do you want to."

If Jock wasn't a skilled lover, and if he wasn't here to see his son born, and if he stepped on the toes of some folks—why, that was just his way. Underneath that mean streak was a man who was gentle with her, a man she could share long silences with, and one who could make her laugh and delight her when she least expected. If she could only combine the qualities of Jock with the good things of Willard—but what man was perfect?

Their union was pretty good, all told, and this baby would seal it. Jock had been a long spell worried when she didn't catch right off, thinking maybe one of them was barren. Even though he didn't say it, Ellie knew he was remembering Willard, too. So it was bet-

ter all around that they were wedded this long before
she brought a child into the world. County gossips had
long memories, but even they couldn't stretch out
time to cover this birthing, rubber-band time back to
when she was with Willard last.

So along with Jock, everybody knew it had to be
his, couldn't be anybody else's. Ellie only left the
ranch when she had to, and nobody ever saw her with
another man, if she wasn't ordering him around on
the place. There'd been an early whisper or two, and
some sideways looks from cowhands, but suddenly all
that had stopped, and she put it down to Jock passing
word and meaning it.

"Uhhhh!" she grunted.

"Right on time," the doctor said. "Any minute now,
Nurse."

Through glazed and slitted eyes, Ellie watched
Granny Richards pucker her mouth like she wanted to
spit, bad. But the old woman only said, "Ten, twelve
minutes, most likely; no more'n that."

Jock. Where the hell was John Ewing? A husband
ought to render unto a wife, too; he sure as billy hell
should be with her now. Not fair, Ellie told herself;
Jock had to be in Austin to beat off the big outfits
again. Aritex was sidling around with some new laws
that would cramp the style of Ewing Oil, but he'd
asked her if she wanted him to stay home. You go
ahead on, she said—but damn a man who took every
little thing a woman said as gospel truth.

Another cry built up in her throat, but she locked
it behind set teeth as sweat broke out on her face.

"Y'all ought to let that be," Granny said as the
nurse dabbed Ellie's cheeks and forehead. "Good for
sweatin' the poison out."

"And you should be out of here." The doctor
bristled his spiky little moustache at the old woman.

Ellie said, "No. She stays. You hear me? Granny
stays with me."

"Just bear down," the nurse said. "Help it a little."

"Him," Ellie grunted. "*Him*, damnit."

If she didn't love Jock, she'd leave him, and he knew it. The ranch was back up, not running rich yet, but with enough in the bank to repay every dime to Jock and have operating capital left over. If she left, he'd accept it as another business venture gone wrong. No, that wasn't fair. Jock would be deep-down hurt, and she knew it. Besides, rarely did one of his investments sour on him.

If he'd just quit trying so hard to be one of the bunch. He was the bell cow and everybody recognized that, but when he was on the Southfork or they went visiting to some party given by one of the old ranch outfits, Jock tried to act like a cowhand wearing his only white shirt. With the oilmen he was one way, with the ranchers, another.

"No sense holdin' back," Granny said. "Your man ain't comin' and the boy is. Let go, child."

Where the hell was he?

Not in South America, drilling for oil in the jungles like Willard Barnes. Word had come back that he'd struck one gusher and was punching down pipe in a new field. Good for Willard, but she couldn't picture him in a white helmet and mosquito net, and how in the world could he celebrate his new well, away down there where most folks didn't even talk his language?

She reached up and took hold of the head of the bed, took a good grip on heavy brass bars, and the image came: Willard wearing a red rose over one ear, popping castanets, and dancing heel-and-toe like they did below the border. It was so damned funny that Ellie started to laugh, and couldn't stop.

"That's the way," the doctor said.

When Representative Frank Kelly's glass tilted and splashed whiskey on his trousers, he made the musical laugh he was famed for, but it didn't sound happy. He said, "Jock, m'boy; this here driver of yours—he ain't a Messican, is he? I mean, the way he took that last curve—"

Leaning forward on the seat, Jock rapped the window and said loudly, "Slow 'er down some, Bond." To the congressman: "Sorry, sir. When he knows I'm wound up, he pushes this Packard hard."

Carefully, Kelly braced himself and emptied his glass. He reached for a cigar and waited for Jock to light it. "Seen them damnfool Messicans bullfightin'; you got to admit they ain't got a whole lot of sense. But this boy of your'n—spillin' good whiskey oughta be punishable by hangin'."

"I'll fill it up for you again, sir," Jock said.

Kelly grunted. "Know you're all in a stew about your wife havin' a baby, but, hell, that ain't nothin'. Women has 'em every day, pop 'em out like slick watermelon seeds."

Jock said, "It's our first, Congressman, and even though she's a strong woman like all the Southworths—"

"Yeah," Kelly said. "I remember now. A Southworth—fine old Texas name; got a heap of kin this end of the state." He drank whiskey and laughed again. "Hell, boy—call me Frank. The way you hornswoggled that Aritex bunch was a sight to watch. Tied their lawyers into a knot they couldn't chew loose. Don't get to see that much, Aritex gettin' raked over the coals. 'Course, I probably won't live to see it again, neither; I mean, you don't buck an outfit that size, less'n they come back hard at you."

"I reckon you're right, sir."

The car hit a bump and Kelly grabbed on, cursing under his breath. "Don't know how I got talked into drivin' all the way down here with—wait a minute, boy. You ain't that little ol' outfit Aritex locked horns with before? Built that pipeline and all?"

"I built a pipeline, and a refinery. Ewing Oil."

"Smith Oil, Jones Oil, Wide-Spot-in-the-Road Oil; state's full of little bitty outfits. Sooner or later, the big ones snap 'em up. Oh, I know you twisted Aritex's tail, but that company's so damned big it won't even *feel* you for months to come. Wouldn't get 'em too mad, son."

"No, sir," Jock said, and refilled the glass. He could make out Bond Whitson's almost-white hair in the dashlight's glow. Representative Kelly, now he had silvery hair because he was old enough and vain to boot, getting it waved and touched up just so. But Bond Whitson was born cotton-headed and stayed that way, almost without any color to him at all, close enough to an albino to make superstitious folks walk wide of him. The boy did have funny-looking eyes, with no more expression to them than a diamondback's, only right pale. He was wild as a pissant like all the Whitsons, but when Jock gave him a job to do, he did it quick and right and was grateful. He was the only person in the world besides Ellie that Jock Ewing trusted.

He sure as hell knew enough about Frank Kelly not to turn his back on him, and it had been a little too pat, the congressman wanting a lift down to the county so soon after the hearing. Voters to get back in touch with, Kelly said, but more likely he was going to come down personal on Judge Eddins for issuing that stay order.

"Ain't been down here in too long a spell," Kelly said. "Near forget how juicy them little country gals are. Expect you know your share of 'em, boy?"

Always pleasure seasoned with business—that was something to depend on with Representative Frank Kelly. His backwoods constituency kept sending him back for term after term, because he was down-home and hard-shell Baptist and didn't hoorah around like the rest of them big-city politicians. Jock poured another drink and said, "Reckon I do, sir. There's this lil' gal got a snappin' pussy that'll fair eat up a man's pecker. I mean, she'll gnaw it off at the roots."

Kelly hung on around another curve, his belly bouncing. "Ain't Messican, is she?"

"Redheaded, tight and young."

"Not too young?"

Jock looked at the end of his own cigar. "Just ripe, I'd say."

Not a big-city politician, no indeed; Kelly was a sly and slippery hometown boy who'd made good because he kept his head down. Smart and careful, the Honorable Mr. Kelly, with a penchant for good whiskey and nubile girls and payoffs that had been going on so long Kelly thought his protection was impenetrable. Maybe getting old and fat caused a man to stop looking behind him, but damned if it would ever happen to Jock Ewing.

"Redheaded gal?"

"Looks like her teensy pussy's on fire. Might be, too."

"Hooie, boy! Fill 'er up again, 'cause you startin' to talk my language. Hell of a way to celebrate, ain't it? I *mean*, you havin' a baby, and we goin' to celebrate by dippin' our wicks."

"Hell of a way," Jock agreed, and Bond Whitson threw the big heavy car on through the night, as he'd been told.

They picked up Patty McCready and one of the Jessup girls and dropped them off with the congressman at the fishing cabin on Whitewater River. Only then did Jock climb into the front seat of the Packard with Bond and say, "Screw down her tail, friend. Let's get home and back real quick."

The young doctor and nurse were all smiles when he came busting up the stairs, so Jock knew everything was all right, even if Granny Richards frowned at him. The bedroom door was open a crack, and as he started for it, Granny said, "Got you a fine, strappin' boy, deserve him or not."

"Thanks, Granny," Jock said. "Oh lord, thank you all."

From the sharp-smelling bed, she said, "Jock?"

He went to his knees and took her hand. Right there against her shoulder was a red-faced youngun with coal-black hair. "You all right, hon?"

"Just fine," she said, blinking drowsily at him. "You see your boy? Ain't he pretty?"

"Looks like a wet monkey, or maybe a rained-on papoose. Hey—I'm only kiddin', hon. You did a right fine job, mighty fine. A boy, a son—what do you know? Another Ewing."

Ellie's smile was sleepy, too. "He needs another name, and you never said."

He kissed her cheek, the sweat-dampened golden hair. "I don't care, Ellie. There's nobody I want to honor. Anything you say. Hon, I'm so sorry I couldn't be with you. Bond drove the Packard like a maniac all the way back, but—"

"Think I'll call him John," Ellie whispered. "John Ewing, Jr. That all right with you?"

"Whatever you say, Ellie. Ellie?"

Granny Richards had slipped up behind him. Now she said, "Quit pesterin' her. Back off and I'll put the youngun in his crib."

Jock stood up. "Take good care of her, Granny."

She rolled her lower lip at him, looked as if she meant to spit. "Knowed Ellie Southworth since she was knee-high to a grasshopper; helped her mama birth her, and a whole lot more. Never did nothin' but take real good care of 'em all."

"I know," Jock said. "It's just that she—she means so much to me, and so does the boy. When she wakes up, tell her for me."

He could feel her tired old eyes probing his back as he turned. "Reckon?" she said.

The doctor and nurse were to stay on, to be certain of everything, and he shook hands with them both. Then he went back downstairs and out to the car again. "A boy," he said as Bond snapped into first and away from the house."

"Good," Bond said. "Most times, that is."

"Know what you mean," Jock said. "Wasn't nobody scared of me, but I expect I'd a' just as soon had it that way, than bein' ignored."

"No, you wouldn't," Bond said, then: "I got the cameras, flash and all, in the trunk with the fat man's suitcases."

"Patty McCready ought to have him screwed to a nub by now, especially if the Jessup gal pitched in. Which one is she, anyway?"

"Sally," Bond said. "Bet a dollar she climbed 'em both."

Jock frowned and braced both hands against the dash as the car slewed around a dirt road ess curve. "She acts normal. You mean she really likes other gals, too?"

"Too," Bond said, his funny pale eyes shining cat-like when light bounced back at them.

Swallowing, Jock said, "Never could understand folks like that. But it'll save us trouble and time."

"Be right there at the back door," Bond Whitson said. "Look yonder—he got every lamp in the cabin goin'." He laughed, a hissing sound he didn't often make. "Could be the gals lit 'em, though. Patty and Sally, they like to *see* what they're doin'."

"Cut the lights and motor," Jock said, so he wouldn't have to comment on anything else.

"You goin' in, ain't you? Stage it all—if you have to."

"Sure. Just don't want to spook him, that's all."

When he got inside, he saw it hadn't taken long, and he was damned glad he didn't have to see anything between Patty and the Jessup girl. Kelly was spilled naked across the bed on his back, bloated belly rising and falling as he snored. Little redheaded Patty grinned at him. "Didn't last no longer'n a fart in a dust devil, you had him so drunk already."

The Jessup girl—Sally?—said: "Kind of a shame." She was dark, and bare-assed too.

Jock waved a big hand at the kitchen door. "Might as well come in, Bond. He's passed out."

"Bond Whitson?" Sally whispered. "Oh lord, don't ask me to—"

"Wasn't meanin' to," Jock said, "but if I say so, you goddamn well *will.*"

Too pale, too white, Bond slid into the cabin, big

camera and flash ready. "Works good, but I got a backup in case. Want me to fix him?"

"I'll do it," Jock said. "Don't mind gettin' my hands dirty, and I owe that bastard for sayin' *sir* to him all the way home."

But after staging the first two pictures, he backed away and let Bond slap Frank Kelly half awake, so he could set the man's head between Patty McCready's legs.

"Leavin' enough face so folks can tell who it is," Bond said.

"You—you ain't meanin' to show these around?" Patty said, head thrown back and her pert little tits standing up. "My daddy would near about *kill* me."

"Be safe to say these'll stay hid until hell and half of Texas freezes over," Jock answered, moving to the table and washing away the taste of what he'd seen with whiskey. The son of a bitch, thinking he could just come stomping into Jock Ewing's county and tear up the pea patch. From now on, he'd be in Ewing Oil's hind pocket, and when Aritex cut off his money for not voting its way, too goddamn bad.

Any one of these pictures passed around Frank Kelly's home graze, and the congressman would be treading water in shit creek. Hard-shell Baptists, the Bible Belt—hell, he'd be lucky to get off with just tar and feathers.

Kelly wobbled around and dragged his face from between Patty McCready's spread thighs, tried to pull his scrotum from Sally's clenched hand. "Wh-what?"

"Get a couple there," Jock said, and took another drink. "He's got his eyes open and up on his knees."

"She—this bitch's squeezin' my nuts off," Kelly blurted, and when the flash blinded him said: "What the hell? What the *hell*, boy?"

"Boy, your fat ass," Jock said. "*Ewing*, you pulpit-thumping, Sundy-go-to-meetin' bastard. To you, it's *Mr*. Ewing."

Struggling, Kelly pushed Patty McCready back and pawed up at the other girl, tried to roll off the bed and get at the camera. Bond Whitson made his strange laughing noise and slapped the congressman back onto the bed.

Kelly said, "Ewing, I'll have your lights and liver for this. Goddamn—you think anybody's goin' to believe—"

"*Everybody'll* believe," Jock said. "Knock his head again, Bond. The son of a bitch forgot to say mister."

Squealing, Kelly backed, hunched for the wall, one hand to his head where cared-for silvery hair was mussed, one hand covering his balls. The girls looked up and when Jock nodded, slipped off to a corner where another bottle stood. They whispered to each other.

Jock said, "I got sworn depositions on file, statements by these two fifteen-year-old girls as to how you seduced 'em. I got notarized statements by four grown-up witnesses, sayin' as how they heard the screamin' and had to bust in to save these underage girls, and found this other man takin' dirty pictures."

"Fifteen years old," Kelly said. "Underaged gals. Migod. And you—you had my face crammed in there between her legs, you two-bit hustler."

Jock didn't have to tell Bond to hit the man. Bond did it on his own, and crammed his fist just about to the wrist in Kelly's puffy gut. Jock took another pull at the bottle of bourbon while Kelly kicked on the bed and made puking sounds.

When the choking noises died down, Jock said, "*Mr.* Ewing, lard ass, and don't ever forget it. You used to be smart, but now you're just one more stupid bastard caught by the short hairs, caught because you got too fat and sassy."

The whiskey was thickening Jock's tongue, but he went on. "You'll be contacted when I want somethin' out of you. Give me one second of trouble and you might as well light a shuck for somewhere the state of Texas can't extradite you—or the daddies of these girls get at you. Better have a heap of Aritex money put by, I'd say."

Sick, Kelly whispered, "You—you got me, I reckon."

"Right," Jock said. "Practice sayin' it."

"M-mr," Kelly mumbled, "Mr. Ewing." The words pained him more than his aching belly.

"Fine," Jock said, and while Bond drove the car and the man to the hotel in town, Jock took the cabin truck and the girls to the Jessup gate and paid them, let them out. "I don't have to tell you, do I?"

Sally said quietly, "And get that scary Bond set after us? No, sir. I been with him once—just once."

Patty McCready said, "That's all you want, Jock? I mean, Sally's folks are clear over in the next county, and it's so early—"

"Night," Jock said, and drove off, leaving them. He drank whiskey all the way back to the ranch. Asking him to stay over, those kids, those girls who played with each other; what did they think he was?

Staggering from the parked truck, he thought, hell —he was a father himself.

CHAPTER 9

Pregnancy was more a bother the second time around. So much to get done, to check into and oversee around the ranch, and this grotesque belly always in the way. Ellie's belly. She made a face at it, wishing she could time her kids better. They should all be born after fall roundup and before spring calving, but they had their own stubborn way of coming about.

She leaned forward so she could massage the small of her back. From where she sat in the rocker on the front porch, she could see dust rising from a catch corral, and hear the bellow of outraged calves being

branded. That's where she liked to be, pushing critters
into a chute, examining for pinkeye; she didn't much
care for dehorning, but dirty work went along with
the good.

It was where JR ought to be, time he could sit a
horse, too. JR—funny how quick her "Johnny" had
been turned into JR by Jock. "Junior's no name to
call a boy," he said. "Brings him nothing but trouble."
So JR it became, like everything else Jock wanted
done with or to his son.

"Like I had nothin' to do with making him," Ellie
said, resting hands on her distended belly. "And JR
will never ride drag on a cattle herd, nor even learn
to throw a rope."

It was easy to see already, she thought. The boy was
home now, but gone about half the time. Only pushing five years old, and his daddy was already hauling
him around to oil wells and offices, hardly giving JR
time to *be* a boy, to play. In a few more years, he'd be
Jock all over again.

Feeling movement beneath her hands, she swore
that this baby wouldn't be dragged away from her
right off, if ever. A girl—she wanted a nice little girl,
but Granny Richards had just about gone blind with
cataracts and wasn't all that certain.

Ellie sighed. Maybe she ought to be happy that Jock
was such an interested father, and damned glad she
was as hard to catch as a mare with one ovary. The
time Jock did stay home—well, most of it was spent
in bed, and "spent" was the word. But it seemed as if
nature decided when Ellie Ewing would be pregnant,
for they never used anything.

Probably it happened when they got fierce, the way
it was when they were making up after a particularly
mean fight. She smiled and watched dust rise from the
corral. They really went at it then, kind of like one
was trying to punish the other, or maybe as if one had
almost walked away and been forever lost. The bed
caught hell, made so much noise that Ellie was sure

the servants could hear all the banging. And Ellie probably got pregnant.

Jock would like it to happen more. If he had his way, four or five younguns would be tagging behind her by now. But the one she did have *wasn't;* he was in his daddy's pocket, Daddy's boy.

Awkwardly, she hefted from the rocker and stood duck-footed, breathing deeply. Jock didn't butt heads with her so much anymore; he'd learned to stay out of ranch business, learned that she would holler for help when she couldn't get by, and not before. And so long as beef was up and the rains on time, there was no point in him running over the land, drilling holes in every likely arroyo.

"If ever we flat-out *need* any oil that might be under the Southfork," she'd told him when Jock accused her of being as muley as her pa, "then *that's* the time to tear up the land looking for it."

"Just like old Sam," Jock argued. "He never could understand that oil is money, and if it ain't being used, it's going to waste."

She said, "You have all the money you'll ever use," and knew it wasn't true, that Jock Ewing would always want more.

She went into the house and along the hall to the kitchen for a bite of something. The little scudder she was carrying was always hungry. She was munching on a buttered cold biscuit stuffed with a slab of red onion when Lupe came in from the back.

"Ah, *señora,*" the woman said, "this one will be big and strong."

Flenching, Ellie said, "I wish he'd wait till he's out here to show his strength."

"*Cómo?*" Lupe was puzzled for only a moment, then laughed. "So—that is the way of the strong. To push, make themselves felt."

The woman turned away, began to take fresh vegetables from a sack and put them on the drainboard. Ellie drank some milk and asked, "Is that what they're sayin', that Jock is pushin' too much?"

Lupe's shoulders rolled expressively; her back remained straight. Still facing the sink, she said, "I would not speak against the *patrón*."

"But others do?"

"Small people, *señora*. And yet—"

Ellie finished the milk. "Some are respected, *es verdad*? Some are the old families?"

"The old *Norteamericano* families, *sí*."

Leaving glass and plate on the table, Ellie grunted up and held her stomach. Nothing was ever forgotten in this part of the country—the wrenching of Texas from Mexico, surviving Apaches and Comanches blaming both countries and each other, the War between the States—every injury, real or imagined, was huddled jealously to the heart.

Though she understood the attitude, Ellie was often irked by it. Lupe and Manuel and their kids had practically been part of the Southworth family, ever since she could remember. The baby kicked again, and she gnawed her lower lip. Her day for facing up to the truth, she guessed. Sure, the servants had been here forever; their ancestors owned the land. As for being all that much family, if Ellie didn't have to make out their paychecks, she'd have a hard time remembering Lupe and Manuel had a last name—Vasquez. The upstairs maid was Maria, the older daughter; the yardboy was, ah—Guadalupe. No wonder she couldn't recall it all the time, and used Chico instead.

Waddling into the parlor, Ellie thought about the bit of gossip passed on. The cattle families had never really accepted Jock, though some of them had been glad enough to come running with leases in hand, after that last bad spell with the weather. But it was as though there were two classes of folks, cowmen and oilmen. That was funny, since some of the cow outfits were just scraping by, and some had never been more than shirttail operations anyhow.

Of course, Jock did lean a little heavy sometimes, and stomp some toes he didn't really mean to walk on. But it was mostly because he didn't notice, or kind of brushed other folks aside in his impatience to *go, to be, to do.*

If she mentioned it to him, it'd be like him telling her which bulls to cull and which to run with the herds. She'd tried to show him how it was, a time or two, but Jock only bowed his neck and they'd had one of their fights. She'd drop some more hints about getting along better with neighbors and maybe he wouldn't sull up like a possum.

Heavily, she sat down in her pa's big chair. A girl— this baby should be a dark-headed girl who would grow slim and straight and maybe have hazel eyes that could sparkle with laughter. Someone to read to in the evenings when Jock wasn't home, to explore poetry with.

Poetry and Willard Barnes—they'd always go together in Ellie's mind, and often make her sad. Maybe only sad people became poets, crying out against loneliness, singing of hope and of lost loves . . . oh, yes, the lost loves.

Where was Willard now? Nobody seemed to know, or at least word hadn't come back for quite a spell. What with all the war clouds gathering, there was no telling what Willard would do. He was romantic enough to enlist in some foreign army, expecting banners and drumrolls, anticipating trumpet calls to glory. Heroes were always immortal and bigger than life. It was what Willard needed.

And every woman needed a Willard Barnes in her life, if only for a short while, if only once. He was something to be savored, then put by in a memory box with an old rag doll and high school graduation pictures, with all silly, crazy, sentimental things. It didn't hurt to take them out once in a while and fondle them in nostalgia, to daydream. It was foolish only when you fought to forever look like the graduation pictures or expected comfort from that favorite old doll.

Ellie sighed again and felt a contraction. So soon? The baby wasn't due for another two, three weeks.

Maybe it was only a cramp, but she had better call Jock anyway. She reached for the phone and gave his office number in Dallas.

"Leaving right away," he said. "Don't want to miss this one. You call the hospital?"

"After I call Granny," she said. "Might be a false alarm."

"You ain't the kind to spook, hon. I'm leavin' right now."

Sitting beside Bond Whitson as his driver tooled the tailor-made Continental through city traffic, Jock propped his head back against the seat and closed his eyes. It had been a good week all around: crude prices had damned near doubled, the oil senators introduced by Frank Kelly were most amenable, and the other independent outfits had elected him head of their coalition. And there was the government contract.

Kelly was still toeing the mark, with no sign of kicking over the traces, and he'd better bigod not. It was pretty impressive to have senators from California, Oklahoma, and Louisiana in his corner, and they were foxier than Frank Kelly. It had been easy to show them the trouble that could be avoided by using independent oil companies, that "monopoly" was a dirty word surfacing too often in legal circles.

It was a great time to be in the oil business. Every time Hitler made another move in Europe, prices jumped. There'd be no staying out of the war for the U.S., despite all the isolationist talk in Washington; it was only a matter of when. Roosevelt had started getting his feet wet already, by setting up Lend-Lease. The army and navy knew we were about yay far from getting up with the shooting; that's why defense oil contracts were being given out, and security jerked tight around the navy's Teapot reserves.

"How was Washington?" Bond asked.

Jock kept his eyes closed. "Tirin' but profitable."

"Can't see you flyin' around like that. Damned planes ain't safe."

"Fast is first, then comes safe, and don't go bad-mouthin' airplanes, good buddy. Uncle pays high for that fuel, and we just happen to have a new high-octane cracking plant at the refinery."

Bond said, "Old fat man didn't give you no trouble?"

"Uh-uh. Kelly flat knows how to put a shine on things. Comes grinnin' and howdyin' up to me like we been asshole buddies all our lives. He'd sure appreciate gettin' me off his back, but ain't come up with a way yet. I keep a close watch on him." Jock cracked one eye and saw they were out on the highway heading northwest, that traffic was thinning and dusk coming down from the foothills.

Bond snapped on the lights. "Them little old girls gone from the county."

"What girls?"

"The ones we trapped the fat man with—Patty McCready and Sally Jessup. Been gone a long time."

Jock turned his head and sought comfort, sought sleep. He didn't answer Bond. Thinking on it now, it didn't seem near as bad as he'd made it out at first. Hell, in Dallas and Washington, men were always joking about going down on some woman: *Man, oh man; I'd eat a foot of her hockey, just to get to bite it off at her ass.* Could be it was only joking, and if it came right down to it, nobody would respect a man who put his mouth on a woman like that, or the other way around.

"Expect them gals out whorin' on their own," Bond said, "but there ain't no word of 'em in Dallas. Too easy for their daddies to find 'em there, I reckon. I'd say California, out where that airplane factory is. Hear them factory fellas make pretty good wages, and the gals, they'll sure know how to get hold of some."

Jock stayed quiet, but vivid images of those kids came back, and pretty soon got mixed up with the secretary in Frank Kelly's office, because she had red hair, too. She always gave him a special smile and a straight look that said: *Come on, baby.* But Jock

Ewing wasn't fixing to get tangled up in the same net he'd used to nail Kelly's hide to the wall.

True, it sometimes got hard on a man when he stayed away from his wife so much, and it was rougher than a cob to get home with her too swelled for loving. Dallas was too close to home pasture, and Washington was Kelly's stomping ground, so it was grit your teeth. Besides, when Ellie wasn't carrying a baby, she was as much woman as any man needed. Still, being gone so long did make you dwell on pretty young things with skirts whispering around full thighs, leggy young girls with high tits and bouncy, tight asses.

Damn, Jock thought, it would only be twelve, thirteen years before JR would be sniffing around split-tails—if not earlier. What with the war coming on, it seemed like regular manners and morals were headed for hell on a downhill slide. War was good for business but rough on families with kids, and from the looks of things, this war could drag on for a long time.

"Buncha goddamned idiots in Washington," he mumbled.

"Sure," Bond Whitson said. "Everybody knows that."

Sorry he'd spoken aloud, Jock scrunched his body around for more comfort. Bond kept talking awhile, but when Jock didn't answer, he fell quiet and pushed the Continental hard for Travis City.

Still unable to sleep, Jock thought of Ellie and the coming child. He was glad for another youngun, and would like a few more, but Ellie was difficult to catch. Maybe if he was home more and could work at it, she'd be in foal every year until she hollered enough.

Ewing & Sons. It wouldn't take much of a change, and that a tax write-off. He'd have men around him he'd be able to trust because they were his own blood, young Ewings standing to the world. They'd be proud of the name and the blood, tied forever to the company *and* to the land, having the best oil *and* cattle could offer. Even if he hadn't loved Ellie, marrying her would have made a heap of sense. It didn't do for folks to run off without a home to come back to. Rootless men just weren't worth a damn, looked like: Digger Barnes, his own pa, most wildcatters and roughnecks. Oil made the money, but land made it worth working for, land and the family it grew.

But some folks were *too* damned tied to the land, stubborn and a little stupid and independent as a hog on ice. The McCreadys and Jessups, setting away back up in the hills on their few hundred acres, not wanting anything else, letting their younguns go bad and slip away. Then there were the bigger ranchers—the Onstadts, Barkers, Rogerses—trying to act like God gave them the holy say-so in the county, hollering about seepage ruining water sources, about taxes overlapping from the oil industry onto their land—or leases pushing cattle from government range they'd grazed so long the ranchers thought they owned it.

The big cattlemen had been in political control so long, it was a real burr in their hide when oil outfits brought in their own men, from county to state to federal. Of course, the ranchers fought for every vote, for every office, once they realized what was going on. But money was the crude oil that refined politics, greasing skids or buttering up, as the occasion called for. There were times ranchers got caught short, low beef years, bad drought years, and the intransigent ones found themselves out scuffling for credit.

Oil had no bad market now; wet or dry didn't matter—only good sense and good luck.

"Southfork comin' up," Bond Whitson said. "Miz Ellie made some changes while you were gone."

Rubbing his face and sitting up, Jock saw a new gravel drive circling in, taller gateposts, something done to the front porch. He saw cars out front—the new Ford from the hospital, that old rattletrap belonging to kinfolks of Granny Richards and held together with baling wire and faith. Have to see about getting Granny something better, Jock thought; Ellie believed so in the muley old woman. But he'd have to fix it so those Richards younguns couldn't get hold of a new car and tear it up; worthless bunch of bastards, running off green bootlegs or just lying around, never doing an honest day's work.

No Ewing would turn out like that. He'd see to it that every Ewing stood head and hat above anybody else in the county. He looked up when he got out of the Continental, looked up at the master bedroom that now was his and Ellie's, since the shade of Sam Southworth had faded with the lingering, old-man smell of him. Electric lights were bright up there, and as Jock trotted up to the porch, he heard the uncertain, angry wail of a baby's first cry.

CHAPTER 10

Ellie shifted on the propped-up bed and twice called out for Lupe. Then she unglued her eyes and remembered that Lupe and Manuel and the young man she often called Chico had left the Southfork a while back. Hell of a note, and so much for the loyalty of old family retainers. Maybe they had gotten their backs up about the time Jock brought in the coloreds to help. Jesus—talk about prejudice! Mexicans were worse than anybody about that.

The pain came dully at first, pushing against the tight band of her stomach. It was stronger than the ache behind her eyes and the brassy taste in her throat. Ellie remembered she wasn't at home, wasn't in her own familiar bed on the ranch. This room was institutionally cheerful, a sunshine yellow, its smell of roses fragrant, but not quite covering up the odor of fears and chemicals and forgotten death that had been painted into the walls.

After this long, a goddamned hospital. Nothing to replace Granny Richards when the old midwife passed on—only a sterile, spooky hospital.

Then she thought: The baby! My God, what about the baby, my daughter?

Turning, wincing, she fumbled around and found a push button. The belly-hurt knifed a little bit sharper, and she used its cutting edge on the nurse who came rustling in: "My baby—where's my baby?"

"Mrs. Ewing," the nurse said, pushing up her heavy-rimmed eyeglasses with a quick, jerky finger, "we must be calm, take it easy. Your son is just fine, breathing normally, prognosis excellent. And you—we really shouldn't be awake yet. That's why doctor isn't—"

Reaching for the water with its bent glass straw, wanting to press hard on her belly and make the pain quit roweling her, Ellie thought: Migod, another boy. Three in a row, and wasn't that supposed to be a charm? Well, there'd be no goddamned way of finding out, even if she was looking for one. "My husband," she said around the glass stem between her teeth, "did he get here?"

The nurse pushed at her glasses again, fiddled with the nameplate that read CAXTON and drifted crackling over to brush deftly and uselessly at the bed covers. "He called, Mrs. Ewing. He's still in Washington, and—"

"The bastard didn't even try, did he?"

Leaning to straighten the pillow, Nurse Caxton said, "I—he sent a message after Doctor told him you were in no real, immediate danger. Mr. Ewing—" she said the name with a certain grudging reverence— "Mr. Ewing said to tell you he'd be here tomorrow or the next day at the latest. Now, if we can just take a look at our bandages—"

"Get away from me!" Ellie said fiercely. "If *we* have bandages, peep at your own, but meantime, go chase that damn doctor in here. What the hell am I paying him a fortune for?"

Eyes squeezed shut against the threat of tears, she

cursed Jock Ewing and Washington and oil. He'd missed all *three* births, damn him. He'd come close on the first two, getting there just behind JR, and almost making it for Gary's appearance. For this one, he hadn't even tried. Jock Ewing was so gaddamned important to everybody else that his own wife and baby didn't mean anything these days.

He'd wanted sons, and she sure gave them to him: three boys spaced over ten years, and married longer than that. And maybe that was it. He was tired of her, and kids weren't a big event anymore. But Jock Ewing never tired of working at oil and politics and playing at gentleman rancher.

"Mrs. Ewing."

Dr. Woodall moved as if he was always walking on tiptoe to make himself taller, and his eyes blinked, peered, and blinked again, over and over. But Ellie knew him for a smart, efficient little bastard. Little men were often that way, sometimes overreaching to prove themselves. *Like Willard Barnes?*

"My baby—my son's okay?"

"Fine, just fine." He came around the bed and lifted the sheet. Behind him, Nurse Caxton pursed dry lips.

"And me, Doctor?" Why should Willard come to mind at a time like this?

"You're great, too. A week, maybe a little longer, and you can go back to that beautiful ranch." He touched her gently, drew back, lowered the sheet. "Does it hurt?"

"Goddamned right it hurts. And I still don't see why you couldn't have—done what you did out at the house, instead of this, this—" Ellie waved her hand at the too-cheerful walls, the bank of red and white roses, enough for a funeral, for *two* buryings. *Maybe Willard was dead.*

"I explained that, Mrs. Ewing. The operating room, the urgency—"

She wanted more water and when her hand moved, he brought the glass straw to her lips. The water tasted like chemicals, like Jock Ewing's filthy oil smelled. Ellie sipped and nodded and said, "You've been my doctor for more than ten years. I reckon that's long enough for you to be able to call me Ellie. Or does Jock Ewing scare you, too?"

Dr. Woodall came up on his toes, settled back down, motioned for the nurse to go away. "Only death frightens me, Mrs.—Ellie, and that's because it defeats me too often." He blinked, frowned, and blinked. "But this time, I win. You'll probably outlive most of the county."

"Useful as a barren brood mare." Ellie didn't mean it; she just had to snap at somebody, and Woodall was close.

"Oh, come on, Ellie. How many children did you intend to produce? You're healthy and the child is too. You're way ahead. All that baby-making machinery; you're better off without it."

"I did want—" she began, and stopped. It would seem juvenile, to prattle about the slim, dark girl she never had, never would have. "I'll take your word for the baby's condition, Doctor. Something like pulling a hind-to foal, I guess; if it makes it through birthing, it's usually okay. I thought I wanted to see him, but— seems like I'm pretty damned tired."

Woodall motioned to the nurse. She rustled close and swabbed Ellie's arm. The needle bite was only a twinge. Ellie closed her eyes and the doctor said something about take it easy, about seeing the baby later, and she nodded. Later was soon enough, and Jock could damned well name this one, for she didn't mean to fight him over the latest Ewing.

He had JR, but she'd managed to keep Gary close to her and at home on the ranch. He was a quiet kid, keeping to himself most times and more confident around animals than people. Nothing wrong with that, although she had to nag at him to keep his school grades anywhere near JR's, and Ellie would bet Gary was smarter all around.

Gary—eight years old, wearing a name she'd pulled out of the air because she liked the sound of it.

She'd thought of Samuel, for her pa, but it just didn't seem to fit anybody else. Now Jock could pick a name, whether to "honor" anybody or not. If he didn't, she swore to start calling the new kid Ewing.

Jock could have made it, if he tried. He was flying most everywhere now, mixed up in so many deals, pulling strings everywhere. The way a lot of folks in Travis City looked at him, he could climb on top of his big office building in Dallas, flap his arms, and make it home on his own.

Drifting . . . she was drifting now and the pain in her belly stopped. Not fair to Jock, she realized. He was just the same when he was home, and they could laugh together, make love like newlyweds. But he wasn't home enough—and making a duplicate of himself in the oldest boy. Men did that, without thinking that maybe the boy didn't want to be like his daddy, that he was part somebody else and the blood cross made him one of a kind.

Still, JR took to his daddy's shaping, and Gary took to hers, and she wondered drowsily how the boys would be if they'd been let alone. Maybe she'd find out with the new one, if Jock didn't start hauling him off, too. . . .

Funny how she'd thought of Willard Barnes; she'd seen Dr. Woodall for all these years, and never compared him to Willard before. He hadn't consciously been in her mind for—oh, when was the last time? When the papers ran the story about him winning the Silver Star in Europe?

Jock hadn't ignored that; he'd been a mite too casual about it, though. "Once a fool, always a fool," he said. "Says here that Sergeant Willard Barnes led his Engineer platoon into attack to save an infantry squad."

"What's foolish about that?" she asked.

"Engineers build roads, bridges, stuff like that. Digger must have had his men too far up, and he risked a whole platoon to bring out less than a quarter as many men."

She'd leaned over his shoulder to look at the old picture of Willard. It was a blown-up snapshot, taken when he was probably drunk, but she could see the devilish gleam in his eye and the tenderness of his mouth. "Army thought he did all right," she said.

He didn't rumple the paper and throw it in the fireplace, as she'd expected. Instead, Jock folded and put it aside. "I don't feel a damned bit guilty about being draft-exempt. If the troops, planes, and ships don't get oil, they don't go anywhere."

She had leaned her head against the mantelpiece and looked into the fire, where flames danced and skipped in open, shameless passions. "I never faulted you for that, Jock," she'd said. "*Women* know all wars are stupid."

But Willard was a hero, now. She hoped it made him happy. Thinking about it, Ellie floated down through the hospital bed, through cool marble floors, and out into the swimmy, flowered green of a place where it was always April.

It wasn't spring in Washington, but a chill and thunder-shot night. Jock Ewing looked at his watch, the telephone, the door to his suite. Damnit, he'd play hell explaining this delay to Ellie, and how bad he felt about it, but she never understood how it was in this town. And Roberta Lessing made it plain she had something of value for him. Representative Frank Kelly had dropped dead this morning, and any information his secretary had might be important.

She couldn't compromise him now; she was the woman who'd always smiled at him with that direct, sensuous look. With Kelly gone, it didn't make sense for her to try and trap him. But Bond Whitson waited in the room across the hall, his pale, cold eye to the door crack, in case anybody tried coming through a locked door after Roberta was inside.

Walking to the bar, Jock poured Scotch neat, drank it off with a flip, and lighted an imported cigar. He rolled the mild smoke inside his mouth, let it drift upward. Rarely did he roll a cigarette from the sack of Bull Durham always carried in his shirt pocket, tag dangling. Nowadays that was mostly for show. It was funny how a man's taste changed.

Her knock at the door was like what he knew of Roberta—straightforward, a little sassy. He let her in and caught a trailing of crisp perfume, something different and lively. Jock slid the door bolt and watched her walk saucily to the bar, her trim tail swinging. A ripe woman, he thought for the hundredth time, with boiling juice beneath that cool, challenging manner. Roberta wore her red hair short but loosely curling over an aristocratic neck, a pert face.

"Help yourself," he said, noting the big purse she toted.

"Thanks." Her eyes were watchful brown, her skin a polished cream and rose. Roberta's mouth was a melon slash, wetly daring. She moved without lost motion, agile and smooth, pouring her drink, saluting him with it.

"You're not all broken up about Frank Kelly," he said.

"Neither are you." There was a throaty quality about her voice, the sort of huskiness singers talk with. "Jock, you should celebrate."

He came over slowly, freshened his glass. "I didn't hate Frank."

"He despised you." Roberta's eyes looked into his. "Frank hated you so much that he spent half his time trying to get back at you for setting him up."

"He told you about that?"

She tilted her head and traced the outline of her lower lips with the tip of her tongue, slowly. Still watching him, Roberta opened her purse and took out a thick manila envelope. "He wasn't far from hitting you with this. It's his dossier on *your* activities."

Gingerly, Jock opened the file and sat on the couch to scan through it. The old bastard—he's really dug after some of this stuff. Nothing sexual—Jock had always been clean there—but there were many notes

of various dealings with certain politicians; photo-
stats; bank-slip copies. Perhaps the most damaging
was the long string of entries in Kelly's own hand—
dates and times of money received from John Ewing,
Sr., in behalf of Ewing Oil. Each entry was notarized
by Roberta Lessing.

"I don't think he'd have bothered me much," Jock
said, and noticed his cigar had gone out. He flicked a
gold lighter at it.

"No bother is better," Roberta answered. "Frank
had a lot of connections; some you know, some you
don't."

"And you do? What do you want for this, Miss
Lessing?"

Her smile was sultry, and she stood hipshot like a
trim mare, one knee out and relaxed. "Nothing for
what I gave you there. For other goodies, I'd like a
steady job—as lobbyist for the Texas Independents.
I'll be good at it, Jock. I'm good at everything I do."

"I'll bet," he said, and had to glance away when she
rolled her hips just that little bit. Damn, but the
woman had a great body, and she'd been one of Frank
Kelly's play-toys, maybe the main one. It wouldn't hurt
to have a woman like her on the payroll. "You've got
a job, Roberta. Make the pay big enough to take care
of everything; expenses will be separate."

She arched a dark eyebrow. "You trust me to set my
own salary?"

"I know you're smart. That means you won't take a
bite so big it'll make the T.I. board edgy."

With another drink, she saluted him. "Thanks.
Here's to Texas Independents and its president. Drink
to that with me?"

His glass clicked hers, and again he drew in that
oddly appealing scent and tried to drown it with
Scotch. She was too damned close, and he had a kid
just born in Texas. He inched back from her and
found a barstool at the base of his spine. He said,
"The announcement didn't cover much, just that
Kelly strangled in his sleep."

"Sleep, sure. He passed out after a gigantic dinner and too much whiskey. Sometime in the night, Frank Kelly threw up, but not all the way, and choked on his own sickness. I know because I was on the couch. I always slept on the couch when he got stinking drunk."

Roberta placed her glass on the bar top, then reached down to cup Jock between the thighs. She stared right into his eyes when she did it, this sudden and surprisingly direct thing no woman had ever done to him. He braced there, taut and shaken, and when she continued to hold him, when she leaned the top of her body over and covered his lips with her hotly seeking mouth, Jock quivered.

It felt like she was the male, that she meant to take him, mount him, rape him if she had to, and there wasn't a hell of a lot he could do about it.

He didn't want to do anything, didn't want to back off. His rod swelled and pushed against her caressing hand; his tongue clashed with hers, and his arms went around her narrow waist. Big and full, Roberta's breasts cushioned to his chest; her mouth drank greedily of him.

Thunder rolled outside and wet wind rattled the hotel windows as Jock reached the floor with her. She didn't have anything on under the tailored dress, not a stitch of underwear except a lace garter belt to keep her nylons smooth. His pants were still tangled about his ankles when she guided him into her violently heaving body, satin and lava and practiced skill.

A long, long time since he'd touched another woman; years and years of knowing only Ellie. This wasn't love; it wasn't even tenderness. Her naked belly slapped an urgent rhythm against him, as Roberta twisted and writhed, gripping him, urgent. Not love and not tenderness, but a fierce battle for dominance that he had to win.

Driving up into her, digging into the flexing heat of her, Jock felt her shudder to completion and tried to impale her upon that vibrant moment. She snapped off him and slid up his chest, a blackwet thrusting at his face.

He slapped her hard, and she rolled off him. He saw blood on her mouth as she whipped around and took him into her lips. He tugged at her, but Roberta let him feel the warning edges of her teeth, and he gasped.

Calling her bitch and whore and cunt, he found his hands tangled in short, bobbing hair. She moaned with him, writhed with him, and when a thunderclap shook the room, it seemed appropriate.

CHAPTER 11

Ellie's words dripped a cold venom that stung more fiercely than if she'd come at him with a buggy whip. "You miserable son of a bitch," she said. "I can just about understand you gettin' mixed up with another woman, but to name your youngest son after her—"

"Ellie," Jock said. "Now look here, Ellie—I didn't have anything of the sort in mind. I mean, she'd already called you with that lie about me wantin' to call him Robert—"

"For Roberta," she said, coiled against any approach by him, ready to strike. "Callin' *my* son after your mistress, goddamn you. With the other boys, naming was left up to me. You said you had nobody to *honor* —until her, is that it?"

"I swear," he said helplessly, "I *swear*, Ellie—when I knew what she'd done, it was already too late. I couldn't tell you then; damnit, you can't *expect* me to have told you then."

"Five years," she said, putting her back to him and staring out their bedroom window. "Five long years,

and that—that bitch just had to be certain I knew.
Can't change the boy's name without mixin' him up
good. We call him Bobby; you call her that—Bobbi,
with a cute little feminine *I*?"

"Ellie"—he drank the Scotch in his glass without
tasting it—"how you expect me to tell you how it is,
unless you let me?"

Whirling on him, eyes sparking-cold blue, she said:
"Oh no, I'll tell *you!* She wants something, real bad—
like your name, so she can strut biggity around Washington. Or she'll kick over your playhouse; that it,
lover? Can your connivin' slut put you on the griddle,
chase you back to little ol' Muleshoe County with
your ears cropped and your tail between your legs?"

"Just about," he admitted. "I knew she was one hell
of a smart woman when she came to me with all that
stuff Kelly put together on me. A lobbying job and
good money; that's all she asked—then. Now it looks
like she wants it all."

Jock got up and stalked to the bar, poured another. "Yes, damnit; she can kick slats out of the
structure we got built from here to Washington. She
kept certified copies of the Kelly information, and
she's added a heap more to it since. She can only
bruise a few of the bigwigs, but *me*—" He looked
down into his glass. "How long have you known,
Ellie?"

"I didn't know," she said. "I suspected, which
counts the same in a woman's tally book. Tell me,
Jock, why? *Why*, damnit? You never had time for me,
let alone another woman. Did I get too old, too fat?
I only put on about four pounds since we got married, and my hair hasn't started turning yet. Is she
better in bed, doin' for you everything you won't let
me do?"

He said, "Damnit, Ellie—a man don't discuss that,
especially with his wife. A wife's one thing, a—a—
mistress is another."

"We're both women," she said, tight-lipped. "What
do you mean to do about this mess?"

Rolling whiskey glass between his palms, Jock said, "Don't know yet. Whole lot is ridin' on you, I reckon —how you take it."

She stared hard at him. "How do you suppose I take it? My ranch, my house, *my* kids—"

"Your husband?"

"Is that the way you want it, Jock? Do you still want a wife and sons, and—"

"I never quit lovin' you, Ellie; not for a minute. I—oh hell, I don't know how to put it, how to explain."

Her back straight and stiff, she looked as young as ever in faded jeans and open-throat shirt, in scuffed boots and her hair twisted up somehow in a bandanna. She said, "There is no explanation, unless you figured this to make us even."

"I never thought—"

Ellie said, "I loved Willard Barnes, or thought I did, and he was *before* you. Does it still bother you so much?"

"No," he said, "and it isn't like that at all. It never was."

"All right, then. What are you aiming to do about this woman?"

Jock frowned. "Don't know yet; I'm still thinkin' on it. She won't keep the stuff where I can lay a hand to it. Not that much of a hurry; she gave me a week."

"Good of her." She started out of the room.

"Where you goin'?"

"Not to the lawyer, just to pack a bag. Believe I'll take me a trip."

He put out a hand. "Please—"

"Oh," Ellie said, "and since you don't use Bond all that much these days, you won't miss him and the car for a spell. He mopes around when you're not here, spooks the rest of the help."

Jock poured another Scotch, lighted a cigar that tasted bitter, and sat down. Married near half his life to that woman, and she still popped surprises at him. He'd expected her to be mad as the devil in a snowstorm, but about him shacking up these last five years, not about naming the youngest boy after Roberta.

And Roberta—back when she had pulled that trick, calling Ellie, posing as his secretary, and saying the boy's name was Robert—he'd been about ready to slap the hell out of her. Except she got so damned cute and soft-eyed about it, crying some and saying how she'd had a brother Robert who'd been killed just before V-J Day, and how much loving Jock meant to her, and since they couldn't be together *all* the time—

One name was as good as another, he'd figured, and let it slide. Just like he let himself keep on slipping around with Roberta. Damnit, no matter what Ellie thought, he never called her Bobbi; nobody did. She was too high-nosed, too royal-looking to ever wear a nickname. A fine, aristocratic lady on her feet, on her back she was the randiest, wildest woman he'd ever run across. The things she did to him, the crazy things that shocked him, then got him all tangled up. . . .

And all the time, she was priming him for a mess of trouble. But not if he would shed Ellie and marry her. Like he ever would. Only a walleyed fool would leave a good woman for one as sly and slippery as Roberta. How many other stupid bastards did she have on the same trot line?

He was hooked good, swallowed clear to the sinker with the barb in his guts. Knowing in general what information she had, he might be able to cover most of his tracks, but not all the way. A congressional investigator with half the nose of a bluetick hound could sniff him down.

Carrying his glass back to the bar, Jock took the Scotch bottle over by the window and drank from it. Damned stuff had a flavor like iodine, and he wondered just when he'd started drinking it instead of honest bourbon.

It seemed he was puzzling a lot over things of late. It was as though he didn't have a clear objective for himself, like he was setting out across the desert and couldn't see a landmark, only shimmery heat waves that played they were water and weren't.

He wasn't that *old*, even if there was a little silver feathering in his hair just over both ears. Roberta said it made him look distinguished. Jock drank some more and watched slategray haze come easing down over the foothills. On the ranch, everything was clear, the operation laid out plain. All you had to stand off was bad luck and the weather, sickness and a low market. A full half the herd didn't ease around, trying to figure out a way to gore you in the back.

Dusk crept over the mesa, while a high cloud picked up a slash of red from the dying sun. It wouldn't be all that bad, if he was to pull in his horns and stay here, keep out of big-time politics. But since he'd got his feet wet in Washington, the Korean war had come along, following so close on the heels of World War II. It could be that War Number III was brewing in Asia. Wars meant juggling priorities, greasing the way for projects, keeping pipelines open and crude flowing, picking a way through a jumble of politicians. It couldn't be done from headquarters on the ranch.

Jock's cigar was cold. He dropped it in an ashtray and clicked on a lamp. Across the field, all he could make out was the high cloud, and it was fading, its life bled out into blackness. He was chewing this over as if he had a choice, as if he could decide for himself to stay in Texas and make damned sure Ewing Oil was nailed down tight for his sons, when it came time.

Look how JR did in school, high marks in mathematics, reading business magazines and trade journals as if he was grown up already, instead of just turned fifteen. Was it that long? Seemed that 1954 sneaked up before you knew it was coming, and next time you turned around, it would be ten years more whipped past.

JR would be ready to take a hand in the business pretty soon, with Gary coming along behind him, and backing them both up, Bobby. It would go on and on,

Ewing Oil passing down to their sons. That was how immortality worked. If somebody didn't come along to screw it all up.

He was about half-drunk and finding it tough to concentrate. There was Ellie and Roberta, and too bad it wasn't the way the Comanches had it in the olden days, when a brave had all the wives he could steal or buy and feed.

Pretty goddamned silly, he told himself, very carefully placing the empty Scotch bottle on the bar. Pretty damned silly, because Ellie and Roberta would be at each other with skinning knives and war axes before the teepee flap dropped.

"Wonder how the Injuns made do," he said, and again with caution, steered himself upstairs and to bed.

As the plane nosed down for a landing in Washington, Bond Whitson bored his fingers into the seat. Every time he had to fly, it spooked him bad. It was about the only thing that scared him, and he tried not to show it to Miz Ellie right beside him, hoping his sweat didn't shine that much.

He was damned glad when the noise stopped and the door opened. Bond relaxed and let the other thing nag at him. It was too late to wonder if he was doing the right thing, because Texas was long behind them and Miz Ellie was standing up, ready to walk the aisle. He had to go with her. He had known that from the time he opened his door to a knock and saw her standing there sad-eyed but with her jaw set.

It was to protect Jock, she said, and made it plain to him why. He'd never liked Roberta Lessing anyhow. She always stared at him from the corners of her eyes, like he was some kind of peep show; like folks in Travis City used to do until he got them set straight. But Jock said screw them, what the hell do they know. And Jock let him wear sunglasses and put on fake suntan and use gloves, so he wouldn't stand out in a crowd. So he wouldn't be a freak.

"I'll find the luggage, if you bring the car around," Miz Ewing said. "You did say Jock keeps one here?"

"Yes'm, a Caddy sets in the parking lot till we need it, or some big shot comes in he wants me to pick up special." Dropping his voice, Bond said, "Miz Ellie, you didn't have to come all this way. I can handle it by myself."

She put a hand on his arm. "I know that, Bond. I only wanted to see her once, give her a fightin' chance."

He wanted to say something else, but hurried away, powerful shoulders swinging, wearing sunglasses at night, and seeing good through them when lights didn't flash his eyes. That damned Lessing woman, letting on to Miz Ellie about getting her own name used on the littlest youngun. That was worse than trying to bust up Miz Ellie and Jock, meaning to take Jock away and live here in Washington forever.

If she could come between two fine people like that, it wouldn't be long before she'd have Bond out. She could tell he didn't cotton to her, the bitch—always cutting her eyes at him like he ought to be in a cage.

He found the Caddy and keyed the door, the ignition, and let the motor warm up. It hadn't been his place to say anything all this time, but when Miz Ellie came right out with how bad she needed his help, there wasn't nothing he could do but come along.

"And glad for the chance," he muttered, flicking on the car lights and circling out of the lot for the baggage pickup stand. It had been a long, dry spell, and he was beginning to get excited, to feel his belly tighten and his mouth go dry. He'd sworn he wouldn't turn loose again, that he'd never be as bad as he'd been down in Mexicali that night, because he didn't want something he did to backfire and get Jock.

But this time it was for Jock's own good; Miz Ellie said so, and he could go just about far as he wanted to. His hands clenched on the wheel. Roberta Lessing, slick and sly as a diamondback easing up on a meal. She didn't know how he'd done rattlers when he was just a youngun, and barefoot to boot, running them down and pinning their head with his naked heel. Then he grabbed a good hold on the rattles and swung the snake around and around, so it couldn't ever take a bite at him. And when he got tired of the game, Bond would pop the diamondback like a whip, to see its head go flying off.

That time, that one time, when the bloody end of the head flipped back and hit him in the mouth, he'd stood there spitting and laughing and laughing. He didn't stop chasing snakes.

Pulling up in the no-parking zone, he slid from under the wheel and took the bags, stored them in the trunk. "You want to go straight there?"

"Please," she said as he opened the back door for her. "To her—their—apartment. She probably doesn't keep the papers there, but I think she'll tell us where."

"Me," he said, closing the car door. "She'll tell me, Miz Ellie, and that's for certain sure."

Bond knew the streets here, and tooled the big car along quickly, but not drawing attention to it. He checked mirrors and side streets, and soon brought it to a stop down in the garage of an apartment building. She was out before he could help her.

"Nice," she said. "Discreet and well guarded, I guess."

"If you hadn't took his keys, we couldn't get in at all," he answered. "Big one's for the elevator there; little one for her door. There's a watchman around somewheres, but the garage door works on a signal from the Caddy. He don't expect trouble from anybody gets in legal."

Ellie let them into the elevator. "Was this his place first?"

"Hers," Bond said. "He keeps rooms at a hotel across town; it looks better."

The elevator rose quietly, discreetly. Ellie said, "Will she be home?"

"Reckon so; it's pretty late, and she don't want to spoil a good thing—yet. Tenth floor; this is it."

Thick carpet muffled their steps, and soft lights showed the way to 1021. Ellie used the door key in an oiled lock and felt Bond brush by her in the secret dark. A wall switch apologized for making a gentle click, and there was light. It was a nice place, richly subdued, tastefully furnished, spacious. To the left, a door was ajar, and she questioned Bond with her eyes. He nodded, and she whispered, "We don't want her screaming."

Nodding again, he went soundlessly across the living room and into the bedroom. Ellie listened hard, but all she heard was a kind of choked gasp, and no more. Then Bond reappeared, carrying a redhead in his arms, one hand clamped over the woman's mouth. She struggled and kicked in desperate frenzy, sheer nightgown hiking up to her rounded buttocks. When she saw Ellie, she stopped fighting and hung limply against Bond, only her toes touching the carpet.

"You know who I am," Ellie said, "so I guess you know why I'm here. Bond's goin' to take his hand off your mouth now, but if you try to scream, he'll hurt you. I swear, he'll hurt you bad."

Leather-gloved, Bond's hand slid away and poised, ready to smother, to throttle. Roberta Lessing said shakily, "What do you—my home—you—I'll have you both arrested."

"No," Ellie said, and Bond shook his captive a little to prove the point. "The blackmail evidence on my husband; where is it, *all* of it?"

Her brown eyes were wide, the rich mouth curled. "You're out of your mind. Do you think you can scare me into—"

"Bond," Ellie said, and turned her back. As she found the bar tucked into a corner, found the bourbon, and poured it, she heard a faint sound behind her. Ellie drank, and there were more muffled, thrashing noises. When they stilled, she said, "Well?"

Bond Whitson answered her. "Passed out, but she's goin' to be tough, real tough."

Behind the bar was a curved spout; she washed her

whiskey glass under it, dried it with a paper napkin. "Will she finally tell?"

"Yeah," he said. "Best you take the car, Miz Ellie. Button on the dash'll open the garage door, then straight ahead two stoplights and turn right; Franklin Hotel's three blocks down. There's a key in the glove box."

"All right, Bond. I'll wait in the room."

"Take a nap," he suggested. "I won't let you down, Miz Ellie. I mean, it's for Jock and you, and that's enough. You're the only folks ever treated me decent. And this is goin' to be a pleasure, anyway—so I reckon it's for me, too."

The back of her neck felt chill as she let herself from the apartment, but Ellie took a deep breath and forced herself to walk calmly to the elevator. It was like using a hoe on a snake, she told herself—like Sam Southworth sniping rustlers, on her granddaddy taking hair from Indians while keeping his own scalp intact. That was the rule: protect yourself and what belonged to you. She pushed the Down button and waited for the elevator.

In the suite, Bond stripped the silken nightgown from Roberta's limp body, then tore it into lengths. Good body, he thought as he tied her wrists together, then to the head of the bed. He wanted to be able to turn her like he wanted, and keep her legs free. For now, he stuffed some of the ripped material into her lax mouth. Later, when he had a use for her there, he'd take it out. Yeah, a very good body, cream and rose—just the color he'd pick for his own dead-white skin, did he have the choice.

Roberta's eyelids fluttered and he cupped the springy dark-red hair of her mound. Her eyes came open, vague and pained. Bond used his thumb, and she tried to scream.

"Whole place is near about soundproof, anyway," he said down to her as she writhed and tried to fling her legs. "Holler all you want, bitch, till I get around to your mouth. You'll be hollered out by then."

Brown eyes in a cream-and-rose face distorted by the gag; brown eyes pleading with him, but Bond only made the hissing sound that passed for laughter. "You waited too long, Miss Lessing. Yes, mam, Miss Smart-ass Lessing, always wrinklin' up your nose when I come around, always pullin' back your skirts like you don't want the freak dirtyin' you. Well now, I'm purdy glad you wouldn't tell about the papers you're holdin' over Jock. Let's see how low-down dirty we can get."

And he added fingers to his buried thumb. One hand was enough to shuck his own clothes while she kicked and arched her back, while she squirmed that good body and her eyes rolled like a weanling filly with coyotes close after her.

She tasted good and perfumy, gone sweaty with fear, and quivering against his teeth. She was one woman and all the goddamn women who'd ever laughed at him or pointed fingers at him, all the whores who went stiff when he mounted them, closing their eyes and making like they were somewhere else. She was all the bitches who never loved him and never would.

He heard her shrieking against the gag, and that was good, too.

CHAPTER 12

Ellie said, "Yes, yes," her fingers going white around the phone; then she whispered, "Thank you, we will." When she leaned to replace the phone, it fell to the carpet and lay there buzzing.

Jock said, "What is it? Somethin' wrong with JR? *Ellie!* What the hell is it?"

Her hands were shaking, so she laced them together in her lap. "Bond," she said through numb lips. "Mexican police checked his ID with the sheriff."

Lurching from his chair, newspaper scattering, Jock jerked a thumb at the boys. "Out! Right goddamned now—*out!*"

Gary leaped up, tripping over his feet; Bobby was slower, reaching to click off the TV set, looking back over his shoulder as he followed his older brother. Behind his father's back, he imitated the thumb-jerking motion and scowled terribly, but his mother was staring down at her hands. Bobby shrugged and eased on out of the room.

"Where is he?" Jock asked. "What'd he do?"

She put a hand to her throat. "Bond is dead. Sheriff Brian is sendin' after the—the body."

"Oh damn," Jock said, "oh damn. I kept tellin' him he'd pile up a car down there. Sit down, Ellie; I'll bring you a drink."

"Not the car. He—the sheriff wouldn't say *how,* just that a—a woman killed him."

Red whiskey spilled over the rim of his glass. He drank quickly, refilled, and drank again, blinking. Jock coughed and found some water, then he poured Ellie a glass. Taking it to her, he said, "Not her; it couldn't be *her.*"

Bourbon seared her throat, but her eyes were already burning, already swimming. "No," Ellie said strongly, "they'll never let her out. Anyhow, if they did, you'd know in a minute." She blotted the corners of her eyes with the folded knuckles of her right hand.

"Bond," Jock muttered. "He seemed indestructible, like a—a steel derrick standin' against fire and tornado and just about everything."

"Except the strike of his own lightning, maybe; the destruction he carried inside."

Jock frowned. "I don't know what—"

"Oh, the *hell* you don't! You just don't *want* to

know, and when you don't, you're like a plow mule wearin' blinders." She came up suddenly and went for her own refill. "Six years ago, when I came back from Washington and told you that your tail was out of the crack, you didn't even ask how."

He stalked across to his desk and opened a box, took out a cigar. "I figured you bought her off."

Making a face, Ellie choked down the drink. "And never wondered how come Roberta Lessing went crazy?"

"A nervous breakdown," Jock said, clipping the cigar end. "Guilty conscience, I expect."

"Jesus! You're talkin' to *me*, Jock Ewing. You, me, that poor damned Bond Whitson, that slut Roberta—if any of us had consciences then, have 'em now, they're blacker'n coal."

"All right, all *right!*" Savagely, Jock bit into his cigar, snapped the lighter, snapped it again. "I didn't want to think how you and Bond made her—that way. I was damned glad to be off the hook. And yes—I knew he was dangerous. When he was a kid, the poor little bastard *had* to be mean, to make the others let him alone. I can remember grown-ups pickin' at the kid, tellin' him he looked like the belly of a snake, that he had eyes belonged to a white rabbit. Like Bond didn't know. Ellie—oh hell, Ellie, ain't no sense us fightin'; Bond's dead and we always knew somebody'd kill him one day, and we never took him to a head doctor because we'd be the last he'd expect to slap him in the face."

"Yes," she said very softly, "and knowin' that, we used him."

He put down the cigar and crossed to her, put an arm around her waist. When she didn't pull away, he said, "I'll call the sheriff back, go down there with the deputy, and help clean everything up, do all I can."

"Yes," Ellie said again, and silently began to cry.

Bobby Ewing slipped down the hall and stayed tight to the wall as he went upstairs. If he kept close and skipped the fourth step from the bottom, nobody would hear any squeaks. It was one time he didn't mind being only ten years old and the littlest, because nobody else in the family could sneak up and down like he could.

Gary would want to know about Bond, even if he'd been scared walleyed by him. Most everybody was, but nobody on the Southfork wanted Bond dead—except maybe some Mex riders and the niggers. The Mexes were always making the sign of the cross behind his back, and the niggers rolled their eyes and shied far from him.

Dead. Dead with his chalk-white face and pinky-blue eyes and his sunglasses and his laughing like a snake. Gary would want to know. Bobby hesitated outside the room he shared with his brother, figuring what kind of trade he could make. But when he walked through the door, he couldn't hold it a speck longer and just blabbed it right out.

Gary's shoulders hunched over and went tight. He was sitting at the table. He didn't say anything for a minute, didn't move. Bobby flared his nostrils and caught it—the smell of beer. He said, "Reckon you're safe; won't nobody come in tonight."

"I'm full eighteen years old," Gary said, "and do a man's work. Ain't nobody's business if I want a beer—you hear that?"

"Don't you give a good goddamn Bond Whitson got killed? They say a woman did it, and Pa's goin' over the border to carry back his body. Reckon they'll bury him on the place? Can't put him in with Grandpa and the others; he was too goddamn funny-lookin' and no part Ewing. Can't put him in with the Mexes, neither, seein' he wasn't Catholic and the live Mexes'd squall like stuck hogs. Dig a place for him by himself, maybe."

Gary drank his can of beer, dropped it in the waste-basket, and opened another. "Quit sayin' goddamn, and quit talkin' about Bond Whitson."

Sitting on his own twin bed, Bobby said, "You

just don't want to hear about him being dead. It spooks you, don't it? You oughta hear the riders hoorahin' behind your back, how you can't shoot a cow caught in a bog, how you're scared to—"

"You little bastard!"

Bobby skidded across his bed and lined up with the door. "If I'm a bastard, you been one eight years longer."

Gary didn't say anything; shoulders tucked like he was bent over a pain in his belly, he drank beer and stared at the tabletop. Bobby settled back on the bed and watched his brother, thinking that none of them looked as though they came out of the same litter. Gary was only two years behind JR, and about a mile different. JR was a smart-ass, lording it over everybody because he was in college. He was big and burly and loud; he had blackish hair and a kind of fat-square face. Gary was light-haired, not brown, not cottony; he was shorter with graygreen, speckledy eyes. And most times he stayed to himself, reading; he even carried a book in his hip pocket when he rode out to work every morning.

And himself: Bobby didn't have the heft of his brothers and never would. He was curly-headed and they weren't. He ran off at the mouth a lot, funning and lollygagging, but the family was pretty used to it by now and didn't laugh like they used to.

"Gary," he said, "I'm sorry. I don't know what the hell—what the heck—gets into me. I mean, you're the only one *listens* to me."

"Okay," Gary said.

And Bobby said, "Look—I don't like to kill anything either."

"*Okay.*"

The kid wasn't all that bad, Gary thought, more clown than anything else, and he could understand that. Bobby must have come along at a bad time, when the only way he could get attention was by cutting up. There was the old man's shadow, JR. When Jock Ewing huffed, JR puffed; if the old man itched, JR scratched. The thing was, could JR ever do anything on his own?

And now to Gary Ewing, he told himself, and drained the beer can; reaching for another, he hesitated. Tomorrow was a workday, and only Mom said different on the Southfork. Maybe she'd stay in town when Jock got back with Bond's corpse, seeing to burial details. What the hell; he opened another beer, because it wasn't like a man could get drunk on a six-pack.

Besides, if Gary didn't show up, Angel Lopez and the other hands would be just as glad; they didn't like taking orders from a kid, even one named Ewing. They were straight when Mom was around, but screwed up when she left, and he didn't much blame them. He'd never been asked did he *want* to run the whole damned ranch, and even after years of working his ass off evenings and weekends, nobody ever said, hey—you think it's too much?

It was all laid out for him, just as it had been for JR. His older brother was meant to take over Ewing Oil; he was set to run the ranch. JR was in college, but Gary—

Hell; he might have made it, if he'd paid attention in school, but his grades were so lousy no college would let him in, and he wouldn't have gotten through high school if his dad wasn't Jock Ewing. But from the first day in first grade, it wasn't right for him; he was lost and lonesome and didn't know anybody. All he wanted was to run back home.

They didn't understand that. "Goddamnit," Jock roared, "get your tail back to school and don't ever let me hear you whimpering again. Hold your head up, boy! You're a Ewing, you hear—a *Ewing.*"

So when he cried for a mangled bird or dying calf, when tears clouded his eyes for the agony of a fence-gutted horse, Gary had to do it out of sight. Jesus, you'd think Mom would know pity and feel hurt; she'd grown up with animals, too. If she did, she never showed it, although Gary knew she could be tender and loving, a comfort and a buffer. But the ranch came first—the goddamn ranch where, almost daily, death and pain and killing was supposed to make you grow a callus around your heart and soul.

If you couldn't do that, there were books to go sailing off in; there was beer or elderberry wine, and sometimes a stolen sip of whiskey from the liquor cabinet. Whiskey was too bitter at first, and beer foam better than the beer, and maybe wine was easiest, if it was sweet. A slow numbness came to cloak anything you didn't like, and hid anything you wanted to keep secret, even from yourself.

Looking over at Bobby, he saw the kid had fallen asleep. Better to be like him, maybe; nobody gave Bobby a bad time. Dad barely knew he was around, and Mom sort of patted him on the head from time to time. No blueprint had been drawn up for Bobby; he could go to college and into oil, or stay on the ranch. He could even take off and do something on his own, something he might really want.

For Gary Ewing, what would that be? "Nothin'," he said to the last can of beer. "Not a damned thing I know about." A woman, he guessed, but he'd been wantin' an easy woman for years and had never done anything about it.

Because he had to get up his nerve with a few beers, and then took sick or drunk or both, the girls at school gossiped about him or laughed at him. It was a lousy circle going around and around. If JR knew he was still a cherry, or Dad—

Sure now that his mother would be in town and too busy to check into ranch affairs, Gary got up from the table and hid the empty cans in the closet. "Thanks, Bond Whitson," he mumbled. "Thanks for the excuse."

Then, his head spinning some and with a faint buzz in his ears, Gary went out of the room and down the steps. Outside, he leaned his forehead against a porch column and cried just a little. For Bond Whitson, the

poor son of a bitch. Bond had looked like Gary felt
inside, underbelly pale and washed-out, wrung-out.

In the parlor, Ellie heard the stairs creak and knew
the cause to be Gary. He'd be going out to the bunkhouse, or making a round of the barns. She appreciated him taking care of details like that. It was good
to have her own blood seeing to the place, instead of
depending upon a foreman. Her pa would be proud to
see it, and his pa before him, and it was a lot easier
to think on Gary and the Southworths tonight than
about poor Bond.

So damned faithful, willing to do anything on earth
for Jock Ewing, and for her. When Jock had brought
him to the Southfork to live, she'd been surprised. It
was not like her husband to take to collecting strays,
and she'd steeled herself to show nothing, to act
normal around him. After a spell, Ellie really didn't
notice anything different about Bond Whitson; she
got used to the glasses and covered hands and strange
laugh.

And she was to blame for him doing something to
Roberta Lessing, had known there was something to
the ugly whispers about him visiting whorehouses and
hurting women. But there was nothing else she could
have done after the redhead refused to talk. If she
believed Bond had made her unconscious on purpose
so she *couldn't* talk, Ellie had lifted a small corner of
her mind and swept that guilt under it.

Bond had called the hotel the next morning, and
asked her to meet him at the airport. There he said
yes, he had it all, had everything Roberta Lessing
meant to use against Jock. She didn't ask to see it,
and Bond brought the big packets intact to Jock. It
was done, and nothing would have nagged at her,
except that Bond slumped in the plane seat beside
her and slept all the way to Dallas. She remembered
thinking it was as if he'd eaten such a heavy meal that
it drugged him.

At home, he was like that for days, like a denned and sated animal that had never gotten its fill before. He stayed in his room over the garage, and if he came out at mealtimes, Ellie never saw him, since the help ate in the kitchen.

It was nearly a week later that Jock came to her with the news. He was jumpy, the way he always got when he had to talk about something unpleasant, and she halfway sensed it had to do with Roberta Lessing. She sat there in the parlor, refusing to help him as he mumbled around the subject; she wouldn't say just forget it, darling. He still had some misery coming, so Ellie sat there and pretended it just might be something she could help him with.

"Ellie," he said, after a couple of drinks, "you never looked at that stuff she had, that Roberta had."

"No," she answered. "I figured if you want me to know, you'll tell me."

He walked up and down, strong white teeth worrying at his cigar. "None of it had to do with women, Ellie. I swear it."

"All right, Jock." She kept her face quiet, placid.

"Oh hell. I got to talk it through just this once, and then I hope you'll forget it, and let me forget it, for it's never goin' to happen again. Like with her, I mean."

So he told her about the tricks it was necessary to use in Washington, how the big outfits were always there with their lobbies, with all their wealth, pushing and pulling to move the laws around to help themselves. He had to beat them off, outsmart them as best he could, or every independent in Texas would be knuckling under, getting taken over, selling out.

"It's already happened in more states than I like to count," he went on, moving back and forth now in a haze of cigar smoke. "I don't much give a damn for them, but it's a sign we'll all be gobbled up. So I spent money—more of mine than Texas Independents', —and I bought some folks and backed some down and blackmailed a few. Reckon I left a trail, because ol' Frank Kelly, he couldn't get it out of his craw that I had him by the short hairs, and he just kept sniffin' until he had it all. He meant to hang me and T.I. but the bastard dropped dead before he could haul on the rope. Roberta Lessing brought me the stuff, and that's how it started."

When Jock paused for another drink, to relight his cigar, Ellie said quietly, "If I hadn't gone to her, what would you have done?"

She'd never forgotten the set of his face, the flatness of his eyes when Jock said in a near-whisper: "Before I'd have lost you and the boys, Ellie—I expect I'd a had to kill her."

That helped Ellie some, but didn't prepare her for what he went on to say—that Roberta Lessing had lost her mind, that she'd been found wandering in Virginia woods, cut and bruised and incoherent.

"And the doctors don't figure she'll ever be normal again. I don't reckon you mind if I put her in a hospital."

No, Ellie had said back then, back those years it took to smooth things over between them; no, she didn't mind. It didn't bother her then, either. She could close her eyes and see the Washington apartment, see the woman who had been Jock's mistress, who knew all things about her husband, maybe more than Ellie did. So she hid the idea of Bond Whitson doing such awful things to the woman that she went crazy with them, such awful things that he was stuffed and swollen with release of them.

Now Bond Whitson was dead, killed by a Mexican prostitute who couldn't accept that kind of terror, that mind-destroying degradation.

Ellie lifted from her chair and looked at the bottle atop the bar, at others tiered high, row upon row, the nirvana of the weak. She went out onto the front porch and looked instead at the soft night, lights still burning yellow in the bunkhouse, emergency lights guarding barns and stables.

Tasting rich air, picking out her special star, the one that she used to dream on when she was a child, Ellie lifted her chin. Yes, it was worth it. Anything was worth this.

CHAPTER 13

The scout from Texas A&M said, "There! That's what I meant. They're double-teamin' the kid, and he's not big enough to handle 'em."

"Took 'em a while," Coach Larkin said, "and they had to stretch for that three yards. He goes down hard and gets up quick. That boy's never been clobbered so he don't get back up and hit 'em again. Laughs at 'em, on top of it; makes the other side ashamed to be gangin' up that way."

The scout watched the play through his glasses. "He slows 'em up so the linebacker can get over to plug the hole, even two on one. He ever been hurt?"

"Everybody gets hurt," Coach Larkin said. "He recovers quick when they put out his lights. Damn! Delta just about scored on that drive."

Lowering his glasses, the scout said, "Is he brittle? You never meant to use him in the backfield?"

Coach Larkin said something to his quarterback, and waved on his offensive line. "Mite too slow for the backfield, and he wouldn't like it anyhow. He'd heap rather be in the trenches, and no—he don't break easy. Too stubborn to bend much, too tough to break. Ain't you interested in anybody else?"

"Not sure of him," the scout answered. "A good big man'll run over a good little man every time, and it gets rougher the further along you go."

Coach Larkin jerked off his hat and flung it on the ground. "You see that? Son of a bitch threw the ball when he didn't have no *idea* where it was goin'—time, damnit—*time!* Onstadt, get your ass out there and see can *you* do some quarterbackin'." ·

A&M's scout said, "Delta High's not as sharp as usual."

"My boys are," the coach said. "Just ain't got the material this year. You'd do worse than my tackle."

"I don't know; *might* give him a try. They're comin' down pretty hard on our scholarships this year."

Coach Larkin recovered his hat and brushed it off. "That don't bother the boy. You don't know who he is, do you? That's Bobby Ewing, youngest of old man *Jock* Ewing's kids."

The scout looked down the bench where Travis High's defense and substitutes were leaning forward, hammering their knees and each other, yelling at a Travis score. There in front of the bench, using two helmets as if they were pom-poms, was Bobby, turned high-voiced and swishy kicking cheerleader.

"Ewing Oil, huh? What's the matter with the kid— queer?"

"Hell, no," Coach Larkin said. "Just the school clown."

After Travis won the homecoming game 14–6, the Travis Tigers hit the locker room, to cavort and holler and pop asses with wet towels. It was a winning season, even if they hadn't gotten to go for the state championship, and about half the first string were seniors. They showered and yelled and tried not to show they might be feeling a little last-game sad, because so far only one had been offered a scholarship —Willie Murchinson, the second-string quarterback.

At the mirror, he said, "We tyin' one on, Bobby? Whooie—let's us bust trainin' with a big ol' bang!"

"Don't know big ol' bang," Bobby said, skipping from the shower, "but I'm more'n passing familiar with big ol' Betsy . . . or was that big Chiquita?"

Somebody else hooted. "You familiar with near

about every whore from Mextown to Big D, Bobby."

"Try to be," he said, toweling himself roughly, except for the tender place over his left rib. Delta High's opposing tackle had purely sharpened his elbows for the game, Bobby thought. "But seems like I can't keep up with the new ones, they come and go so fast. 'Course, I'd rather come." On the heels of the general laugh, he said, "Sure—let's tear up this town's pea patch and if the sheriff gets the red-ass, we'll cut out for Dallas. I'll carry many as the van holds, and the rest can try to catch up."

He ached beneath the bruises, deeper than the welt that puffed his cheekbone and his usual collection of bumps and scrapes. But he was flat ready to tree the town, because, bigod, Bobby Ewing had stayed first string for three long damned years when they said he'd never make it. Too small for a tackle, they said, like 185 pounds on six feet of ranch-toughed frame was little.

It was *light*, when all that beef was stacked opposite, but like some cowboy philosopher put it, it wasn't the size of the man in the fight that counted, but the size of the fight in the man. The old cowhand probably never came down off his real tall horse, but there was something to be said for his sentiments.

Combed and school-jacketed, and pretending he didn't hurt, he clowned out with the bunch while some collected girls and broke off, and some paused to tell their folks sure, sure, they'd be in early, anyhow.

Then they roared off for Mextown, carrying on and acting the fool because they were young and had just whipped the school rival and would live forever, those that knew a way to stay out of Vietnam.

All wouldn't be going to college, and those would feel the cold draft on their necks. It didn't seem right to just take guys whose lack of grades or money made them vulnerable. But then, a lot of things didn't hold together these days, Bobby thought, braking the van around behind the Cantina Luisa.

"Bobby Ewing," a girl said, so close to his ear that

her hot breath tickled down into it, "Bobby Ewing, if a ruckus starts in this place, don't you dare run off and leave us, hear? I *mean*, my daddy would peel the hide off my tail if word got out I'm hangin' around a place like this."

"Linda Ann Rackley," he grinned, "if your daddy don't want the job—"

"Oh you!" she play-slapped at him, and Mel Onstadt pinched her butt good, so that she squealed out of the van and after the others. Bobby opened his door. The bruised ribs bothered him; he slid out easy, and from the back of the van a small voice said, "Bobby?"

"Hell," he said, "that you, Karen?"

She crawled into the vague cloud-scudded moonlight, a slender girl in a bulky cheerleader sweater, white skirt, cowboy boots with tassels. She dropped to the gravel beside him and just waited, little flower face looking up.

"Karen," Bobby said, "oh hell."

"Linda Ann and Sylvia are with you all," she said.

"You're not like them, and you know it. How'd you get with 'em, anyway?"

"I hid in the van as soon as the game was over," she said. "Why'd you mean to leave me?"

"Just because," Bobby said. "Damnit, because this is probably the last night we'll all be together; because come graduation, everybody'll be goin' separate ways. And one other thing—you got no permanent claim on me, Karen."

Another cloud wiped at the moon, and the girl seemed to shrink in the shadow. "If I—put out like them in there, would it be any different?"

Putting an arm around her shoulders, he said, "Your way suits you just fine; I appreciate you standin' up for your beliefs. It's honest."

"And lonesome. I—I won't ask any promises, Bobby. I know you're not studyin' on being engaged or anything like that."

He hugged her, shook her some. She was so little and kind of lost, humbling herself this way. "Miss

Karen Rogers, if I was even half a mind to *de*-flower you, like the books say, it wouldn't be here, like this—" Bobby tried to move her in a dance. "Oh, I would deflower, but for the sour hour—"

"Bobby, damnit! Don't laugh at me."

He stopped goofing around. "Beats cryin', Karen; I thought you knew that. Baby, baby—you're just too sweet and nice, and if I had marryin' in my mind you'd be the one, I swear. But next year this time I'll be gone—in Vietnam, I reckon."

Up close to his, her eyes grew big and sad. "But—but you're goin' on to college, to A&M."

"Guess I surprised myself much as you, baby. Must have been thinkin' on it without knowin'."

She stamped a tiny boot. "But it's so stupid, and you don't *have* to go, and—"

He moved her back to the van, cupped her elbow and helped her into the seat, then went around and got behind the wheel. It was warmer inside, but Karen didn't stop shivering right away. Bobby said, "You know, that just might be why I'll enlist, because I don't *have* to. I never planned on A&M. It was laid out for me, account of JR went there and Gary's already runnin' the ranch, or supposed to be. They never came right out and said *go*, or help with the Southfork, but then they don't say much to me; never did."

Putting her dark head on his shoulder, she said, "I just don't understand you, Bobby Ewing, and I reckon that's the problem."

Her hair smelled of next springtime, the hinted softness of unborn flowers. He stroked it gently. "I been goin' my own way ever since I can remember. Played ball because everybody said I was too little and I had to prove different. Guess I'll sign up for the war just because everybody says it's dumb. What I'm tryin' to say is I have to see things for myself."

"You're different already," Karen said, "when you're not being funny all the time. Maybe I saw that when we got away from the others once in a while. But that

still doesn't tell me how come you won't—do it to me.
I know you've been with other girls, lots of 'em."

Finger under her chin, he lifted it, brushed the
lightest of kisses across her trembling lips. "Karen,
what you're offerin' me is about the finest gift a man
can have, and only a damned fool would turn you
down."

"Then don't," she said fiercely. "I'm not doin' this
just because the other girls do. And I haven't held out
all this time because my mama said to. You have to
see for yourself? Then so do I—and is it wrong to want
you to show me?"

Bobby leaned away, started the van, and turned on
its lights. "They can find a way back," he said.
"They'll be *some* put out, but it don't matter."

"Bobby," she murmured, snuggling close, "Bobby—"

"I hope you won't be sorry," he said as he guided
the van along the highway, and wished the same for
himself.

In Ewing Oil's Dallas offices, JR Ewing shrugged
into his civilian jacket and was surprised at how light
and loose it felt. The weight he'd put on in Japan
didn't hurt a bit; it just filled him out, made him more
mature. JR glanced in the mirror and smoothed a
hand across his too-short hair. That would grow out
soon, but not too long—only enough to make a gesture
toward fashion, but to stay within conservative bounds.

Checking the mirror once more, he realized his
tailor would have to be alerted, and looked at his
watch. She'd better bigod get here quick, or somebody
would get racked. Never this kind of holdup in Japan,
and those fine little women, busting their delicate
trained asses to please a guy, raised from childhood to
know about sex and everything the man liked.

It had been damned good in Japan, especially for a
lieutenant who could outspend a general any time he
wanted. The only thing about the army that bugged
JR was being told when and what and how; it was
better to do the telling, better yet to run the whole

damned show. Of course, being a medical administrative officer beat hell out of anything a line outfit could offer; it also kept him a long way from Vietnam.

If he'd never seen Japan and Tokyo's Shimbashi district, JR might have gone on thinking that what Sheila Barker did to him was a twisted and perverted thing. He might have kept right on feeling guilty about being a part of it, that he was perverted too, for allowing her to do it. What did he know? He was just a kid then.

Then the submissive but wild little whores of Japan showed him that nothing was wrong, if the *man* wanted it. Just thinking on them, JR felt the heat mounting in his groin, the trembly feeling he got when a good time was close.

Sheila Barker . . . he'd just about exploded when she got him alone in the cotton crib that time. Fifteen, he'd only been fifteen, and she was a married woman damned near twice his age. She was big-titted and sway-hipped, with long smooth legs that drew his eyes every time she went by, all wiggles and slidy roundnesses. She was a certain woman and all women, always the ultimate mystery who walked his fevered nights in aching, shamefully released dreams.

He was visiting Billy Barker that day, not because he liked the kid, but to get another long, yearning look at Sheila. She was Billy's aunt, married to one of the Barker men gone overseas, and had two little towheaded younguns of her own. Somehow, that just excited him more, her having kids.

Thinking back on it, JR realized she must have been noticing his hungry stares for a long time, but never had a chance to do anything about it. Maybe she wasn't horny enough until that particular time, what with her old man gone and all. But it was possible she'd seen the bulge in his pants he tried to hide. When she was near, it was something he just couldn't control.

It was a Saturday in early fall, and a bunch had come out with JR; the Barker place had a good catfish

creek on it, and Billy Barker knew every fishing hole,
knew where the fall huckleberries grew ripe and juicy.
There were always Barkers coming and going out
there, big and little ones. The main ranch house was
center of a hub of smaller log houses occupied by sons
and daughters and grandkids. Scattered farther back,
they'd put up barns and stables and cribs for cotton
and corn, since they farmed about as much as they
ranched.

That day, JR kept hanging back, loath to follow
kids yelling off toward the creek with hand-cut cane
poles and old coffee cans made heavy by dirt and red
worms. He was going to do it again, though he fought
against it, not wanting to break out in pimples or go
crazy. But he'd caught a good look at Sheila's legs
through her thin dress, when the sun outlined them.
They were more beautiful than he'd imagined, and
when she leaned over to give one of her younguns a
biscuit, JR actually saw those big, wonderful nipples.
It was enough to drive him out of his mind, and he
eased into the cotton crib to do something about it.

It was cool and kind of dark inside, piled high and
soft with fluffy, seeded cotton that hadn't been ginned
and baled yet. JR had his pants open when he sensed
her, when he heard the warning creak of the door. She
didn't wear perfume and didn't need to; Sheila
Barker's sweat was golden and spiced with a heady
musk all her own.

JR tried to hide in the cotton pile, but she knew
he was there, and when she stroked his hair, he had to
lift his red face. His eyes popped wide and he thought
for a second he was strangling, that he couldn't
breathe, because she was *naked*.

In the half light, there was a shimmer about her, a
glow that haloed every magic inch of her bared for
him, for *him*. JR couldn't move, react, think. He held
his breath until he got dizzy and it cycloned from him.

Throaty, purring, her voice caressed him. "Just keep
real quiet, honey. I'll dig us a hole in the cotton, case
anybody comes by."

Hypnotized, fascinated, he watched her burrow a place and heap cotton high around it. When she reached out, he jumped at the touch of her hand. JR felt like the biggest fool in the county when she undressed him and his thing started leaking. Every brush of her stiff nipples shivered him, and his nostrils flared at her randy scent.

"Right pretty," she breathed when she had him stripped. "Young and hard and pretty as any picture. You ever had a girl, JR?"

Speechless, he could only shake his head, but not widely, for his eyes never left the meloned breasts, the beguiling nipples, except to dart covetous glances at the midnight piling of the tightly curled black hair between rich, smooth thighs.

"That's just fine," she murmured. "That makes it better, you bein' a cherry and so hard up. But you're goin' to pop off quick as a wink, and that's for certain sure, honey. So Sheila will take care of you thisaway first—"

JR was horrified, turned numb when she kissed it, when she covered it and he squirmed, gasped noisily for air, and went off, just like that. The explosion tore at him, ripped him up and down, and when it dropped him, JR wanted to crawl off and hide.

No way would she let him, and shocked him more by smearing her mouth into his, that quickwet tongue darting, racing. Sheila took him into her searing, wondrous woman's depths and showed him the secret.

Now, a century and as many women away, JR poured a drink from his pa's private stock and saluted himself in the mirror. "Never got caught out," he thought, "and a good thing we didn't. That ol' Matthew Barker would of turned me every which way but loose, if he didn't take pity on my tender age and kill me."

They'd had a lot of fun for nigh onto a year, until her husband came back from the army. Sheila'd taught him a whole lot. But he never recovered from her mouthing him like that, and it got so she had to do it every time before he could get hard for regular screwing. He knew it was dirty and against the law; it was worse because she was a well-thought-of married woman, but he needed it.

"Messed me up," JR said to the mirror, "and damned near ruined my love life. None of them little ol' girls around home would even *think* on such a thing. They quit goin' out with me, when word spread around."

He downed the drink of twelve-year-old Scotch and had turned for another when the tap came at the door. JR strode across the office and let her in. Tall and lissome, expensive and showing it, the call girl said, "I thought somebody might be putting me on. I mean, this is my first time in an office."

"Mine, too." JR grinned. "But there's a big ol' couch yonder and a bar, and any damned thing else you want." She stood smiling at him, cool and almost regal, until he brought out his wallet and lifted out a hundred-dollar bill. Her smile stretched itself when he added another.

"You'll earn 'em, baby," he said.

"Anything except getting hurt, dear."

"Nothin' like that, pretty girl—but everything else."

She shrugged off her coat and lifted the glittering dress over her head. She was cool and almost regal and her expression was just a little bored.

Down the street and around a couple of corners, a graying police lieutenant hung up the phone and hit the intercom buzzer with a splayed thumb. "Charlie— send down to the tank and fish out the Ewing kid. *Ewing*, damnit! Just give him back his stuff and turn him loose. What? I don't give a good goddamn what the charge is, long as it ain't murder. His name's *Ewing*, and I just got done listenin' to the Ewing family lawyer *and* the commissioner. Oh, and clean off the blotter. We ain't seen hide nor hair of him, does anybody ask."

The checkout sergeant pushed wallet and watch,

all personal effects across the board. "Sign here, sport. Be to your best interests was you to stay away from Mextown and niggers, too. Lucky you still wearin' your head."

Gary Ewing mumbled thanks; his hands shook as they gathered things. "Guess I got a little drunk."

"Yeah," the sergeant said, "and you oughta know how it feels by now. Sport, I seen a few winos in my time, but you the youngest of the bunch."

"I'm no . . . no wino," Gary said, stomach churning as he crammed wallet, comb, and bandanna into back pockets. He missed a loop when he put on his belt.

" 'Course not," the sergeant said. "Nobody is."

There was money, so he bought a flat pint of vodka, and ducked into an alley to drink about half of it. Gary's eyes blurred and it damned near came back up, but he choked it down, needing the stuff so he could remember where in hell he'd left the pickup. As the night came back in jagged bits and pieces, Gary's head cleared some.

Yeah, yeah—that lot across from the station; he'd put away the truck because if he picked up one more moving violation, one more drunk-driving bust, he'd lose his license. Or go to Mom to stop it, and he didn't know which would be worse. She never said much, just sat there and looked puzzled at him, as if he could explain what went wrong, if he was only of a mind to.

Well, he was just as confused. There wasn't a cause, wasn't a reason he could make out, and he'd gone over a number of them in his head. Thinking on old wrongs set him off again most times, so it was better to figure drunks just happened, like rain or winter northers or prairie fires; they just happened.

Tucking away his bottle and making the street again, Gary brushed at his clothes and combed his hair. The cab stopped, and he hauled back to that parking lot, paid up, and got his keys. Hell—Vera leaving him didn't make all that nevermind. They hadn't been together but about six months when she cut on out, saying she couldn't stand it a day longer, the way she was treated.

Gary drove out into slow traffic and pointed the truck's hood ornament for Travis City; the miniature oil derrick always led the way, but sometime he meant to knock off the damned thing. Vera Rodriguez Ewing was treated pretty good, he thought. Of course, she didn't go up to the big house much, and if Mom and Dad were a mite standoffish to her, that might have changed around in time. It was mostly a surprise to them, Gary guessed, account of he brought home a wife without them knowing her first. But hell, he didn't know he'd gotten married himself, until he woke up with one piss-cutter of a headache and Vera in the sack next to him.

She wasn't the first woman he'd come to with, but this time there was a piece of paper, and the whole Rodriguez bunch yammering at once, and Gary didn't remember anything about the last three days or so. It wasn't the first blackout either, but no other had lasted more than a few hours.

When Vera lit a shuck, it surprised him some, but didn't hurt. She was a pretty good girl in her own way, and Mom saw to it that she got enough to salve over any sin Vera felt about a divorce. Mom saw to everything, smooth and easy and not saying much; she just looked at him sad-like, the lines around her eyes and mouth grooving a little deeper.

A semi crowded Gary's pickup and he blasted the horn and slacked off speed. He wasn't in a hurry. Maureen would give him hell, that was for certain; she wasn't easygoing and ladylike. He had often wondered what Mom saw in her, how come Maureen Stanfield was underfoot every time he turned around, invited to dinner and for weekends. She got after him to cut down his drinking, but it was no business of hers, long as he kept the ranch running. She was pretty enough, and had two years of college she was right proud of. After a while, it had seemed easier to marry her than fight her off.

Now she had something else to beat him over the head with—little Lucy, three years old and a heap like her mother, sometimes like no youngun he ever knew. Hadn't planned on her either. Six months with Vera Rodriguez Ewing, who wasn't fixing to commit mortal sin by using anything protective, and no kid. Better than a year of bedding Maureen Stanfield Ewing, more or less, and nothing in her belly either. Gary figured he was sterile, and just as glad of it. Then, after he took that two-week trip to pick out a set of champion Santa Gertrudis bulls, damned if she didn't catch quick as a mare wide open in foaling heat.

It was just before JR got his commission as second lieutenant in the army and left for Japan. Gary knuckled his right temple; it was beginning to throb. He pulled the truck into a Fireball gas station and went into the toilet to drink more vodka and chase it with lukewarm tap water. Japan—and the farthest Gary had gotten was old Mexico, and not many miles there.

Outside, he paid the attendant for a fill-up and said no, the oil ought to be okay. His head kept aching as he pulled onto the highway. Japan and England and Spain—so many far places to be seen; England first, because even if they said Camelot was never real, it would be nice to wander around and play like it was. There'd be armor and pennons, lances and jousting, and nothing heavier than metal weighing him down. A man could hide his face behind a helmet visor and nobody would even know who he was, nobody keep after him in a hundred quiet, little bitty ways.

One long swallow, and the vodka bottle was dry. Gary spun it out the window just ahead of the Travis City sign. He slowed for the stoplight, then turned right and carefully drove three blocks before parking the truck.

BEER, the sign blinked, and DRINKS.

He was ready for both.

CHAPTER 14

Ellie paced the parlor, one slim finger holding her place in the book she carried. "I don't know, Jock. This sounds like Gary, and again, it doesn't."

He looked up from his notebook, from the ledger he was bringing up to date. "You readin' those books again?"

"A new one. We've got to do something about him."

"Doin' it," he grunted. "Dryin' him out at another fancy sanatorium; gettin' him healthy so he can pitch another big drunk."

She moved back to the bar, looked at a bottle, and walked over to the easy chair. "I hate to say it, but I expect Gary is an alcoholic."

Jock made another notation, cross-checked the notepad, then slammed the ledger shut. "Alcoholic, alcoholic! What the hell is that, except a fancy name for somebody drinks too damned much? Gary can quit any time he wants to."

"No," she said. "He's tried too often, and it never takes."

"If he *wants* to," Jock repeated. "Willpower, that's what he needs. Goddamn—the boy's had everything, so it *has* to be Maureen. Wife can drive a man to drink quicker'n anything else. He didn't want to go to college, and his grades were too bad, anyhow. He didn't want to fight so I wangled him an out from the draft board. He's been ramrod of this ranch, like he wanted, biggest damned spread in the county, and what does he do? Neglects the job and runs off three, four days at a time, a week. Piles up trucks, cars; gets throwed in jail. You got any idea what that boy cost me so far?"

"Us," Ellie said, opening the book upon her knees, "what he cost *us*."

"Yeah; he costs you more than he does me, I reckon. You were always closer to Gary."

"As you are with JR."

Jock lit his cigar. "Natural thing with the firstborn. I purely thought we both had what we needed—me, my own blood to follow me in the business; you, a son to help with the Southfork."

Ellie pressed the tips of fingers over her right eye. "And neither of us payin' attention to Bobby. We *should* have changed his name, you know."

"No, I *don't* know! Bobby turned out all right, just fine. Went to Vietnam and did himself proud, and has the medals to prove it."

"And the scars."

"*Life* puts scars on folks; doesn't have to be a war." Jock dragged on his cigar, rolled it in still excellent teeth. "The boy wasn't ready for college then, but look at him now, always on the whatchacallit list—"

"The dean's list."

"Yeah, that. Settled down and comin' right along. I'm ready to take him into the company any time he wants to come, diploma or no. Bobby'll do right well in public relations; he still tells a joke a minute if you get him wound up, and he's damned near pretty; won't be no trouble for him to impress all the ladies."

Ellie rubbed the spot over her eyes, but it wasn't going away. She was about to have another migraine. They had started right about when Gary's problems had—or maybe before. Ellie wasn't certain anymore. It seemed to her they were getting worse all the time. "Is—is that what Bobby wants?"

"Sure; told you he settled down. Couldn't you tell, time he came back?"

Carefully, she stood up. "He's quieter, more thoughtful. Bobby doesn't really show anybody what he thinks, least of all us."

Jock peered at her. "You gettin' another one? It's worryin' over that damned kid; that always starts you off."

"Maybe I can kill it, if I catch it now. Jock, it wouldn't hurt if you drove up to see Gary sometime."

"He'll be out soon. If he won't listen to you, there's nothin' *I* can say. You better talk to him, Ellie; talk to Maureen, too. He's liable to smash up somebody out of state, get himself charged with manslaughter where I can't help him. Then where'd his pretty wife be, Maureen, and that cute lil' Lucy?"

Now the pain was a weight growing heavier by the moment, pressing inward, blinding the right eye, and feeling sharp flashes into her very brain. "Here," she said, "they'll be right here on the ranch, where they belong, no matter what happens to Gary."

Feeling her way, head tilted to one side, Ellie made it to the bathroom and fumbled for the codeine, the Valium. Dr. Woodall said it wasn't wise to take them together, but *his* head wasn't threatening to bust wide open like a dropped, ripe watermelon. Running water until it was almost blistering hot, she dipped a washcloth in it, and when it cooled just a speck, pressed the cloth to her forehead.

Across the main yard and down the winding road where Gary had his house built, a car eased dark and silent behind the screen of cottonwood trees. JR slid from behind the wheel and closed the car door with caution, for sound carried a far piece on a still night. He couldn't see the big house or bunkhouses from here, and that was just as well.

The house was dimly lighted, candlelit, the way he had come to like it since Japan. JR catfooted up on the porch and tapped, just three times. She must have been waiting because the music died down and the door opened. He went in quickly and she shut it after him, clicked a bolt into place.

He only had time to ask, "Is the kid asleep?" before she was wrapped around him, pressing tight and lifting to her tiptoes, pressing urgently against him. Maureen's mouth was wet and fiery, her teeth scraping his, her heavy breasts filling his hands.

Breaking away, JR hissed, "Not right here, damnit. She might come out for a drink of water, or go piddle in the bathroom."

"Scaredy cat." She teased him with swift, deft fingers. "Come on into my room, then. I've been waiting all week for you, darlin'."

"Couldn't bust loose," he murmured. "The old man's dumped near about the whole load on my shoulders—in Dallas, anyhow. I just couldn't get free."

Honey-blonde hair swung free as Maureen Ewing opened a silken wrapper and let it drift to the floor. Darker pubic hair caught and held candlelight. His fingers jerked at zippers and buttons, and he was half-way up by the time she kneeled before him and did it so slow and tantalizing, did it so practiced and eager.

They went from there into the bed, and when he got back his strength, JR topped her the way she liked it—rough and mean and driving. He always worried about the kid hearing them, Maureen sobbed and carried on so, moaning and clawing at him while the bed complained.

When they lay with sweat drying on tightly coiled bodies, when he was melting and in that special drowsy place, she started in on him again. Not nagging, not whining, just pushing a little more . . . each time a little more.

Why couldn't she get a divorce over in Nevada, where nobody gave a damn about Jock Ewing? They wouldn't have to get married, not right away, although they should know their own minds by now. She could find a place in Dallas, and he wouldn't have to come to the ranch so often; they could be together.

"It's just not enough," Maureen said now. "I never get enough of having you, of that big studhorse pecker. Not since that first time when you carried me along looking for Gary on one of his running drunks. It was natural for us to make love then, and it's a right thing now, JR my darling.

"Just like it's natural I don't love Gary anymore, if ever I did. You changed me when you made me pregnant. Did you know I hadn't slept with Gary for more than a month, a whole blessed *month,* and even when he made it to bed he was too damned drunk."

She stopped to take a drag from his cigarette. "You know she's yours? No doubts about that?"

He took back the cigarette. "Uh-uh. Just have to look at her once to know she don't belong to Gary. Funny nobody else sees it."

"Not so funny if they do," she said. "It would ruin everything. That's why I think I ought to leave Gary and leave here—before we get caught."

"Give me time," JR said. "I need to think it through, and it's not like Gary'll bust in on us. He's still locked up in that nuthouse."

She took another pull at his cigarette, and when she gave it back, JR ground out the butt and stared at the ceiling. There was a whole lot to think through, not just what Maureen wanted, but all that had to be done. Better than seven years, he'd been making it with his sister-in-law, and he'd never found a woman fitted him better or suited him more.

But there was no way on earth he'd ever marry her, because of Jock and Ellie and Ewing Oil. Knowing her as he did, JR realized that after a while, Maureen wouldn't be satisfied with living in. The pushing would begin all over—a small jab here, a little insidious pressure there. He felt around his side of the bed for the night table, and another cigarette. Damn her, anyway.

Bobby Ewing lay on the couch, feet up, watching TV. His off-campus apartment was small, and it was often a hassle driving out to A&M every morning, but he appreciated privacy now, *really* appreciated it. Three years of breathing other people's air and smells, of hearing snores and belches and farts; it built up until just being alone was precious.

Sure, he needed people sometimes. Everyone did, because man was as much a herd animal as a horse or cow. But it was better to take them in smaller doses, to pick friends and acquaintances. Having folks shoveled all over you was just too much.

He sipped at a can of beer and watched colored figures moving on the screen without really seeing them. His nights were quiet, too. When he first had come to school, he'd snapped awake a dozen times every night, made alert and quivering by some sudden noise. Nights were when Charley did his best work, when the Vietcong hit hardest. Back in the Nam, nights were a series of small deaths; for some, the final blackout.

Nights that pulled tight as a recruit's bedsheet; jungle hot and wet and brooding—that's when you needed someone else to touch, so you could help keep each other alive until morning. If your luck held out.

Even during the day, deep patchwork jungle played tricks on your eyes; greenblack shadows threatened, but turned out to be only shadows—after you fired a long burst into them. And the slope-headed son of a bitch you never saw; he whipped a bullet through your head and planted shit-smeared punji sticks and trip-wired grenades.

If you let it, the Nam took away everything you arrived with—self-respect, pride, honor, a sense of humor. It turned men into hollow shells that moved and fought, thin, empty containers that poured water and food and dope into themselves.

On Bobby's TV, somebody said something funny and the audience laughed like crazy. Putting down his dry beer can, he framed the set with sock feet where jungle rot still lingered. He usually made notes of really comic lines, so he could rework them or deliver them verbatim, sometime in the future. People didn't hear, or weren't watching, or forgot. They thought he was one hell of a storyteller, and everybody liked him, missed him when he didn't show up for days on end.

Those were times like this, when he was plugged into aloneness and getting recharged. He had the fridge stocked, door bolted, phone off its hook. By Monday morning, he'd be okay again, not looking over his shoulder for slopes, not feeling like he'd stuffed himself into a bamboo tiger cage and it was being pulled smaller every hour.

No problems, no trouble with his journalism and business courses; no hassles with men or women or another part of the world. When he needed a woman, he found one in town, kept it no-promise and casual. Life was simple and easy; life was going to sleep in a safe, locked place with solid walls; it was knowing you had a pretty fair chance of waking in the morning.

Back home, Dad had been delighted with his decision to go to school, with his plans for coming into the company. His mother hadn't seemed surprised. They'd both been upset when he signed up for the army, and Jock called him a damned fool for not going for a commission or ducking the whole asinine war. It was the first time Bobby could remember them being concerned about him.

He wouldn't rock the boat again. He'd finish school and go into Ewing Oil to be the country's most expensive pimp and court jester. Someday he'd marry a girl his family liked and they would produce 2.3 kids, or whatever the hell the average was these days. No revolts major or minor, no nothing but sidestepping anything that smelled remotely of trouble. Bobby Ewing was going to live life one sweet, fat, and beautiful day at a time.

Gary Ewing watched TV also. He had to fit in, not make waves, don't give his temper any slack. Any deviation from the group norm, and it would be that much longer before they'd let him out of this plush-lined squirrel cage. If he took a swing at some professionally whispering, simpering attendant, they'd swarm over him, an army of white jackets and muscle.

Then they'd hit him in the ass with a horse needle, and he'd wake up about eighteen hours later in a rubber room.

You beat the bastards by knuckling under, going along, being oh-so-honest with the shrink, and after a while they patted your head, said to be a good boy now, and turned you loose.

Until the next time.

Gary retreated behind glazed eyes while the TV screen jiggled and sang. The patient beside him asked a ward boy for a light. Inmates weren't allowed matches or drawstrings in their pajamas; they shaved one by one, with a blade that could be locked into the razor and an attendant watching. No shaving lotion, because someone would drink it. No knives or forks in the dining room, only dull spoons, and wherever you turned, chairs and tables were bolted into the floor.

He'd been in worse places—drunk tanks, the county jail, state hospital, without ever quite knowing how he got there. But before too long one of Ewing Oil's lawyers would get him freed and maybe give him money to get back on. Back where? Southfork, of course; that was the limit of his world and every time he tried to find a hole in the fence, they caught him and dragged him back.

Gary dreaded that more than anything, facing up to them at home. Maureen's horseshit he could close out like he had little doors in his ears, but the old man kicked down those doors to chew ass, and over in the corner, there'd be Mom, silent and suffering. In his own place, Little Lucy would sidle away from him as if he was full of cactus needles. Hell, he hardly knew the kid, hardly knew what went on at the Southfork either.

Mom had brought in a foreman, some grizzled old codger who talked and walked like he came out of a cowboy magazine. When Gary was home and sober, everybody pretended he'd never been away, pretended he was still running the ranch and old Fred Krebs was just hanging around to lend a hand.

It might be different this time. When he got out, he could go somewhere else, get a job doing anything. There ought to be jobs for good ranch hands. Even if the pay wasn't much, if he kept his nose clean for a long spell and saved up, Maureen and the family would see he meant business. She and the kid could join him, and maybe his dad would spring for a good-sized loan, so Gary could start up his own little place, now that he was serious and had cut out all his foolishness.

"Okay, everybody up," the attendant said. "Bedtime comin' around, and you all wouldn't want to miss your good pills."

Obediently, Gary took his place in line and shuffled across the hall to the heavy steel door. Inside the ward was a dayroom, with a hall that led off to the patients' rooms on one side. On the other were the padded cells and treatment rooms; shock therapy was at the end—nobody could look at that door without wincing.

He turned right and went into his own room: single bed with a place for restraining straps; table and chair bolted down; metal mirror screwed into the wall above the sink; window of heavy wire mesh. The communal toilet and shower was at the end of this hall, so that sometimes patients got mixed up and thought they were being carried for shock treatments; they'd holler and kick.

For one long and shuddering moment, he felt like putting down his head and running into the wall just as hard as he could. Then Gary took a couple of breaths and made his hands unfist. He'd be all right now, until they brought him his sleeping pill.

CHAPTER 15

It seemed like every time he stopped in one place for a spell, trouble caught up with him, but Digger Barnes was damned tired of running. He was a whole lot older and tired; he got drunk quicker and his kids were grown, without him ever knowing them.

Oh, he stopped by from time to time—a couple of weeks after working in the Kilgore field, two months after the Mexican government grabbed every gringo-financed well south of the Rio Grande. Then he stayed home nearly a year, after Venezuelan bandits shot him up some at a drilling site down yonder. The kids had been too small then, and by the time they got used to him, he was gone again.

Digger stared morosely into his glass, remembering. Penny: She'd been a good woman who deserved better than him and his rambling. But what the hell could he do but hunt oil? He didn't know anything else and didn't want to learn. And whatever he did was just fine with her; Penny looked up to him, never complaining when so many things kept going wrong.

She'd been quiet and shy, a mild and patient woman. If he sometimes compared her to the fire and power of Ellie Southworth, it wasn't because he meant to. Once a man had known a woman like Ellie, she stayed in his blood forever, like malaria. Both could be pushed under, contained, but the bug only lay dormant, surfacing at unexpected moments.

Sipping his drink, Digger glanced down the bar and saw that it was nearly deserted. Early in the day for roughnecks to come hollering in, ready to buy drinks, more than willing to listen to his stories about the old days and better times. He might as well finish this lonesome shot and go back to the house.

As he walked slowly around the corner and headed for a side street, Digger admitted he wouldn't even have this, if his sister hadn't found him after he was full grown. Maggie Barnes was a stranger, but looking for some kind of permanency, a blood tie. They were the only ones left, she said, and she'd never married. Maggie looked and acted like what she was, an old-maid schoolteacher.

But she took in Penny and the kids, when he'd had all that bad luck, and they got along just fine. When Penny died, Maggie was with her; he had been in Chile or Algeria, somewhere like that. Then she mothered the kids, making the most of the chance, since she'd never have any of her own.

She doted on Pamela and Cliff, but didn't spoil them. Maggie was also a teacher at home, and made them study, made them work. After her heart stopped one night, the lawyer got hold of Digger in Oklahoma and said the house was his. Good thing, too; he and the kids had no place to go.

He went through the little yard and up board steps to the narrow porch. Since the kids pulled out, he'd let Maggie's yard and flowers go all to hell, but it just didn't seem right for a grown man to be piddling around flowers and such. His back bothered him ever since he fell off the platform out in the Gulf and a wave slammed him against that big steel corner leg. Wouldn't do to throw it out, messing with a lawn.

Maggie's house and Maggie's bank savings doled out piecemeal, her little pension every month, the social security check—starvation wages for a man who knew what it was to spend a thousand dollars a night. Christ. It was always money, money—and bile rose bitter in his throat because of the millions Jock Ewing stole from him.

As he did every time he stood on the porch, Digger Barnes lifted his head and turned it, to look away off and up to where the Ewing Oil Building stood like a tall, pointed club against the sky over Dallas. And as always, before he went inside, he likened the structure to a giant prick, poised to screw everybody in the world.

Across town in the apartment she sometimes shared with her brother, Pam Barnes hung up her phone and frowned before she remembered it would line her forehead. Smoothing the lines with fingertips, she glanced at the notepad. It was strange that Ray would want to attend a fraternity party, but the thought of a weekend with him brought the familiar tingle to her skin, that insidious tightening of her nipples.

And it wasn't as if most of the time had to be used up traveling; the college kids were throwing their bash in Dallas, at the Alamo Roof. She thought it must be nice, having money to throw around like that. But Ray would be out of place among those rich kids, and so might she.

Nothing formal, he'd said, and she was just as glad; she owned one evening gown and the only time she'd worn it, some klutz had spilled his drink on her. She'd scrubbed hard at the spot, but it still showed and was difficult to hide.

Casual, Ray Krebs said. The boys are out for a blast and we might as well get in on it. She didn't ask how he got the invitation; Ray worked out on the South-fork, beyond Travis City, for those Ewings. It was kind of silly, but she got this twinge of resentment at the name. Did the Hatfields and McCoys, those feuding families of legend, still hate each other down through generations?

She made a face, unbelted her robe, and did a tricky dance step into the bathroom. Under the shower, Pam ran slidy, soapy hands over her skin, caressing the excited body that would so passionately respond to fondling later tonight. Ray Krebs always did that to her, made her acutely aware of every inch of her flesh. Perhaps every woman's first lover reacted upon her like that. All Pam knew was that she had never been able to stay away from him, not since that first time he had made love to her. She had been fourteen.

Rinsed, Pam stepped from the shower and rubbed wet feet upon the bath mat, enjoying the tickle. Not that she hadn't tried to break Ray's sensual hold upon her. No longer a lonely, uptight teenager, she'd tried on a few guys for size. They didn't measure up to Ray's raw, driving power; nothing they did could lift her to such blinding heights. One man proposed, but she couldn't see trading orgasms for dull security; she was young, vibrant, and in no big hurry. Besides, Ray Krebs might ask her someday.

"Never happen," she said aloud, spreading the towel to dry and feeling deliciously sinful as she moved naked to the bedroom closet to search for something to wear. "Ray Krebs isn't about to give up his tomcattin', and I've been poor too long to set my sights on a ranch hand, even if his daddy is foreman."

Her brother would raise hell, anyhow. Cliff was such a dedicated climber that anybody less than the governor's son wasn't good enough for his baby sister. In all their lives together, the only conflicts they'd had were over Ray.

Lifting out a dress and spinning it slowly upon its hanger, Pam thought that Cliff was probably the best thing to happen to her, more than just her brother. In their loneliness, with their father practically always gone and maiden-aunt Maggie a chilly disciplinarian, she and Cliff had clung to each other. At first for comfort, then for understanding, and later for something they couldn't share.

Oh, Cliff Barnes was an up-and-coming young attorney, everyone said, a crusader like that fellow Nader, but a Texan to boot. Busy as all get-out, they said. No time for girls or marriage yet, but—no siree! —he sure wasn't one of those gays; a way too manly for that.

"Still," she mused, holding the dress to her and searching her reflection in the full-length mirror, "still, it's good that Ray caught me when I was just turning ripe." Pam cocked her head and grinned into the mirror. "Young, but exceedingly ripe."

She held the dress aside and pulled in her tummy, pushed out her breasts, put a hand on her hips, and stood posed like a model—for about five seconds. Then she broke up in laughter and, as it subsided, thought she'd better get ready for her date.

In an office building miles from Pam, Cliff Barnes worked late, his small office showing the only upper level light. He added another sheet of speculations to a thick file, rubbed his eyes, and leaned back. By now, Pam was at the Alamo Roof, already being introduced to Bobby Ewing and getting over being stunned, he hoped.

Ray Krebs owed Cliff, and he owed Pamela. Cliff never forgot what the big bastard owed Pamela, and it might take him the rest of his life to pay up. Right now, he was meeting the first installment on the due bill by bringing Bobby and Pamela together. It would be up to her to take it the rest of the way.

Cliff knew his sister. Pamela would consider Bobby Ewing a challenge and turn the full force of her beauty upon him, do her damnedest to charm the boy. If Prince Robert, third in line to the throne, had any blood to him, he'd be interested in Pam.

Naturally, she'd only tease him, play around with him until all the fun was squeezed out, then drop him like the cow turd he was, like all Ewings were. But in the meantime, she could milk information from him, once the kid got taken into the company. That wasn't far off, for he'd be graduating from A&M—when?—no more than a year.

No hard-won scholarships for Prince Robert; he didn't need them, didn't have to work his tail off and study at the same time. Everything was laid out for Bobby Ewing, not for commoners like Cliff, and that was the way of things, wasn't it? The rich and the

poor, the inheritors and those who got by on crumbs;
it was the age-old order of things.

"Bullshit," Cliff said and stood to stretch, to rub
the back of his neck. The Ewing organization had long
fed on its own corruption, growing fat and careless, its
flabby underbelly open to a hungry hunter. "And I
mean to rip it," Cliff said. He meant to spill their guts
for what they did to the people of this state, stop them
from doing any more damage. And Pamela would
help, knowing or unknowing, she'd help; she had as
much reason.

North and west out of Dallas, a man thanked a
trucker for the lift and dropped down from the cab
to stand and watch its lights dwindle up the road.

Gary Ewing pulled air into his lungs, dry air tangy
with sagebrush, filtered through a million glittering
stars. The highway was dark, and when the clatter of
the diesel faded, he could hear the ghostly quaver of
a screech owl. Smiling, he pictured the little guy, not
much bigger than a fistful of feathers, and half that
taken up by eyes.

The turnoff was there, across the highway, and he
could make it out fine, once his eyes adjusted to the
night. Hoisting the surplus GI duffel bag to one
shoulder, he started to walk it by starshine. Gary tasted
the night and liked its flavor. He thought of the spice
ahead, of Maureen and the grubby kiss of their little
girl. He didn't fret about Mom and his father because
he was sober and ready to face up to them. If they
wanted, he'd work as an ordinary hand and be glad to
sweat his own juice instead of recycled booze.

Laughing into the night, Gary lengthened his
strides, daring any late-hunting diamondback to zigzag
in front of him. He was going up his own road to his
own family, and he'd been dry just about a year. Out
on his own, too; not locked away where he couldn't
get at whiskey. He'd held a bunch of two-bit jobs in
that time, dishwasher, pumping gas, setting fence,
bucking hay—anything and everything to keep busy,

to stay straight. Now he figured he had it made, and when they got a look at him, when they listened, they'd accept him again.

Maureen. She must have guessed by now. He'd sent her some of each paycheck to prove he was staying clean, not because Mom would ever let her lack for anything. But she didn't know he was coming home. Anticipating her surprise, Gary laughed again. Far off, the mournful cry of a whippoorwill answered.

He was sweating when he reached the leg of the V that led to his house, but it was clean, good sweat. Gary glanced at the big house on its low knoll and lit like a birthday cake, spared a quick look at barns and stalls and bunkhouses, gratified by their stability, their unchanging presence. Duffel bag under his arm now, he trotted toward his own house.

"No," Maureen said, from inside, as he reached the porch. "No, damn it! I'm a decent woman, and I don't mean to wait any longer. I've had it up to here with this place, havin' to bow and scrape and say yes'm."

Quiet, slowing his breath, Gary heard a man mumble something, then Maureen again: "Oh sure, sure—I'm their brood mare and your slut, that's all! You think they give a good goddamn about *me?* All they care about is this precious grandchild, seein' it's the only one they got. Only that's not how I want it."

Who was his wife talking to? Not the old man; nobody stood up to Jock Ewing like that. *Slut*—she'd said, *his slut.* Oh, good Christ. Easing down his bag, Gary locked his fingers together. His fault, being gone so long. Couldn't blame a lusty woman for taking up with somebody when her own man was knocking around the state, or put away on some funny farm. It was his fault, not Maureen's. If he held on tight, he could make it work.

Whatever else they said got lost in the roaring of his ears, and he forced himself to slip from the porch, to sit hunched and taut away from where light could reach him. Gary continued taking an occasional great gulp of air and kept a grip on his bent knees, rocking back and forth on his heels. It was good he'd made it off the porch, because he didn't want to know who the man was. It was damned good he hadn't put his eye to the crack in the drapes to look at them.

Minutes dragged by almost as slow as doing time in a padded cell with nothing to read and nobody to talk with, no window to look out of. It took some doing to live with only your own thoughts for company. It took some doing now, because Gary didn't want to mull over what he'd heard, taking it apart bit by twisted piece in his head. He used to do that, sitting in a straitjacket and not able to scratch anywhere; he'd listen to noises that came under the green steel door and try to put actions to them.

There was the floor mop sloshing, gray beard straggled and snaky; the roar of water—if short, a toilet; if long, a shower. Picturing them was busying, for he had to create every small detail of stained porcelain and silvered metal, had to form the floating of rainbow bubbles and how steamy water felt on the skin. It was better during the day, because he could keep his eyes open and unfocused. At night, things hovered dark and drear; if they got close and he couldn't beat them off, he had to yell. They didn't like yelling on the ward and punished him for it.

Flinching, Gary stared around at the quick-open, quick-shut door, the rattle of the screen. There was only a pencil flash of yellowed light upon the man moving across the porch. His tread was heavy, certain, as he walked toward the screen of cottonwood trees that made his house private. A hidden car pulled out with its lights off, the sound of its motor also heavy and certain. When it was gone, he went back onto the porch and pulled open the screen door, turned the doorknob.

"Darling," Maureen said, "you came back!"

"Yeah," Gary said. "Surprise."

"God in heaven!" she said, backing from him in a translucent, very short nightgown that revealed every curve and crevice of her body.

"Maybe," Gary said. "I'm not all that sure where he hangs out."

Her hand was at her throat, her eyes big and scared. "G-Gary—did you just get here? I didn't—didn't hear a car—"

Watching her, hands hanging at his sides, he said, "No, I came a spell back. You were busy, so I waited."

Maureen cut her eyes at the closed bedroom door, back to him. "Then you—?"

"She asleep in yonder?" he asked. "She always sleep through it, or does Lucy get curious sometimes?"

Backing another step, she put her hind side to the lamp table with a drawer in it. Gary remembered that drawer; it was one that didn't stick. She said, "You saw him leavin'. So what? I mean, you expect me to set and wait forever?"

"No," he said, "reckon I didn't expect that, when I think on it. That's not devilin' me much right now. I just want to know if Lucy sees anything, hears anything."

Maureen put both hands behind her, and he made out the little woodenish whisper, as the drawer opened. She raised her chin and looked him full in the face. "She's not blind or deaf, and my kid doesn't see anything wrong in kinfolk visitin'."

"Kinfolk," he said.

"He's got the right," she said, bringing the chromed .38 Bulldog from behind and showing it to him. "He's got a better right than you, but here you come at just the wrong time, messin' up everything."

"JR," Gary said. "Couldn't be anybody else. JR."

"You didn't see him," Maureen spat. "You didn't even know who he was, and you come slippin' into my house, wormin' it out of me—"

He went in under the pistol, fisting it from her shocked fingers, chopping his other hand into her silken belly so she couldn't get the breath to holler.

Methodically then, with great deliberation and coolness, Gary Ewing began to beat hell out of his wife. When he was done, he left her bloody on the bed and backed panting out to look awhile at the other bed-room door.

He found bottles in the cabinet and carried them two by two onto the porch to stuff in his duffel bag. The last one he held in salute to Maureen, beginning to stir and moan on spattered sheets.

The wiskey burned all the way down, but he just didn't give a shit anymore.

CHAPTER 16

The formal dining room was baronial, all glittering chandeliers and tall-back chairs, a vast expanse of polished pecan-wood table. It was seldom used, except for company affairs, but three of them sat at one end of the table now.

"Servants can't sneak up on us," Jock said, clipping the end of his cigar. "It's not being paranoid either. Never know who works for who anymore, which one is gettin' paid off. Last week, Ben Kelso showed me where somebody'd bugged Ewing Oil's boardroom, so I have the whole damned building swept regular, and I reckon I'm about to start in on the house. There's just no tellin'."

Ellie took a sip of sherry from a stemmed crystal glass, and pressed fingertips to her temple. "But this—distasteful as it is—is family business, nothing to do with the company."

"Everything's got to do with the company," Jock said. "In Texas, if a Ewing gets a bellyache, bankers fidget and listen for their phones. So let's see what we can do about this mess, and get on with it."

JR clipped the end of his own cigar, the same brand

as his father's. Have to start watching his weight, he thought; even with a loose belt, the belly-band of his pants felt tight. He said, "When did she leave?"

"I'm not sure," Ellie said. "It was—difficult all around, from the time she went crawlin' to the nearest bunkhouse for help, until after she was out of the hospital. Maureen didn't want much to do with us, and stayed to herself a lot. I went over every day or so, to see how she was makin' out, and to check on Lucy."

"Lucy," JR said. "That's the point, isn't it?"

"Goddamn right," Jock said. "If Gary came home and knocked knots on his wife, must have been he had good cause. Overdid it some, I'd say, and if we'd caught up to him then, it was Katy-bar-the-door."

Surprising himself, JR said, "I think we can write off Gary. He may come home someday, and he just might not."

"No," Ellie said. "He's my son, too."

Cocking one grayish eyebrow at JR, Jock said, "We ain't abandoning him, Ellie. *He* run off on us."

"He—he probably thought he'd hurt Maureen much worse, imagined he killed her. He's scared, spooked out of his head, and—and—well, I know he wouldn't have done anything like that if he wasn't drunk," Ellie pushed her own glass from her.

JR blew cigar smoke. "Still and all, he ran off, Mother. And because of him, your only grandchild is gone. If Maureen doesn't want to come back, that's her lookout, but Lucy—"

"Lucy's blood kin," Jock said around his cigar.

"Exactly," JR agreed.

Ellie said, "Please—don't do anything to be sorry for."

" 'Course not." JR stood up. "If you'll excuse me, Mother—Dad, I'll see to it."

When he'd gone, Jock took Ellie's hand. "You cold, honey? Don't worry. JR'll make that woman see. Kind of rearin' up on his hind legs for a change, you notice? Reckon I can have him tote some more weight."

"Gary," she said, holding tightly to his hand. "Gary is gone, Jock."

"Honey," he said gently, "the boy's been gone a long time, ever since the first time he crawled up into a bottle and stopped it up behind him. We don't aim to forget him, and I'll have a watch kept, but what we have to do now is think on our other two. JR yonder is feelin' his oats, and Bobby—we'll wait and see what he amounts to, soon as he gets out of school. Offhand I'd say we got two fine boys left, and that's to be proud for."

JR got on the library phone and gave crisp orders. Outside, he climbed into the dark Mustang and kicked it off, went wheeling for Travis City. At the branch office there, he parked the car and eased into the back-seat of the company Cadillac, using the car phone before the driver had him well on the highway east.

Sure, Maureen would light a shuck for Forth Worth; it was where Gary had met her, a cocktail waitress in a sleazy bar. Trust younger brother to screw up like that. She must have hooked him on sex, right off; it was what she was real fine at. But the bitch didn't have good sense, splitting that way. If she had the brains God gave a horned toad, she'd realize that Gary wasn't about to come back. But no, she kept bearing down on divorce, just too stupid to see he wasn't studying on marrying her.

It would have been okay if Maureen just stayed put, where he could bed her near about every week. The old man would see that she never wanted for anything. Hell, they could have met a couple of times a month in Dallas, but Maureen wanted more than that. She wanted too damned much, more than the money he offered, the considerable sum he carried now.

Compounding her stupidity, that's what she was up to. The first dumb move was admitting to Gary that Lucy wasn't his own youngun, and the next was putting a pistol on him, when a bottle would have done a heap better job. Then slipping away from the ranch when it finally soaked in that JR wasn't about to marry her. She thought she had a hold over him, and said so on the phone: *"Blood tests will tell whose daughter Lucy is."*

Like hell; a test like that only showed who the father wasn't, but it sure wouldn't be good to have it turn out Gary fired blanks. The finger would point somewhere, and with Maureen acting the woman scorned. . . . He dismissed the thought, and put his head back on the seat and catnapped. Ewing Oil's security branch had contacts all over the state. Men would be scouting motels for the pickup she'd taken, going over lists of her known friends. They'd find her, all right.

"Yessir," the driver said, "Fort Worth comin' up."

The phone buzzed and JR said yes into it, listened, then gave his driver directions. She was running true to form. Maureen Stanfield Ewing had checked into a motel within walking distance of the Longhorn Bar, where she used to work. The limo pulled into the motel lot, and JR got out. Three men were waiting.

"She's in the bar," one said. "The kid's in the motel."

JR looked around. "Take the youngun' to the Southfork. Two of you bring the woman to the motel when she's gone. What room?"

"Give me five minutes," a man said. "Room two-eleven. The door'll be open."

"Yes," JR said, and looked at his watch. The three men faded away, a pair sauntering for the bar, one homing in on Room 211.

When JR spotted the guy with a blanket-wrapped bundle getting into the ranch pickup, he walked through the parking lot to Maureen's room and sat on the bed. A pillow was rumpled from Lucy's head and the TV was on. He clicked it off. The security people were good. They'd picked up Lucy without a sound and she was on her way home, where she belonged, where she'd stay from now on.

The door opened and they trundled Maureen into

the room, a wristlock keeping her tippytoe. Her face was chalky, her eyes bulging, and her hair mussed.

"Had to stiffen the bartender," one of them said. "Old friend of hers. Nobody else horned in, but it'd be better if we didn't take long. Some sport'll use the phone."

"Cover her mouth and twist her arm a little," JR said, moving away from the bed. He watched Maureen's knees buckle and saw her strain for air against the callused palm clamped over her mouth.

"Okay," JR said, "wait outside." The man dropped her pale and shaking upon the bed. JR said then: "You holler just once, and they come back to break your kneecaps, Maureen. If I say to, they'll snap your neck and drop you in a deep river, after they open your belly and load it with rocks."

She lay trembling, eyes showing him the lasting memory of Gary's beating. "Lucy—where's my baby?"

JR inspected a cigar, bit off an end with a sharp click of teeth. "Lucy Ewing, you mean. Miss Ewing's just fine, I'd say. She's goin' to stay that way, Maureen, no bother, no problems."

Mouse-small, her voice quavered. "The—the courts, JR. I'll take you to court an—"

He shook his head, used a heavy gold lighter on his cigar. "Once I thought you had ordinary good sense, but that's not the case. A *Texas* court, Maureen? Ewing Oil versus a woman sleepin' around with so many men who'll swear she's a pretty good lay. A good screw, but an unfit mother, your Honor."

Maureen put both hands to her face. "You'd do that. Oh my God, you could get away with it, too. The folks you don't own, they owe you favors. JR, please, *please;* all I wanted was to be with you all the time, to make love with you without sneakin' and hidin'. That's all I ever wanted."

"No," he said, and blew on the spark of his cigar, "you wanted to be my wife, and that's a heap different. Goddamn, woman, you think I'd *marry* a bitch cheated on one husband?"

"Then you n-never loved me?"

Blank-faced, JR stared at her. "You were just handy and did the right things."

Jerkily, she sat up and crossed her arms over her stomach, swaying back and forth in little painful arcs. "You've got Lucy. What else do you want—to turn those apes on me, kill me?"

He reached for his inside coat jacket, brought out a sheaf of bills, and dropped it on the bed. "There's fifty big ones here, fifty thousand dollars, more than you ever saw at one time. More than you deserve, but Jock's gettin' soft in his old age. Now you take this money and get as far from here as you can, quick as you can. If I have to tell you never to show your face in Texas again, you're dumber than I figured."

Dropping her hands, Maureen said, "You bastard, you puffed-up, righteous bastard, makin' me sell my child, like I'd take money for flesh and blood."

He flicked ash from his cigar. "You will, baby, you will." He left her sitting there, drawn and faded-looking. He wondered what he'd ever seen in her.

Bobby Ewing brushed at wavy dark hair and hoped the mod style would last a long time; he'd always thought his ears were too big, but this way he could halfway hide them. Tonight especially, he wanted to look his best, and grinned when he thought of how his father would react if he knew why.

Bits and pieces of the story, Bobby knew, most of it hearsay picked up in Travis City when he was a kid. Probably, he'd never know all of it, a purely unbiased look at a blowup between two young wildcatters, away back when. All this time, both men carried a grudge, but it was easier for Jock Ewing to handle, since he was wealthy. According to his daughter, Digger Barnes was much more bitter, and he was broke.

It was nobody's business that Bobby was seeing Pamela Barnes. It wasn't all that often—maybe five, six times during the past year—and it couldn't be considered serious. Pam didn't exactly fall all over him, although he sensed turbulent currents below that lovely surface, a fiery wonder held in check by her determination not to cheapen herself.

Normally, he'd have dropped a chick like that real quick. There was too much stuff running loose all over the campus, in any town close by. As for Dallas-Fort Worth—the happiest of hunting grounds for a cocksman. Jock Ewing happily promoted those expeditions, even paid the freight for call and party girls. Won't always be able to find amateur nooky when you need it, Jock had said. Make connections, boy—let them know who you are, so you can get back to them when you start work for the company.

And the Cowboys, Jock pointed out, you make yourself liked by the Dallas Cowboys, take the trainers out for dinner, the bench warmers; get around to knowing everybody. You'd be surprised how many deals you can swing just for scarce tickets to a big game, followed by a juicy little piece of tail; that's what Jock said. It was as close as he'd ever come to camaraderie with Bobby, and likely ever would.

So why was he taking out Pamela Barnes again? He liked her. She was good not only to look at, but worth listening to. She was bright and ambitious, and she knew how to enjoy, to laugh. If she said she didn't want to screw, he had to believe her, for he knew she wasn't being coy or playing hard to get. There was a directness, an honesty about Pamela Barnes that intrigued him, and though he had wondered how Ray Krebs knew a woman like her, he'd never made a point of asking.

Ray was okay around horses, cows, and beer busts. He just didn't seem to fit with Pam, but when he first introduced her to Bobby, he'd done so with an easy kind of intimacy. Bobby grinned again and checked his pockets for car keys, wallet, and credit cards. Ray Krebs wasn't dating her. These days he was pretty damned busy taking up the job his father left off. He was young to be ramrod of a spread like the Southfork and busting his hump to prove he could handle it, that he'd learned from following Fred Krebs around the place.

Fred's horse had popped a leg in a gopher hole one day, a few months back, and rolled over Fred when he came down, fourteen hundred pounds of hurt animal. Next day, Ray was at the big house, dressed in a black suit for the burying yet to come, and asked Jock Ewing for his dead pa's job. Jock appreciated his guts and gall and gave him the chance, on trial.

Bobby was glad for that; otherwise he'd never have met Pamela. She was part of the take-it-easy life he was into now, the cool-it, don't hassle, don't hurt lifestyle. Pam knew where she was going, up from copywriter to an underboss at her ad agency, someday vice-president, someday married to the right man, but not now.

Not like little Karen, he thought. It had been embarrassing for her to run into him when he was first back from Nam. When her letters slacked off, he had a hunch, but in the jungle that didn't matter. The important things were staying alive, keeping sane, making it back to the real world. But meeting her on the street had shaken him some, anyway. It was the baby, big enough to push in a stroller, bigger than some little slopes chopped down at close range with their mamas in that stinking village with no goddamn name.

"Bobby," she'd said breathlessly, sunnily, and just a little too fast. Karen had put on a little weight and cut her hair. "Bobby, I just couldn't write and tell you—"

"It's okay," he said, and it was. Except for the kid that old already, and a virgin cheerleader turned mama so damned quick.

"Well," she said, "I have to get the shopping done."

And he said, "Sure, sure—happy for you, Karen," looking after her as she pushed the stroller in that harried housewife way. Bobby hadn't asked her new name, because she wasn't waving pom-poms now and maybe there had never been a big homecoming game.

Maybe there'd been no careful penetration in the back of a van, when a young girl trembled and cried, twisted and cried so that he could taste tears on his lips.

For about a hundred years, the only reality was jungle and the dirty little shits infesting it. But back in the dreamworld they didn't know that, and went right on pretending cars and sweet-smelling women and money were all there was. But few in the dreamworld were dying mean and ugly on purpose, or torching huts and standing back from the sizzle of crisping bodies.

In his apartment, Bobby swallowed and blew memories from his nostrils and adjusted his jacket, the new throat jewelry. He looked good and felt great. When he went out, he could damned well leave the lights on if he wanted.

At the Southfork, in the foreman's house set apart and aloof from the bunkhouses, Ray Krebs stumbled from the shower. He was too tired to make more than a couple of swipes with a towel before falling into bed. It was rough as a cob, but he was hacking the job; he was making the hands respect him and if old man Ewing wasn't pleased, Ray would have heard before now. Foreman of the Southfork, biggest outfit in Muleshoe County, bigod.

Punching his pillow into shape, he stretched on the bunk and flicked off the light. Bare-assed, he thought about women and when he was going to get around to some. Thinking on women naturally brought him around to Pamela Barnes, and he smiled in the dark as he caressed himself. Man, how she'd taken to it when he pinned her down and threw the meat to her the first time. Fourteen, she was, carrying her cherry and anxious to be rid of it. He was nineteen, and had dicked every Mex gal in Travis City—some of the white ones, too.

Once he got her broke in and she quit being sore, Pam Barnes was the best diddling of all. If she was here tonight, she'd hump and buck and carry on like a she-panther while she loved every minute, every inch of it. All he had to do was run one hand down her arm, or a finger down her back, and she was ready to drop her pants. Pam wasn't the kind that quit after just one go-round, either; she needed more and demanded it, liable to get pissed as all get-out if she didn't make it three, four times running.

Now what the hell was Bobby Ewing doing with a fine piece like Pam Barnes? Getting some, no doubt, but if the kid wasn't careful, he'd be so pussy-whipped he wouldn't finish up at college.

And how come Cliff Barnes wanted his sister running around with Bobby? You'd think, after listening to old Digger mouth off about how Jock Ewing screwed him out of millions, that his son would want to put the blocks to the Ewings, good and deep.

Could be, that was happening, but Ray didn't know how yet. Long as all the wheeling and dealing didn't screw up Ray's job, he didn't care what happened. The Ewings could stand being took down a peg or two, and Cliff Barnes was so goddamned prissy-holy, it wouldn't hurt him to get squashed like a cinch bug, if he stung the Ewings too hard.

And that's exactly what would happen. Cliff Barnes was a tumblebug rearing up at a freight train; him *and* his little ball of shit would get run over.

Turning onto his side and curling up to the other pillow, Ray made a couple of dry humps and hoped Pam wouldn't get caught in any crossfire. It was a pure shame, to waste ass like hers.

CHAPTER 17

Bobby tooled the Mercedes 450SL along the freeway, leaving the red-neck part of Louisiana behind, glad to be past Alexandria and its suspicious, closed-tight faces, past Shreveport. They couldn't outrun sunrise, and its advance scouts of brightening pink raced them across into Texas.

"Home," Bobby said, "home is the hunter, home from the hill—"

"In New Orleans?" Pamela asked. "A *hill?* Well, there is the levee, if you're counting manmade bumps."

"I'd like to be counting a couple of yours. What say we find a neat motel and—"

"I'm willing," Pam said. "Oh boy, am I ever! But now that we're reasonably sober, eminently respectable, old married folks, we can't just be pullin' in at every motel. But only, my dear," and she drew her hand lingeringly along the inside of his thigh, "only because your family's expecting us. Not me, exactly— but the youngest Ewing and wife. Are you nervous?"

He dropped a hand from the wheel and caressed hers, pressed it into his leg. "No, just proud."

"I don't believe you."

"Hey! Our first fight already. You're callin' your husband a liar, when all I'll admit to is a couple of butterflies, maybe a Miller moth. You?"

"More like bull hornets," Pam said. "I keep figurin' your folks will throw me right off the ranch."

"No way, honey. You're my wife, family, *Ewing.* It'll sink in, and they can't help lovin' you the way I

do. My mother's been pushing me for years to get
married, and the old man—well, he keeps checking to
see if I walk funny."

She laughed, and to Bobby the sound was a small
celebration of temple bells, a call to worship. How
could he have been an atheist so long? From the corner
of his eyes, he admired her profile, the pert cameo of
her face—mostly big, dark eyes and ripened mouth
and a cute little nose. He was glad she wore her hair
shoulder length, a floating, not curly, not-straight
frame for the morning glory look of her.

It was weird, come to think of it. Here he'd known
Pamela Barnes since a frat party away back when, and
even if they never saw each other often, he was comfortable with her. He'd balled her when—two years
ago, a little less? And what a surprise she'd been, after
too many dates of coolness and tongue touching and
feeling the lithe roundness of her wiggling to him, but
no thanks, friendly and firm.

When she did turn loose with him, it was with all
stops pulled, like one of his old man's gushers blowing
in, all power and fury, without an emergency cutoff
valve. There was nothing mechanical about Pam's
loving, but something old and experienced, something
new and improvised. She was wonderful to him and
for him and with him.

"I should have married you right then and there,"
Bobby said.

"When and where?" She turned her face upon him,
the look into his soulful eyes, and the half-smile saying
she knew his flaws and accepted them.

"When we made it the first time in Dallas."

Her smile was bigger, softer. "Thank you, sir," she
said. "But I wasn't ready then, not for such—permanency. I only knew for certain that I wanted you so
much I ached inside and out, but mostly inside."

"You reckon being who we are held us back?"

"Subconsciously, maybe. The front of my mind
never paid any attention to that Barnes-Ewing stuff,
and it never was a real feud. Digger never has been

competition to your father. He just—talks. It's about
all he has left. I kind of dread tellin' him, but I will."

He lifted his right arm and put it about her shoulders; she snuggled close, smelling of newness and
fresh things, delicate excitements and new adventures.
Bobby watched the freeway and said, "Breakfast soon's
I see a good place. You hungry?"

"Hmmmm," she answered, burrowing into his
shoulder.

Something to do with Kismet, she thought: her in
New Orleans, and suddenly there *he* was, in the
Mariott's lobby, laughing and boyish as if they'd been
together only yesterday. Hey now, he said happily,
and when he quit talking close up into her ear, when
he let go her elbow, they were in the rooftop restaurant that looked like an old-time river paddlewheeler.

She'd come on business for her agency, and Bobby—
well, he was doing what he generally did, hustling
around for Ewing Oil, glad-handing, passing out
goodies to Louisiana-Texas oil legislators, their friends
and families. Bobby Ewing was perfectly suited for the
job: if someone was sad, Bobby got the blues; if somebody told the dustiest old joke, he laughed. And it
wasn't a put-on. His moods reflected those of people
he was with; he adapted, sympathized, understood.
Bobby Ewing had a million friends, if Ewing Oil did
not.

Pamela breathed more deeply, bringing through his
open-neck shirt mingled odors of soap, lotion, and
clean skin. It was aphrodisiac, and she lifted her chin
to take a teensy bit of skin between her teeth.

"Hey now," he said, "we're slap-dab out in the
middle of nowhere, and you start carryin' on like
that."

"Okay, I'll be good," she murmured.

"Didn't say it wasn't *good*, honey; there just isn't
a whole lot of room in this buggy. We'll have to get a
—station wagon with those one-way decal windows all
around, and never put up the backseat. That's it; a
station wagon."

Why the hell hadn't he said what he started to—a van? There had been other girls before virginal Karen in the back, rolling and giggling, sweaty flesh and slippery noises. Pam didn't fit into that picture. No, not a van.

Of course she wasn't a cherry, and never pretended to be. He never expected that, but respected her for being choosy. He wished he'd been as picky over the years.

A sign flipped by the window and he said, "Breakfast comin' up and funny thing: It's a motel café. Marshal, Texas, next, and Dallas, two hundred *more* miles. Good thing it's a *motel* café."

"You wouldn't," she laughed.

Bobby was sympathetic to people, she thought, not a chameleon. Beneath that agreeable charm lurked a steadiness others might not sense, a hidden core of something very hard and unbendable others didn't dream of—but then, others weren't crazy in love with him. It might be she was blinded by what she felt, and by the abrupt coming together of them.

They'd done Bourbon Street's shabby strip joints— clip joints, mostly because they were reluctant to part after an exotic dinner and easy, rambling talk. There was that electricity when their hands brushed, when their eyes, full of sensual memories, touched.

Over obligatory chicory coffee and rich, square doughnuts at the Morning Call, he said it would be nice if they could have a lot of breakfasts together. Pam said yes, it would, and first thing they knew, they were having a last long drink in hurricane glasses at Pat O'Brien's—while they waited for a doctor's office to open.

For blood and urine tests, because even if they crossed over into St. Bernard Parish, as so many folks in a hurry did, they still needed the test results.

To get married by a justice of the peace; a goodly chunk of Texas money standing before a sleepy old JP and his witness-wife.

She said against his throat, "It'll be right for us, Bobby. I'm determined to make it right."

"Yes," he said, and stroked her shining hair before turning in at the motel café.

A lot of freeway further on, and some hours later, JR Ewing stood with his arms folded before a huge color TV set, staring hard at it with the corners of his mouth folded down. The years were starting to show on JR and he was aware of it. He knew damned well he had a running start at a double chin, and knew damned well his short, almost GI haircut was out of style. But it was thinning, and this way he could pretend it was on purpose.

On the screen, a chunky guy with hair clear over his collar was hogging the camera over older men, much more important men, making the most out of his moment of glory. "How long did you work for Ewing Oil, Mr. Bradley?"

"*Mister* Bradley," JR mimicked. "*Mister* Bradley—hell, old Phil won't know who he means."

The TV camera changed angles, picking up a weasel-faced man. "Five years, Senator."

JR grimaced. "Phil, you damned old hammerhead, you know he's not a senator—only a two-bit lawyer playin' big man for the committee."

The woman crossed the big, opulent office behind him, carrying a silver tray heavy with coffee and sweet rolls. "Are you talking back to the set again?"

"Just watchin' old Phil showing his ass and tryin' to be cute. Julie, you know well's I do that he'll be fallin' over his own tongue, come dinner time."

He looked at her and when she gave him his cup, casually ran one hand up and down her thigh. A handsome woman, JR thought; yessir, a mighty handsome woman who looked like she was on the right side of thirty instead of past it. Julie had that knack, and she was something else in bed. He said, "Wonder if the old man's watchin' this mess."

Julie didn't move away from his hand; she simply

stood there and waited. "You know he is," she said.

At the ranch, Jock Ewing was listening and muttering, bootheels cocked up on his study desk, chewing a cigar. Once in a while he snorted and ashes dribbled onto his vest.

Ellie sat near the door, watching him more than the TV set. "You'll catch fire," she said.

"Goin' to do some burnin' of my own," Jock snapped. "See a couple of right familiar faces there, old boys supposed to be helpin' *us*." Picking up the phone, he punched out a number and waited impatiently—then: "JR—you watchin' the hearing? Who the hell let 'em pick up Phil, and why ain't our good buddies there doin' something?"

Blowing smoke, he coughed, listened a second, then cut in: "Where's Bobby, damnit? You get him on the horn in New Orleans and tell him I said haul his tail down to Austin and collect what's owed us; spread some more bees around, if he has to—yeah, *yeah*, I said!"

Ellie shook her head, her fingers not so deftly manipulating her embroidery needle. Why did she embroider? It was boring as hell, and Dr. Woodall knew it. Stay off horses for a while, the old coot said; best you stay off them forever, but I know better than to tell you that.

Like *he* wasn't all stove up, too; like *his* hands weren't all spotted and wrinkled and the hell with having to look at them. She put down the round frame and said, "Why don't you stay out of it? JR's no youngun, and you taught him all your tricks a long time ago."

He dropped his boots and swung the swivel chair to face her. "Woman, don't you care that they're hollerin' bribery and collusion and what-all?"

"Hollerin' true, I expect," she said.

Jock glared at her. "You think this ranch could've turned itself into anything near *about* like Ewing Oil? I don't know how many times this spread would've gone under, if it hadn't been for oil money holdin' it up."

Ellie said, "You never got over bein' mad at me for holdin' you to your word not to drill anymore here. And what makes you think I *wanted* anything near big as Ewing Oil? Was somebody to breed a nineteen-hand horse, I don't reckon he'd be better than a fifteen-hand one—if as good."

"We ain't talkin' horses, we're a-talkin' oil." Jock caught sight of movement in the hall. "Lucy—you Lucy!"

The girl stopped and turned slowly into the study. Jock couldn't hold a frown on her, never mind how she deviled him. Such a pretty little thing, bright hair and a saucy way of moving. She looked better in a dress, but insisted on wearing those worn-out jeans and some kind of top that outlined too much tit. Hot-blooded young filly like her, she oughtn't show too much.

"Okay, Grandpa—I did it again; shut off the alarm and just zonked."

Ellie said sharply: "Not so you can miss a whole day's school. Get hold of Ray or one of the hands to drive you, hear me?"

Lucy dimpled at them, green eyes mostly on Jock. A little girl not so little these days, all filled out and busting at the seams. She said, "Meant to do just that. Bye, Grandma, Grandpa."

"She wasn't carryin' a single book," Ellie said. "Likely she didn't come home with any, either."

Getting up, Jock stamped to the TV and turned it off. "Give the child some rein, Ellie. You was the one always hankered for a daughter, and she's next thing to it."

"No," Ellie said, "no more than she's a *child*."

He turned and snapped on the set again. "Barnes, goddamnit—has to be a *Barnes*. Thought I was shut of that name for good and all, but it keeps followin' me around like—like—" He looked at Ellie, but she'd left her needlework on the chair seat and was going straight-backed and high-headed through the door.

Damned fine-looking woman, Jock thought, and clicked off the TV; muley as ever, but a whole lot of woman still.

The hay barn was farthest from the big house, one of several spotted about the ranch, but the others were a mile or more in any direction. It was easy for Lucy to cut through the long garage where family cars were kept, and scoot around the shed where ranch equipment not in use was kept—rolling stock, hay wagon, cat, pipe trailers, and the rest. Then up the ladder and high to a flat spot where soft old quilts were spread, and feather pillows sneaked from attic storage.

Come fall, she'd have to move the bedding somewhere else, make a hidey hole far back in the hay, against the wall. They'd reach it through a secret tunnel, while ranch hands worked the other end of the barn, hauling loads of hay to feedlots. It would be kind of kinky, having to use a secret tunnel. Ray would bitch, but she knew how to take care of that mood.

She heard a voice calling, and eased to the edge of the top layer on her belly. Down by the stables, she saw Jock Ewing stomping up and down, hollering for Ray Krebs; old Grandpa on the loose. Ray came from behind the shed, where he'd been on his way here, and Lucy watched him nod agreement when her grandpa said something to him. Whatever the chore was, Ray wouldn't do it until after he saw her.

The old man pulled off in his station wagon, coming right by the open barn, and Lucy scooted back to the pallet. In a minute or two, she heard the ladder rattle, and stretched her arms above her head so her boobs would stand out better, lifted and bent one knee.

Ray Krebs climbed up and said, "Damnit, that was close."

"Bullshit," Lucy said. "He'd never climb up here. Probably can't 'cause he's too old. You're just runnin' scared."

He moved to her, stood looking down, his eyes touching her all over. "If the old man had any idea, he'd kill me, blow me away. Damn right I'm scared."

She ran a redwet tongue over full and pouty lips. "Well, *I* sure ain't goin' to tell him. Come on down here, scaredy cat; see if you can't turn into my tiger."

Heavy-shouldered, intriguing faintness of mansweat, fluffy chest hair reaching past his open collar, flat-bellied and big in the thigh, Ray dropped to his knees on the quilts. Square, tanned hands reached for her and Lucy's body arched to meet them.

Her mouth raced over his, tongue darting, lips and teeth nibbling. Ray held her tightly as she fitted her young, eager body to his, squirming and thrusting. Their breath mixed, and she raked his back with her nails.

"You're still goin' to town, makin' it with other women," she panted.

Cupping her breast, face buried in bright hair, Ray said, "Why not? Expect me to carry *you* to some juke joint?"

She twisted just enough so that he couldn't peel her jeans. "And her—that Barnes woman—still seein' her?"

"You little bitch—no, not for months. Come here."

"She screw any better'n me, any different?"

Ray Krebs pinned her down as she laughed and kicked off her boots. Shiny and pulsing, very soft, her mound rolled against his palm. Lucy reached for him, held him. "You ever slip up and call her my name?"

"Goddamnit," he said.

Laughing, she held him away as he struggled to reach her. "That'd be funny," she said. "Probably fuck you up good with another woman. *I* wouldn't mind, if you called me *her* name. Be kind of kinky. Go ahead, Ray."

"What! You're out of your gourd."

Lucy kept wiggling, turning away. "Do it, do it."

"All right," he said. "Pam—Pamela."

CHAPTER 18

Ray sat on the pallet, pulling on his boots. Lucy, little flakes of alfalfa clinging to her golden hair, put her eye to a crack in the barn siding. "Bobby's home; thought I heard that ol' Mercedes purring. Well now, what do you know? He's got a woman with him."

Standing up, Ray tucked in his shirt, zipped up jeans, and buckled his belt. "Bobby don't usually bring his kind of women to meet Miss Ellie."

"His kind of women, your kind; can't tell 'em apart without brands. Oh-oh! Oh man, this is unreal!"

He stooped for his hat. "Half the world's unreal to you, Lucy."

"Yeah? Well, trot on over here and take a look at who's gettin' out of the car. Come on, before Bobby carries her inside the house."

"I got no time for games," Ray said. "I have to show myself somewhere besides this barn."

Lucy snickered. "You'll find time for this game, lover. Down yonder is none other than the woman you've been makin' it with all these years—Miss Pamela Barnes."

"What?" Ray's hand clenched on his hat. "You sure?"

She laughed again, in pure mischievous delight. "Surer than that, stud. From what I can see, Bobby's *married* her."

"Goddamn!" Ray grunted, striding across wire-baled hay to her peephole. "If you're puttin' me on—"

"She's spooky about goin' up the steps, and yeah—he's sàyin' something to her and twistin' rings on her finger—*left* hand, stud; I can see a big diamond flash from here. They're married, all right. It sticks out all over them—her, more than him, I reckon. Jesus Christ! Bobby the pimp bringin' home a *Barnes*—oh wow."

Three long strides, and he had her by the arm, yanking her back. Ray stared down, focused on the pair at the car, the look of them. "Son of a bitch," he breathed.

"That's *funny*," Lucy giggled. "Oh man, is that funny."

Moving away from the peephole, Ray said, "Shut up, damnit."

She put both hands behind her head, rolled her pelvis, and gave a bump. "But don't you see what a crack-up it is, stud? It'll be a blast, tryin' to figure who's screwin' who."

His voice was gritty, ominous. "I said shut the hell up, you little bitch."

Surprised at his intensity, Lucy went quiet. He brushed by her and climbed down the ladder. When he was out of sight, she extended an upright thumb. "Sit on it."

At the big house, Ellie Ewing moved onto the porch and the screen door swung shut behind her. The girl was lovely, she thought, straight and graceful; she'd sit a saddle well. It was about time Bobby brought someone home; he was the last unmarried son, and she could stand another woman in the house, somebody she might possibly talk to. You couldn't talk with Sue Ellen, JR's wife; all that one knew was beauty contests and new kinds of makeup and what everybody was wearing.

Eyeing this girl, Ellie sensed a difference, and something else she wasn't quite certain about. Somehow, there was a familiar quality about her face, possibly around the eyes, or the mouth—

"Mother," Bobby said, "this is Pamela. We were married in New Orleans."

Ellie felt a flutter in her chest and held a deep

breath to still it; then she said, "You might have let us
know, Bobby. I'd have liked to—welcome, Pamela,
and I'm sorry for runnin' on like this. It's a surprise."
She held out her hand.

Pamela took it and thought, what a strong, handsome woman. "It was a surprise to us, too, Mrs.
Ewing."

Bobby's laugh was relieved. "Not that it was love at
first sight, Mother. We've known each other for years,
but when we met in New Orleans, it just seemed like
fate or something. So we got married next day, and—
well, here we are."

"Come in, come in," Ellie said. "If you drove all the
way from New Orleans, you must be tired and hungry.
I'll have Millie fix you something, and see to your
rooms, and—oh my, I do carry on when I'm caught
off balance."

In the foyer, halfway across a gigantic living room,
Pam touched Bobby's elbow and stopped. "You'll have
to tell her right off who I am. Would you rather do it
alone? I can use a powder room, anyway."

He hesitated, then said, "Down that hall, hon. Yes,
I'll go tell her. I guess nobody else is home, except Sue
Ellen; that's my brother JR's wife."

"Don't talk to me," Pamela said. "Talk to her."

At the kitchen door, Bobby caught up with his
mother. "We don't need anything, Mother. We had
breakfast a spell back. I—ah, maybe it'd be better if we
talked in the living room. Wouldn't want the servants
knowin' before the rest of the family."

Again, Ellie felt that faint hint of familiarity, and
now a foreboding. The girl—something about her
son's bride.

They sat on a couch and he took both her hands.
"Mother—Mom—she's Pamela Barnes, or was, before I
changed her name."

"Barnes? She can't be related to—"

"Yes, Cliff Barnes is her brother. I've never met her
father, but he's the old-time wildcatter; Dad knows
him already."

It was a struggle to keep her face steady, but Ellie managed. Good God—could this be *Willard* Barnes's daughter? In her house, married to her son, in this house where Ellie and Willard used to—"You wouldn't know her pa's name?" Ellie asked.

Letting go her hands, Bobby said, "Don't think she ever calls him anything but a nickname—Digger."

It hit her low and mean in the belly, and she squeezed both arms over the shock. After all these years, and no wonder the girl seemed familiar; it was her way of talking, the stubborn chin, the quick, damned-to-you eye.

"Anything wrong, Mother? Look—I know Dad's ticked off at these hearings and Cliff Barnes is easy to focus his mad on. But Pam has nothin' to do with all that. I hope you'll accept her for what she is—a fine, beautiful woman who is now my wife."

Ellie rubbed at both temples. "Bobby—I can and will accept her, make her welcome here," she said with difficulty. "But JR and your daddy—well, Jock and Digger Barnes used to be partners, but they had a fallin'-out many years ago, and there's been nothin' but bad blood between them ever since. Now, with Cliff Barnes headin' the investigating committee—"

Frowning, Bobby said, "I didn't know all that, but it wouldn't have made any difference. I'd have married her anyhow, because I guess I've been in love with her for a long time and just never realized it. If Dad carries so much grudge that he doesn't want my wife here, then we'll both move out."

Tiny bird-wings continued to beat within Ellie, and Willard's name echoed through long-closed corridors of her mind. Of course he would have married some-time; he was always a footloose rover, but he would need some place to come back to—or someone. Seeing Cliff Barnes on TV wasn't the same as meeting Willard's daughter face to face.

Willard's daughter—would she quote random bits and pieces of poetry, at times misquote them? Had she carried a book everywhere she went, and did she. . . .

Certainly not; Pamela hadn't ridden the rails and read by firelight in a hobo jungle. She was a young woman grown, and times were good, work and money plentiful. Who even remembered the Depression—or Willard Barnes?

Ellie said, "This is my house as well, and Pamela's welcome here."

Bobby patted her hand. "Thanks. Dad and JR still in Dallas? Maybe I ought to call and tell them the news."

"Let me," Ellie said. "They're getting plenty of news as it is. You've been too busy for the hearings, I reckon?"

He lifted an eyebrow. "They started already?"

"First thing this mornin', with Phil Bradley on the spit, and Cliff Barnes basting him every time it turns over."

"I ought to be in Austin, then."

"See to your wife. I expect this other news will bring your pa and JR home a-runnin'."

Willard's daughter, she thought again, and a ghost arose—a girl-child never born, slim and dark-haired and filled with fairy laughter, a kiss soft as thistledown and doe-eyed; she was a child of the mist who danced on moonbeams, and she would know those precious, precious silences so warm and still, more golden for the sharing.

Shaking herself, Ellie dialed a number and spoke into the phone, cutting off JR's questions, cutting off Jock also. It was done, she said, and that was that. And if they wanted Bobby to be of some use, they'd better hightail it on home.

"Jock," she said, "both of you mind your manners. You make that boy turn on you, and you'll wish you hadn't."

When she hung up the phone, Ellie sat looking at it for long, introspective moments. Jock Ewing took JR when the clay of him was soft, and formed him to his own image, made him driving and ambitious and oil-wise, company-wise.

Ellie Ewing had sworn he wouldn't take her next born, and he didn't. She kept Gary home, mothered and guided him, but tried to make him strong. Something went wrong in the core of him, and when he'd fled his own home, his own battered wife, Ellie was left more alone.

Because neither father nor mother took much hand in the upbringing of Bobby Ewing, like a weed in an unnoticed corner of a garden, he flourished untended. Jock didn't manipulate him, and Ellie didn't guide him. Whatever Bobby Ewing was—and Ellie began to realize that nobody really knew—whatever he'd grown into, he'd done it on his own.

Playing tackle on the Travis High team, when everybody said he was too light for it; enlisting for Vietnam and winning the Silver Star there, getting shot; not whining and not bitching about lost time and real-world pain. Bobby came home and finished school and did what his father wanted, the obedient son doing for the company what he'd done best for himself.

"We shaped him," Ellie whispered. "We shaped him by ignoring him, and it wouldn't take a whole lot for him to ignore us, in turn. We never saw behind the jokes and clowning because we never looked. And now"—she pressed hard against her temple—"now I don't think I *want* to know what's behind that painted-on face." There were times when she'd had a glimpse of his eyes when they weren't hiding behind a twinkle, and they were not funny.

My sons, she thought, as pain spread from her temple behind her right eye, spread down the right side of her neck, *my sons*—we gave you too much or too little, but we never shared, never listened. It must have been hell growing up here, if ever you did.

Covering her right eye with her palm, Ellie got up and walked carefully to the stairs, climbed them slowly, and reached her own bathroom. She took pills quickly, running water hot in the sink for the washcloth she'd press over the pain.

Pamela came to him, lay her hand against his cheek. "All talked out?"

"With her," Bobby said, taking her wrist and turning the hand so he could kiss its palm. "The others are something else. But no matter which—"

"Have I been missing something?" The voice was little-girlish, carrying a hint of petulance. Pam looked partway up the stairs to see the woman, sleek and polished, every red-brown hair neatly in place. She had high breasts and a sinuous body, long legs, everything just where and how it should be molded. But somehow, she gave off no aura of sensuality. Pam might have been looking at an animated clothing mannikin.

Bobby said, "Come on down, Sue Ellen." And to Pam: "Sue Ellen was Miss Texas, nineteen-seventy-five. My brother married her before she could go on to the Miss America contest. Hey, Sue Ellen, I want you to meet the newest Ewing—my wife Pamela."

"Hey there." Sue Ellen flashed a brilliant smile, came to stand with a tilt of her head and one foot out just so far, posing. Pam thought the woman didn't realize she did it, the movement was so much a part of her.

"Hi, Sue Ellen," Pam said. "It's nice to know that someone near to my own age will be here to sort of show me the ropes."

"Sure," Sue Ellen said through the brilliant smile, "of course."

They waited, but Sue Ellen didn't say anything else. Bobby took Pam's arm and made excuses, then led her up the stairs to his room—their room now. Once inside, with the door closed and Bobby's arms around her, Pam said, "Is she a little strange, Bobby?"

"No more than the rest of us." He nuzzled her throat, moved his hands over her back, down to her hips. "Sue Ellen spends half the day spit-shinin' herself, and the other half standin' around, waiting for JR. He takes her out sometimes—when he needs to act the family man, or when he particularly wants to show her off. My wife—Miss Texas, you know."

"That must be rough on her," Pam said, breathing a bit harder, glancing around the room her husband had spent his childhood in, his teen years. It didn't show much about him, except for the books, row on row; a junior-sized lariat hanging on a peg; a beat-up western hat.

Grinning, Bobby pointed out keepsakes: "That lousy pair of bookends I made in shop class, my trophy as part of the high school team that won the conference. Nothing much—all of Bobby Ewing tucked into a corner."

"And your war medals?"

"Put away," he said. "Nobody was proud of that war, Pam."

She moved restlessly about the room, touching books, the trophy. "Will the rest of them be here this evening?"

"No doubt. Mother called the office to sort of prepare them."

Pam said, "I can understand your father, a little, but what's your brother got against the Barneses?"

"No cause, hon. When my old man chews tobacco, JR spits. The old man was supposed to retire last year and the year before. Technically, JR runs the company, but anytime we get caught in a tight place, here comes Jock."

"So your brother's the big gun at Ewing Oil, and you're—what?"

"What I want to be: public relations. Keeps me out in the sun, and night lights. Dad calls it the *bees* department—booze, broads, and booty. It's my job to distribute wealth where it'll draw some kind of favorable interest for us. Somebody has to do it, you know. That's the way independent oil companies stay independent."

She sat on the bed, then lay across it, hands behind her head. "And you've never wanted to make company decisions?"

"Nope, and do you realize you're forcing me to make

a decision right now? To lock the door or hope nobody comes bustin' in."

"Lock it," Pam said.

They had time to shower and change before cocktails. Pam brushed at her hair, plucked a thread from her blouse, smoothed her panty hose for the tenth time.

Bobby chuckled. "You look just fine, hon. Miss Texas is already downstairs. You know, it's a good thing you didn't compete with her; she'd have never made it."

"Thanks," she said. "About that time, I was tryin' to be something besides a typist and worrying how to pay the rent. I don't imagine Sue Ellen ever had those problems. And she's already in the family. I still have to be accepted."

Putting his arms around her waist from behind, he snugged her to him, inhaling the freshness of her hair, feeling the supple curvings of Pam's marvelous body. "They'll accept you. Just be Pamela."

"Barnes," she said, "Pamela Barnes—Ewing."

"Bear down on the Ewing, baby. If you're ready, we'll take a stroll through the lion's den."

"Maybe I can find a thorn to take out of a paw?"

They laughed together, tension gone, and she knew it would be okay, that Bobby would make it so. Downstairs, the Ewings waited in a semicircle, low rumble of conversation ceasing when they heard Bobby and his bride coming. Heavy furniture, rich coverings on walls and floors, the dull gleam of silver everywhere— the pack ready to spring. It was how Pamela felt, but she strolled in to them, holding hands with Bobby.

"Dad, JR, Lucy—here she is; this is Pamela, and I'm sure you'll make her welcome. She's met everyone else." He eyeballed his father and JR until they grudgingly rose. Jock grunted something inaudible, and JR said, "Another real beauty in the house; us Ewings can't be faulted for our taste in women."

Bobby mixed drinks with Pam at his side, mixed for

themselves, because all the others were holding glasses, except for Lucy. She sat on the arm of Sue Ellen's chair, wearing a T-shirt and cutoffs, swinging one lushly shaped leg back and forth. Sue Ellen had changed clothes; her gown was deceptively severe and clinging, deeply veed front and back.

Pam glanced at Ellie Ewing—Miss Ellie, near legendary rancher who still controlled this vast spread and made it pay. Then Jock, another legend in his time. He was a hard-looking man, heavily creased around the eyes and mouth, with eyes that kind of stabbed out at the world, and a stubborn chin. He didn't look as if he was nearing seventy; he looked like he could climb derricks and run a drill and do about anything else around an oil well.

Bobby saluted them with his glass. "Here's to the quickest marriage I ever made. I've known Pamela for a spell, ever since we met at a frat party." He was going to say Ray Krebs had introduced them, but some warning buzzed in the back of his mind. It would be a mark against Pam that she'd gone out with a hired hand. "But all of a sudden, there we were in New Orleans, not only talkin' marriage, but going for the tests and headin' out of the parish to a J.P. For your sake, Ma, I asked him was he a Baptist, and sure enough—"

Like a windup doll with a button pushed, Sue Ellen said, "I didn't know you were so impulsive, Bobby."

He laughed. "Neither did I."

Ellie said, "You meanin' to stay in your old room, or in Gary's house? It's been closed up a long time, but I'll have Millie go air it out."

She had the feeling she was being talked around, so Pam said, "Anywhere will do tonight, Miss Ellie. I only have one bag, and I'll have to go right back into Dallas tomorrow for my things."

Jock stirred on the couch, crossed his legs. "If you see your brother, let him know we're not a den of wolves out here."

She looked directly at him, this weathered, hard old man. "My brother and I are different people."

Bobby edged between them. "Thought we made it a rule not to talk business or business problems until after supper."

"That's right, Jock," Ellie said. "Will you give me a refill, please?"

And Pam said to Bobby, "I think I'll have another, too."

Lucy's clear, pouty voice lifted. "Oh my, here's our foreman. Do come on in, Ray."

Clearing his throat, Ray Krebs said, "Sorry to bust in on you, Mr. Ewing. Lucy said you wanted to see these tallies—"

Jock frowned. "Did I now? Well, seein' as how you're here with the ledger—"

Lucy bounced over to them. "Get you a drink, Ray?"

He shook his head and Jock's glare told her plain as anything that hired help didn't drink with family. She grinned and shrugged. "Oh yeah, and this here is the newest Mrs. Ewing. Pamela, our ramrod, Ray Krebs— but it seems like you two met before."

"I didn't know that," JR said.

"Small world," Lucy said. "Lil' old bitty world, really. Ray was tellin' me just the other day, while he was carryin' me to school, that he once had a passionate thing goin' with this Pamela, but I didn't connect *that* girl up with Bobby's new wife."

Jock said, "Here, I'll sign the book."

Ray took back the ledger and cut his eyes at Lucy. "Yessir, well—good night. And congratulations, Bobby—Miz Ewing."

Bobby said, after Ray was gone, "Now what was *that* little byplay about, missy? It's no secret that Ray Krebs introduced me to Pamela, years ago."

Lucy shrugged again and sway-hipped back to her chair. JR said, "I'd like to show Pamela our little house, if you don't mind, little brother. Maybe Mama's gardens, if the light holds."

"Look—" Bobby said, but JR had her by the elbow,

and she couldn't pull away without a scene. She nodded at Bobby and walked away beside his older brother.

Outside, JR said, "I apologize for my father—different generation, and he tends to speak his mind. He doesn't expect you to reveal anything about your brother's activities."

Moving her arm from his grasp, Pam said, "I don't know anything. I hardly ever see him, he's in Austin so much."

"Of course," JR said. "Well, here's where Sue Ellen and I stay—kitchen, sitting room, two bedrooms; one was meant for a nursery."

"Oh," Pam said, "is Sue Ellen going to—"

"Not yet," JR said, "but it's a matter of time. The old man is anxious for an heir, someone to run the business for the next generation."

Moving aside, Pam pointed at another house, one barely seen through a shielding of cottonwoods. "Who lives there, the foreman?"

"Oh no, your—friend stays in the bunkhouse. Cattle folks are democratic, but not to *that* extent." JR smiled, but his eyes didn't. "No, that house used to belong to our brother Gary and his bride. He came very close to beating her to death in there, and the incident may have affected little Lucy; she's their daughter, you know."

Pam said softly, "N-no, I didn't."

In the same conversational tone, JR said, "Did your brother put you up to this?"

Swinging to face him, Pam could only stare.

He said, "It's not an unreasonable question, Miss Barnes."

Bracing her feet apart, Pam said: "It's *Mrs.* Ewing." She started off the porch of the small house, but JR blocked her way.

"How much?" he asked. "We're willin' to spend some money now to avoid a hassle, but if you insist on bein' chased off, you'll come out with nothing—*zip*,

baby. A quick annulment, our lawyers handlin' everything—"

"Back off mister," she said through set teeth. "If you
don't, first I'm going to kick you in the crotch, and
then I'll start screamin' until they hear me in Travis
City."

Coming across the yard, Bobby said, "Hey, what are
you guys doin'?"

JR didn't change expression. "Talkin' some; gettin'
to know each other."

Bobby said, "Well, come on. Mama has supper waiting."

"You'll learn to know our mother . . . Pamela,"
JR said. "She's old-fashioned—family loyalty and all
that." He looked after her as Bobby led her off. His
thin, confident smile said he was in control.

CHAPTER 19

In the flare of the lighter, JR watched his father's
craggy face but couldn't read it. The front porch was
dark, but there was still movement behind them in the
house. JR said, "I thought the doctor said you're not
supposed to smoke those things."

Jock grunted. "Man can't do a little of what he's
not supposed to, he ain't much of a man."

There was nothing to read in his father's voice
either. Most times, JR thought, he could figure just
about what the old man was thinking, knew instinc-
tively what he wanted done. Right now, it was all out
of kilter. What the hell got into Bobby? First that off-
the-wall marriage, and to Pamela Barnes, for chrissake;
then him popping off at dinner about how he wanted

to come off the road, take a guiding hand in the business.

Damn. Bobby was just a kid; he didn't know his ass from his eardrum about the company or the Texas Independents. He was good for setting up parties, for furnishing party girls and booze and discreet motels. Maybe it was that woman Pamela putting little brother up to being something he wasn't. A Barnes, a goddamn *Barnes*.

JR said, "I tried to find out her price."

"You did what?" Jock's voice was sharp.

"Figured on payin' her off, getting rid of her."

"You're a jackass."

JR flinched. It wasn't like his father to come down on him like this. "Cliff Barnes is crucifying us on TV; now you want Bobby married to his sister?"

"Didn't say that, but there's ways to go about things, subtle ways that don't get everybody's back up. You ain't learned 'em yet."

From upstairs, JR heard Pam and Bobby laughing, cutting the fool and not caring who was listening. "She put him up to it, I reckon—Bobby an executive. *Her* idea, and he goes along like she's got a twitch on his lip."

Jock said, "Could be it's time he went to work."

"But PR is plenty important, especially now that we're gettin' mud slung at us."

"Nothin' but pimping and such; any good bell captain could handle the job."

JR's fists pushed against his thighs. "You put *me* in your chair."

"Reckon you'll stay there, too. But it don't hurt to have another Ewing keepin' an eye out. Don't recall as I said you had to run the whole shebang yourself." Jock drew on his cigar, cocked his head at another outburst of hilarity from the second floor. "Better see to Sue Ellen, boy. Sounds like my first grandson is liable to be theirs."

In darkness, in silence, JR hunched in his chair long after his father went back into the house. Jesus. He hadn't even thought about that angle until the old man made such a point of it: the next Ewing generation, the next *male* Ewing. Lucy didn't count, in Jock's estimation, because women didn't run big oil outfits. And Lucy was a living symbol of a failure: Gary. Oh God, if the old man ever knew the truth!

But there was no chance of that. Maureen was smart; she'd taken the money and run. Wherever Gary got to, he'd never shown his face at the ranch again, and most likely never would. By now, he was dead from booze, or some other drunk had killed him.

Little Lucy didn't recall anything important from her early childhood, or she'd have stuck it to him already. His own daughter, and the kid hated his very guts; he didn't know why. He'd always been good to her, good as he knew how, but she looked at him sometimes like she'd be happy to see him dead.

Bobby and Pamela—that was something else. Suppose they produced a kid right away, a male heir? That might just tear down JR's playhouse, and, damnit, *he* was president of T.I., president of Ewing Oil. Bobby nor any of Bobby's brats would steal that from him. Maybe if Sue Ellen—but shit, he couldn't ask and she wouldn't anyhow. All those luscious looks, that entrancing wiggle, and she was a lifeless slab in the sack. Still, he might have to go through with it, work out his own hang-up somehow, so he could knock her up.

Off to the right, he saw the spark of a cigarette brighten and ebb. JR got up and walked toward the intermittent glow.

Ray Krebs said, "Thought you might want to see me."

"How the hell did she end up marryin' him? Thought you had that little ol' girl peter-whipped and hand-trained. How come you introduced them in the first place?"

Pulling on his cigarette, Ray wondered what old Big Dog Ewing would say if he knew why, if he knew how Cliff Barnes got some juicy tips. All the money JR handled, and the cheap bastard hadn't boosted a ranch salary in four years; he thought it was a big deal to take Ray whoring sometimes; made him real democratic. Ray said, "Just happened to run into Bobby at that dance, and couldn't *not* introduce 'em. She was my number one lady; how'd I know she would flip out over baby brother—or the Ewing money?"

JR said, "We can't sit still for it."

"We? *Us*? She got you runnin' scared, JR?"

"I don't like her old man spoutin' off how Jock Ewing screwed him out of millions. He ought to have been shut up long ago. Who knows what this bitch has in mind? She's already got my little brother chompin' at the bit, wantin' his own office."

Ray dropped his cigarette butt, ground it out with a bootheel. "I wouldn't mind havin' Bobby's old job. Sure no place for me to go on the ranch."

"First things first," JR said, "and first we bust up Bobby and Pamela."

Upstairs, Bobby and Pamela came together gently, with much tenderness. Fresh from their baths, they were dewy and eager, delighting in each other's body, loving and being loved.

Entering her, Bobby breathed, "Lord, but you're wonderful. I'll never have enough of you."

"Don't," she said, moving to meet his body. "Don't ever, ever have enough."

But the next day the honeymoon was officially over. Jock Ewing wanted Bobby in Austin—quickly. It would be his last smoothing-over job, the old man said. After that, his own shop in the Ewing Oil Building, a near-about free hand with his part of the company.

So Pamela was off in the Mercedes for Dallas, relieved to find that family breakfasts weren't important, that each member went his own way at his own pace. She sang, she whistled, she beat time to radio rock; the world was bright; the world was sunny. She'd passed muster with the Ewings, and if she hadn't exactly been accepted, she hadn't been outright rejected either.

When she pulled the 450SL up in front of her garden apartment, her brother was sitting on its steps, chin in hand.

She stood beside him, keying her door. "You're a far piece from Austin."

Following her inside, he said, "And you're out of your head."

Pamela went into the bedroom, pulled suitcases from a closet, and opened them up on the bed. "I see you've heard the news. How?"

Cliff Barnes glowered at her. "I have friends. Why, damnit? Why marry a Ewing?"

"I married a man I love."

"You used to be worse than me about revenge for what they did to Daddy. You broke more windows, threw more rocks—"

"I grew up," Pam said, stuffing clothing into a bag and clamping it shut. "Did you?"

"They're leeches, bloodsuckers, tyrants. They're ruining air, land, and water, and somebody has to stop 'em; someone has to show the goddamned Ewings they can't *buy* everything they want in this state. Texas would be better off without 'em."

She looked at him. "I wonder if you'd be so noble if you were going after somebody named Jones." Hauling more clothing from dresser drawers, she packed them into the other suitcase.

He said, "When I knew you were running around with Bobby Ewing, I didn't say anything. But *marrying* him—have you told Digger?"

She shook her head, hefted both suitcases after a quick look around the room. "No. I'm not up to that yet. Guess I'll send for this other stuff."

When Cliff reached for a bag, she wouldn't let him take it, but carried both out to the Mercedes. He said there, "Here's one good reason for marrying him, and you don't have to write that crappy ad copy anymore. Big cars and furs from now on."

She put down the bags and unlocked the car trunk. "You really don't have to try hard to be a bastard, do you?"

When she lifted in the luggage and closed the trunk, Cliff caught her arm. "Damnit, Pam, we shouldn't be fightin'; of all people, *we* ought not fight. And the Lord knows, you'll need every iota of your energy to stand up to what that family will throw at you. They'll cut you to ribbons."

"I'll buck them, don't worry. Do you want to follow me in your car, or ride in this symbol of decadent Ewing wealth?"

"Where are you going? Don't expect me to set foot on that ranch."

"Digger," Pam said. "I might as well face up to him now, because nothing he says will change anything. That's if I can find him."

"I'm comin'," Cliff said. "Try the Longhorn first, maybe the Goliad Saloon."

Downtown in Ewing Oil's headquarters, Julie Parsons brought rolls and coffee to JR. He patted her rear and asked, "How's baby brother doin' in yonder?"

"Not so babyish," she answered. "He wants the safe combination."

"Damn! Why would he want that? After all the routine garbage I dumped on his desk—"

"Look," Julie said, "maybe it's none of my business, but offhand I'd say that kid is no kid."

"I'll talk to him, then." JR rolled a cigar in his fingers but didn't light it. Crossing the waiting room, he reached the smaller office where Bobby had been set up. It was formerly the file room, and some of the confidential stuff was still there in locked files, the small wall safe. Before JR opened the door he lit his cigar and put on a fresh smile; Julie followed him.

"Hi. Finish goin' through all those papers?"

"Pretty boring stuff, JR."

"Nobody said nuts and bolts are interesting, but they hold it all together. Julie said somethin' about combinations—"

Bobby leaned back in his desk chair. "Look, JR, I

mean to be here for a spell, so I'd like to know what's goin' on—*all* of it. Like the red files."

JR started. "Red files? Who told you—"

"Just a good memory," Bobby said. "When Dad technically retired, he made a big to-do about presentin' you with the key to the red files."

"Bobby," JR said, "why don't you just playact, or go back on the road, where you'll do some good. Or don't do anything; go for a trip around the world."

Levelly, evenly, Bobby said, "Those files, JR."

"Kid—"

Bobby sat very still, his palms flat on the desk. Julie was standing off to one side, notebook in hand, and it seemed as if the air conditioning had been turned up full. My God, she thought, his eyes have gone all funny, like dark icicles that don't reflect light.

He pushed himself up and started around the desk, slow and deliberate. JR bit through the end of his cigar and it fell onto the desk; nobody moved to pick it up. JR said, "Bobby—Bobby, there ain't no call for—goddamnit, Bobby—*here!*"

Dropping a key on the desk, JR wheeled and trotted from the office, almost running over Julie. She stood a moment longer, seeing Bobby sit down again, watching him reach for the key; he didn't touch the lighted cigar, but let it smolder against wood. Holding her breath, she eased to the door and sidled out. He didn't look up.

In JR's plush, airy office, it all seemed incongruous: the silent, terrifying threat; JR's fear—

He said, "I ain't no coward. You know that, Julie."

"Of course not," she said. "It—that surprised you, and after all, he's your brother. You didn't want to—to hurt him."

He poured coffee from the silver pot, spilling some. Then he took the cup over to the guest bar, and topped it with bourbon. Back to Julie Parsons, he said in a brittle voice that didn't sound like his own, "I've always been big for my age. I was big then, at seventeen, lots of muscle and pretty fast. Bobby—you know

I'm ten years older than him?—he was little and skinny and never said much. That was before he started clownin' around; he was about seven, I guess. Anyhow, he was workin' on one of those plastic airplanes, puttin' it together, and I stepped on it.

"Well, he waited for me to say I was sorry, and I didn't feel like apologizing to a little shit seven years old. So I just told him to keep his crap out of my way, and kicked the rest of that plane over the side of the porch." JR pulled at his laced coffee, waited a moment, swallowed again.

"I was seventeen, remember—near big as I am now. He just looked at me with his eyes gone kind of flat, and went into the house. I said somethin' after him, like go tell Mama, crybaby. Only he didn't tell anybody. He never said a goddamn word to me or anybody else, and when he came back out that door, the first swipe he took came *that* close to cuttin' my head off."

JR drank the rest of his coffee, turned around to look at Julie. "Shit. I mean, who the hell expects a seven-year-old kid to come at him with a butcher knife? I fell off the porch, because it was the only way to get away from him, and the little bastard flat-out meant to *kill* me. You hear that? *Kill* me over a plastic airplane. I mean, he just kept a-comin', not cryin' or anything, just comin' sure and certain, and cuttin' at me every step. You're goddamn right I busted and run. I stayed a good ways from him for a long time, and I reckon neither of us said anything to Mother or Dad about it."

Splashing pure bourbon into his cup, JR drank, wiped his mouth. "Don't forget—he was in Vietnam a spell, too. His citation says somethin' about him killin' ten gooks with his rifle, then beatin' two to death with his entrenching tool. That's a foldin' shovel. *Damn*— a shovel!"

He carefully put down his cup. "Bobby's about half loco, and fightin' that war didn't help him any. So you're damned right I gave him the red files key. I'd give him the whole fuckin' building when he gets like that."

Julie said, "Darling, you don't have to explain any—"

"Just so you know," he said, bending to open the lower right drawer of his desk, "and so you'll put these special files in the office safe."

She smiled in admiration. "You thought it out in advance. But he'll get around to that safe, too."

"Not before you get over to the bank and put 'em in *your* safety-deposit box."

Julie stared. "But I don't have a —"

"Sure, you do; as of this mornin'."

"JR," she said, "nobody will ever get around *you*."

"That's for sure," he said. "Like my daddy said, do things subtle."

Pamela and Cliff found him in a seedy bar not far from his house, the house they grew up in. He was telling the same story, acting it out with Shakespearean gestures. A half-circle of men in work-stained clothes applauded Digger, bought him another drink.

"Kill 'im," he said. "Had me the chance and never killed Jock Ewing. 'Thirty-three or 'thirty-four—ah, death where is thy sting? Just think on how much better off this country would be today."

"Dad," she said, "please?"

He wobbled with them, jacket rumpled, hair uncombed, smelly. He said. "Stole millions off'n me, you know. Who steals my purse steals nothin' but the food outa my mouth—or somethin' like that."

Cliff said, "Please get in the car, Dad. We'll carry you home."

In the backseat he said, "But the night is young, and she's so beautiful—there among the shadows, beautiful."

Cliff said, "Pam, maybe you shouldn't—"

"He's been a lot worse," she said. "Dad, Daddy—I came to tell you I—I'm married."

"Ha!" Digger said. "Across the threshold led . . .

and every tear kissed off soon as shed . . . his house
she enters, there to be a light . . . shining within,
when all without is night . . ."

She said, "Daddy, please don't be hurt. I married
him because I love him, but he—he's Bobby Ewing."

Digger Barnes leaned forward and stared at her.

Cliff looked at her and shrugged. She said, "Bobby
Ewing, Daddy."

Digger made a strange sound, a noise halfway between spitting and throwing up. "Ewing."

"You're just not goin' to *let* yourself understand,
are you?" Pam threw the car into gear and burned
rubber away from the curb. She swung corners and
pulled up before the house they'd once shared. "Take
him in, Cliff."

Digger grunted out, half-supported by his son. He
didn't look back at her, and Pam crossed her arms on
the steering wheel, buried her face in them. She didn't
remain there long. Wiping at her eyes, she took off
again. Cliff could find his way back to her apartment
and his own car, and Digger could. . . .

Like the old folks said, here was Pamela Barnes,
between a rock and hard place. No, damnit—not
Barnes, but Ewing. She'd made the choice and taken
the step, and she'd stick by her decision, stand beside
Bobby. She was pretty well cut off from her own
family, and the Ewings were lined up against her in a
solid bloc.

She made it through town and onto the freeway,
whipped around a big semi and hauled out for Travis
City and the ranch beyond. There was one other little
problem out there—a golden, randy stud named Ray
Krebs, which was a hell of a place for an old boyfriend
to be, right now.

CHAPTER 20

Ray Krebs watched her slide from the Mercedes, a
flash of long, exciting legs and the briefest glimpse of
lace frill panties. Pamela got better looking every day,
seemed like; more ripe and lush. He felt a sense of loss
at her being married, especially to one of the family.
But with JR working on a bust-up, Ray thought he
wouldn't be missing any of that fine, special stuff for
very long—if at all. Pam always craved more meat than
most men could furnish at one time.

He grinned; he sure as hell ought to know. For
about five good years, he'd taught Pam Barnes all she
knew and had her coming back for more. Any time he
called, here she came, switching her eager ass and
jiggling those high, firm knockers. Whatever he was in
the mood for, she met his desires more than halfway,
turning on, getting high on sex as other people did on
grass or dope.

Of course, as she got older and went to work, and
after he had to back down half the cowhands on the
place to get his daddy's job, they didn't get together as
much. But the fact that Pamela was still single, listening for her phone to ring some weekend, was a sign
that she was hung up on him for good. It would be his
ass if JR found out he'd introduced her to Bobby because Cliff Barnes had wanted him to. Hell, how was
he to know Cliff was going to come down on the
Ewings so hard with the state investigating committee?
No more than he could figure that environmentalists
from all over the country were also behind Cliff now.
Because Cliff was Pam's brother and a lawyer, Ray had

gone to him about that statutory rape mess with another kid, and Cliff got it smoothed out pretty cheap.

Wasn't like actual *rape*, by a long shot. That hot little chick had kept after him worse than Pam had, until he thought some on soldering shut his zipper. But when Cliff wanted a favor, Ray owed it, and he figured it wasn't any more than trying to get Pam in with the big wheels, find her a rich husband. Ray didn't mind sharing juicy stuff with another guy, so long as there was plenty around for everybody. But her marrying a Ewing—oh man, JR was right. It had to be busted up, quick.

He sauntered toward her, watching the slick rhythm of bare, tanned legs as she went around to the trunk of the Mercedes and opened it. "Hey, Pam."

She looked over one shoulder, heavily lashed eyes, full mouth, hair floating. "Hi, Ray."

"Let me get those suitcases. I just wanted to say— well, I never expected you to marry him, but congratulations. Cost me my best gal, but I hope you're happy. You won't get hassled from me. There'll be enough of that around here."

Her eyes were direct, warm—remembering the sweaty, gasping passions? "Thank you, Ray."

Hefting the suitcases, he said, "If you ever need— forget it. I'll just tote these on up to your rooms."

Heat stirred in his belly, and he dropped his eyes to the hypnotic rolling of her haunches as she went ahead of him onto the porch and into the house. There she surprised him by cutting off toward the living room where he could see Sue Ellen and Miss Ellie arranging flowers. All he could do was keep on to the stairs.

Pam looked after him, wishing she didn't recall the salted flavors of him, the madness he could arouse. She smiled brightly at her new in-laws. "Hi. You all look busy. Anything I can do?"

Sue Ellen's lacquered face showed nothing at all. Pam expected it to crack when the woman said, "No thanks. We got sort of a—sort of a routine."

Ellie Ewing turned a vase just so. "Appreciate it, Pamela, but I reckon we're about done. Some folks comin' in this evening, is all."

"Well," Pam said, quietly put down, closed out. Whirling, she went quickly upstairs and along the wall, one trimly booted foot propped behind her, arms crossed just below young melon breasts whose tops were exposed by an open shirt collar.

"You ain't got a chance," Lucy said.

"What?" Through the partly open door, Pam could see her luggage, but not Ray Krebs.

"He cut on out," Lucy said. "Ray won't embarrass you none. Oh, I know you were his girl for a long time. Saw him carry you to a motel in Travis City once; listened in on another phone a time or two, when he talked to you in Dallas."

"You're a busy little—thing," Pam said, brushing past to enter her rooms. A separate house, she thought, like JR and his wife had; maybe the empty one still farther out. The Ewing mansion was big, but no house could hold all the women and this sullen girl.

Lucy followed her inside, toed the door shut. "Bobby tell you about me?"

Lifting a bag to the bed, Pam said, "No."

"My daddy—that is, Gary Ewing, was the middle brother. But he was a drunk that run off. I reckon you know about drunks, from all they say. I know, too." The blue eyes blinked hard. "Goddamnit, I *know,* even if they keep tellin' me I was too young. I—I saw things and heard 'em and—well, they'd flat be surprised at some of the things I know. Like JR—I know goddamned well JR run off my mama, and I know—I know that he—*he*—"

The eyes filled and Lucy brushed angrily at them. "They tromp on anybody gets in their way. So you ain't got a chance here, Mrs. Bobby Ewing. They'll bust you and tromp on you and—oh hell!"

"Lucy—" Pam reached out a hand, but the girl was already slamming out through the door, a whirling of sunshine hair, of faded jeans. Maybe, Pam thought, if she could reach this kid, she might find a friend in this armor-plated household, anyhow.

She bathed, washed her hair, blew it dry, and stayed in her rooms listening to country music and hanging up her clothes. With Ray Krebs lurking in the background, and JR openly antagonistic, other Ewings turning on the chill, Pam certainly didn't need any involvement with a teenage neurotic. But the kid was so vulnerable, despite her outer shell of toughness, and Pam could see herself only a few years back, walking the edge of a precipice. Pam Barnes could have gone either way then, slipped down and out, or climbed up to being her own woman—up to finding and loving Bobby Ewing.

Yes, she knew about drunks, as Lucy said; and a hard-faced bitter old woman who knew everything but love. Tangled so deeply with Ray Krebs, needing his maleness so damned much, the sexual reassurance that she was *somebody*, she might have wound up hustling on the streets. Ray was only solid when he was making love; reach for him any other time, and he was a handful of nothing. But Cliff had been there, too, to fill up the lonely times, to hold her hand. Digger was seldom there, but Cliff was, before and after Ray Krebs, and until Bobby.

She must have lulled herself into a light sleep, because she jerked awake when Bobby galloped in. "Baby—hi, baby!" He was sweet and nuzzly, boyish and kissable, rolling across the bed with her, and everything was all right. "Hey, Pam—how come you're not gettin' ready for the whooptedo?"

She kissed his throat, his chin. "The what?"

"Party, like—not a *big* affair, but still a party; some of the neighbors and most of the Texas Independents company heads. No dinner, but dress-up. Didn't anybody tell you?"

"No," she answered slowly, "they sure as hell didn't."

He frowned. "Must have forgotten, what with all the uproar down in Austin. Come on, let's get dressed.

I have to split for the capital soon as I can, first thing in the mornin', after they hold this—kind of informal meetin'."

Pam sat up. "You're playing fetch for them again? I thought that was done."

At the closet, he searched for a tux. "Maybe JR can go. I'll see."

But of course JR couldn't; Bobby was used to handling things like this. He knew which good old boys down there owed the Ewings, and which others could be put in debt. Still three or four days to get to them, JR said; no, it wasn't only business, it was family.

Hard-eyed, teeth clamped on a long cigar, JR said, "This investigation turns into legislation, all us independents might's well sell out, turn over our holdings *and* our ranches and run. You want that to happen, boy?"

"I just thought—" Bobby said, trapped, his father looming in the background, "I just thought—okay, damnit. I didn't know I was the only man in Texas who can whoa up this catastrophe. Didn't know I could be all that important."

JR eyed his brother, seeing the retreat, the duty. All Bobby's early—and damned deadly—rebellion seemed to have faded, and JR was glad. He pressed his advantage now: "Anytime, Bobby. I can call in the chopper and you'll be settin' down in Austin before breakfast, before our enemies know you're comin'." He flicked a look at Pamela. "Long as somebody don't warn 'em."

Pamela put her empty champagne glass upon a passing waiter's tray. All around them, music was old-fashioned and mechanical; across the patio, a black group pumped out rhumbas and fot-trots, an occasional waltz. People more or less danced, and voices were getting louder, drunker; smoke thickened.

She smiled sweetly, moved very close to JR, and lifted her lips to his ear. "Go to hell," she said.

JR grinned after them, Pamela as she strode angrily away, Bobby as he trailed arguing in her wake. He'd lay odds they wouldn't ball tonight, and lifted his glass to a short honeymoon, to red files back where they should be, and Bobby where *he* ought to be. All was right with the Ewings, and so, with the world. But there was one more scene to set, so he put down his glass and waded through the crowd, nodding and patting backs and howdying everybody important.

Ray Krebs had his butt propped against the back porch, and when some little split-tail heard JR coming, she gasped and moved out of his arms, faded swiftly into the night. Ray laughed and picked up his drink, rattled ice in it.

JR said, "Jailbait's goin' to hang you out to dry some day. That wasn't the Layne kid, was it? Ol' man Layne, he's mighty high up in T.I."

"And his little ol' gal is mighty *hard* up," Ray laughed. "But bein' a gentleman, I ain't tellin'."

Hunkering down on the porch, JR said, "Might's well get rid of the Barnes woman right quick. Carry her off sight-seein' after breakfast, down yonder to the line cabin by the lake. I'll see that the chopper's late, and drive him out there, instead of to the pad. When we get there, son, I want to see you and her and plenty of shinin' ass."

"JR," Ray said, "she's actin' funny. I mean, she may not come with me and damned if I know—"

"You find a way," JR said. "You damned well find a way, you hear?"

He went back through the kitchen, scattering black servants and Mexicans. Take an ordinary cowhand under your wing, carry him along tomcatting, and pretty soon he got uppity, got to feeling he was near about family. Well, Ray Krebs had him some learning to do and it was schooltime.

Just because that bastard could whistle up women anywhere he went, and mostly young ones, mostly married ones, he thought he could get away with damned near anything. Who had to pay the freight, once the party was done? It sure wasn't Ray Krebs, the whoring foreman.

Mood changing almost immediately, JR said, "Whorin' foreman," and laughed like hell over another glass of champagne, because good old Ray would do like he was told. And Pamela Barnes-turned-Ewing? Ray said he'd dicked her since she was fourteen years old. Bitch that took to screwing so early didn't back off just because she was married.

JR looked across the patio at a crowd of admirers around his own wife. Look yonder at Miss Texas, would you? She was purely strutting her stuff, posing, cocking her head, and batting false lashes. She accepted a drink like a queen doing mere commoners a big favor; she allowed some asshole to light her cigarette, and he like to wagged himself to death account of he got to hold her hand. Sue Ellen glittered and she smiled; she sparkled and she smiled; and smiled, and smiled. It was about all she'd ever learned to do.

That and soak in the bathtub for an hour straight. Then put some kind of grease all over her face, and it looking naked with lashes, eyebrows, and dark-red mouth all wiped off; so much time to paint her toenails, to peel every tee-niney little hair from armpit and leg, uproot hints from thigh and belly until he thought she was for sure going to shave her nooky, too. One hundred and one goddamned strokes of the hairbrush every night, and if he got pissed at her, she batted her big eyes and looked dumb.

What the hell could he expect out of a woman who'd spent her life in beauty contests or getting ready for them? Miss Pretty Baby, Miss Pre-Teen San Antonio, Miss Sweet Sixteen—and on, and goddamned on.

JR put a hard hand against a waiter's chest and nearly made him drop the tray. But it balanced and JR took it, told the spooked nigger to go get another. He drank down a glass, and another, but sweat broke out on him anyway, like it sometimes did when he thought too long on Sue Ellen. Because her body was real: every wiggly, jiggly inch of that spectacular, beauty-contest body was solid and perfumed and hand-slicked. It was enough to make a man pitch a squalling fit.

Because three times—bigod, only *three* measly times —he'd worked himself up and felt her all over, caressed goldeny tits like honeydew melons, run his shaking hands over flank and thigh and into that musky dampness. Kissing her hard, tonguing her mean, and pretending some other woman was getting him set with her mouth, that was how often, in near to four years married, JR had been able to strain himself up to do it.

And every time, Sue Ellen just lay there. She didn't even play she was doing it back, just lay there like she was dead and just hadn't cooled off yet. And when he drooped, when he stared down into that naked, greased face—at least she wasn't smiling for a toothpaste ad. She was biting her lips like she was nailed to a cross, but in some way keeping herself holy; keeping herself lovely, gorgeous, pure Miss Angel Food Cake.

Planking the serving tray on a table, he spilled empty glasses; two rolled and splintered on the flagstones, but nobody could hear over the music, the babble. A salvaged drink in his right hand, JR inched through the dancers, eeled among serious drinkers along the bar. Now Sue Ellen was out on the floor, dancing with old man Layne and the old roadrunner was trying to feel her up, but her delighted-with-this-pretty-world expression didn't change.

Never would, JR thought, unless somebody got between her legs. He caught himself a nice, round handful of evening-gowned ass. She backed into him and shook it, and he just let it go, turned loose somebody's hot-to-trot wife and went wobbling off to one side to sit down so the sweat might dry. Pamela Barnes, he thought, taking it from good old Ray when she was only fourteen. Ray must have turned her every whichaway but loose, and she'd know how to make a man studdy, swell him up like a barber pole.

JR drank, hurled the glass into an oleander bush

and patted his face with a handkerchief, but he kept
right on sweating. He was drunk and horny and if he
ever took a chance on getting into Pamela's drawers,
it would be after Bobby cut her loose. If he kept pulling the right lines, he was sitting high in the catbird
seat. A woman was just a woman, but slick old JR was
Ewing Oil.

CHAPTER 21

She didn't sleep worth a damn. It hadn't exactly
been a fight, but close enough to be upsetting—and
disappointing. The last time, Bobby said, "I swear,
baby, it's the last time they'll maneuver me into doing
any more dirty work." And she said, "Yeah, sure. The
last time was it, remember?"

So Pamela had two cups of black coffee in the
kitchen before anyone else came down for breakfast,
and went walking in the dew-cool freshness of the day.
She didn't want to see Bobby or anyone else, not JR,
arrogant and domineering; especially not Jock Ewing's
hawkish old eyes so weighing and watchful in the
rumpled parchment of his face.

Maybe she'd come down too hard on Bobby. She
didn't want to be a nag, pushing and pulling him all
out of shape and fighting with his family. Maybe she
couldn't battle them; it was possible they'd chop her
into painful confetti and strew her to the wind.

Strolling past the stables, Pamela smelled horse and
alfalfa, and the barest hint of nippy fall hanging in
the shadows. Hands in jacket pockets, she moved on
toward the barn, wondering if she ought to go back

and tell Bobby good-bye, let him off the hook, show him it was okay.

It wasn't, damnit! He didn't have to be the Ewing clown, pimp, fixer, briber. Bobby was far better than that, stronger than he knew, and shouldn't let them push him. What did *she* want for him? To be himself, tender and thoughtful when it was that time; considerate and fine when that moment came. But not to run scared before his brother and father, not to give up rather than argue, subordinate his own ideas to theirs, always knuckle under.

There was courage to him; she knew that. He'd married her knowing the storm that would gather flashing around his head. And she had run exploring fingertips, sorrowing lips, over the ugly wounds in his body, still angry, their indented scarlet fading slowly. His courage hadn't run out with the leaking of his blood in Vietnam, but maybe ambition had.

"Pamela."

She flinched, her head snapping up.

"Hey now," JR said. "Didn't mean to spook you. Bobby and us missed you at breakfast."

"Thought you might," she said, and started around him.

"No sense in jumpin' salty," he said, business-suited, ready for the office, only his puffy eyes indicating JR Ewing had had a long, wet night. "I mean, since we're in the same family, we ought to get along."

"Oh sure," she said, "you're *my* big brother, too."

"I'd like to be."

Not trusting herself to speak, Pam pulled her neck deeper into the collar of her jacket and swung off for the barn, the stables, anywhere. She didn't hear him following, but after a while, JR's dark Mustang flickered up in front of the house. Last night they'd been talking helicopters, but today there were only cars—and the out-of-nowhere jeep that screeched up to her.

"Hi, Pam—want to see some of the place? I have to

check out a line cabin, and look to some cow critters back up the lake draw, so—"

She looked at the house. "I don't think so, Ray. Cow critters?"

He chuckled, morning sun picking up his light eyes, sun-faded hair beneath a beat-up straw work hat, showing her the familiar cleft of his chin, Ray's laugh lines. "Well, I have to *sound* like a shore-nuff cow-puncher, don't I? You should see that lake, Pam; it's blue and clear and beggin' for somebody to swim in it."

She made a face. "Chilly as it is?"

"Be near scorchin' in a few hours. Who you afraid of, girl? Bobby, the family, me—or you?"

"Nobody," she said, and looked at the house again. The Mustang squatted out front; the open garage showed Bobby's Mercedes, the pair of Cadillacs, a white Continental that could only belong to Miss Texas of Whenever. Bobby didn't come onto the porch, wasn't looking for her, nor worried about her. JR had things well in hand.

"Okay," she said. "Let's have a guided tour of the homestead, what we can reach of it without goin' on safari."

Ray's teeth flashed. "Good gal. Knew they couldn't put you down and make you like it."

She didn't look back as the jeep went whirring over a dirt track, bounced in a grassy sea going brown. Behind this line fence, chunky whiteface cattle; past the other one, Santa Gertrudis, humpier, more likely to be horned. Then no fence at all, the land waves rolling higher in air cleaned during the night, pulling at her hair, tingling her eyes. No stink of oil dirtied it, and Pamela was glad.

At the house, Bobby hesitated on the steps, looking past the hot-walkers and holding corrals, looking around loading chutes for Pam and not seeing her. He wore a western-cut suit, tailored Tony Lama boots, and a pearl Stetson that was a month's pay for a cowboy. With his cowhide briefcase, he'd look like a hundred other cattlemen, lobbyists, oilmen, or legislators in Austin. It was a uniform, and those out of it were suspect.

"Thought I'd see Pam," he said. "Guess she's still miffed."

JR moved down the steps. "She's a woman, and one who ain't used to our ways yet. She'll come around."

In the car, JR drove not for the front gate, but angled off into the ranch itself. Bobby said, "What the hell?"

"The chopper," JR said. "Got word on CB they'll have it fixed by the time we reach that back line emergency pad. Be a heap quicker all around, if we meet it there. Besides, you ain't seen much of the home place of late. Mama has a lot of changes goin' on: crossin' one stock on another, tryin' for the perfect beef cow—heat and cold resistant, bug proof, all brisket and short on bone."

Bobby grinned and settled back. The air had a spiced smell of sage and mesquite, cow and dust, and carried memories on the wind. It had been pretty good being a kid here. Off by himself lonesome didn't matter, because everything out here was a moving part of the Big Lonesome, coming together with another moving thing only in passing. How long did wideblue and empty sky remember the cruising hawk, or brown dust form the track of a rabbit?

There had been Gary, sometimes; at a slow lope so Bobby's short horse could keep up, Gary explaining about cactus and rattlers, telling tall stories of Gilas, tarantulas, and Indian ghosts. But it wasn't all scary; some of it was measuring up to Gary when they hauled an orphan calf out of a bog, when they fought blowflies or blackleg. Some of it was good tiredness, good closeness and purple twilight blanketing down in warm quiet.

"Gary," Bobby said. "I just realized I haven't even thought of him in years. Our brother, and we don't know where he is; we don't care. Dead or alive, he could be found, but we don't care."

"That's right," JR said. "Rogue, locoed, or diseased, you cut that animal out of the herd, right? So it don't infect the rest, don't hurt the good stock."

And Bobby said, "And you sure as hell don't hand-raise its get, if the cull was so dangerous to the strain."

JR turned off onto a road little more than a wagon track, slowing to save the Mustang's shocks. "You talkin' about Lucy? People are some different than cows."

"That's what I was saying," Bobby commented.

"It ain't up to me," JR said. "That's for Jock and Mama to decide." Changing the subject swiftly, he said, "You could have had your pick of any woman in Texas. How come a Barnes?"

"I got tired of picking any woman in Texas," Bobby said. "They all got to look alike, sound alike; they even started to screw alike. And a Barnes? At first I didn't put it together—Pam's name and what went on between the old man and Digger Barnes away back. After a while, it didn't matter. Come down to it, if anybody should carry a grudge, it's Barnes, not Ewing."

"See, damnit? She's got you thinkin' their way. What's so special about a woman like that? Hell, Ray Krebs has been tellin' me about her for years."

Quietly, Bobby said, "That's your ass talkin'; your mouth knows better."

"Okay! All right—I tried to do it proper, without makin' a mess, but I can see there just ain't no reasoning with you. You always been a knothead, just had to have everything spelled out in black and blue." Slewing the car around in a cloud of dust, JR rabbited it along a dim track that circled a high rise in the ground. "Tried to save you this," JR went on, hanging to the wheel as the Mustang slammed over bumps and dry wash ruts. "But I reckon you'll believe your own eyes."

Pam stood on a ledge of soapstone, jacket on a bush behind her, shirt open and sleeves rolled up, face lifted to the wind. "Beautiful," she said, "the lake's everything you said it would be, Ray. I wouldn't mind staying in that line shack for a while, away from everything."

Shucking his shirt, he held his arms horizontally, cooling in the light wind. "And every*body*? It ain't workin' out, is it? Hooo! Told you it'd get hot today."

She fluffed her hair and looked away from the bronzed, bared chest and muscular arms. "I don't know if I can buck the whole family, but I have to try."

"To them, there's blooded, pedigreed stock and grade stuff; they build high fences so the two don't mix. For you and me, it's damned near the same; you know they never let me use the *front* door? It galls 'em to have you do it."

She rubbed her forehead, stared down into the water. "I didn't believe that, before. But the way they act, the way they cut me off from Bobby—"

Ray put a hand gently upon her shoulder. "You and me, we fit better, alway did. Guess I had to lose you to know it."

She didn't answer, and he could feel her stiffen beneath his palm. He looked at his watch. "Okay, I'll back off. Just wanted you to know. Say—maybe you're tryin' to do too much at once, makin' the big change-over too quick."

"What do you mean?"

He smiled. "Used to be, you wouldn't take a dare. You did what you wanted and be damned to the hindmost. So let's go swimmin'."

Laughing, Pamela shook her head. "I don't know; the water looks cold."

"Cool, baby—"

She shrieked as he scooped her up, tossed her far out. Pamela hit the water and rolled, its chill at first numbing, then invigorating. As her head broke surface, she saw Ray kicking off his boots, saw him arching high in a dive. Its wave swamped her again.

Giggling through water, striking out strongly, she stayed ahead of him to reach a low spot in the bank.

Pamela climbed out, shaking herself all over like a spaniel, throwing her hair forward, and rolling it in her hands, wringing it. "You big fool! We—oh migod, my feet are sloshing—we aren't kids anymore—and I'm d-drippin' ice water."

"To the line shack then! A fire, dried beef and beans; what could be better? Race you!"

"Not fair, not fair! You're barefoot!"

It felt so crazy-free, so young-happy, that she was still laughing when she stumbled into the shack. Ray was already out of his clothes and wearing a ragged blanket like a sarong, putting a match to kindling in the cookstove.

She hung one blanket down between the upper bunks, feeling dumb about it because Ray was familiar with all her body, inside and out. But it would also be dumb to turn Ray on, to start something she didn't want. Pamela used a thin quilt to knot a sari for herself, and took her soaked jeans and shirt to the sink.

"They'll never dry," she said.

Ray said, "Coffee and chuck comin'. Sun's hot outside; give me your stuff and I'll hang it."

"You keep playin' belly robber," she said. "I'll find the clothesline." She noticed he looked at his watch every few seconds. "Ray—is anything wrong? Are you expectin' any riders?"

"No," he said. "Just figure we'll be splittin', soon's we can. Lot of work to catch up on. Here—give me those wet things."

"I *said* I'll do it." She started for the door, got to it, and stopped. A car was coming down the hill, a plume of dust lifting behind. Backing a few steps, Pamela dropped her soaked clothing atop a war chest. "So that's it, Ray. All that crap about pedigree and grade stock; you're *mongrel* stock, Ray Krebs, mongrel that should have been culled and cut years ago."

"Pam, I couldn't help—"

"JR and *you*, setting me up. Bobby's in that car, right?"

"Now look, girl—"

"No, you son of a bitch—*you* look! JR doesn't know my brother had you introduce me to Bobby, does he? JR has no idea you even *know* Cliff Barnes, and I wonder what he'll think about it—that you're an informer, a spy?"

"Jesus," he said, "you wouldn't—he'd fire me, black-ball me all over Texas—"

She heard the car muttering close. "One more thing, lover boy. Knowin' your penchant for young girls, I'll bet you're balling Lucy Ewing, and I'm goin' to swear I *know* it."

Ray lifted one big, helpless fist. "JR'd kill me for that. Oh damn, Pamela—don't tell him anything like that. I wouldn't live through the day; don't you *see* that, damnit?"

"All I see is a sneakin' bastard trying to ruin me with my husband. So if you don't back me up all the way, you're in bigger trouble than me."

When the door opened, she went to meet Bobby, lifting to kiss him. "Hi, honey. I'm glad JR knew *exactly* where to find us. We might have been here for hours more, dryin' out."

JR glared at Ray, waited, his eyes urging the man. Ray said, "My fault, I reckon. Took her too close to the edge, showin' her the lake, and the bank gave way. More busted under me when I tried to reach her out."

JR grunted. "Now, ain't that a pretty story? Two ex-lovers that don't look so ex."

Pam kept her hand on Bobby's arm. "Ray—whose idea was it to show me the ranch? Who knew we'd be at this line cabin?"

Ray wouldn't look at his boss. He spread his hands. "JR, I reckon. I mean, he said—"

Bobby said, "Austin, the helicopter's mechanical trouble, the ride across the ranch—all ducks in a row, JR?"

"Boy, it's for your own—"

Pam had never heard the cold edge of Bobby's voice before. He spoke very softly, almost in a whisper, but his words reached every corner of the cabin, changing the expression on Ray's face, making JR's mouth twitch. Bobby said, "All this bullshit stops here and now. I knew about Pam and Ray, but it didn't make a dime's worth of difference. When I married her, my wife's life started *then;* so she's just three days old. Let her alone. Don't put your hand to her; don't put your mouth to her. If I hear about any more trouble, any more gossipin', I'm goin' to waste the asshole did it."

He drew a deep, shuddering breath and Pamela saw his eyes. They were flat and obsidian hard, and a terrible eagerness lurked in their dark depths. "You civilian shitheads know what *waste* means? It means, frag, blow away, zap. It means you're *dead.*"

His eyes touched his brother, raked Ray Krebs in turn, and Bobby said, "Make me show you I'm serious. Give me the slightest damned excuse."

Quiet . . . the line shack was so still that only the crackling of wood in the cookstove dared probe the silence. Ray Krebs let out his breath; JR shifted his feet. Bobby took Pamela's hand, walked her outside.

JR fumbled out a cigar; lighter flame trembled as he lit up. A car motor sounded, and Ray said, "He's takin' the Mustang."

"We got the jeep," JR said.

"JR," Ray said, "she got the jump on me, had it all figured out. I—I couldn't do much, and I'm sorry."

Letting smoke curl from his mouth, JR said, "My fault. I underestimated her."

"Jesus," Ray said. "Bobby—I never saw—"

"Yeah," JR said. "Crazy as a bedbug. Might have to do something about that."

CHAPTER 22

Lucy softly walked the palomino gelding until she was beyond earshot of the buildings. Circling into a draw, she bent low over the horse's neck and squeezed him into a gallop. When they reached the highway where the Southfork mailbox stood, she pulled him to a sliding, stock-horse stop and bailed off before he quit skidding.

Rifling the box, she found the letter from the school and crammed it into a pocket. She swung up into the saddle and spun the gelding, moving him fast back along the way they'd come. At the barn, she walked him on a loose rein and grinned. When would those dummies at school wise up? If they were no smarter than this, they couldn't even teach her anything.

She unbuckled the cinch, lifted off saddle and blanket to drop them on a tack stand; then she slipped Gold Penny's bridle and watched him trot into the near pasture. Must be hell to be a gelding, she thought; never any screwing, and when a horse was cut it took most of the fire out of him.

Ray Krebs had plenty of fire, but lately she had to keep fanning it. Something to do with Bobby and Pamela, and mostly Pam. He wasn't banging her, but she turned him on; Lucy could tell, because Ray's eyes followed Pam whenever she passed.

Some kind of stud, Ray Krebs, and Lucy could dig that. What she couldn't understand was what he saw in a woman that old—nearly thirty, at least. It wasn't like she was fresh stuff, either; Ray had balled her for years and years.

Moving around the stables, she scooted across open space and behind the house. Maybe she'd get knocked up and Ray would have to marry her. Uh-uh; she'd thought of that before, and there were some things wrong with the idea: one—Jock Ewing might cut Ray in two with that big old shotgun; two—Ellie would ship her off, lock her up somewhere, and three—Lucy wasn't all that sure she wanted to tie herself up to any one guy. There were so many good-looking guys around, and now that she knew how to handle them, all the kinky ways to stay boss, what was wrong with looking around some, trying on a few?

It was such a pain in the ass, having to playact a little girl when she was as much woman as Pamela, and a whole lot more than Sue Ellen. Like going to school, and dressing up cute, and all that old-fashioned crap. Cutting out with Ray Krebs when he was supposed to be driving her to school, that was a blast. If he argued about it, she just slid her hand over between his legs and took a good hold; she just eased over next to him in the jeep and ran her tongue into his ear. He zigzagged all over the field, ran off the road, and finally pulled off into the brush somewhere, or took her to a line cabin.

Ambling up the back steps and through the kitchen, she stopped to tear the school letter into tiny strips and drop it into the trash barrel. Through an open door, she could catch sight of Sue Ellen, all spit-shined. What a kick in the head—Miss Old-time Texas, frigid, a nothing in the sack. Lucy eased out through another door, thinking that a cold wife was just what JR deserved, the bastard—the dirty, dirty bastard.

In another corral, Bobby gave Pamela a leg up. "She's a good old baby-sitter, Stella is. Try to stay off her mouth; the bit and reins are for her control, not *your* balance. Sit up straight, baby; you don't ride on your tail, but on your crotch."

"Mis-ter Ewing, how you do go on!" Pamela grinned down at him, delighted he was back from Austin and they had a whole day to themselves. "In any part of Texas, I'll have you know that a girl—oops! What's she doin', Bobby? Hey, damnit—don't be so bumpy, S-Stella—"

Bobby laughed. "You squeezed her, signaled a trot with pressure from both legs."

"N-no such d-damned thing! I'm just hangin' on."

"Lighten up," he called. "Catch your balance and keep your legs away from her, let 'em hang naturally."

The mare dropped to a walk, plodded around to the gate, and stopped. Pamela said, "Call me a cab."

They laughed together when he helped her down, clung and laughed and kissed.

Upstairs, Sue Ellen Ewing dropped the window curtain, mouth thinning at how the newlyweds hung onto each other, putting their hands just everywhere; it was disgusting, so animal. She went to a mirror, checked her lipstick, her hair. Breakfast was behind her, and there wasn't anything to do until dinner. Miss Ellie wasn't going into town, and JR didn't like her going by herself. There just wasn't anything to do.

Sue Ellen didn't like horses or dust, and vast, open places made her feel insignificant and scared. It was much better with walls all around. Of course, where she liked best was a *big* walled place, all filled with upturned faces. The music, the big intro, and the eyes like a million jewels, watching *her* as she came on stage with just the right rhythm, just enough swing and wiggle to her beautiful long legs.

The best sound—her name followed by a thunderous crash of applause, and the flashbulbs and the roses and another crown and. . . .

Hands clenched, Sue Ellen went over to the little TV and turned it on. Careful not to muss her skirt, she sat down in a big chair and stared dully at the set. JR was in Dallas or somewhere, and it wouldn't help if he was home, anyhow.

She would have to watch her diet again, cut down on starches and fried stuff. She had the willpower for that; her mother used to say it all the time; "Sue

Ellen, you mean to stay so beautiful, you got to have willpower. Girl, you got to suffer to be beautiful, and it's all you got, your face and your body, because the good Lord knows you ain't very bright."

"I am, too," Sue Ellen said to the game show flickering behind glass. "I could of been as smart as any other kid in San Antone, but Mama kept me out of school so much, travelin' to all the contests. I'm glad, Mama; I'm glad it like to broke your heart when I didn't go on and be Miss America. But you got it all anyhow, Mama—you got a house all paid for and money every month and I got—I got—"

Reaching for tissue, she dabbed carefully at her eyes. Sue Ellen swallowed and focused on the TV show. After dinner, there wouldn't be anything to do until supper.

Ellie passed the cream pitcher to Jock, so he could use just the right splash in his coffee. She stirred her own, thinking how she'd gotten a sweet tooth when she didn't have any teeth of her own. Sure they were her own, bought and paid for.

"That girl," she said.

Jock wrinkled his forehead and squinted at her. "Barnes woman?"

"No Barnes woman here," she said, "just Ewings. I'm talkin' about Lucy."

"Good kid," he said. "Good youngun. A mite flighty, but that's as it ought to be."

"She's a heap older than her age," Ellie said, "and a sneak. That girl ain't been to school in I don't know how long. Thinks she's Indianing on down to the mailbox every day without me knowin'."

Jock sipped coffee. "What'd she be doin' at the mailbox, gettin' love letters?"

"Stealin' letters that report her skipping school. What's the matter with those jarheads at school—don't they know how to use a phone?"

"You sure, Ellie?"

"I don't miss much goes on here," she answered. "Best we think on that private school."

Jock rattled his cup on the table. "But damnit, the girl's my only grandchild. Her ma's blood, I reckon, or—" He clamped his jaws, unwilling to say the name of a son he considered dead.

"Just think on it," Ellie said. "For right now, anyway. You ain't noticed, but Pamela seems to get next to her. Maybe she can help."

"I don't—Ellie, I ain't taken that one serious yet. Why Bobby, damnit? Spy for her brother, maybe; hopin' to bleed money out of him, from all of us."

"Or maybe just in love with him," Ellie said. "It happens to women."

Jock grunted and looked into the bottom of his coffee cup. "Used to know this ol' Indian woman claimed she could read coffee grounds. These days, coffee don't taste the same, and there ain't ever any grounds left in the cup."

"No sand burrs either," she said and got up. "I'm goin' out to my garden. You set your mind on Lucy; can't have her runnin' wild as a mustang filly in first heat."

Ellie walked her garden, more taken by brown stalks and withered blooms than by late asters still flinging color about. A kinship, she thought. Old and shriveled calling to its like. She heard a footstep and looked around. "Pamela. Thought you and Bobby'd be enjoyin' the day."

"Me too," Pamela said. "But JR came up with something important and hauled him off."

Putting a hand against the small of her back, Ellie said, "You wouldn't believe it now, but this garden's a shinin' glory all summer long."

"I can see you put a lot into it."

Ellie gestured. "This is one thing I don't let the yardman mess with; it's mine, and I take credit for its success, blame for any failure."

"It's a good rule," Pamela said, "all around."

"If you care to," Ellie said, "you can help me pick up. Such a sorry charade . . . sorry and tacky."

Pamela looked puzzled. "I—don't understand."

"Lucy. She don't even pretend to take books anymore. Mavericks get into trouble. Ever see a maverick bull that won't stay with the herd? Goes off on his own and, used to be, a panther or bear picked him off, maybe a hungry Indian. If he stayed lucky for a spell, and tried to get back with the bunch, the other bulls, they'd gang up and run him off again. He was strange to 'em then, you see; he didn't belong. It's lonesome out yonder in the cold, for cows and folks alike."

As Ellie snapped dry stems and pulled sere grasses, Pam raked them into piles, followed along with a garden cart to collect them. Ellie was pleased; the girl didn't mind working with her hands and she knew how to listen. It wasn't a quality most young folks had these days.

Sneaking quick looks at Pamela now and then, Ellie caught a certain play of light about the mouth and eyes, a fleeting angle of a cheekbone, and her heart turned over. In that fragment of time, she had seen a shifting image of herself blended with young Willard Barnes, an overlapping likeness of them both. Ellie put a hand to her ribs and closed her eyes.

"Miss Ellie—something the matter?"

There was an ornamental bench close by, and Ellie sat on it. "Catchin' my breath. Get a stitch in my side once in a while; age does it, I reckon."

Uncertainly, Pam said, "Are you sure I can't get something for you, call somebody?"

Ellie put out her hand and Pam took it, held it. Ellie said, "There was a time when I purely craved a daughter, but could be a good thing I never had one." She didn't take her hand from Pam. "Ewing men are strong—Jock, JR, Bobby, if they look to see it. Gary now—Lucy's daddy—he just didn't *want* to compete, seems like. He kind of folded up, and lookin' back, I fault myself. Tried to keep him tied to me, make him do what I wanted, since I'd lost JR to his daddy."

She stopped talking, gently removed her hand from Pam's, and stared at her faded garden. "Bobby now, he came up on his own; Jock was busy with JR, me with nose-leadin' Gary. I reckon it's the best thing ever happened to him, growin' up his own way; that, and findin' himself a woman with backbone. The others didn't."

"Thank you, Miss Ellie," Pamela said.

Ellie smiled. "Expect you know the difference between backbone and bullheaded. Lucy is bullheaded because she's been spoiled rotten by Jock; JR doesn't pamper her, but seems like he can't say no to her either. Bobby hasn't been around her enough, and she slips around me. Sue Ellen—well, Sue Ellen lives inside herself too much. If Lucy don't straighten up, she's goin' to be hobbled and twitched and shipped off to a boarding school."

"I'll try," Pamela said. "I can relate to Lucy because I see myself in her, when I was about that age. My brother pulled me out of what might have been some messy incidents and set me straight."

"We'll all appreciate it," Ellie said, rising from the bench. "Right now, reckon I'd better go change and collect Sue Ellen; she probably forgot we have a luncheon in Dallas today. If you like, you're invited to the next one, but they're borin' as hell; mostly old biddies carryin' on how women voters are goin' to change the world."

"Next time," Pamela said, and watched Ellie walk firmly, erectly from the garden. At the gate, Ellie turned, her voice just reaching Pamela: "How is— Willard What's your father doing now?"

Willard. It was a name she'd never heard applied to Digger, Pamela thought. "He—I guess he's making do, Miss Ellie; just making do."

Dryleaf soft, Ellie Ewing said, "You might say howdy to him for me, next time you see him."

"I'll do that," Pamela said.

Back in the house, she looked out to see them getting into the White Continental, Miss Ellie and Sue Ellen in expensively severe suits, hats, white gloves. Pamela felt pretty good, wonderful, in fact; a crack had developed in the Ewing armor. Miss Ellie had opened a little, asked for help with Lucy, and that was good.

Pamela drew coffee from the party-sized percolator that was kept simmering all day, and sipped it as she looked around the family room. The phone rang four times before she realized she was the only one home, and picked it up.

"Yes, this is a Mrs. Ewing. Who? Oh yes, I'm Lucy's aunt. She's not in school again? No, there haven't been any letters. I'll see that she's in school today, if I can find her—and I think I can."

The Mercedes made good time to the line shack because Pamela didn't give a damn about shocks and springs. She saw the jeep parked there and slid to a stop beside it. While dust was still rolling, she was plunging through the cloud and banging open the cabin door.

Ray Krebs sprang naked from a lower bunk, face twisted in shock and anger. Lucy was much quicker, zipping out the back door with a flash of creamy buttocks gleaming below an unbuttoned shirt. Pamela dove after the girl, her longer legs eating up the distance between them. Lucy shrilled in outrage when Pamela caught the flapping shirt and spun her around. She clawed one hand for Pamela's face, and Pamela slapped her hard.

Wide-eyed, face gone chalky in utter, disbelieving surprise, Lucy put a hand to her cheek. Pamela snapped: "Back in there and finish dressing."

Dropping her hand, Lucy said, "Throw my clothes out here. Then you can take seconds with him. That's what you really want."

"This time," Pamela said, "I'll close my hand and guarantee to knock you flat."

Lucy flinched and stepped back. "You—you wouldn't. I'll tell Jock and—"

"Tell him what? That I caught you balling Ray Krebs? After Jock and JR get through with him, they'll turn his remains over to the cops and he'll do about five years for statutory rape. Now *move!*"

Inside the shack, Lucy snatched up panties and jeans. Ray already had his jeans on, but nothing more; his face was dark and ugly. He said, "What the hell is it with you, Pam?"

"Haul it out of here," she said. "Alone."

"Goddamnit, I didn't *want* to drive her to school. It's old man Ewing's orders. She gets to me every time."

Lucy said, "You ought to know how to do that, *Auntie* Pam. Or maybe he's changed some since your day."

"Ray, just get out," Pamela said, "while I'm still inclined to save your miserable hide."

In moments, he dressed and was out the door without a backward glance at Lucy. Dirt and gravel flew as he roared the jeep away.

"Now," Pamela said, "we're goin' to school. Your counselor called."

Wriggling into her jeans, Lucy said, "That nerd. Jock won't believe *him* against me—or you, either. You tell him about me and Ray, and we'll swear it was the other way around, *you* and him."

Pamela said, "Look, kid, when I was your age I was waiting tables nights in a greasy spoon, gettin' pinched and goosed and taking it because we needed the money. Then I worked in a store, being nice to spiteful old hags who snapped and snarled and breathed in my face. When I got up to making it with an ad agency, I thought I was in hog heaven."

Curling her lip, Lucy said, "So?"

"So I was never petted and pampered. I worked like hell *and* went to school. So don't try to shine me on; don't hustle me. I've been there, kid—and I'm strong enough, mean enough, to whip the pee out of you every time you mouth off. You want to make the first time right now?"

"Hey," Lucy muttered, "now wait—"

"You can walk out there and get in my car, or get dragged out by the hair. Take your pick."

"All right, damnit! Don't you put a hand on me, you hear?" Sullenly, Lucy stamped out and got into the Mercedes.

Pamela strolled around the car and sat behind the wheel. "When we get there, tell your counselor the truth. Mr. Miller sounds like a straight guy; maybe he can lay on some makeup work, so you can graduate."

"And if he don't? If I don't give a damn about their stupid ol' graduation?"

"Then you'll be on your way to a boarding school; as Miss Ellie says, 'hobbled and twitched.'"

Lucy's lip poked out and she sat hunched over. "Jock wouldn't let her do that."

But she continued to frown into the windshield and picked at a thumbnail.

CHAPTER 23

Julie Parsons stood near the coffee maker, looking thoughtfully at the office Bobby Ewing had taken over. JR was taking chances, bringing his brother into Dallas on every little excuse. She knew what he was up to, hoping that by cluttering the new executive with detail work, trivialities, Bobby would soon tire of playacting and stop bugging JR.

But this Bobby was shrewder than big brother figured; he picked up on every small item, and delighted in nosing into obscure files. That's where the

bodies were buried, in those innocent-looking inconse-
quential folders. JR had the "smoking pistols' squir-
reled away in a safety-deposit box, but there was so
much telltale stuff here yet, material that could point
a finger.

Drawing a mug of coffee, she stirred a sugar and
brought it into Bobby's office. He looked up and
smiled his thanks. She said, "What is it today, ancient
drilling records or just Dick and Jane?"

"It's nearly that bad, isn't it? But these minutes of
the Lone Star Oilmen Association—"

Julie arched an eyebrow. "I prefer Harold Robbins."

Bobby sipped coffee. "I don't know; seems Ewing
Oil is swingin' a lot of weight here, too. Texas Independents, I can understand, but we don't carrying
enough votes here to—unless we're workin' through
dummies, some front men."

She said, "JR's been lucky, I guess. He can be very
persuasive."

"I have to ask him how."

"Oh hey," Julie said, "he needs a bunch of this stuff
for his signature. I have to make the afternoon mail
with it."

"Leave that Association file, please."

"Oh, did I grab that, too? Sorry. Boy, JR would
think I'm taking trips on something besides the elevator." Smiling brightly, Julie crossed the waiting room
and entered the inner sanctum where JR was punching buttons on a calculator.

"You ought to keep the kid out of here," she said,
"not drag him in every chance. Now he's picking
through the Association minutes and putting things
together. He's no dummy, JR."

He stopped figuring and slid an arm around her
waist. "Damn, but you look good, honey. What's all
that you're totin'? Besides all that good stuff up front
here, I mean."

"Camouflage. I tried to scoop up the minutes, too.
He wasn't having any."

JR pulled her to his knee, cupped one full breast.

"He'll get tired of playin' big man. What's he goin' to do, anyway—blow the whistle on his own family? Ummm—that's some set of knockers you got there, lady. I ever tell you that?"

"Not lately," she said. "Do you have any idea how long it's been, JR? Not weeks, but months—*months*, damnit!"

"Honey," he said, "you know how hectic it's been, and here lately I don't know what's got into her, but Sue Ellen just has to come into Big D with me. Now it ain't like Bobby and his bride, hard up for livin', but it sure puts a leash on my tomcattin'.'"

She sat quietly under his caressing hands. "I didn't know your wife came in with you."

"Didn't I tell you? Wish she hadn't, but she's downtown right now." Playfully, JR tweaked a nipple. "Tell you what honey: I'll be certain sure to keep next weekend open for you. How's that?"

Julie stood up quickly. "Gee, thanks. Thanks a whole hell of a lot."

JR grinned because the door was self-closing and she couldn't slam it; that made her madder than ever. Do her good, he thought; she'd been around so long Julie got the notion she was kind of a wife. He didn't mind banging her every so often, because she was good at it and knew exactly how to take care of him. But he got tired of her, just like any man got bored with his real wife. It took new stuff to keep the blood rising, make the old hammer jump up.

Confidential secretary, confidential mistress, Julie Parsons had been with him quite a spell, and knew almost as much about the business as he did. But she got damned well paid for her services—both kinds. Smart woman like her wasn't about to tear up the pea patch.

Julie marched to her own desk and banged down into her chair. Right there on the notepad—Mrs. John Ewing, Jr., and Mrs. John Ewing, Sr., called: personal, from Travis City.

The smug, arrogant son of a bitch. Julie Parsons—
Ms. Julie Parsons was getting pretty damned tired of
being taken for granted. He could plug her in or turn
her off like a piece of office equipment, at his pleasure.
She'd more or less accepted that in the beginning, but
in the back of her mind was the hope, unspoken and
repressed, that someday JR might say—come on, kid,
let's make it legal.

But now he was married, and still she hung on.
Political marriage, he'd said, like one of those alliances
old-time kings used to arrange for their sons. Old
Jock—he's after some leases this girl's family has, and
he wants me to show her off at parties—Miss Texas,
you know.

Oh, she knew, all right. She'd seen the gorgeous,
sexy, vacant-faced bitch too often. Julie opened her
center desk drawer, stirred through it as if she were
searching for something important. If she really was,
she couldn't see for blurred eyes, and Julie wasn't sure
which made her cry harder, the hurt or anger.

Lucy Ewing lounged on the wide marble front
steps of Braddock High, legs sprawled, elbows hooked
back. As each boy straggled from the school, he slid
his eyes greedily, longingly, over her small, ripe frame.
The girls, dressed differently than Lucy's jeans and
shirt, whispered to each other and hurried on, eyes
averted.

One boy slowed, stopped. His school sweater carried
a football letter and three stripes on the sleeve. One
foot set only inches from her hip, he stood looking
down at Lucy. "Hi there. I'm Roger Hurley."

She didn't glance up, just kept watching the street
for Pamela's Mercedes. He sat beside her anyway. "I
hear you're only down in math."

"What?" Lazily, her blue eyes raked him, cata-
logued, and scorned him.

"Math might keep you from graduating. I heard
your meetin' with Miller a while ago." She didn't
answer, looked away, and Roger went on: "I'm presi-

dent of the letter club and our office is right next door. We provide services, tutor history, biology, math—"

Lucy said, "And sex education—with a note from Mama, of course."

He cupped her arm, caressed it. "Hey now, a terrific sense of humor to go with that terrific bod."

She didn't move her arm, only her head, to stare at his hands. Flustered, Roger moved it. "Well, if you need some help—"

The Mercedes purred up, and Lucy strolled to it, trailed half a step by the boy. Pamela opened the car door and said hi to him, but Lucy slid onto the seat and put her back to Roger and the school.

Pamela said, "Nice-looking guy, big and clean-cut. It wouldn't hurt if you dated guys your own age. Getting started too early is a drag, Lucy. It can burn you out, distort your sense of values."

"*You* know," Lucy said.

"Yes, I know. When did Ray Krebs get to you—a year ago, a little longer?"

Lucy stared out the window, bright hair floating in little wind kisses.

Pamela said, "I was fourteen. I thought he was the world's greatest, so much older than me and paying *me* all that attention. He was smart and tender and very cute; he led me slow step by easy step into his kind of sex. The greatest, I thought, and dreamed—do you dream, Lucy?—of the time Ray Krebs would come take me away from everything boring and childish."

Face turned toward Pamela now, Lucy was listening, the hint of a frown upon her smooth forehead. Pamela said, "Ray's good, but he's not the greatest, not by a country mile. It takes *giving* to be a first-class lover, and Ray's only a taker."

"You're just puttin' him down because you can't have him anymore," Lucy said, her lower lip pushed out.

Pamela laughed. "Can't have him? *Any* woman can have Ray; it's only a matter of place and time. No, Lucy—I don't *want* him. I'm happier with what I have, with Bobby. We care for each other—*care;* I don't think Ray has learned the word."

"I'm not listenin'," Lucy said, looking away again.

"But you've begun to think a bit, and that's a start. Hey—know why I was late picking you up? I went shopping for you. Now, I know no woman is supposed to shop for another, but it was spur of the moment. I saw how your classmates were dressed and figured you wouldn't want to stick out, so—"

Lucy lifted and swung around to kneel on the seat. "This the stuff back here?"

"Yes, the orange box is—"

Lucy threw it out the window. Pamela slammed on brakes, flinging Lucy's shoulders hard into the padded dash, rolling her head against the door. "You're not very smart, are you?"

Trying to untangle herself, feeling her head, Lucy said, "Goddamnit, you nearly killed me."

"You did it to yourself. When will you learn that every action has a reaction? Walk back and pick up that box."

"The hell I will."

Pamela leaned and hit the door handle, put a foot against Lucy, and shoved. The girl spilled out onto the shoulder of the road. "The hell you won't."

When they arrived at the house, Lucy darted from the car and pounded across the porch. The yardman stood expressionless until Pam motioned him over. "Raoul, isn't it? Please, would you take in these packages? Just leave them in the foyer, and thanks."

Ray and another man were off-loading lumber from a flatbed near the loafing shed; Pamela drove there. Getting out of the car, she said to the other man, "Will you excuse us, please?"

He glanced back and forth, to her, then Ray, and his grin was oily, knowing. "Sure thing."

She waited until the ranch hand rambled from sight around the barn, then said, "Lucy's back in school. Stay away from her, completely away."

Ray raised one boot, placed it on a low stack of lumber, a consciously macho pose. "Or what?"

"I already told you that."

He thumbed back his hat. "You're new and unwelcome; they'd just as soon be rid of you. Think the family'll believe sweet little Lucy is screwin' the foreman—after both of us swear it's not so, that it was you and me, and you're tryin' to pass your sins off on that innocent child? I might catch some flak—but on the whole, they'd be glad I got you off the place. The old man would probably give me a bonus."

Pamela said, "She's not worth it, Ray. Because I'll prove it on you, sooner or later—pictures, witnesses, tapes; I'll prove it. The way Jock dotes on that kid, it wouldn't be just your job: he'd gun you down."

"What are you?" he said, angry spots flaming his cheekbones. "Some kind of social worker? She's all I got goin' for me around here, and she's fun, baby. Fun like you *used* to be, before you got too damned good for your own kind."

"You want to gamble," she said, "go ahead. There's still Cliff Barnes."

He glared, whirled, and strode away. Pamela breathed deeply, knowing she had an enemy for life, that Ray Krebs would always be alert for a chance to get back at her. If he was fool enough to continue balling Lucy, he'd be leaving himself wide open, and she would stretch his hide to dry. And she meant to make certain she gave him or anyone else no cause to come down on *her*. Pamela was determined to be a part of this family.

After parking the car, Pamela collected the packages from the foyer and carried them up to Lucy's room. The girl lay belly down across the bed, a stereo blaring, and when Pamela opened the boxes, tried to talk about the music, Lucy upped the sound.

Reaching across her, Pamela snapped off the player and said, "That private school in Arizona. It's staffed by nuns who are really tough. It's about eight thousand feet up—clean, cold air. The nearest town is about a hundred miles, and although some girls call it a prison, it seems their grades climb in a hurry once they're there."

Lucy rolled over, and Pamela said, "Hang these, and put away the rest. All right?"

"Yeah," Lucy said.

When Pamela was gone, Lucy opened boxes and bags, arranged things neatly in closet and dresser. The stuff looked pretty good, she admitted, but she'd look just like the rest of those giggly, dumb-head girls at school; she wouldn't stand out.

That fink counselor, that prissy Miller guy; if he hadn't called the house nobody would know she'd been cutting school so much. She stroked the sleeve of a blouse, narrowing her eyes. If she had to stay in that nerd school, somebody was going to pay for it. A sharp yank, and the sleeve parted at the shoulder; another hard pull and the collar broke away down the middle. Just perfect; tomorrow she wouldn't wear a bra, and the fink would get his. Lucy clicked on the stereo and turned down the volume, smiling. This could even bounce back on Pamela, she thought.

She studied that evening, in the living room, so Jock and Ellie would be impressed. Politely, she replied to questions, and gave her grandpa a stronger hug, a longer kiss than usual before she went up to bed. Next morning, everyone commented on how nice she looked in her new things.

Sue Ellen said, "Now dear, if you'd take just a little more trouble with your hair—"

And Pamela said, "You'll knock 'em dead at school."

Lucy didn't miss the understanding glance her grandma and Pamela exchanged. Leaving the table, she frowned. Miss Ellie in that woman's corner? It didn't seem right, but she gave no sign of her puzzlement when Pamela drove her to school.

"Pretty soon," Lucy said, "I'll be driving myself. I mean, if I hadn't totaled out that ol' pickup in Travis City when I was fifteen, and if that dumb cop didn't know who I was, I'd already have my license."

"Stay clean, and you'll do okay," Pamela said. "You meeting with Mr. Miller after school today?"

Nodding, Lucy said. "He's coaching me in math, givin' me some makeup work. Guess I'll be there like an hour after everybody else is gone."

"I'll be there to get you," Pamela said.

"Didn't figure you'd let me alone, Auntie."

Lucy stepped out of the Mercedes quickly and mixed into the crowd. Pamela gnawed her lip as she drove off; Lucy was *too* good, and that made her uneasy, but she had things to do in Dallas—clean out her desk at the agency, have lunch with her husband, see to movers to finish cleaning out her apartment.

When she checked her watch, it was past time to be on her way. For once, Pamela was glad the Mercedes with its personalized plates was known, because no cop looked her way as she threaded in and out of traffic lanes, hurrying. Making up time on the freeway, she reached the school just about right, but no Lucy waited on the front steps.

Pamela went inside and turned down the hall toward Mr. Miller's office. Kids were clustered buzzing around the door, but still no Lucy. The boy she'd seen with the girl the day before parted from the crowd and came toward her.

"Mrs. Ewing, Roger—Roger Hurley from yesterday."

"I remember you. Where's Lucy, and what's all the excitement?"

The boy looked down, shuffled his feet. "Ah—she isn't here. I mean, after that thing with ol' Miller and seein' the principal, she—"

"What thing?"

Roger said, "Lucy busted out of Miller's office, hollerin' and cryin'; her blouse was near about torn off, and you could see she wasn't wearin' a—well, ol' Miller, he tried to make her, and got rough about it. Wow—rape!"

Pamela felt a chill up her back. "Which way to the principal's office?"

He pointed. "Right down there, and, Mrs. Ewing, if I can help—"

"Thank you," she said, "thank you," and hurried along the hall. Through a glassed door, she could see Miller arguing with another man, a round-bellied man with a red face and little hair. She went in without knocking.

Miller said, "Mrs. Ewing, believe me, I never touched—"

"Mr. Daley," he principal introduced himself. "I'm upset indeed at such a—"

"Let's talk it over," Pamela said. "Lucy was wearing a sweater when she left home. How about in your office, Mr. Miller?"

CHAPTER 24

Lucy was defiant, smiling because she'd slipped one past Pamela this time. Dear Auntie would play hell making her go back to school now. "How about that?" she asked. "Got it worked out pretty good, haven't I?"

Pamela looked after the school bus that had dropped off Lucy; no doubt it was the first time poor little rich girl had ridden it. She propped her arm on the Mercedes window and said, "You're dumb."

"Dumb?" Lucy glared. "It's Miller's job *and* his tail, if Jock finds out. Boy, I'll bet the principal was scared spitless, too. I mean, Jock could probably close down that old school, if he wanted."

Pamela shook her head. "You're worse than dumb: You're really stupid."

Lucy balled her hands and took a step toward the car. "Yeah? Well I know you're sweet lil' Miss Bleedin' Heart, and you're worryin' about poor Miller hangin' onto his crummy job, so I've got a backup story. I can always say I stopped going to school because he was after me the whole time, and scared me so bad. This attempted rape—just a misunderstandin'; a story I made up because he threatened me." She stuck out her lower lip. "That's my deal, baby—no school, no letters home, and I don't make a big stink."

Pamela's smile was pitying. "And what—*baby*— happens when you don't graduate with your class? All your lies won't help you then."

Flinching, Lucy said, "I—I can make 'em give me a certificate. I can make—"

"Good luck," Pamela said. "I already straightened it out at school, with Mr. Miller and Mr. Daley. I see you're wearin' your sweater again. You only took it off *inside* Miller's office. The blouse—that new blouse I bought you yesterday—was already torn. Bet a dollar I can find bits and pieces of matching thread up in your room."

Lucy bit her lip. "Pamela—"

But Pamela drove off, and Lucy stared into the swirl of dust behind the car. She wanted to yell after it, to scream at Pamela how damned unfair it all was. She wasn't a schoolkid; she *wasn't!* And it wasn't that school was tough; with half an effort, she could whip right through and probably stay on the honor roll.

But for what? JR wouldn't give a good goddamn one way or the other. He didn't even know she was alive, looking through her and past her and when he *had* to say something to her; it was like he was talking to the yardboy or cook. Hell, he didn't even know she'd been balling Ray Krebs all this long, and wouldn't care if he did.

Why hadn't he just let them alone? He didn't really *want* either one, so why had he brought her back? The stiff-necked, cold, *mean* son of a bitch. Maybe if she got pregnant that would jolt him. Maybe he'd get mad enough to beat her, yell at her, something to show he realized she was still alive, that he cared.

None of them, damnit—Lucy wiped angrily at her eyes—none of them knew how hard it was to carry a secret so heavy for so long. And the longer it stayed on her back, the harder it was to get rid of. Who would have believed her then? Who would listen to her now?"

Walking up the road toward the house, Lucy knew just about how it would be if she stood up in the living room tonight and spilled her guts, just let it all hang out. Now, child, Miss Ellie would say, *child!* She'd stopped being a baby that night in the little house when she heard her mama—the thought made a lump in Lucy's throat, choked her, but she spat and cleared it—her *mama* talking about whose baby Lucy was.

Now, child, Miss Ellie would say, little babies don't remember that much, and you were so tiny back then.

Baby, hell. Not remember, bullshit! Every word, every sound was burned into her head. She'd been thinking that this man was her real daddy, anyhow; he came around more than the other one, the man who staggered and fell down and got sick on the floor. That night proved it.

And when he came after them—Lucy stopped walking and leaned her back against one of the shade trees that stood along the ranch entranceway. When he came after them, Lucy-that-was thought it was wonderful. But Mama—that two-faced, gutless bitch!—darling Mama took some money and didn't even say good-bye to her baby.

But if he wanted his baby so much, if he brought her back and asked Miss Ellie to care for her, why didn't he claim her? Why didn't he hold her hand, or kiss her cheek, pat her head, kick her ass—*something?*

She could have killed him when he brought home Sue Ellen, the beauty queen. Sue Ellen wasn't much older than herself, and wouldn't really get any older —not in the head, anyway. Miss Ellie was *so* old and kind of hard, and Jock was a sweetheart but he was ancient, too. Bobby was gone and there just wasn't anyone she could talk with.

So she'd found somebody. First Kenny, one of the ranch hands, only eighteen and not all that swift, but willing enough when she got him started. Then Ray—he was different, because he talked with her and said he loved her and made her feel loved.

Pamela was stopping that. Pamela came in and took over and acted like she was somebody's—mother, or something. Lucy shoved away from the tree and practically trotted up the road to the house. It would have been a whole lot better if Pam hadn't been screwing Ray for so long.

At supper that night, she wouldn't look at Pam and never looked at JR and the beauty queen, anyhow. So she talked to Miss Ellie and said yes, ma'm, school was going to be fine from now on; no more messing around. Ellie said, "I hope not," and Jock winked at her.

Then the phone rang and Raoul said it was for her.

His voice was all icky, and he laid a threat on her. Roger Hurley, first string on the football team, president of the letter club, and all-American boy; the bastard was trying to blackmail her!

Lucy played along, hearing him say how he'd seen her big fake job on Mr. Miller from the next office, how he'd keep quiet about it if she went out with him tonight, went out and put out.

Lucy glanced into the dining room where the beauty queen was lighting JR's cigar. "You got me," she said. "That new place, the Big-D disco—that's if you've got phony IDs for both of us."

At the table, Bobby was pulling back Pamela's chair and she smiled up at him like it was the greatest trick ever. "Good," Lucy said into the phone. "Eight o'clock's fine. I'll have to hustle my grandpa and get dressed, but—okay. Yeah, I'm sure you'll really get a big charge out of this night."

When she hung up, Lucy's lip curled. Big man on

campus would get a charge out of the evening—right in the mouth if she could swing it, and she was just about certain she could. Ray Krebs was making the Big-D tonight and taking that carhop, Jolene somebody. He wouldn't take *her* out, of course; someone might see them, and Jock find out.

"Okay, mister," she whispered. Bobby and Pamela were coming down the hallway then, and Lucy got it together to give Pam a sweet smile. Maybe it was a mistake, she thought, as she went into the living room to work on Grandpa, because Pam looked hard at her then. Got to watch it, Lucy reminded herself. Pamela was on a different vibe length.

Upstairs, Pamela said, "Lucy's up to something."

Bobby shrugged. "When isn't she? Hit the shower. You know it takes you longer to dress. If we're going' to show 'em how to Saturday Night Fever it, how to Grease it—no, that'll come later, just you and me."

"You're obscene," she said. "I *am* having a tough go with Lucy, though."

"Why put yourself through the hassle?"

Pamela lifted her dress over her head. "Miss Ellie, she as much as asked me to, and—Bobby, I *like* your mother."

He said, "I hoped you would. If anyone's to be liked, it's her. She's learned along the way, mellowed. Oh, she's still a very tough lady, but Miss Ellie has turned thoughtful. The others—but we're not chewin' over family history tonight, we're getting ready to go knock 'em dead. I can see tomorrow's headline: Dozens Decked at Big-D Disco—"

"Do tell," she said, and skipped to avoid a slap at her rear.

Lucy and Roger Hurley made it past a doorman who only wanted to see something on paper to back up the five Roger laid on him. Multicolored lights were spinning and the music loud; if the drinks were weak, they didn't know it. After the first, he was feeling her under the table and she sat quiet for it. Midway through the second round of Tom Collins, Lucy spotted Ray Krebs and a sassy blonde whose hair was as phony as Roger's ID cards.

"Let's dance," she said. "You want to get me turned on, let's dance a couple, then head back to the ranch—and the barn."

"Yeah," he said, all shiny-eyed, and made a path for them to the dance floor.

Lucy switched it on, rocking and banging with each solid beat of the music, half-closing her eyes and throwing back her head, swinging her hips and throwing her pelvis, bouncing her braless breasts.

"Oh wow," Roger said, but she didn't hear him: She was busily working through the crowd toward Ray Krebs and the phony blonde, step by step, every sensuous gyrating pivot taking her just a little closer.

Bobby Ewing hesitated just inside the door and said to Pamela, "Somewhere, there has to be a table. Ahh— never let it be said that Bloodhound Bobby couldn't track a two-seater from yon to yonder. Quick, before migrating midgets swipe it."

On the floor, Ray Krebs eyed the slow grinding of Jolene's hips, and smiled, thinking of the good night ahead, the different night. Jolene was something fresh and unexplored, at least by him, and the whole weekend lay ahead. Away from the ranch and cows and another woman holding a big stick over him. Ray inched near his partner, moving so she'd know what was coming up for her later in the evening.

He wasn't ready for it when Lucy Ewing danced into him, when she wheeled and grabbed his arms. "Oh Ray, please—I have to talk to you—"

"W-wait a—Lucy, this is Jolene and—"

"Now!" she insisted. "You have to help me now." Tugging at him, Lucy pushed-pulled him from the floor, while Roger and Jolene looked at each other in confusion. Then Jolene shrugged and picked up the beat.

Backed against the bar, Ray said, "Now, what the hell is this? And what are you doin' here, anyhow?"

"The guy I'm with, this creep *made* me come with him. He's—he's got somethin' on me, Ray, and he's goin' to make me ball him."

He looked at the crowd, at the boy dancing with his date. "It's not like you're cherry, kid—hey! Don't grab me like that, right out in the open! You lost your marbles? Okay, damnit—"

Ray maneuvered her into a darker alcove. "You're flat-out crazy. What if somebody sees you and me—"

Pressing against him, she said, "I don't care! I won't go home with that guy, I just won't." There, she thought, let the smartass big boy on campus run up against a grown man and see how bad he could run off at the mouth.

At their table, Pamela said over her drink, "Why— there's a friend of Lucy's, a boy from school, and he's with an older woman. I'm sure he's not old enough to be in here."

"A high school kid who's out with an older woman —if it isn't his sister—has already graduated, in my book. I mean, he gets a big A for double smartness. If I'd known back then what I do now—" Bobby broke off and stared, rising a bit from his seat for a better look.

"What is it?" Pamela asked.

"Lucy," he said, standing erect. "Lucy plastered to that goddamned Ray Krebs. Him and *her*."

She reached for him. "Bobby, don't jump to—it may not be what it looks—" and she thought, Oh God, oh Ray, you dumb bastard, bringing it right out in the open like this . . . that kid, that underaged girl in a disco, and pawing her—

Bobby moved swiftly along the edge of the dance floor, circling it, brushing tables and jostling people, his eyes locked to the couple by the wall. A green light played over them and slid away, then a yellow one, reflecting Lucy's wealth of bright hair. In a sudden jerking of strobe light, they looked ghastly, unreal. Hurrying after, Pamela clawed again, and missed again; she couldn't have held onto him anyhow.

Peeling Lucy off the man, Bobby spun her aside and threw a punch almost in the same motion. Ray caught it high on the cheek and went down. A woman screamed and a table crashed over. Pamela grabbed Bobby's elbow.

"No—please, don't, Bobby!"

And a thin voice at her ear: "She came with *me*, Miz Ewing—" The kid from school, something to use: "Bobby! She's with this boy—this *boy*, Bobby!"

Two burly men with marked-up faces were shoving through the crowd, and Bobby Ewing turned to put those flat, unwinking eyes on Roger Hurley. The kid was more than man-sized, so that Bobby had to hook slightly up at him. Roger staggered into the spreading crowd, into yelling women, and went clattering down. Then the men with marked-up faces and folded-over ears reached Bobby.

"Come on!" one of them grunted. "Right on out the back door, champ."

The other one made a smooth, professional move to put an armlock on Bobby. Bobby put his head down and rammed the bouncer in the gut. He was punching good when the second one got to him. He fell away, wobbled, and came back. Both men hit him, and hurled him into the bar. Bobby came away with a beer bottle that broke across a bouncer's face. It gave him a moment to swing a chair, to kick a table leg loose. With that for a club, he dropped the remaining bouncer.

Then he smashed Ray Krebs over the head with it, because Ray was just about to his knees. He went back at the kid then, chopping the table leg, but Roger was scared out of his mind and running. The club only scraped down his back, but with enough force to stagger him.

It seemed as though everyone was screaming then, and a man in a white apron came around the bar with something black and leathery cocked in his hand. Ray threw a rolling block at him, bounced right to his feet, and kicked the guy's head up against the bar. It made an odd *thump!* Feet spread, blood clouding one eye—funny, he didn't remember being hit—Bobby Ewing cleared a space around him.

Swinging—he was swinging and swinging and couldn't stop for even a split second, because if he did, one of those squalling slopehead bastards would kill him. There was only the shovel, and one of the little shits shot him anyhow, even after Bobby hit him with the entrenching tool, hit him again and again, because the taste of fear was worse than the flavor of his own blood. He splashed redgray brains and made redwhite bone stick up all sharp and ragged, and he was grunting, mewling, growling like a damned dog, fighting for his life, fighting for it *all*, man. . . .

"Oh man," the big cop said, "I never seen a guy go total ape like that. Oh man, what he's done to this joint and half the folks in it. Be a wonder if nobody's kilt."

Pamela held herself still inside, with a great effort. She said, "I realize you had to—to spray that stuff—"

"Mace, lady."

"Spray Mace at him, but did you have to hit him, too?"

"Charlie," the big cop said, "that ambulance on the way? Lady, he didn't give me no choice. I mean, he was hog-wild and not even Mace was goin' to stop him. He ain't really hurt, you know. You comin' with him?"

"Of course, but I'll follow. Lucy—get to the car, *my* car, and stay there. If I can find a phone—"

The big cop said, "Good idea, lady; your man's sure goin' to need him a lawyer. Five or six folks hurt here, and a couple boogered up pretty good. Funny, he don't look that big or that bad. Charlie, be sure you get statements from everybody got mixed into this shindig. Yeah, lady, I'd say better call a lawyer right now, for what good it'll do you tonight. Ain't nobody goin' to wake up a municipal judge to set bail account of a juke joint fight. And if one *was* to get woke up, he'd be upset and lean toward makin' that bail real high."

"Oh," Pamela said, as men in white came trotting into the disco bearing stretchers and rolling gurneys, "oh, I don't intend to call a lawyer. I don't even know one. I'm calling my father-in-law, your prisoner's daddy. But I'm sure Mr. Jock Ewing has a lawyer or two he can reach any time of night. And I imagine he can make bail."

"Beautiful," the big cop said. "That Mercedes outside—his, right? That's real beautiful; on top of all this mess, the guy has to be Ewing Oil. That right, miss?"

"Right, officer," Pamela said. "And thank you."

As she walked to the phone booth, the cop said, "Oh, you're welcome, lady. Oh yeah."

Then he said, with feeling. "Oh shit."

CHAPTER 25

Getting into the Mercedes, Pamela cut a hard look at Lucy Ewing, sitting small and humbled against the far door. "The hospital's keeping him overnight for observation," she said. "They don't think he's badly hurt, but that's not *your* fault, is it?"

The car was well away from the hospital before

Lucy said, "I didn't have anything to do with it. I didn't know you two were goin' to the disco."

"But you knew Ray Krebs would be there, didn't you? You deliberately tried to set up that kid Roger for a beating, but it got all tangled up."

"Well," Lucy said sulkily, "he was tryin' to make me—do it with him. Roger knew Mr. Miller didn't try anything with me."

"So much for Junior Mr. Clean," Pamela said. "But all you had to do was tell me, not start all that violence."

"How'd I know, damnit? How'd *I* know that Bobby would flip, turn into some kind of wild-eyed freak? Don't be blamin' *me* for somethin'—"

"Oh, but it *is* your fault. You were the bait, the catalyst, and you'll have one hell of a time explainin' it to Jock and Ellie."

"Do—do *they* have to know?"

Pamela threaded through late-night traffic and pointed for the Travis City cutoff. "They already know, dear child. The police, hospital people, reporters—a whole lot of folks were anxious to do Jock Ewing a favor. What'd you expect—I'd dream up some stupid story to explain Bobby being in the hospital? How about Ray, will he make it back to work Monday? And Roger's parents—"

Lucy put her hands to her ears. "Shut up, shut up! You don't really care about anybody else—just *you*." Whipping around on the seat, she dug her fingers into her knees and said, "You know something? You make Sue Ellen seem sincere. She's a wimp, but she doesn't put on a front like you do. She says how nice I got to look and talk, but she believes it; she thinks it matters how you talk and look. But you—oh wow!—you grab onto Bobby's wedding ring and pull yourself up, climb it to get away from all the Ray Krebses you know. But now all of a sudden, you can't stand to see Bobby Ewing's niece actin' trashy, because you don't want it to backfire on you."

"That's not how it is," Pamela said, touching a button that brought cool, head-clearing air against her face.

Lucy said, "You're a Ewing already, you know that? Because you already learned how to use people and lie about it. Like you're usin' me to score points with Miss Ellie."

Pamela hesitated, then said, "No. What's all this crap got to do with stirrin' up the bad kind of trouble you started at the disco?"

Lucy brushed at her eyes but refused to cry. "Maybe you never wanted to get back at somebody so bad you could taste it. Maybe nobody ever did you so much dirt that you just couldn't *stand* it any longer and had to scoop up a handful of shit and fling it back at 'em—" She stopped talking and turned to stare unseeingly out her window.

After waiting a while in silence, Pam said, "Seems you've been causing all the hurt around here, or is there somethin' I don't know?"

"Oh man," breathed Lucy, "is there ever." Then she shut up for the rest of the way back to the ranch.

Jock and Ellie were waiting for them, Jock's jaw set above a smoking jacket, Ellie's eyes not friendly behind the glasses she seldom wore, a worn robe making her seem older and frail.

"Damnit," Jock began, "police callin', goddamn newspapers callin', folks in the hospital, now what—"

Lucy broke for the stairs, making crying sounds that Pamela wasn't sure were real. She said, "All right, let's sit down and I'll try to fill you in on everything that happened."

Jock said, "Where in hell's JR? He oughta be here right now. You get hold of JR?"

"Mr. Ewing," Pam said sharply, "do you want to hear this, or shall I just go up to bed?"

There was a flicker of something in Ellie's eyes, a fleeting sparkle Pamela couldn't swear had passed. Ellie said, "Jock, set and listen."

When Pamela began to talk, she found herself omitting Lucy's part in the mess and placing the blame upon Roger Hurley. Bobby had made a mistake in jumping Ray Krebs. It was so lightning fast that nobody could straighten Bobby out in time, and then he went berserk; it was the only word to describe his actions, Pamela said.

Jock snorted and poured himself a drink. "Was the boy roarin' drunk?"

"No," she answered. "We hadn't even had our first ones."

Ellie said, "I've been feelin' it, Jock. There's a tension in Bobby, has been ever since he got back from his war, or maybe it was only then I could make it out. He's wound up so tight that somebody's bound to get hurt, once he turns loose."

Jock tossed down his drink and coughed. "Just a youngun and never been trouble to anybody. Musta been plumb out of his head, goin' up against Ray Krebs. It's a wonder Ray didn't bust him up worse."

Pamela made small fists on the arms of her chair. "You don't understand. *Ray's* hurt, and the Hurley boy, and at least three other men I know of. It was like—like seeing Bobby suddenly transformed into a wild, raging animal, something more than dangerous —something *deadly*."

"Made his mark, did he? Damned if he ain't turnin' into a sure-enough Ewing."

"But the damage, the people—Bobby himself—"

"Take care of it all," Jock said. "Already started when my lawyers made the police turn him loose; they comin' down hard on the newspapers, too, account of we don't want this spread around. Won't be no backlash, do I have anything to say. As for Bobby, he done right, even if he was off target some. The boy just got madder'n a clucky hen when he saw his little-girl niece in a joint like that. I don't blame him a lick."

"Jock," Ellie said, "you've been tellin' folks what to do for so long that you forgot how to listen. Pamela, I appreciate you fillin' us in, and seeing to Bobby and Lucy. We'll talk some more about it after everyone's had a good rest."

Though Pamela had a hunch Miss Ellie didn't completely believe her story, she didn't change it in the days and weeks to come. Lucy was overly meek and thoughtful, as if waiting for the ax to fall, despite Pamela's silence, and the girl continued to keep her distance, closed off into a shell of loneliness that Pamela couldn't crack.

When Bobby went back to work at the office, JR walked easy around him; no jokes about fading bruises and a patch of hair growing back over the police-club cut. Bobby found his own secretary, a cute and tidy little brunette named Connie Bullard. She was young and efficient and somewhat shy. Bobby wondered if Julie Parsons had hand-picked her, then thought, What else? Julie could no doubt run the entire office if given the chance.

But within a few days, Bobby discovered something else: a horde of workmen making noise in and around his office. "Got to take them when we can get them," JR said. "You ain't gotten into those union contracts yet, have you?" "Never mind, boy," JR said. "They'll be gone before you know it."

"In the meantime," Bobby said, "I can't work in there. I'm goin' home."

JR glanced at the file holder Bobby held and said, "Hey now; that file's got no business leavin' the office."

"Give me an alternative," Bobby said. "Jock wants the tally *today*, and damned if I can concentrate with all that uproar."

"Just be careful," JR said.

And Julie Parsons said, "I'll ride down with you, Bobby. It's lunchtime."

JR watched the elevator doors close, then saw how Connie Bullard jiggled and wobbled when she jumped as the carpenters fired a rivet. Really put together for a downy young thing; Julie must be slipping, to let a girl this tasty into competition. But to tell the truth, Julie was getting long in the tooth, and fresh new nooky was what it was all about. He stopped at her desk and roamed his eyes over her, grinning when she ducked her face and turned pink. Damned if she wasn't blushing, JR thought.

Outside the Ewing Oil Building, Julie paused on the sidewalk. "I never got to say welcome back, Bobby."

"Thanks for what you didn't say, Julie—like what a damned fool I was. Last time I blew up like that was in the Nam."

She touched his arm. "You're entitled. Do you really like being here instead of in Austin and Washington? And how about being married?"

"Being married, best. I don't feel tied down, either by Pam or the office."

"JR thinks you're bored in the office."

"JR *hopes* I'm gettin' bored. Sue Ellen *hopes* Pamela's gettin' bored. That's a spiteful woman, and I can't understand why. It would have been so damned much better if you—"

She looked out at traffic. "It wasn't my decision."

"Hey," Bobby said, "there I go with a case of hoof-in-mouth disease. Sorry."

"That's okay. It's been accepted all around. Take care." She walked quickly away from him, across the street, and ducked into a self-serve restaurant. Julie didn't want sympathy; she didn't even want JR anymore. But she didn't like smoking either, and kept at it, knowing damned well what it was doing to her.

Going through the cafeteria line, Julie picked a salad and started to scoop potatoes onto her plate, changed her mind and added another salad instead, low-cal milk and a sugar-free dessert. For what, she wondered, for whom?

Lost in sympathy for herself, Julie sat down and made a face at limp lettuce. He sat opposite, and she looked at his food first—toast and tea; somebody worse off than herself. She glanced up and saw Cliff Barnes.

"I know," he said. "The spider is supposed to wait in his web until the poor little flies wander in—or do the Ewings consider themselves mistreated butterflies?"

After scanning the cafeteria quickly, her eyes came
back to him. She liked what she saw, the modish way
he wore his neat brown hair, the directness of hazel
eyes, the determined jaw and set of his mouth. Cliff
Barnes wasn't a pretty man, and taken together his
features were nothing extraordinary. But parts of him,
especially the eyes and mouth, seemed rare. Maybe it
was the intensity of the man, the drive that somehow
lighted him up from the inside. Vaguely, incongru-
ously, Julie wondered if early Crusaders looked like
this on their way to face the Saracen.

"We've talked before, Mr. Barnes. My answer is the
same, but a lot of people know I'm here for lunch,
and if they see us together—"

"Guilt by association, or through fear?"

"You're the enemy," Julie said. "Does Begin meet
Sadat for bagels?"

When he smiled, the inner light spread outward.
He glowed, Julie thought; he really glowed. "Neither
of them is pretty, Julie; you certainly are. If you'd
have dinner with me, we could talk about the PLO
and Sinai—"

"And not even whisper about the Ewings?"

He reached across the table and took her hand. His
fingers were long and strong and warm. Cliff said,
"I'm not asking you to betray your own principles,
Julie, only to stop hiding them, to take an honest look
at things."

"For a change? It would be a change, but I do have
my—loyalties."

Cliff held her hand. "I respect that, even if it's mis-
directed. Being on opposite sides of the fence shouldn't
stop us from having dinner together."

"Right now," Julie said, "it does."

He fished in the pockets of a houndstooth jacket,
then into shirt pockets. "Never do I have any paper.
Here, this'll do—" she watched him write a number
on the back of a laundry ticket. "If you change your
mind—"

"Pick up your shirts," she said brightly, too

conscious of the scent of his shaving lotion, the polished kind of cleanliness, a few golden-brown hairs scattered on the backs of strong hands.

"My unlisted number," he said. "Julie, it would be nice. I don't often do this kind of—"

"I know," she said. "Never a stain upon the escutcheon."

"Something like that."

She watched the rolling rhythm of his shoulders when he left. Julie tasted her salad and found it surprisingly spicy.

Jock Ewing's den was all leather and polished woods, rich metals and the smell of gun oil, cigars, bourbon. He sat at the small, inlaid table across from State Senator Wild Bill Orloff and thought he'd gone to seed—fat and seed, past his prime and showing it plain.

Orloff drew a card, looked at his hand, and muttered. "Barnes is a nuisance, that's all. Hundred just like him, a thousand—seen 'em come and seen 'em go."

"Glad you take it like that, Senator. We depend on you." He reached for the senator's discard, and changed his mind. Two plays later Orloff said "Gin," spread his hand, and chuckled. "You ain't on your toes, Jock."

"Guess I ain't," Jock smiled. "Time for a drink."

"Too early for me, but what the preacher don't know, won't confuse him."

"Bourbon and branch water it is," Jock said, rising and walking to the heavily carved bar. "This Barnes fella—he ain't exactly like the other do-gooders, Wild Bill. Difference is, it's downright personal with him; bad blood between his daddy and me a long time back. This 'un is still carryin' the spite. Got him a bite like a loggerhead turtle, too; gets aholt of somethin', he ain't apt to turn loose till it thunders."

Orloff sniffed at his drink, nodded a great mane of silver hair that was in need of another touch-up, and drank off the whiskey at a gulp. "Got a herd of little snappin' turtles around him, too. This investigator of his was havin' coffee with my secretary the other day. He got around to askin' how come I always got seats on the fifty-yard line for the Cowboy games. Guess he knows about that box *you* get every year. Anyway, my Lillian is smart as a turpentined whip. She says: 'Well now, sonny, Senator Orloff is older'n that stadium. He was probably settin' there when they built the place and nobody had the heart to move him.' "

Jock laughed and nodded, then took Orloff's glass for a refill. The senator said, "Thought maybe when that youngun of yours married the Barnes gal—"

"Not a chance," Jock said. "Cliff Barnes wrote his sister out'n his will, soon's he heard. Too bad; she don't inherit no free hair shirt and two passes to the crucifixion."

"Damn!" Orloff chortled. "That's a good 'un, Jock."

Jock said quietly, "He been much trouble to you, Bill?"

"Just pokin' with a stick, to see what jumps up and runs. What can he find? Most everything between you and me was done on our words and a handshake."

"Yeah," Jock said, and reached for the bourbon bottle again.

Borrowed coveralls flapping and paint-speckled, Pamela was halfway to the main house when she heard the car. She smiled and stopped to wait. When Bobby clambered out with his briefcase, she came to kiss him. "Surprise," she said. "You're home early. Couldn't stand bein' away from me?"

"That and all the hammerin' at the office. Just couldn't concentrate. You smell like paint. How's our house comin' and why don't you send in a couple of the hands to do it for you?"

"Because then it wouldn't be *ours*, silly. Besides, cowhands would slop more around than they got on the walls."

"Hire some pros, then. I don't like to see you workin' so—"

"I like it, baby; really. Oh—Senator Wild Bill Something is with your daddy."

"Orloff," Bobby said. "I've got his story in my briefcase, and I'd better drop in on them." He paused and glanced at the barns. "Krebs—he takin' it all right? I swear, if the old man didn't set such store by him, I'd—"

"Ray stays out of sight and does his job," Pamela said. "And so does Lucy. That's what we want, isn't it?"

He passed a free hand across her cheek. "Good to hear that about Lucy. She used to live in the house we're takin' over. It might hold some kind of—bad memories for her."

"It's something she'll have to face, then. We have to think of ourselves first, and the sooner I'm out from under the same roof as that painted-up little doll— no, that Kewpie doll. You even win one at a carnival? Cutesy curly hair and smily, pouty red lips. It's all hollow inside, and if you mash it just a little, you get a big dent that never pops back out."

Grinning, Bobby said, "Don't dent her, then, and for sure, don't strike a match close by. Kewpie dolls are damned thin plastic."

"Come on back," she said, "and I'll light a match to *you*."

Bobby stuck out his hand. "Senator, good to see you."

"My boy, my boy," Orloff said. "We miss you around Austin. When you comin' back? Got to bring that pretty lil' gal you married, too."

"Learnin' other ends of the business," Bobby said. "You know how it is, Senator."

Jock looked hard at him. "Home early, ain't you?"

"People tearin' up the office, rebuilding. I tell you—"

"Yeah," Jock said. "Excuse us a minute, Wild Bill. I got to put a bug in my boy's ear."

Down the hallway, Jock said, "You got his file with you?"

Bobby patted the briefcase. "What's with Wild Bill? He's Ewing Oil's oldest, and sometimes dumbest, friend."

"Scared shitless," Jock grunted. "Son of a bitch told me a story about an investigator and a couple of season tickets. No way that old windbag can lie to me."

"If he's spooked," Bobby said, "why call in his markers now?"

"That what you think of me, boy? I want to help the old bastard, give him back the damned things."

"Might be a problem," Bobby said. "Some of this stuff is on the record, if they know where to look."

"Well, you see to it a false trail gets laid. Damnit, if you hadn't lost your gumption, you ought to be down yonder seein' that a few other folks get laid, too. Free pussy can do more to change a man's mind than anything else I know."

Setting his teeth, Bobby said, "I'll do just about all you want, Dad. But I gave up hustling whores for good. If you want another pimp, you can hire a good one outa New Orleans."

From beneath thickening salt-and-pepper eyebrows, Jock Ewing peered at his youngest son. "Damned if I don't believe like your ma does, that Vietnam turned you all around."

"No," Bobby said, "I don't think so. The Nam reached down deep and shook loose some things, I reckon. They just naturally came floatin' to the top."

Jock looked at him for a long moment, then nodded and went back into the study.

CHAPTER 26

Bobby stretched upon the couch with his feet up and head pillowed. The Orloff file was done, tucked behind one leg, and he frowned as he read other documents. Pamela skipped in, fresh from the shower, to plant an upside-down kiss on his mouth.

"That feels weird," he said.

Hair hanging over, smelling of soap and powders and her own indefinable woman scent, she kissed him again. He said, "Let's hear it for weird, strange, and all fun-type aberrations."

She came around and squinched in beside his legs. "You've been reading for hours and hours. I wanted an executive husband, sure, but this is ridiculous. Now if you were to take a break—or whatever you big shots call it—I might show you what I've done to our house, so far. And—"

"And?" he said.

"You betcha."

"Magnificent offer," Bobby said, "if you'll give me a couple of minutes more. I'm just beginning to understand something here, Pam—and it's sneaky as hell, also dangerous as hell. Damned if I understand *why* we're doing this; we don't need the money."

Pamela shrugged and reached behind her to hook both arms around his bent knees. "I don't pretend to understand any of it. Oil comes from a hole in the ground; then they do something mysterious to it, and charge too much to fill my gas tank. That's it."

Closing the file, he laid it upon his chest. "All this balanced on a razor edge, and Jock is still playing

games with his statehouse cronies. Damn! *This* is the
danger, the thing that could hang us, Texas Independents, Lone Star Association—everybody. You'd
think that JR could see it, too."

Bobby nudged free of her arms and lifted his feet
high to swing them over her head so he could sit beside her, the file across his knees. "Look, I'll explain it
to you. The old man may call it good business, but I
call it crooked and irresponsible. I can just hear Jock
now, sayin' as how everybody else is doin' it, and we'd
be fools not to. And in his own way, he's right. From
what I've seen here, there are at least seventy-three
independent companies in the Houston area involved
in this rip-off. In Houston *alone*."

Pamela said, "I didn't know there were that many
independent outfits."

"There aren't." Bobby shook his head. "Some of
those titles have to be fronts, with the left hand sellin'
to the right hand. Oh boy. Pam—a few years ago, I
think it was the middle of 'seventy-three, the government set up a price structure. It was meant to spur
new exploration, but there are so many loopholes—
old oil, that's for wells already in production, goes for
five dollars thirty-four cents a barrel; *new* oil can sell
for eleven dollars eighty-seven cents. That's six dollars
fifty-three cents per-barrel spread, and *all oil looks
alike*."

She took his hand. "You mean they—we—are switching old oil for new and getting top dollar? But how
can we do that?"

"Easy," he said. "Just shuffle a lot of paper, because
the enforcement regulations are practically nil. Think
how much money is being ripped off by the independents alone—a hundred thousand, maybe five
hundred thousand barrels a *day*. That is a whole *lot*
of bread, baby."

After a soft whistle, Pamela said, "Yes, it is. And
Ewing Oil is mixed up in this rip-off?"

"Right to our boot tops."

"It wasn't you," Pamela said. "Jock and JR set it up

long before you came into the office, while you were still on the road."

He said, "Same thing, Pam. I'm the company, too. I'll talk to Jock, see if we can't pull out of this before the federal government comes down and tears up everybody's playhouse."

And Pamela added, "If it does any good. Your father won't make any such step without JR, and he won't be home until much later, if at all. So why don't we stop gettin' all hot and bothered over something we can't help right now, and—"

"And?"

"Go get hot and bothered about somethin' we *can* help."

"Woman," he said, "you've got the best business head in this family, among a bunch of other best things."

Sue Ellen drove the white Continental to a slow stop and a precise parking before the steps. Ellie got out of the front, Lucy from the back. Ellie and Sue Ellen carried packages, Lucy her schoolbooks.

"Mom, Sue Ellen—Lucy," Bobby said. "Pam's goin' to show me the little house, what all she's done to it."

Lucy hugged her books to her breasts. "It—I don't *like* that house; nothing can make it look good."

"Hush, child," Ellie said. "Sometimes folks'd rather be to themselves, even if it's in a tent."

"Not me," Lucy said, and stalked into the house.

"Pamela," Ellie said, while Sue Ellen stood like a store dummy, looking at nothing, her arms loaded with shopping loot, "don't be shy about askin' help, if you need it."

"I won't, Miss Ellie."

Ellie smiled. "I'm sure you'll do a fine job."

Sue Ellen's lip quivered; she made an icy smile to hide it and said, "Well, Miss Ellie, I'd just as soon get all this stuff inside, if you don't mind."

"Certainly, girl; no need you standin' here. See you younguns at supper?"

"Sure, Mother," Bobby said. "Senator Orloff's still here, waitin' for you to stuff him like a turkey."

Just inside the door where she'd been waiting and listening, Lucy said, "Let me help you with those, Sue Ellen. Say, how come JR never comes home early, like Bobby? Maybe you two been married too long."

Primly, Sue Ellen said, "JR's work is far more demanding. He's the real boss there, you know. Bobby is just a—just a figurehead."

"Sure," Lucy said, "oh sure. That's why he's here talkin' to senators and JR's back in Dallas."

Sue Ellen tossed her head and climbed the stairs while Lucy headed for the kitchen and Ellie for the den. She entered her suite and locked the door. Dropping packages on the bed, she selected one and opened it, her hands shaking a little. It was so beautiful and yet so—so daring. She'd never minded the skimpy bathing suits for competitions, because all the other girls were wearing them and she had the best body of them all. But this—

She quickly peeled off dress and undies, even her bra, and stood in high heels to hold the nightgown before her, eyeing the full-length mirror. Even doubled, the black, sheer, and clingy material was sinful; it hung to every curve and nestled into each indentation.

There had to be more to marriage than what she had with JR; there just had to. Tilting her head, she heard faint, happy laughter from the house Pamela and Bobby would soon be moving into. Upstairs here in the big house, they laughed a lot, too, especially at night—soft laughter smothered before long. Sue Ellen's hands trembled and she stared at the lift of her nipples against the sheer gown.

It had been so long since JR even tried. Maybe it was her fault at first, because she didn't expect it just that way, and thought that men lasted longer. The few books she forced herself to read didn't say he went soft right away, and had a tough time growing at all. She stared into the mirror. Now she could do it better; she was sure of that.

Forcing her fingers to loosen, Sue Ellen lay the outrageous nightie across the dresser. There; she was stark naked in the daylight. Pretty; she was very, very pretty. Pamela didn't have fine, full breasts with hard pink tips; Pamela's tummy wasn't so flat, tapering just so to a full, pouty mound mossed with gleaming dark-red hair. Even Lucy wouldn't have the smoothness of skin, the flawless satin of flesh—

Her hand moved of its own; she swore she didn't mean it to caress her tummy, her hip like that, so slyly sensuous. And when it cupped her there, when it probed gently but demandingly—oh lord! Sue Ellen snatched away her hand and turned hiding from the mirror. Her robe; she needed her robe. Safe within it, she hurried into the bathroom and only took it off when she slipped under the shower. Sue Ellen gasped at the impact of icy, almost-wintertime water, but huddled under the stinging needles until she felt normal again. But this time, when she was drying with the big white and fluffy towel, it started all over. Her skin was sensitive, as if each minuscule pore was awake and throbbing.

Sue Ellen was conscious of individual hairs upon her arm, those silken things so tiny as to be almost invisible. But she could feel them standing apart, as if they were electrified. It wasn't possible, but she felt as if she were sweating inside and out. Dusting with talc didn't help all that much, and when she dabbed perfume here and there, it seemed more powerful than usual, nearly stifling.

Wishing her old terrycloth robe were rougher against her skin, Sue Ellen went into the bedroom and stood uncertainly in bare feet whose soles tingled against the carpet, her toes trying to dig in and crawl. When she heard the doorknob rattle, she winced, then drew her robe tighter, so glad that JR was home.

"Darlin'!" she kissed him hard on the mouth, and would have held it longer, but he pulled back.

"Damned union carpenters," he said. "First they run Bobby off; then me."

She ran her tongue over her lips. "Well, at least they got you home early. How was your day?" When he shed his coat and tie, unbuttoned the top of the shirt, she said, "I had fun; I did some shoppin' with Miss Ellie, and stopped by school to pick up Lucy. I swear, if she keeps bein' so good, Jock'll just *have* to get back her license and give her a car."

At the dresser, JR held up the black nightie with one finger through a strap. "What the hell is this?"

"I th-thought I needed to change my image."

She didn't like the way he laughed, not like it was funny, but like he was making fun of her. "That'll change your image, all right. Might as well write *whore* right across your forehead. I mean, that's not you at all, Sue Ellen."

Something was pushing at her, the way her mama had pushed at her at first, when she was too scared to walk out on stage. "I don't care. I figured I'd wear it tonight. Just—just once, anyhow."

"Well, you figured wrong. Take that damned piece of trash back tomorrow. No, it's better you don't even show your face in that store again. Throw the thing away." JR moved toward the bathroom. "Goin' to take me a shower."

Sue Ellen watched her hands rise to the top of her robe; it amazed her to see them open it. "JR—maybe you could postpone that shower?"

Mouth open, he stared at her. "What's got into you, girl? Cover yourself up; you're hangin' out."

"JR," she said helplessly, "JR—"

"You actin' plain cheap," he said. "You're my wife, and you're actin' like some Juarez whore. It must be Pamela, our trashy sister-in-law. Stay away from her, you hear?"

"I just wanted—oh God, I don't *know* what I wanted! Somethin'—more than we've got—just a little bit more. I—I want us to laugh at night like they do, like Bobby and Pamela."

"See," he said, "told you that woman had to do with you paradin' around like a bitch in heat!" JR flung off shirt and T-shirt, jerked open a drawer, his closet door. Clean top and shirt in hand, he whipped out into the hall and kicked that door shut behind him.

Sue Ellen swayed right where she was for what seemed like a long time. Then she walked stiff-kneed to the dresser and picked up the black see-through nightie. Holding it against her face, she began to cry.

Julie Parsons lived in a small garden apartment complex. It was on a side street, protected by a wall of trimmed and interlaced oleanders; in its neat little courtyard grew two waxy green Cape Jasmine bushes that had browned their blooms and flung away their perfume long ago.

She was in a loose hostess gown, curled in one corner of a fat, velvety sofa. At the other end JR sat with his shoes off and feet up on the coffee table. Julie said, "It's been a spell."

"Yeah, too long."

She rose and took his glass to a small built-in bar for a refill. "Want to know what I think?"

"Always do. Respect your opinion, and you know it." JR had been drinking awhile, and he was just beginning to drag his words.

Pouring bourbon over fresh ice, Julie said, "Call this one for the road. Then wheel it on home to your wife."

"Hell," JR said, "I don't want my wife."

"Why did you marry her, then?"

"Because—because, oh hell, Julie. We been through all this. Miss Texas—prettiest girl in the whole state—credit to me, to the whole damned family, to Ewing Oil."

"Here's one for the trip home," she said, handing him the glass.

He caught her wrist, drew her down beside him. "Don't put me down, Julie; not you. You're the one always turns me on, honey. You always know just how."

She didn't struggle. "You taught me how, JR; told

me exactly what you liked, what you need. You mean you haven't told Sue Ellen?"

He let go her wrist and drank his whiskey. "Damnit, a man don't—" He moved suddenly and caught her to him, kissing her deeply, probing her parted lips with a hungry tongue. When she didn't respond right away, he released her and stared.

"It's not enough anymore, JR. Not enough for me to catch you on the fly, or when you've had an argument. I don't want you."

"Hell you don't. You always want to screw."

She flared at him: "Not this way, damnit!"

"Any way, hon—and you know it." He had her again, his hands moving, sliding, reaching beneath the hostess gown to part her knees.

Julie might have been asleep, might have been dead; she allowed him to handle, to manipulate her. "I loved you once, JR—long before Sue Ellen. I knew you'd never marry me, and I accepted that. All these years, you've been comin' to see me and I lived for it. But the mornings, JR, the mornings. God, how I hate eating breakfast alone."

Against her throat he said, "Talk all you want, but talkin' ain't doin', and I can feel you gettin' ready, honey, I can *feel* you."

"Let me go," Julie said. "Oh, please get the hell out of my life and give me a chance."

He covered her mouth with his own, and against her will, against all logic and sense, her body betrayed her. It began to buck in a slow, demanding beat. Against her teeth, he said, "Yeah, hon—oh yeah, that's it, baby. Get it, baby—yeah—"

"You son of a bitch," she hissed into his lips. "You overbearing, shit-mean son of a bitch."

JR groaned and kicked from his pants, groaned and reached up for the handholds of her slowly descending head, arching himself to meet her while she continued to curse him. But only for a little while, her breath hot and tingly and maddening. . . .

When he got up and searched out his clothing, part

here, part in the other room, she lay on the bed with her back to him, a pale blue blanket pulled up nearly to her shoulder blades. JR found his coat and cigars, lit one, and inhaled deeply. The dresser lamp was on, and he saw the birthday cards propped around.

"Oh hell, hon, when was your birthday?"

Back still to him, Julie said, "Day before yesterday."

"I ought to be stomped and drugged for forgettin' it."

"It's okay," Julie said. "It's just fine. If you don't have to get back tonight, stay and I'll whip up a good breakfast."

He drew on the cigar, balanced the glowing end off the side of her dresser and looked around for his shorts. "Don't have to get back to the ranch, but there *is* that early plane to Austin tomorrow. You remember takin' the message from Jock? He wants me to sit in on a caucus the boys're havin' about ol' Wild Bill Orloff. So I got to go by the office, then out to the airport. I'll leave my car there, and if little brother don't come in, you run things til I get back, like always."

"Daddy's little helper," she said.

"Hey," he said, "don't go jumpin' salty because I forgot your birthday. Hell, you and me, we're gettin' up where we'd just as lief forget 'em, right?"

Julie could hear him moving around, the creak of wooden flooring beneath his weight. She didn't want to turn over, didn't even want to listen anymore. But he put one hand to her shoulder and rolled her gently to her back, kissed her forehead.

"Here, hon," he said, "buy yourself somethin' pretty."

She lay for a long time staring at the next pillow, where JR had dropped the hundred-dollar bill. She heard the door close, and listening hard, made out the motor of the Mustang when it kicked over.

After a while, she got up and went naked to her handbag. Rummaging through it, she found the crumpled laundry ticket. Holding it, she went back to the bed and picked up the hundred-dollar bill. Turning the list over, she stared at it as she dialed.

"Hello," she said. "I know it's late, but I figure you as a man who stays awake and catches up all his homework. About that dinner—look, let's not wait that long. How about breakfast?"

Cliff Barnes said, "Great with me; when and where?"

Someplace where there's no chance of anyone recognizing either of us. Tell you what—" She gave him her address. "Give me an hour to run out to the all-night market and I'll promise you a feast. Oh no—I'm buying. I just came into—an inheritance, and I can't think of a better way to spend it."

CHAPTER 27

Jock had taken over JR's desk, and JR didn't much like it; he sulked on the leather couch while Julie brought coffee for all of them. Bobby Ewing stood beside the desk while his father went over a list, peering, grunting, and checking off.

From the couch, JR said, "What makes Orloff run scared?"

"He's old and soft," Jock said. "Some men get that way. Some just get tougher, but he ain't one of 'em."

Julie spooned sugar into Jock's coffee, added cream. He didn't look at her as she left the office.

JR said, "I know Wild Bill gave you a hand back when they were hawking oil leases on street corners, but he's collected for it a hundred times over. Now he's got to have his arm twisted."

"Nothin' here than can be traced back to us," Jock

said, glancing up at Bobby. "It's all pretty well covered."

"Well," Bobby said, "there's one thing can tie us to Orloff—that second trust deed on his house, fifty thousand dollars, no payments received."

"No problem," JR said. "I never recorded that. The senator and us have the only copies."

Jock chewed his cigar. "Let's see ours."

Bobby rifled through his briefcase, pulled out each document and file holder to go through them again. "Must have left the damned thing at home."

Sitting upright on the couch, JR said, "Told you I don't like files leavin' the office."

Reaching for the phone, Bobby said, "I'll call Pam. I was on the couch with her—" Punching buttons, he looked at his brother. "And I told you there was no choice, that Dad wanted them soonest."

JR got up and sugared his own coffee, just becoming aware that Julie hadn't done it for him. He glanced at the closed office door and remembered her feeble attempt at resistance, the hot, driving kind of sex Julie was so good at. When he looked back, Bobby was replacing the phone.

"She'll be here pretty soon. Havin' lunch with her brother, but she'll drop the folder off on her way. Right there on the couch, it was—but kind of stuffed between the cushions."

Putting down his coffee cup, Jock said, "Her brother?"

"They're blood kin, Dad. It's only natural."

"Both Barnes, and I don't like it."

Bobby said, 'There's something *I* don't like a whole lot more: this business of switchin' old oil for new. Playin' around with Orloff and his kind, the state investigation—a Cub Scout meeting, compared to what a federal investigation can uncover there, and *will*. No way to hide it from a payoff-proof auditor."

JR snickered. "You know one of them rare birds?"

"Two, three presidents from now," Jock said, "and that's U.S. presidents I mean, boy—a whole regiment

of snoops might uncover a few daisy-chain operations.
I sell old oil to Acme; it sells to BJ Jones; Jones
peddles it to Houston Industries; every time the price
or the kickback goes up a mite. Finally the end user
gets it, but now it's new oil and premium cost."

"Hell," Bobby said. "I could track down a deal like
that in an hour."

Jock lifted a bushy eyebrow. "You ain't a low-paid
government auditor."

"Besides," JR put in, "it's been goin' on so long and
so many different ways that a good part of them government folks are already tied in to the deal. They
can't pull out and can't point the finger."

Bobby walked away from the desk, hands stuck in
his hip pockets. Pamela was forever getting on his case
about that; she said it stretched his pants out of shape.
He said, "Why, goddamnit?"

Jock and JR exchanged puzzled glances; Jock said,
"Why?"

"Yes, why? How come? Ewing Oil goin' broke,
spreading itself too thin in new enterprises, what?
Why the hell do we have to cheat?"

Then Jock Ewing said what Bobby had known he
would say all the time: "It's just good business, boy.
Everybody else is doin' it, and if we don't, we're left
suckin' hind tit."

"What difference does it make?" Bobby asked.

Jock picked up his cigar and blew on the end of it.
"There's times I just don't understand you, boy."

They argued some and Jock stomped around the
office some, still the herd boss, the king stud. When the
dust settled, Bobby had been shunted off into a corner, because he found himself doing battle, making
waves, and that was a country mile from the go-easy
attitude he'd promised himself. He had Pamela and
air conditioning, love and a safe place to sleep. There
wasn't a lot of sense looking for a fight, especially with
his own family. He stared out the window, not seeing
the bustling anthill of Dallas spread far below, but the

rotting primeval green of deadly jungle. It took some doing to refocus.

Julie made her professional smile as Pamela Ewing entered the outer office. "Hello, Mrs. Ewing. It that the Orloff file?"

Pamela crossed to the desk and put the folder in the other woman's hands. "Yes, is my husband around?"

Nodding at the inner office door, Julie said, "There's been some kind of battle going on in there, but it seems to have settled down. I'll go rescue Bobby, if you'll wait in his office."

Expensively dressed now, Julie thought, watching Pamela walk lithely into the smaller office. She could remember Pam Barnes as a grubby copywriter for a small ad outfit, a company scuffling for the crumbs of Ewing Oil's business, a company that would have fired Pam in a second if its owners knew of the bad blood between Ewing and Barnes. Now look at her: acting as if she had been born to the purple.

Julie's fingers tightened on the Orloff file.

In Bobby's office, Pamela looked at pictures on the walls; Bobby in football uniform, in army uniform, at a Booster banquet for the Dallas Cowboys. She looked closer at that one, seeing all the family faces, but younger. In the background: was that her brother? It certainly looked like him, but if it was Cliff, the woman with him had her head turned away.

At least he'd been out with some woman. She'd begun to fret a little over Cliff's life. He was just too much the Ralph Nader to suit her—not the same ascetic, but spotless, blameless, seeming to live for nothing but his work, his sacred duty. It was a little spooky, and more than a little pitiful.

"Hello and farewell," Bobby said, "and did you bring the file?"

She kissed him. "Gave it to Lady Faithful." Pointing at the banquet photo, she said, "Know who you were havin' dinner with?"

"Cowboy fans; the chosen people."

"And my brother Cliff. He wasn't at the big table, of course."

Bobby kissed the tip of her nose. "Probably a spy for the Colts."

"I figured you'd say something like that. When are you goin' to meet him, dear?"

"At dawn. Four-letter words at forty paces."

"Fool," she said and smiled at him as he headed back for JR's office.

With some difficulty, she found her brother's new apartment. He also had to keep a room in Austin because he commuted between the cities, doing research here, bringing the results of his investigations there. Pamela knew Cliff used a couple of assistants, but she'd never seen them.

She buzzed and he let her in, kissed her cheek, held her hand awhile as he used to do when they were kids. Pamela said, "Still not enough room for all the books, the stacks of paper."

"I know where everything is—generally; at least I know the pile it's supposed to be hiding in. Thought you'd rather eat here than out, so we could take all the time we need to talk."

"That has an ominous ring, counselor."

"Oh, come on, I'm off duty. And I happen to know you like tuna-fish salad. Sorry it's not caviar."

She made a face at him. "That's a lawyer-type crack that the jury will be instructed to ignore. But you do get points for the salad—just the right amount of grated onion; you didn't go berserk with the Bermudas this time."

His smile was warm and genuine. "It's good to be with you, Pammy."

"Oh God, you're the only one calls me that—or dares. I tried to get Bobby to come along."

"Good you didn't. I wanted to be with *you*, as we used to be. Remember how we'd play Tell Me Your Dream?"

Pamela poured tea for them both. "After a while, it was no fun with you; you always had the same dream. Be a lawyer and make a million bucks."

"The million stopped being that important; five bucks was, in college. I couldn't think beyond that much."

She patted his hand. "But you hacked it. Hey, you know—I keep forgettin' you went to school with Bobby."

"So did a few thousand other people; Bobby Ewing and I didn't exactly move in the same circles. Sometimes I'd get to clean up his table in the Student Union. I was still a busboy in my senior year; needed the money."

"I know. You worked so hard—any job you could get, *all* jobs you could get. I don't understand how you found time to sleep and study."

Cliff moved his hand from beneath hers. "More tea? Sometimes I didn't sleep, or couldn't study. Scholarship or no, I might have been the oldest senior on record. Then along would come a Bobby Ewing, driving a big car, picking up the check for two or three girls, sailing through classes without effort. And I'd hate his guts."

"Especially Bobby Ewing," Pamela said.

"Damned right! I'd look at him, the millionaire freshman, and think: There, but for the greed of *Jock* Ewing, would go I." Cliff Barnes sat there, angered more by the clean, compelling scent of his sister, by a closeness and beauty forever lost to him now, stolen as his legacy had been. It was so damned much worse, knowing that she ate with them, lived beneath their roof, suffered his hands upon her, his body covering hers—

"I'll clean up," he said.

"Let me help."

"Sit still; I'm used to waiting on Ewings."

"Cliff, I'm one of them now. For better or worse, the man said, and I agreed to it. I believe in it."

"All right!" he snapped from the sink. "How do *they*

feel about it? I'll bet you weren't welcomed with open arms."

She fiddled with her teacup. "All things considered, I'm doin' okay. Bobby—we seem to get happier every day, until I could swear I'm about to bust with it. The old man—he tolerates me; Miss Ellie—a self-taught lady, every inch of her. She's hard but she's fair. Then there's Lucy; the kid acts as if we're mortal enemies, but if our ages were closer we could be out of the same litter. So she can't hustle me.

"And JR; and Sue Ellen—I can't help feelin' that JR is basically evil—no, amoral might be a better description. What's right for him is right for the world, or ought to be. His wife is a windup doll whose mainspring is wearin' thin; I don't ever want to see into her clockworks. Something's mixed up inside her."

Cliff said, "You forgot somebody—Ray Krebs."

"That was, is, and will be—*done.*"

He came back to the table. "Then what was that brawl at the Big D disco about, if not you and Ray? If Jock hadn't pulled some quick strings, there might have been a rash of lawsuits over that little affair. What's wrong with your husband—did he freak out in Vietnam?"

Coldly, she said, "Question one: The fight was about Lucy being where she wasn't supposed to be. Question two: No, Bobby didn't freak out in Vietnam; surely your spies have told you he won medals in combat. And while you're thinking on that, Mr. Investigator, remember he didn't *have* to do, that he didn't *have* to be an enlisted man. While he was bleedin' over there, where the hell were *you?*"

"Becoming a lawyer, so I might have a hand in stopping the next bloody, senseless, unforgivable war."

Suddenly contrite, she stood up and put her arms around him. "Okay, dear—a truce? You're still my brother and I love you."

"Yes," he said, holding her tightly for one haunted, vibrant moment, then pulling himself free. "Yes, Pammy."

The street was quiet, tree-lined, residential, and the dark Chevy seemed to belong there. Julie Parsons put her head back on the seat and said to Cliff Barnes, "Do you mind me just camping here awhile? The office was so busy today there just has to be some overflow, and they're liable to call me at home. Anyhow, I don't usually get to have breakfast *and* dinner with a handsome, attentive man."

Quietly, intensely, Cliff said, "I'm not very good at this. I haven't much experience. I only know I don't want this day to end. Please, Julie, let me drive you to my place, where no one will call and nothing break the spell."

She turned her face to his, intrigued by his boyishness, his uncertainty. He didn't quite land squarely upon her mouth either; she soon corrected that, and a great, joyous brightness leaped within her. She liked it, liked *him,* and exulted in a heady new sense of freedom. When she could breathe again, Julie said, "Let's go."

She was reasonably certain no woman had ever spent the night in his apartment. There were none of the touches of the swinging bachelor; one bottle of good Scotch, no wines; bluegrass eight-tracks, no mood music, no McKuen. She couldnt' even find a candle or incense. There were books everywhere, spilling off chairs, propped high against a wall, stuffed into cases. There was a heavy metal file cabinet, chained and locked.

He shifted behind her, cleared his throat. "Ah, if you don't like Scotch—"

"It's just fine," she said, "and I like bluegrass, too."

After that it was easy in a way, wondrously exciting in another. Cliff talked with her, not *to* her, and his nervousness dissipated after two drinks in his home surroundings. When he kissed her this time, there was no hesitation or awkwardness, only a hungering, intense need that seared into the depths of her.

She borrowed his beat-up robe and took a shower, all

her flesh in tune with the hammering in her temples, the pulse-beat at her throat.

Hair loose and floating free, she went out to rejoin him, excited as she hadn't been since the beginning with JR Ewing. This was the real good-bye, the genuine severing and—oh God, how very glad she was to be cutting dark and cruel bonds, for she had tied the Gordian knot herself.

He was waiting in the bedroom, a discreet night-light the only guide; he was under the covers and her side of the bed had been turned down. There was such purity to it, such simplicity, that Julie's happy laughter rang out as she let the old robe drift away from her body.

Proud of his eagerness, of the effect her naked body had upon this new man, she stood beside the bed while he kneeled upon it, gently caressing her, kissing her breasts and stroking her hips, her thighs. Then, when he was shaking and she could hear his breath hanging in his throat, Julie Parsons slid into bed and fitted herself to him.

He was a man long deprived of love, of women, and went into her too swiftly, too fiercely. Julie didn't mind, for this was a true need and she met him gladly, gladly. When he shuddered and caught at her haunches, when he gasped her name over and over, she kissed his hair, his eyes, his cheek and throat.

Slowly then, she coaxed and teased him back to desire, using all she knew but moving carefully, experimenting, lest she shock him. Only when he didn't resist or tense up, did she progress, her flesh reading his, fingers and lips Brailling him. Julie said everything to him through her newborn body; her old one had been discarded, peeled away like an old, tired skin.

Because it was a strange bed in an alien room, Julie came awake at a sound she couldn't identify. Blinking at the ceiling almost in panic, she turned over and smelled his scent in the other pillow. The night came

back and she smiled languorously, with a lazy content-
ment.

There was another odor—crisping bacon, the vitaliz-
ing nectar of chicory coffee, and suddenly she was
ravenous. Migod, Julie thought: *It's the crack of day,
and somebody's making breakfast—for me.* There was
no time for a shower, only for hurried unsnarling of
tousled hair, with *his* comb. Her purse—where the hell
was her purse, lipstick, eyeshadow? There—it lay upon
a chair; she leaped for it and did things to her face.
Thoughtfully, she stared into the open purse.

"Sorry," Cliff called from the kitchen, "but I have to
get with it early. If you're hungry—"

"Believe it," she said, carrying the purse with her
and sitting down. There was even freshly squeezed
orange juice beside her plate.

"Julie," he said, and for an awful moment she
thought he was going to apologize, or worse, thank her.
But he said, "I wish it didn't have to be like this, but
well—I'd appreciate it if you walked down to the
corner and took a cab after I've gone. You see, some
people would like to get something on me, anything
to sling mud. I think I could take it, but I wouldn't
like any rubbing off on you—despite the new mo-
rality."

Afraid to speak, her eyes blurring, she nodded. But
when he kissed her cheek, she said, "Wait," and handed
him the Xerox copy. "You never asked for this, Cliff—
but maybe you should call a press conference before
you leave. I think this is something you've been waiting for. It's a copy of a second trust deed on Senator
Orloff's home; the Ewings hold it."

CHAPTER 28

Cliff looked good and knew it, felt good and showed it. The setting worked well for him, too—the busy hustle of an office-building lobby, with people stopping to gawk at the portable TV camera, the reporters shoving recorder mikes at him.

Tilting the paper so camera lights wouldn't bounce, Cliff Barnes said, "I have here a second trust deed on Senator Orloff's home, for fifty thousand dollars. I can find no records where the senator has paid back any part of it."

Right on cue, the TV reporter asked, "Who holds the deed, Mr. Barnes?"

"John Ewing, Sr., his heirs and assigns," Cliff answered. "If you can move in—the date of the loan is here: ten years ago."

He waited until the camera moved back and a newsman said, "Would you call that bribery, Mr. Barnes?"

"Not yet." Cliff smiled quickly. "There may be many answers forthcoming—a favor, a loan somebody forgot to pay and somebody forgot to collect. After all, what's a mere fifty thousand dollars between friends?" On the subsiding chuckle he said, "I'm presenting this to the committee in Austin. I imagine they'll want to talk to the senator."

"Mr. Barnes," someone asked, "do you want to tell us how you came by this incriminating document?"

"Sorry," Cliff smiled boyishly, "but I don't, gentlemen; at least, not yet."

Breakfast at the ranch was most often leisurely and

relaxed. Ewing employees knew this, and were reluctant to break in on the family for anything less than catastrophe. So when the phone rang, JR got up and frowned his way to answer it.

Pamela was laughing over something with Bobby when the silence caught up to her. She looked a question at her husband, but he only took her hand beneath the table and shrugged.

JR hammered the phone at its cradle, missed, and slammed it furiously into place. Every face at the table turned his way, and he said, "Cliff Barnes just held a quickie news conference. Real sudden and real cute. Had a document in his hand, a copy of that Orloff deed—right out of the file that little brother forgot to stick into his briefcase yesterday. That was the same file that little brother's wife brought to town—where she just happened to be havin' lunch with *her* brother—the said Cliff Barnes."

Everyone but Bobby swiveled heads to stare at Pamela. JR said, "I wonder how that two-bit crusader got hold of a private paper. You reckon we got us a spy in the house?"

Pulling free of Bobby's hand, Pamela leaped to her feet and ran from the room, from the house. On the front porch, she braced herself against one of the tall columns and fought a losing battle against tears.

At the breakfast table, Bobby said, "You're accusin' her without a damned speck of proof."

"Who else?" JR asked. "Me, you, Dad?"

"I don't know," Bobby said. "I *do* know Pam didn't give him that copy."

JR banged his fist against the table and cups rattled in their saucers. "Then who did—*who?*"

Ellie said clearly: "Stop that hollerin' in my house. Sit down, JR."

"Sorry, Mama." JR took his seat between Sue Ellen and Lucy. In a calmer voice, he went on, "You left that file home yesterday, Bobby. Pamela brought it to the office, and as far as I know, the only time that file was out of my hands, or yours, was while she had it."

Bobby's eyes traveled from face to face around the table. "You all think she sold me out. I don't. Now, is anybody here on *my* side?"

After a dragged-out moment, JR said, "You're askin' too much, little brother."

Standing up, Bobby leaned to press his fists against the table. "Okay, you've passed judgment on me as well as my wife. One thing you *can't* do, and that's remove me from the board of Ewing Oil, not without turning over to me a full twenty-five percent of all assets—and that means *all* holdings, in cash. Dad, you should remember how you had the bylaws drawn up."

"I do," Jock said slowly. "I just never had an idea you'd—"

Bobby cut him off. "JR, I'm not goin' to tell you again: Don't call be little brother anymore, or you'll find out how often I can come up side your head with my little fists."

"*Bobby!*" Ellie said.

He stamped from the room, rolling his shoulders and breathing hard in the anger that rode him. He caught up with Pamela halfway to their small house. "Let's pack," he said.

"I—I didn't do it, Bobby."

"Hell, I know that. But did you stop anywhere on the way, leave the file unattended—oh, never mind." He put his arms around her, looked her in the eyes. "Damned if I'm goin' to stay here and let them snipe at you. I can take it at work because the old man won't say anything and JR sure as hell better not."

Her eyes were big and dewy, showing her hurt. "I don't mean to c-come between you and your family, Bobby. But I didn't do anything wrong."

Kissing away her tears, he said, "There's one way to solve all this. Will your brother tell you where he got that paper?"

"I—I don't know," Pamela said. "I can ask him."

"Come on," Bobby said. "We'll get a place downtown, and I'll go right on into the office."

"Can't they—won't they stop you?"

His smile was grim. "No way, baby. They can out-vote me, but they can't keep me from meetings or records or any damned thing else. I can write checks to beat hell, and I mean to hang right in there—at least until I clear up this crap about you. Then I might tell 'em to stuff it. Please, let's get out of here before JR comes out from under Mama's protection and I start takin' him apart a piece at a time."

They took a suite at the Dallas Hilton, and Bobby left the Mercedes with Pamela, catching a cab to the Ewing Oil Building. He got up to the main office in time to see attorney Ed Heartrow's expensively tailored back going into JR's lair. Bobby followed the man inside, and without a word, plopped in the corner of the couch. Behind the desk, Jock didn't show surprise, but JR's mouth hung open for a second.

JR left the couch, crossed the office, and took a chair. Ed Heartrow sat opposite Jock, alligator briefcase at his right foot, and leaned against the chair leg.

Jock fiddled with an unlighted cigar. "How bad is it, Ed?"

"Well," the lawyer said, "back-dating a bunch of payments is risky; chemical tests can fix the age. You have the right to call in the loan, demand payment in full. Technically, you'd be off the hook."

Bobby said, "Orloff will lose his home."

JR didn't look at him, but at Jock. "He knew the risk when he took the money."

Nodding, Jock said, "Thanks for comin' over, Ed. We'll let you know."

"Not much choice," Heartrow said, retrieving his briefcase and rising, readjusting his coat, smoothing a sleeve. "Daddy says howdy to everybody."

"Tell him be particular," Jock said, and when the man was gone, said, "It's always hard when you have to come down on a friend."

"You and Wild Bill have been close for a lot of years," Bobby said. "There has to be another way. He's an old man—"

JR said then, "If you're too tender, little—ah, Bobby, *I'll* let Orloff in on the facts of life."

"I'm still part of this firm and this family," Bobby said, "like it or not. Calling in markers has always been my job—the shitty end of the stick. I'll go see the senator." He went to the door, stopped, and turned. "I see how far old friendship goes; I wonder how much farther it is for blood kin."

At Cliff's apartment-Dallas office, Pamela was almost head to head across his desk with her brother. "I don't understand, Cliff."

He moved away from her, leaned back in his swivel chair. "There's nothing to understand. Wild Bill Orloff has blocked every piece of creative legislation my people have been involved in."

"And you don't care if I take the rap?"

He made a steeple of his fingers, looked at her over them. "Never crossed my mind they'd blame you, but I don't guess I'd have backed off, anyhow. You wouldn't want me to."

"You never asked, and here I am, between my husband and his family—"

"Ewings," he said. "It figured they wouldn't trust *you*."

"Evidently, you don't trust me either. You won't tell me who copied that paper for you."

Cliff smiled. "Ethics, my dear. The Ewings wouldn't understand it."

Pamela backed away and found a chair. She looked at him, examined her brother closely for the first time in how long? Maybe ever. The phone rang, and when he answered it, his conversation was guarded—from *her*. Damn Cliff Barnes for what he was doing to her. She knew he had worked long and hard against almost impossible odds, that he'd struggled and fought to get where he was. Pamela didn't think Cliff meant to stop at this level, and the statehouse couldn't hold him long either.

"Tonight," he repeated into the phone, and hung up. Then: "Pammy—"

"Forget it," she said, standing and making for the door. "You're eatin' this up, relishin' every dazzling second in the spotlight. The hell with me, with anyone else. Well, that's no game of solitaire, Cliff Barnes; the hell with you, too!"

Bobby walked slowly with Orloff, moving along the street in Deely Plaza, toward the School Book Depository. Symbolic, he thought; another assassination was about to take place here, but the killing wouldn't be as quick, would not be merciful.

Orloff paused and watched the people passing. He took off his Stetson and wiped the sweatband with a bandanna. "You been out to the house plenty of times, Bobby. You know, that's one thing me and Dorothy done right, pickin' that house. Had chances to get bigger, fancier ones, but passed 'em up. That house *suits* us."

"It's no good, Senator," Bobby said. "We're callin' the loan."

Orloff put on his hat. "I ain't got the money just now."

"Let's keep walkin'," Bobby said. "Less chance of a directional mike pickin' us up. Look—we'll pass you the money tomorrow."

"Godalmighty," Orloff said. "Never get away from that. I mean, IRS will want to know where it come from, all them reporters—never be able to hold onto my seat in the legislature. They been real touchy since Watergate, Koreagate, and all that crap." He looked at Bobby and almost ran into a passerby. "What you mean?" he asked. "You tellin' me that ol' Jock Ewing is boxin' me in so tight I have to give up my seat, resign, or lose my house, my *home?* I can fight this, I got a heap of friends—clear my name—"

Bobby said, "Barnes has that paper. Who's going to stand with you?"

Orloff took off his hat again, patted his forehead.

The great silver mane of hair was damp, and in daylight Bobby could tell it was thinning. "Guess I got no pick; I got to resign."

"I'm sorry, Senator—purely sorry."

"Yeah," Orloff grunted, turning his Stetson in both hands, "I reckon everybody's sorry. Just one thing, son—how'd Cliff Barnes get hold of that trust deed to copy it?"

Bobby looked at him. "We don't know yet, but we mean to find out."

He was glad to leave the old man, gone stooped and bent now, made a hundred years older by the loss of a friend—a man he *thought* was a friend for all those years. Bobby hurried to the hotel, eager to wash off the grime, yet knowing he'd never reach the place he felt dirtiest.

For the first time in many nights, he didn't make love to Pamela. There was strain between them, even when she snugged to him in the darkness. "Cliff wouldn't tell," she murmured.

"Didn't figure he would."

"He's so—so damned intense, he scares me. And today I saw something else in Cliff—a diamond-hard ambition, and behind that, gloating."

Bobby didn't say anything, only held her close and breathed the good, clean scent of her hair. "You, me, JR, and—Julie. You passed the Orloff file to Julie, didn't you?"

"Yes, for a few minutes, I guess. But she—"

"She's had something goin' with JR for years, or at least *he* had something goin'. But she's been with us so long, I just don't see—"

"Unless she's breaking up with JR," Pamela said. "Any hurt woman is capable of striking back in a fury; almost any woman will, given the chance."

Across town, Julie Parsons was also snugged to a man, the sweat of their passions drying upon sated bodies. She tasted his skin, his hair, the very essence of him.

He said, "You're kind of anxious about the press conference, huh?"

Smiling into the dark, she said, "Well, we could talk about how Tom Landry never smiles and how the Cowboys ought to make it to the Super Bowl. Sure, it shook me, hearing you on radio, knowing you were on TV; I mean, the Ewings were outraged."

"I'm sure even Mata Hari had a few bad moments."

Julie propped up on one elbow. "Just before they shot her? Cliff, if you simply wanted Orloff out, why didn't you confront him head-on?"

He turned onto his back and clasped hands behind his head. "If I'd just shown him the copy, he'd have been on the phone and Jock Ewing would have come up with a secret account or lost receipts—anything to cover him. This way, Orloff is in the spotlight and can't make a move. Don't feel sorry for him; he's as crooked as they are, if anybody can be crooked as the Ewings."

"I still feel kind of funny—"

"No," he said, hand sliding over the touchy connection of her hip and thigh, "no, you feel just great."

"You make me feel fantastic," she answered, hooking one leg over him, moving bit by bit to cover him with her needful softness, the smoldering heat of her. "*You* make me feel, and feel, and—feel. . . ."

Bobby Ewing had to show ID to the suspicious security guard downstairs, and use the same plastic card in a slot in the office door; a light flashed and a buzzer sounded. He stepped inside and flicked on the overheads.

"Maybe we should have waited until tomorrow," Pamela whispered.

"Could you have slept? Not me, not until I take a good look around. And when you mentioned that Cliff moved recently, and has an unlisted number—"

Pamela said, "As a one-time secretary, I'd say she filed his number somewhere—ah, the Rolodex file.

Let's see now, Baker, Bandon—here it is: Barnes, Clifford."

"I'll be damned," Bobby said. "So simple and so close nobody could see it. Are you sure that's your brother's new number?"

Pamela punched out the numerals. "No better way to find out. It's ringing, and again—Oh, hello, Cliff? So I've changed my mind and I'm speakin' to you again. When can I see you? Oh, not tomorrow—*when?* No, I won't get on your back; this is—personal. Right. Bye now. Oh, and tell the lady you're with that I can hear her panting."

Bobby stared. "Is she there with him now? Julie? Is that how he's payin' her off?"

"Somebody is," Pamela said. "And, my dear, virtuous brother didn't even bother to deny it."

"I suppose it's better than sellin' out for pieces of silver," Bobby said. "And now we know."

"What we *don't* know," Pamela said thoughtfully, "is what JR did to her to bring this about."

Bobby said, "Whatever it was, Julie sure as hell got over it quick."

CHAPTER 29

Cliff Barnes was preparing coffee the old way, with a percolator. Up almost an hour before Julie, he was already showered and shaved, brushed and rolled-on, ready for the new day. His kind of day, not one for the Ewing empire.

Listening to Julie in the shower, he hummed as he set out sugar and cream and the toaster. Cliff was eager to be off, to get into Austin and see what the committee—surprised and elated by his announcement of yesterday—meant to do in moving against the Ewings. It was great to have them by the short hairs, to make them sweat and look over their shoulders to see if he was gaining on them.

"Damned right, you old thief, you creaky old rip-off artist—I'm gaining on you, Jock Ewing. And I'll keep catching up until I run right over you and all your family." He whispered the words, savoring their taste, wishing he could make lyrics of them and set them to music.

The radio music was light, matching his mood, and Cliff tried a couple of dance steps. "Hey, Julie! I'm making coffee and toast—you want anything else?"

The sound of the shower diminished, and Julie called back, "No thanks; I have this wonderful guy who likes my bod just the way it is, with no added poundage."

A news announcer came on, breaking into the music. "A special bulletin from Austin: Senator William Orloff has just resigned from the state senate, effective immediately. This action follows revelation of an ethically questionable loan accepted by the senator and revealed at a Dallas press conference yesterday by senate investigating committee counsel Cliff Barnes. At the conference, the attorney displayed a document which said—"

Cliff snatched at the radio, snapped it off, and stood holding it in both hands, his jaw set. When Julie came from the bathroom wrapped in a towel toga, he didn't glance up.

"Hey now," she said, "how come you shut that off? It's just the perfect way to begin a day."

Jerking the cord loose, Cliff threw the radio against a wall. It shattered, plastic and wire insides spilling out. "Damn!" Cliff said, "Damn, damn, *damn!!*"

Julie clung onto her towel, eyes widening. She had never seen this white-faced fury of Cliff. "It—isn't this what you wanted, Cliff? You said you wanted the crooks out of office; you said you intended to give government back to the people. Then what—"

"I do!" he snapped. "But I needed Orloff; he's the key. He can help me open up that snake pit, show the goddamned Ewings so all Texas can see them for what they are."

She took a backward step. "It's *them* you're after. You're carrying on a vendetta with the family. You don't really give a damn about ethical government, do you?"

He stooped for the radio, tried to poke back its entrails. "We can still do it, Julie. You have access to all the files; they trust you."

Julie ran back into the bathroom, closed and locked the door. His voice struck through the wood, through her shaken defenses: "Julie, you must have something on the land deal JR pulled off two years ago."

She started to cry and he said, "And remember those oil leases he bought for two bits on the dollar?"

Julie clamped hands over her ears, but she could still hear him inside her head, and the echoes rang there long after she dressed and made up her face. But when she went out to confront him, Julie didn't want Cliff to know she had been crying.

But he didn't notice, didn't even look up. "Ready for that coffee?" he asked.

Just like that, goddamn him; as if any wound he made should heal right away, ought to scab over, grow a scar immediately, and be forgotten as quickly. What gave *them* the holy *right*, the power, the balls? "No," she said. "The sooner I'm out of here—"

"Wait," Cliff said. "What about us? That was no act—Julie—we're real, you and me; what happened to us is real."

She faced him, hands knuckle-white on her purse. "What makes you think you're a damned bit different from JR Ewing? Do you actually believe you're any better?"

"Yes. I was honest with you all the way. I said I'd pry information out of you, said I'd use you. I'd use anybody or anything to put a stop to those bastards and what they've done, what they'll go on doing, unless someone like me—"

She started for the door and he didn't put himself in her path. Julie said, "Isn't there something about the end justifying the means? Oh yes, Karl Marx, wasn't it? You make yourself sound so *noble*—"

"I'm the good guy; he's the bad guy," Cliff said.

"No difference to me," Julie said, turning the doorknob. "Whatever the reason, I've been *used*—a dirty handkerchief, a greasy condom—a rose is a rose, or isn't that in the manifesto?"

JR made it into the office before anyone else, frowning and rattling his keys. Both secretaries were usually here and the coffee bubbling by now, and so much for that liberation crap; any woman that worked for JR and sulled up at making coffee and serving it could go get a job with one of those damned lesbians.

He went to the window and looked down at morning-time Dallas. The old man had been content to go just so far, get only this high, but not so JR. He was making Ewing Oil a true power to be reckoned with, swinging more clout, raking in more profits. This generation of Ewings would leave a mark on this city that could never be forgotten. At least, *one* Ewing would make them sit up and take notice.

Bobby's secretary came in, bobbing her head and giving him a quick, shy smile. Neat legs, fine little ass, nice way of moving, and those quiet, shy ones were most often hell in bed. Little brother Bobby wasn't dicking Connie yet; too busy with the bride, but when the newness wore off he'd be a fool not to get next to this little lady. Watching the fluid action of her body beneath a pale orange dress, JR thought he'd beat Bobby to it. No sense in wasting all that good, ripe stuff, and it'd be pretty easy to work it in between stands with Julie.

The outer door opened and JR looked there, but it was only Bobby. What the hell was with Julie? It wasn't like her to run late. Old reliable, old dependable, that was Julie. He said to Bobby: "You hear from Julie?"

Propping one hip against the door frame of his own office, Bobby said, "She just might be out givin' Cliff Barnes some more papers."

"What? What the hell you sayin'?"

"I figure Julie passed the Orloff deed to him."

JR felt in his coat pocket for a cigar. "You been grazin' on loco weed, or just smokin' it? That's ridiculous—*Julie*? You're really reaching, tryin' to take the weight off your bride."

Bobby said, "I don't give a damn if you believe me, but it figures. Pam gave the file to Julie when she came in. How long would it take to make a copy?"

Lighting up, JR blew smoke and said, "You got to have some kind of proof, some motive."

"You didn't give Pam that benefit."

JR backed off, crossed almost to his office door, then said, "Julie's been with us a long time, and entitled. Your wife hasn't earned anybody's trust yet."

Glancing at Connie, Bobby closed his door and moved into the middle of the reception room. Softly, he said, "If I have to give the family another suspect, you won't like it, because that will mean blowin' the whistle on you and Julie."

"Now wait," JR said, "now wait. I've got a wife, and Sue Ellen would just—"

"So—*your* wife needs protection; mine doesn't."

"But damnit, Bobby—"

"Think on it," Bobby warned. "You've got the rest of the day."

Uncertainly, a slow anger building, JR stood glaring as his brother slammed out. He was just turning around for his own office when Julie entered. JR gave her some of his intense stare, but dropped that when she yanked open a drawer and began clearing it of personal items, scooping everything into a brown shopping bag.

"Julie," he said, "how come—"

She kept gathering things, a crazy doll, a date book. "I quit."

JR's teeth almost met in his cigar. "You *what?*"

"Cliff Barnes; he got that file from me."

He felt mule-kicked, all the wind driven out of him by a hard hoof in the belly. "W-why? You sell me out, after all these—"

Now she lifted her face and looked at him. "There was no money offered or taken. I guess I liked the way he made love and thought he deserved a reward, a little bonus, for being so damned good in bed. At least he stayed for breakfast." Julie's face was set, and her eyes showed she had been crying, but they were dry now. "Do I love him? You won't ask that, but I don't even have that excuse, because I don't love anybody. I don't think I've even cared for myself—not for a long, long time."

JR said, "Tell me *why*, Julie."

She hefted the shopping bag and took a final look around the office. "Because you have to ask, that's why." She didn't slam the outer door; in fact, Julie left it open, so he could see her reach the elevator.

Its light blinked, the door slid open, and Pamela stepped out to stare in surprise at Julie. Julie said, "Okay, I told him," and stepped into the elevator. "You take care now, hear?"

Starting into his office, JR was stopped by Pamela's chilly voice: "Were you going to keep quiet about it, JR?"

"I figured you'd tell him quick enough."

She came nearer. "And you? Is that all I get from you? No apology?"

He eyed her, this pushy, always crowding kind of woman who had reached so far above herself when she married the youngest Ewing. JR could see that she was determined to stay where she was, entrench herself with the family so there would be little chance of tossing her back out onto the street. His mother, the old man, possibly even Sue Ellen, would be leaning toward her side now. For JR had twice been wrong, twice underestimated Pamela Barnes Ewing and been made to look like a fool.

He said, "Would an apology mean anything?"

"Not really," she said, "not comin' from you."

"Hey, look," he said, "I put my foot in it twice already, but that don't mean we can't start all over, be friends and kinfolk."

She flashed him a smile as false as his overture. "You've been after me ever since I married Bobby, after my blood. I haven't tried puttin' my knife in you, JR—not yet. But if you don't stay on your side of our little demilitarized zone, don't be surprised to wake up some morning and find your throat's been cut while you slept."

Snorting with disbelief that she could possibly do anything to hurt him, JR didn't entirely disregard the faint warning signal in the back of his mind. He said, "Okay, then—a truce. Do we kiss and make up, or shake hands on it?"

Pamela's smile was bright, the same kind of smile one woman would show to her rival. She said softly, "No, thank you. I'd just as soon kiss a diamondback and shake with a tarantula."

He wanted to slam a fist into her painted-up mouth, teach this trashy bitch a good lesson. But JR still had good sense; Bobby would flat-out kill him if he laid a finger on this woman. Reaching back inside his head, he could still bring out the vivid memory of little seven-year-old Bobby and the butcher knife. All a combat tour in Vietnam had done to Bobby was toughen him, make him even more volatile. Look what he'd done to that whole damned bunch in the Big D disco, including Ray Krebs. Could be Bobby Ewing was suffering from combat fatigue, crazy enough so that he might be dangerous to himself and others. It was a pretty good idea, to be filed and kept for future reference.

Pamela dipped to him in an ironic mock curtsey, then walked lithely into Bobby's office. JR thought on how she'd look, stripped to the skin and tied down on a bed, arms and legs jerked wide apart and fastened so she couldn't do any more than buck and wiggle. Be fun to see how uppity she'd act then, how she'd roll her eyes and try to beg when his thumb dug in to open her jaws, when he fed it to her, forcing her to do what was good for him. The bitch; the strutting, sassy bitch. One of these days he just might find out what made her so attractive to Bobby, what power she carried between her legs to make Bobby Ewing kick over the traces when he had all the fine women in Texas he wanted.

In Bobby's office, Pamela said, "She admitted it. Poor Julie admitted giving the trust deed to my brother."

"*Poor* Julie? She just about got the roof caved in on you and you're sorry for her?"

"Because I think I understand," Pamela said. "Because I'm a woman. It had to do with JR's treatment of her, which caused her to strike back at him—with the paper. She is, or was, sleeping with Cliff, and didn't look too happy about it this morning. Yes, I say poor Julie. She quit her job and probably has no place to go or anyone waiting for her, and it's sad; it's sad as hell."

Bobby took her in his arms, kissed her ear. "If you can feel so deeply for Julie after she put you in such a bind with the family, then somehow it must not be all her fault. Don't look so down, hon. I'll see that JR doesn't blackball her, or better still, maybe I can get her a good job in Austin with one of the state senators. She *is* a fine secretary, and we can lay off her quittin' to something else, personality problems with JR, say."

He felt good, felt tender and comforting, but Pamela drew back and looked at him. "So long as you aren't plannin' to keep on usin' her. Don't be another JR, darlin'—please don't let this business turn you into another JR. And damn me for gettin' so paranoid as to think you might."

Pulling her back into the circle of his protection,

Bobby nuzzled into her hair. "The business itself is paranoid, baby. But maybe—just perhaps—I can straighten out this end of it, and make Ewing Oil a respected name."

"Is that so important to you?" she asked into his chest.

"I guess. I wouldn't be here if it wasn't. The old man wouldn't like it, and Mother would be hurt more than she'd show, but we could walk right now. I mean, with enough money to do nothin' but have fun for the rest of our lives." Bobby stroked her hair and tried to put it all into words. "But having fun and doin' nothing—that just doesn't hack it, Pam. Everybody has to point in some direction, have some kind of goal. If he doesn't, nothin' makes a whole lot of sense. If you're wrong, if you got pointed the wrong way—all right; turn around and take another shot at it."

Gently, he moved her from him, sat her in a big leather chair that made her feel tiny. Leaning against the front of his desk, Bobby continued: "In the Nam, there might be weeks when nobody did anything—not us, not the slopes. Everybody was all pulled up tight with the waitin', with nothin' happening, and scared that it might *start* happening. Civilians can't understand that, maybe. I got a chance to think a lot in the Nam, to point myself somewhere. But still it took *you* to get me started, move me away from the fun and nothin'."

She tilted her head. "You'd have done it anyway."

"Maybe, but maybe never. It's so damned easy to just slide along—if nobody's shootin' at you. But somebody's always shootin'; in real life here, the bullets may be paper, but they're damned near as deadly. Since I've been in the office, I've gotten a feel of Ewing Oil, and it's not just folks carryin' the name. It's a lot of others, drillers and survey men and riggers and just about every kind of job you can imagine. *And* their families, so many wives and so many kids. It's paid holidays and pension plans and new cars. What's done in this set of offices affects that many people."

"I can see that," Pamela murmured. "But are you certain about what you want, about your direction?"

His face was serious. "I think so, hon. I think I want to reshape this entire company, turn it into somethin' real and good and honest."

Standing up, Pamela reached her hands to his face, lay her fingers lovingly upon Bobby's cheeks. "I hope you can, darlin'. I just hope the business doesn't reshape you, instead."

CHAPTER 30

He always got this lift in his belly when he opened the door of a motel room for a new woman. JR was expansively drunk, but not beyond his capacity. And the woman—she was pretty as any you'd find, a mite better looking than the one Ray Krebs had in the room next door, and this was as it should be.

The woman—what the hell was her name?—swung on inside, carrying mix and glasses. JR already had the ice and there was a machine close by in case they needed more. Good old Ray, he thought, eyeing the attractive play of light upon nylon-sheathed legs. Ray Krebs could find women anywhere in the state, good-looking women who were more than willing.

Wanda, that's who she was, and if she had a last name he'd never heard it, and didn't want to. In the next room, with the connecting door wide open, was good old Ray with a woman called Mary Lou. That one was trim and black-headed; JR's was a redhead, chunkier and chestier.

Throwing off his coat and tie, JR worked the cap off a bottle of CC and poured healthy shots into plastic glasses, added ice and cola. When he turned around, Wanda was out of her dress but still in bra and panties, and she purely looked fine—big old knockers spilling out, plump white thighs and a flat belly. And no whore; Ray'd been definite about that. These two were housewives out on the town, and that made it better for JR, knowing he would be putting it to another man's wife, screwing somebody else's old lady.

"Here's to," Wanda said, lifting her glass in a way that made the boob on that side damned near jump out of its basket.

"To what?" he asked, sitting on the bed beside her. He could just about see through her panties and she wasn't a true, complete redhead, but what the hell.

"To us and everything," Wanda said.

"I'll drink to that," JR said. "And to a mighty pretty woman."

She grinned. "Good to hear that from a man once in a while. My old man, now, he don't ever say nice things to me; not no more."

JR said, "Not even when he's mountin' you?"

Holding out her glass for more, Wanda said, "Especially not then, and that ain't all so often, nohow. Acts like I'm a piece of meat, like a side of beef or somethin' and ain't got no say-so in what's to happen. The uptight bastard screws like a missionary; know what I mean?"

"Yeah," JR said, refilling her glass and freshening his own. "Ain't it hell bein' married to somebody don't even know *how* to screw?"

"Bet your ass," Wanda said. "Well, here's to."

"Here's to," JR echoed and peeped around into the other room. Mary Lou was already bare-assed, sitting on the bed with her legs crossed and drinking whiskey like it was pink lemonade and she was at the circus. Not much tit but nice long legs, JR thought, and got another good idea: later on, when they each got tired of screwing the women they had, him and Ray would change over. There was always something new to be tried out, and that's the way it ought to be.

"That buddy of yours," Wanda said, "seems to be a whole lot of man."

"Reckon you can try him on for size after."

"Hot damn," the woman said, "here's to."

A sure-enough fun night, JR thought, because a woman like this was in it to get all the good she could, while her old man was out of town or wherever. He figured she wouldn't mind doing him, and she didn't; went right after it like she was starvation hungry.

He wallowed her all over the bed after she got him up good and strong, and she gave him back lick for lick, grunting and sweating to him, with him, as he plowed up another man's pea patch. Wanda was a talker, too; she kept telling him what to do to her and exactly what it felt like when he did. She made him feel good, calling him lover and studhorse and complimenting him on the way he used his rod. JR hung onto her for a while after they both made it, account of she was a prize of sorts and he liked her.

Then, as he was mixing more drinks for them, he looked into the other room and got turned on all over again. Old Ray Krebs had really laid it to the slim girl, to Mary Lou, so she was sprawled panting and twitching across the bed.

Wanda said, "Cute ain't she? My brother's wife, and he ain't a bit better'n my old man; that's how come she's out with me. Them damned dirt farmers don't care none about *us*, just in gettin' fed and their clothes washed, and a sometimes piece of ass."

"Well now," JR said, "if you ready for it, trot on in yonder to Ray and send your sister-in-law here to me. Tell you one thing; we're sure meanin' to show our appreciation to you fine young ladies, yessirree. Now, I know you girls ain't the commercial type, and I don't mean to insult you none. But I guess any lady can use a crisp hundred-dollar bill to buy her some pretty lil' things."

Stark naked, the marks of his passion still upon her, Wanda came around the bed to kiss him. "Knowed you was a true gentleman soon as I laid eyes on you—

and I'll be back, sugar; back for the rest of the night, if'n you can stand it."

Slapping her on the butt, he said, "Don't you fret about *me* makin' it, Wanda. Just don't let ol' Ray burn you down."

"No man ever did that yet, sugar."

He watched her roll her tail sassily as she went into the other room, and watched with just as much interest when Mary Lou came back. Mary Lou was some shyer, and had a towel wrapped around her hips. JR howdied her and sat her down; he mixed drinks while he smoked a cigar and let her keep the towel. Those little knockers of hers were pert and their nipples stuck out cute.

Just to make talk, he said, "You-all do this a lot? Run around to juke joints, I mean?"

Softer-voiced, younger, she said, "Gets right borin' to home, and a gal's just got to have a little excitement, a little spice to her life. Ain't that so?"

"Right as rain," JR chuckled. "I got some spice right here, do you want to taste it."

The towel dropped away when she scrooched over to lay her face against his belly. "Looks kind of used up."

"Just hidin', sweetheart. See can you find him and haul him out to do his job."

She nuzzled closer, and with a mischievous giggle, said, "Hell, big man—I'll make him think he's a flagpole in a high wind."

And the woman knew what she was about, JR admitted; old Ray and him would have to come this way again. It was turning into one hell of a party, and it took a lot of firewater to keep it wet down.

Resting, JR stared blurrily at the ceiling and thought it was big of Ray to forget and forgive like he did. Damned Bobby had just about tore off his head back in that disco, and for nothing. Ray filled him in on exactly what happened, how Lucy came to him so he'd get that smart-ass Roger kid off her back. And yonder comes Bobby all lit up like a Mexican fiesta, not giving anybody a chance to explain, poleaxing Ray when he didn't expect it, then busting him over the head with a chair leg. It was a prime wonder Ray hadn't give notice at the ranch, but JR told him that bigod, Bobby Ewing wasn't running *anything* yet, much less the ranch.

"Huh?" he said, and "Huh?" again, when Wanda crawled back on the bed with him. Good thing she was drunk as he was, else he'd have been forced to face up that he was getting old. About then, all he wanted to do was sleep, but no—she kept yammering about them hundred-dollar bills until he hauled out his wallet and gave her a couple. Spilled everything else, though, and was too damned wore out to care; he just let it be and lay back on the pillow.

About thirty seconds later, seemed like, Ray Krebs was shaking him by the shoulder. "It's that time, boss."

Head aching, mouth all matted, JR whispered, "Don't wake 'em, for chrissake. Gimme a second—"

He pissed, stuck his head under the cold shower, and wrapped his hair dry with a bath towel. His stomach churned, and JR thought he'd put off trying a cigar for a while. He was still rubbing his hair when he came out into the room and fumbled with his clothes.

"Ought to get goin'," Ray said.

"Yeah, yeah; just a minute. Looks like I spilled everything here—no, I'll pick it all up. Gave her some money for both of 'em."

"You didn't have to do that, boss."

"Know it," JR answered, scooping up business cards and credit cards and bills, stuffing them back into his wallet. "But next time we come this way, won't they be hot to trot?"

Ray laughed without making much noise. "Damned if you ain't somethin' *else*, JR."

There was about an inch of bourbon in the bottle. JR closed his eyes and forced it down, waited a second for the warm bomb to go off inside his belly. Feeling better, he said, "And one thing's for damned sure—I get the clap, you got it, too. Share and share alike."

Shaking his head, looking fresher than he should, Ray Krebs eased them out of the room. By the time they reached JR's Mustang, JR could work his lighter at a cigar. He jerked a thumb at the other Mustang in the lot of the Tropicana Motel, a dented and dusty orange, its seats covered with fake leopard skin. "Ain't that somethin'? Them old gals sure know how to get around. You better drive, Ray—my eyes ain't exactly workin' yet."

As Ray eased the car out onto the highway, JR locked the cigar between his teeth and put his head back on the seat. The shot of bourbon had made him just about human, and he could go back over every detail of the night. Some party; *some* goddamned party.

The man driving the '61 Ford half-ton was called Luther, and his parents named him right. He had that set and somber look of a man of purpose, the humorless, hard-lined face of a believer—in something. He said, "This here motel's about the last I'm tryin'. Them bitches ain't found by then, best we go on home and lay for 'em."

His partner was younger and would have been handsome but for the narrow setting of his eyes and the permanent half-smile that showed his teeth. "Wanda never was much account," he said. "Now she's got Mary Lou doin' the same thing."

"Shut up, goddamnit," Luther said. "You didn't have that much to say when I courted her, Payton Allen."

The vapid smile flickered. "Uh-uh, account of I figured you'd take her slap off'n my hands. Never figured on you movin' in."

"Brought my share and do more'n my share of the work," Luther said. "Who's bustin' his ass while you out slippin' around town and the stills?"

"The Lord didn't mean for Payton Allen to be no raggedy-assed poor dirt farmer."

"Your ass ain't covered no better'n mine. What's the Lord a-waitin' on?"

"Not for you to be trompin' on your old lady."

Muddy eyes cut a spiteful look at him, and Luther said, "You ain't goin' to whup on Mary Lou?"

"Sure, but not so's to bust her snatch or somethin'. If'n she means to screw around, she might's well get paid for it."

Luther spat from his window. "*My* lawful wife ain't about to be called no whore."

"Shoot," Payton said, his upper lip curling up and back again, "ol' Wanda was screwin' for a bottle of Nehi Orange and a Moon Pie by the time she was twelve years old."

"Goddamnit," Luther said, "looka yonder. That's sure'n billy hell her car."

"Screwed for that, too," Payton said. "Growed out'n Moon Pies, I reckon."

"You walleyed son of a bitch," Luther said, "quit talkin' about your blood sister thataway. Hand me down that rifle from the rack."

Shaking his head, Payton said, "You just don't go hellin' into a fancy motel totin' no rifle. Folks'll call the law, sure'n shit. You got your short gun, ain't you? Besides, you a plain fool, do you plan on bustin' caps around here. Highway patrol be here quicker'n you can say scat."

Luther parked the battered pickup next to the orange Mustang. "Which 'un you reckon they in?"

Payton climbed out and shrugged. "Start with the first and go ahead on."

Hammering on the door, Luther stood squat and dirt-stained, heavy head and beat-up hat thrust forward. Somebody mumbled behind the door and Luther hammered again. The door opened and a man in flowered pajamas stood there rubbing his eyes and saying what the hell. Luther pushed on by him and looked around. Out again, he said, "Ain't here."

The man said, "You slap out'n your mind? I'm gonna call the law and—"

Luther showed him the handle of a pistol under his patched shirt. "And you'd be dead, time I hear that sireen squallin'. Get on back and forget it."

It looked like fun, so Payton tried the handle of the next door and showed more tooth when it turned. Peering in, he motioned to Luther. "There she lays, and a door open to another room." He took out a knife and snapped open a long blade. "Expect somebody might be in yonder with Mary Lou. Wanda's alone."

He slid through the rooms, smiling, always smiling. Luther went over to the rumpled bed and looked around at the empty whiskey bottle, the glasses, the cigar butts in an ashtray. Then he leaned over and took his wife by the hair.

"Hey, baby," she said, pawing at his arm. "Cut that out; you're hurtin' me."

He used her hair like a whip, and flung her head into the wall. When she moaned and fell off the bed, he wheeled to check out the bathroom, disappointed to find it empty.

From the connecting door Payton said, "Mary Lou's by herself, too. What kinda whorin' around is this? You expect these here women gone queer for each other?"

"Not less'n one of 'em smokes big cigars," Luther said. Back at the bed, he straightened out a sheet and came up with a business card. "Well now," he said.

Payton eeled by him and stooped over his naked, dazed sister. "Ain't this a howdy-do?" He snatched and showed his hand to Luther. "Two hundred dollars; you ever see hundred-dollar bills afore, Luther? Shoot; get rich slicker'n greased owlshit, thisaway."

"Bastard," Wanda said, pushing herself half erect. "That money's mine and—and Mary Lou's."

"Hooie!" Payton said. "How'd you run a hundred men through here in one night?"

Still groggy, Wanda came to her knees, heavy breasts sagging. Brushing hair from her eyes, rubbing the back

of her head, she said, "Luther, I don't know what got
into me, I swear."

Luther said, "I know what got into you, all right.
About six inches got into you, bitch. What I mean to
find out is *who* got into you, and damned if'n it don't
look like my hard luck's fixin' to change. Got me a
business card here, all fancy made so the letters stick
up. Tells me just *who* mounted you in this bed."

Wanda said, "Luther, make him give you one of
them bills. Won't do you no good to stir up a mess
about this."

He slapped her, hard. Wanda's head hit the wall
again and her eyes glazed; a spot of bright red appeared at the corner of her mouth. Luther said, "You
Babylon whore! How poison drippeth from the mouth
of a woman—you think I'm about to take this last
piece of shit lyin' down? I been gettin' hit with shit
every born year of my life, and I'm goddamned tired
of it. I'm right up to my craw with it, and I mean to
do some turd-chunkin' myself."

"Got us two hundred dollars to do it on," Payton
said. "Can't the chunkin' wait till we has breakfast in
a shiny café, get us a couple bottles of store-bought
whiskey? Hooie! Pay for it with a hundred-dollar bill."

"Yeah," Luther said. "Yeah, then we hightail it out
to the place on this card, and you know what we're
goin' to do? We're goin' to pay 'em back in their own
dirty coin. We'll fuck *their* women like they fucked
ours."

"Good," Payton said. "For a second there, I thought
you meant to give 'em back this-here money."

CHAPTER 31

The radio played country and western, and outside the car windows, country flowed past. Traffic was light and Ray Krebs handled the Mustang smoothly, expertly. Eyes shut, cigar gone out, JR said, "Wish to hell I could sleep in a car. I need it. Them women like to have ate me up."

"Ought to be home in a couple of hours," Ray said. "All the hands are takin' the day off for fiesta. Slow season, anyhow; nothin' heavy to do until the last cuttin' of hay, now that the spring herd's been sold off."

Shifting his cold cigar from one corner of his mouth to the other, JR said, "Sure happy you needed me out here to give you some help with the sale."

Ray chuckled. "Figured you to be overdue on really gettin' your ashes hauled. No matter how much a man's got at home, he has to dip his wick in somethin' new."

"Shit," JR grunted. "What I got at home ain't worth the time and trouble. But speakin' of wives— *you* oughta know how come Bobby is so pussy-whipped he can't think for himself no more."

For a while, the car hummed along, then Ray said, "You mean that, JR? I don't aim to be puttin' down nobody in the family—"

"That nut damned near killed you; you don't owe *him* nothin'. Yeah, I want to know, because that woman's leadin' him around by the cock. Bobby never messed into things that didn't concern him till he tied up with Pamela Barnes."

Slowly, Ray said: "She's a whole lot of woman, and she does it all, man. She does it and *enjoys* what she's doin' and that makes all the difference, I expect. I ought to know, because I broke her in, got her cherry when she wasn't but fourteen. And I hand-raised her careful, one step at a time, brought her along slow and easy. She just might be the—well, the best I ever had."

"Damn," JR muttered. "You figure the boy knows what to *do* with all that?"

They laughed together and Ray felt easier in his mind. He'd been on edge ever since Bobby Ewing hit him that cheap shot in the disco, halfway expecting to be given notice, told to draw his time. Where else could a guy young as him get a job on top of the pile, drawing down the kind of money he was making? And if old Jock got mean about it and blackballed him—forget working in Texas and maybe a couple of other states too. But as long as JR was on his side, Ray planned on staying around for a long time to come.

The radio music stopped, and an announcer cut in. "A sudden tropical storm is blowing up from the Gulf of Mexico and has practically sealed off the city of Houston. Telephone communications have been cut, and gusts of up to one hundred miles per hour have closed the airport and major highways. The storm is moving northwest across the state; small-craft advisories have been posted along the coast, and—"

JR sat up. "Twist her tail, Ray. We best get home before that thing hits."

Ray put the gas pedal to the floor and the Mustang leaped out.

The drapes were pulled and Ellie Ewing's bedroom was dark. She lay atop the covers, her eyes closed, hoping the codeine she'd swallowed would take a better hold. Just so many of those pills, and the stomach went out, turned sour, and refused to accept any more. And the pain went on, the over-one-eye nail that pene-

trated bone and brain and tried to come out the back
of the neck.

Trying to pull her mind off the migraine, she
thought of Pamela, that cast of face and glancing eye
that reminded her so much of Willard Barnes. She
would carry his image all her life, what was left of it.
First love, the only poet, wild and footloose and often
crazy man—Ellie didn't know if she ever wanted to
see him now, to know the awful changes time made
upon face and body.

She touched her own cheeks, their skin toughened by
sun and wind, seamed with much age and a few deep
sorrows. Would she want him to see *her?* Perhaps he
held the young picture of her in his mind, as she carried him. Now, with the wrinkles and seams and faded
hair, the shoulders stooping no matter what she did to
hold them up, the other sagging places high and low,
she lived in a body she could not herself recognize.

Ellie pressed the heel of one hand against the right
side of her forehead. She hadn't been unhappy with
Jock, and if they didn't often climb the pinnacles of
rapture together, so be it. He was solid and she knew
him to the core; she was old-shoe comfortable with
him, and they had mixed their blood in the boys.

The boys . . . a girl such as Pamela might have
been better, somewhere in between. Pretty as a bluebell, and underneath, tough as whang leather. Ellie
had been elated to get word Pamela wasn't the spy, and
carried a load of guilt for not standing up for the girl
when JR came down so hard on her. She would apologize, Ellie thought, in front of the whole family at the
supper table. *If* Pamela and Bobby came back to the
ritual suppers; if they moved back into the small
house.

Back in her own young time, Ellie Southworth
might not have come back so easy. She might have
made some folks eat humble pie for a while. But then,
Ellie Southworth hadn't been all that easy to get along
with.

Ellie Ewing had mellowed, settled herself as the

years went by. If the ranch got into trouble, a lean year or two hadn't meant so much after she married Jock. What beef couldn't do, oil made up for. She rubbed her head, turned over and thought of her pa. If he could see the ranch now, he wouldn't fault her for breaking that promise so long ago. She'd kept it ever since, though Jock brought it up from time to time that they ought to drill on this section or that. Just that once, and her move had saved the Southfork, backfire or no, for out of it had come Jock Ewing.

"Miss Ellie? I brought you a tray, if you can manage to eat somethin'."

She turned onto her back. "Thanks, Sue Ellen—but not now. JR back yet?"

"Any time, I expect."

"Set awhile, Sue Ellen." Ellie took a series of deep breaths; sometimes they helped against the pain. "You think Pamela can be comfortable here?"

Sue Ellen hesitated. "Well, JR says—"

"JR's muley as Jock. But far as I can see, Pamela's good for Bobby, good for us. Jock thinks so, too—but won't admit it."

"I—I don't know, Miss Ellie. I mean, it's kind of like she doesn't fit—but I reckon that's up to you. She—she came back about an hour ago and I told her you had a sick headache."

So she was back. Ellie smiled and reached for another long breath, more oxygen. Bobby couldn't have driven that girl back if she didn't want to come. No more than young Ellie Southworth could have been gee-hawed into doing something she'd bowed her neck against.

"Tell you what," Ellie said, "if all of us thought more of her as Bobby's wife, instead of Digger Barnes's daughter, we'd get along better."

"Yes'm," Sue Ellen murmured. "If you say so."

Downstairs, the phone rang and Pamela picked it up because the upstairs extensions would be unplugged. They always were when Miss Ellie had a headache.

"Bobby—yes, dear. No, I've only seen Sue Ellen so far. Your mother has a migraine. What?"

Bobby said, 'Storm warning. You hear about it out there? JR, Ray—oh hell; they're off somewhere, and the hands are gone, too. Big wind, Pam—things have to be buttoned up on a ranch, taken care of."

She said, "Hey, I'm a Texan, too—remember?"

"This thing turns into a twister, you'll find out how different it is in town and on an open ranch. Look: If JR and Ray aren't back in an hour or so, call me and I'll come runnin'. Right now there are some people to see, and with JR out of the office—"

"I know," Pamela said. "Don't worry. If it looks bad here, I'll call right away. Love you."

When she put down the phone Sue Ellen said from close by, "A tornado? I heard somethin' on the radio, but never paid a whole lot of attention—"

"I don't know the difference between a hurricane and a tornado, a cyclone—whatever they call it. Bobby says a very strong wind is headed this way and he's worried about the ranch, with no men around."

Sue Ellen put one hand to her mouth. "I don't like tornadoes. They scare me bad, and I don't think this place has even *got* a storm cellar."

"Maybe we'd better check the radio," Pamela said. "And Lucy—what about her, off at school? Somebody will have to go after her."

The front door banged open, then shut, and Lucy Ewing said: "No way *I'm* goin' out in that! You-all know they let school out for the day, ran everybody home account of the cyclone comin'?"

"I'm glad you're here," Pamela said. "Were you ever on the ranch in a windstorm?"

"Not like this hundred-mile-an-hour stuff," Lucy said, dropping schoolbooks onto a chair and running both hands over her hair. "Wow! The wind was rockin' the school bus like crazy, and the *big* blow is still on the way."

Sue Ellen said, "I—oh God, I'm scared of it. But we have to—have to— Lucy, you know where Miss

Ellie keeps the coal-oil lamps? Bring 'em in the living room. Pamela, make sure all the windows are closed tight and the drapes drawn. I'll find flashlights and the battery radio. We could lose power any minute— Oh yes, I'll start drawin' buckets of water for the house. No tellin' if that emergency gas generator will work, so in case—"

She was gone, and Lucy put her fists on her hips as she looked after Sue Ellen. "What bit her? I mean, who does she think *she* is, givin' orders like that?"

"Somebody who's been through a bad storm," Pamela said, "which makes her one up on us. Let's get with it, girl."

In the Ewing Oil Building, Bobby hauled out his briefcase and snapped it open. "Connie," he said to his secretary, "I don't like the looks of that sky, and the wind's rising. Suppose you take off the rest of the day and head for home."

"Thanks, Mr. Ewing," Connie said. "My mom gets kind of worried in bad weather. If you don't mind, I'll just hurry on now."

At the outer door, she passed Jock Ewing, said howdy, and her heels went clickety-click to the elevator. Jock said, "Nice girl, but it'll take her a spell to measure up to Julie Parsons."

Bobby put papers in his briefcase. "She's learnin'; we all are. How was the luncheon?"

"Those things never change, not even the menu. That's why I fill up on Mex chili first. Gives me a good excuse to leave the table if some windbag goes on too long." Jock looked around the office, at Bobby. "You goin' somewhere?"

"The ranch; big storm just about gave Houston religion and comin' this way. With JR gone and all hands off for fiesta, includin' the servants, the women are alone out yonder."

"And more'n a bellyful for a tribe of Apaches or a little ol' tornado." Jock moved to the desk and flopped in the big chair facing it. "Ran into Bronk Anderson and some of them old boys; got to tellin' them about how you turned into a first-class, jump-up-and-go-get-'em executive and—"

Bobby saw his father had been drinking through the Chamber of Commerce luncheon, smelled the rich fumes. "And they didn't believe it. We'll show 'em some other time."

"You already checked to home? Well then, wait up a spell and give 'em another call. I made these here dinner arrangements that just ain't goin' to be all that easy to break. Ol' Bronk Anderson now, he's been hearin' things about federal men in Houston." Jock chuckled. "Maybe the storm blowed 'em all away. Sure hope so, account of that investigation's bound to spread a wide loop."

Bobby stopped filling his briefcase. "You mean that old-oil–new-oil scandal that's brewing. *That's* where we should have been trying to clean our britches, instead of worryin' over that piddlin' thing in Austin. Hell, I hear business is *too* good for Houston lawyers, that firms there are sendin' prospective clients far away as New York and Washington."

Peering from beneath bushy brows, Jock said, "You're right, son. But this was closer to home and JR—well, he ain't seen it yet. That's how come we better go talk to Bronk Anderson and them others tonight."

"Oh hell," Bobby said. "Okay then; I'll stay. Here, put your boots up on my desk and take off your hat. I'll shut the door and wake you in a couple of hours."

"Be the damned day," Jock grumbled, "that *I* need to sleep in the middle of it." But when Bobby took his papers into the outer office, his father's eyes were already closed.

Wind fisted the old pickup, rattled a loose fender on it, rocked it on the highway. Luther cursed in a flat monotone and tried to get a clear look through the dust and sand blowing across the road. "Ain't so far now, and don't choke onto that bottle. Pass it here once in a while."

Payton yawned through his smile and said, "How— we just goin' to walk in on them folks and tell 'em we're there to screw their women?"

Luther drank from the bottle and gave it back. "Not hardly, but this here storm's liable to help. If it don't knock out the lines, we will. Hell, I hope them bastards are to home. I'd just as soon make 'em watch where I put it to their old ladies."

Grunting, Payton said, "Hope they ain't all that old."

"If'n they are," Luther said, as a heavy gust rocked the truck and threatened to push it off the road, "then they got daughters, or granddaughters; I don't care which."

"Hey now," Payton said through his teeth and curled-up lip, "hey now, but I ain't knocked off no real young nooky since I got old enough for it to be against the law. Leastwise, I can't recall no ten, twelve year olds of late. Fifteen, maybe."

The wind howled, chopped at tree limbs and uprooted tumbleweeds, hurled them across the land, into the side of the barn, the house. When Ray Krebs stopped the car before the house, JR had to yell at him: "Check the womenfolks, meet you here—bring the jeep—maybe we can herd the young stock into that near gulley—"

"Yeah!" Ray shouted back, and wheeled the Mustang for the barns and loafing shed. So JR was about to help with the ranch, but only because nobody else was there, and he'd be about handy as shoes on a snake. Run around and make a big to-do about rounding up cattle, like he could do something with them afterward. Wasn't a bad idea about putting the yearlings into the gulley with its mouth facing away from the wind. It would give them some protection, if they didn't panic and come boiling out right over anybody or anything holding the draw.

JR fought the wind to keep the back doorknob from being torn from his hands. When he won, he bolted the door and panted into the kitchen.

Sue Ellen said, "Oh, honey, I'm so glad you're here. You know how I'm scared of storms—and Miss Ellie has a migraine—"

"Jesus," he said, "will you quit yammerin' and fetch my jacket? Got some boots in the mud room here—"

Pale, she stared at him. "You didn't call and say you were stayin' over last night."

Peeling his coat, kicking off shoes, JR rummaged for boots. "Got too late, and this mornin'—*will* you get that damned jacket?"

She wheeled and ran from him. The wind rattled windows, moaned around the corners of the house, and the lights dimmed, then came up again. JR stuffed his feet into his boots and snatched the jacket from Sue Ellen when she came back. "What the hell you lookin' bug-eyed at me for?"

Swallowing, she answered, "I—I'm just scared of storms. We—my mama and me—we got caught in one and a big tree fell over on the house and—"

He strode to the door. "Bolt this thing after I'm gone. If the wind gets in here, it'll smash everything. Oh—and see to Miss Ellie every few minutes."

She worked the bolt when he left, then put her forehead against the door and said, "Sure; yeah, all right. All right, JR." In a while, she stepped back and looked through the glass to see the jeep go off with its lights on. So black, so dark in the daytime, she thought, and backed out of the kitchen with her hands clenched.

The front door; something was beating on the front door as the lights flickered again, then dimmed to a yellowish glow. Tree limb, fence post—something. Sue Ellen made out a voice then, hollering. She worked at the front-door lock, and spiteful wind sucked at the door, at her. Two men hunched there, making motions at her, through the snarling wind, and Sue Ellen let them in. One got the door shut, and the other smiled at her, just smiled and smiled.

"Hooie," he said then, "ain't this 'un somethin'?"

CHAPTER 32

Sue Ellen took a backward step, one hand rising to her throat. "What—what do you want?"

The smiling one didn't wear a hat, and there was dust speckling his wavy hair. The other one, the dark and somber man, took off his rain-shaped felt and said, "Ain't no need to fear, missy. Just need a phone, account of our truck broke down back yonder."

Smiling, the other one probed Sue Ellen with light-colored eyes set too close together, and she felt as if he were seeing through her dress, right down to her skin. He said, "Probably the carb got blowed full of sand or somethin'; thing is, can't be workin' on it out yonder in the tornado."

She said, "Well—you're welcome to stay here—awhile."

Luther glanced around the room, at the stairs, the hallway. "Your men all gone?"

"Just—just seein' to the cattle with—the rest of the hands. I expect they'll be back right soon."

"Expect?" Payton said through the fixed smile that bothered her more than anything else.

Why should Sue Ellen be afraid? They were just ordinary men, and only the worst kind of fool would bother any of the Ewings, especially on Ewing land. Lucy and Miss Ellie and Pamela were all in the house, and surely JR and Ray wouldn't be gone very long. There was no reason for fear, and yet. . . .

"Visitors at a time like this?" Lucy skipped into the room, and the men looked at her. She was a little high on the storm's excitement, the way horses get edgy and silly at a sudden weather change.

"Just hidin' out from the wind," Luther said, eyes checkin her tied-off shirt and tight jeans. "Gettin' a mite cool, and I'd be proud to build you a fire, give a hand doin' whatever you ladies need."

Tossing her head, Lucy said, "My, that'd be nice. Wouldn't that be nice, Sue Ellen?"

"I—I guess so," Sue Ellen answered. "Coffee; I'll fix coffee and sandwiches, because the men'll be back soon—"

"Huh!" Lucy said. "Might be hours tryin' to herd those spooky cows, might be even longer."

Sue Ellen fled into the kitchen and said to Pamela, "Two—two strangers in the house; truck broke down, need the phone. Somethin' about them, the look in their eyes—I'm scared, Pamela."

Pamela took her hand. "We can handle whatever comes up. You're afraid of storms, but look how well you did preparing the house and overcoming your fear. You did a great job, Sue Ellen, a great job."

Staring, Sue Ellen said, "Do you r-really think so?"

"We wouldn't have done it without you."

"Gee," Sue Ellen said, "that's the first time in my life—"

"We'll see about those men. Did you leave Lucy with them? How about Miss Ellie—has she come downstairs?" Pamela was still talking as she led the way back into the living room. Sue Ellen stopped her in the hallway and whispered about coffee and food, so Pamela went in alone.

She saw one man kneeling at the fireplace, touching off kindling there; Lucy was standing close by, sway-hipped and with her breasts thrust out, combing at her flowing bright hair with hooked fingers, to draw attention to it and to herself.

Luther was saying, "—and how many hands? Big ol' spread like this oughta hire a passel."

"Don't know offhand," Lucy said. "About twenty at roundup, I'd say, but they're all off celebratin' the Feast of San Antonio, even the blacks. Most of the hands are Mexes, you know."

The little fool, Pamela thought, flirting with these men who carried the hungry, sullen look about them; telling them anything, everything. She said sharply, "Did you men want to use the phone? It's right over there."

"Hooie," Payton whistled from the hearth, "if it ain't another fine 'un. House is plumb full of purty women."

Keeping her chin up, Pamela said, "The phone?"

"Well now," Luther said, shambling toward her, greasy hat in his hands, "seems like the lines is down. Since we can't see to the motor in such a storm, looks like we just got to stay right here. What's your name, purty miss?"

"It doesn't matter," Pamela said. "The men will return in a few minutes and—"

"Sure they ain't off celebratin' some Mex feast, too?"

"Indeed not," Pamela said. "Lucy, come here. We need your help in the kitchen."

"Hurry back," Payton said, winking at the girl, and when they were gone, said to Luther: "Man, man— you ever see three in a row like that? Fine as frog hair, all of 'em. Goin' to be hard pickin' which to screw first."

"Makes no never mind," Luther said. "Mean to stick 'em all, make the high-tone bitches crawl and beg. Goddamn *rich* bitches; you see this here house, all the stuff in it? Hell, the rugs costs more'n all my ol' furniture put together."

"Works out real good," Payton said. "Hands all gone, men gone, too. Wonder which of 'em belongs to the fellas fucked our wives."

"All, I hope," Luther said. "They'll feel it that much more."

Bobby Ewing went to look from the window. The

sky looked yellowish, angry to the east, and the window quivered as a high gust explored it. On his desk, the small radio bleeped and music stopped for an announcer ". . . did so much damage in Houston earlier today is moving quickly for Dallas. Winds in the Waco area are reported at close to one hundred miles per hour . . ."

Bobby moved to his own office and opened the door. Jock was slumped in the big leather chair, boots up on the desk. Behind Bobby the radio rattled on ". . . windows shattered . . . heavy damage . . . Rangers asking that everyone stay off the highways . . . driving hazardous. . . ."

"Dad," Bobby said. "Dad!"

Jock slid his boots off the desk and grunted. "I hear you."

"I'm headin' home. The phone's out and I've got a gut feelin'."

Rubbing his eyes and reaching for his hat, Jock said, "Get a hunch, bet a hunch. If you're frettin' over the womenfolks, best we head on out."

"But the dinner," Bobby said. "Bronk Anderson and the others."

"Act of God," Jock said. "They won't understand that till I explain it clear to 'em."

"It's dangerous," Bobby said. "The Rangers are keepin' all nonemergency traffic off the highway."

"Then you need me more," Jock said, climbing up and shaking himself. "Know every one of them Rangers by name—and what the hell you think—that I'm made outa pink icing or such? Besides, I got the Continental in the garage, and it's heavier than that play-pretty of yours." He started across the reception room. "One more thing besides: Your ma would nag me everlastin' if I let our youngun get blowed away by himself."

Bobby grinned and put a hand on his father's shoulder. "Let's go then."

At the mouth of the narrow draw, JR stood up in

the jeep, waving his arms and his hat at a white-eyed
cow that tried to break past. Sledging him, as if trying
to upend him, the wind nearly threw him out of the
jeep. He sank down and raced the motor, flipped on
the headlights and brights, hit the horn. Useless
damned horn, he thought; couldn't hear it any more
than hollering. The wind sucked all sound out of
your ears and only let in its own wicked howling.

Raising to one knee on the seat, he cupped a hand
beside his eye so he could make out Ray Krebs through
flying bits of brush and a horizontal curtain of stinging dust. The man was using a post setter, hammering
hard to drive a steel post in the side of the draw.
They'd hook field wire to it, use the jeep to draw it
tight to two other posts already sunken, and make a
barricade to keep this bunch of cows out of trouble.

They could get killed here mighty nigh easy as anywhere else, JR thought. Hell, the barns could go, or
the bunkhouse, in a bastard wind like this. The big
house would hold; it had, for a hundred years or more.
JR saw a splotch of white cowface and jumped out of
the jeep to yell and flail his arms. The stupid son of a
bitch ran on past, with no damned idea where it was
headed. Goddamn cows were all stupid, and horses
not much better.

Sand slapped into his cheek and made him spit.
Hanging onto the jeep, he tried to see Ray Krebs and
couldn't for debris and the water in his eyes. Arm
across his face, he plowed around the jeep and bumped
into him. Mouth to JR's ear, Ray roared something
about the wire. They worried one end of the roll free
and Ray fought it to the post, did things with wire
cutters. The wind tried to tear away the wire and JR
hung back against it.

Together, they straightened the wire and got the
jeep rolling; JR held the jeep in place until Ray tied
in to the middle post, then eased it along as the field
wire unrolled.

It was when Ray was securing the final post that
another steer came snorting out wild from the bunch

humped with their tails to the wind. It skidded into Ray and pinned him to the post, bending it, before rocketing back to the herd.

Ray couldn't get up and JR tugged at his arm. Pulling him close, Ray yelled to drop the roll off the jeep, then back it to him. "My—leg! That damned cow—"

Then JR got a shoulder under him, got him lifted to where Ray could help, and he was in the jeep with one leg stuck outside. Lights bobbing, piercing a dust cloud now, the jeep felt its way toward home. JR hoped he was headed for the house, because he'd lost all sense of direction in the blinding, yammering wind, the whirling dark.

Upstairs in the big house, Ellie Ewing eased to her elbows and immediately knew more pressure over the right eye. Setting her teeth, she sat up and put her stocking feet over the side of the bed, then eased herself to the bathroom, where she soaked a cloth in cold water and applied it. Holding her head back, she filled the basin with hot water and plunged her hands into it, holding them there long as she could stand it. The medicine cabinet gave up two Fioranols, and blessedly, they stayed down.

In a few minutes, Ellie felt better. The tom-tom was still behind her eye, throbbing maliciously, but dulled now. Patting her face with a towel, she had just reached her bed again when the lights went out. Because she always kept emergency candles in the bedside table, Ellie had no trouble finding and lighting one.

Better than the brightness for her eyes, she thought, and remembered the days when no electricity reached the ranch. Coal-oil lamps glowed warmly golden then, and nobody stayed up late anyhow because sunup came too fast. They'd hauled water up from a hand-dug well, and kept milk and eggs cool in a rock springhouse. And the smokehouse—what a wealth of hickory smoked meat hung there, sides of beef, hams, slabs of bacon. Lord, who smoked meat nowadays? It was too easy to freeze things, but somehow they didn't taste the same.

"Must be gettin' better," Ellie muttered, "when I can think on something to eat."

Shielding the candle, she got up and walked to the closet, where an oil lamp was stored. Bringing it back to a table, she put it down, lifted the glass shade, turned up the wick, and used the candle to light it. Shade back, wick adjusted, she basked in its glow and said, "There."

Wind hit the house hard, jerked at the eaves, and tried to shake out windows. No such a thing, Ellie thought; this house has stood against the worst northers in Texas, and it'll be firm when all of us are gone, when new generations of Ewings sheltered in it.

She knew every board, every handmade brick of this house, each split shingle of its roof. And Ellie knew its moods, the cranky settling of it in the winter as it complained in creaks and dry groans. She responded to the rattle of it freshening in spring rains, the opening of the old house to summer.

And it was why she knew—through the blunted migraine that something was wrong in the house now, this moment. There was a tightness, a waiting—and not for the storm; the house had faced to the wind and defied it. No, it was something else. Ellie put her feet into soft slippers and drew an old robe about herself.

Downstairs, Luther said, "You women—set over yonder on the divan."

"Why?" Pamela asked.

"Don't give me no sass, woman. Do like I say, or I'll knock a knot on you, sudden."

She swallowed and held her chin up. "Do you know *where* you are, *who* you're messin' with? This is Ewing land, mister—and we're Ewing people, all of us. What Jock Ewing doesn't own around here, he runs."

"Jock Ewing," Luther said. "That'd be John Ewing,

Jr., like it says on this here card?" He flung the bit of
cardboard at her face, but Pamela didn't flinch.

"That's one of his sons," she said. "JR's got a long
arm, too. You hurt anybody in this house, and you'll
be a long time runnin', mister—or a long time dead."

Two swift steps, and Luther backhanded her, the
meaty sound loud in the room as Pamela staggered and
fell on the couch. "You think I give a good goddamn
about Ewings or President Johnsons or any other *rich*
bastards in Texas? Son of a bitches piss on me ever'
time I turn around, grind my face in the dirt, keep one
hand in my pocket and t'other at my neck." His dark
eyes were distended, marble-shiny. "I'll just burn this
fuckin' house down to the fuckin' ground, if'n I got a
mind to!"

"Luther," Payton said. "Now, Luther—"

"Now, Luther, *shit!* It ain't enough a bastard like
this robs me on company store books, and sweats me
to a nub, now he's screwin' my wife, just like I'm a
goddamn *nigger* and got no say-so to it." The pistol
snaked out of his back pocket, short and ugly, efficient.
Luther said, "Well, I got me a say-so. You, yella-
headed gal—hist on over yonder and bring me some
whiskey. I say frog, you *jump!* T'other woman, set
yourself on the divan next to the sassy 'un."

Payton said, "Make 'em name theirselfs, Luther.
Hate to get 'em mixed up."

He pointed a grubby finger, and Pamela gave her
name through rapidly swelling lips. Lucy answered
meekly, and Sue Ellen spoke up, her voice too loud
and too high. Pamela glanced at her and saw the strain
around eyes and mouth, the quiver of barely contained
hysteria.

Pamela said, "Don't worry, Sue Ellen. If this one's
got no sense, maybe the other doesn't want to be run
down and stomped like a bug."

"You better hush, woman," Luther grated. "You
just better hush. Now—which 'un belongs to that John
Ewing, Jr.?"

"Don't say anything," Pamela warned.

Cat-quick despite his chunky bulk, Luther snatched out and caught her hair. She smothered a scream as he jerked her off the couch and flung her to the floor.

"Hooie!" Payton chortled, "You see them slick legs and lil' old frilly pants? I just as soon take dibs on this 'un, Luther."

"Take what I give you," Luther said. "Sloppy seconds, maybe. Now who's this Junior's woman?"

"I—I am," Sue Ellen said.

"Why looky here," Payton said, "if'n it ain't the same woman in that big picture yonder, her with the ribbon crost her titties. Says Miss Texas on it. That true, woman—you Miss Texas?"

"I w-was," Sue Ellen said. "Please, if—if my husband did somethin' to you, wronged you, why don't you t-take it out on me, and let the others go?"

"Get up," Luther said, nudging Pamela with his foot. "Rise up and set, so you all look like them three wise monkeys, all in a row." He glared at Sue Ellen then. "*If* your husband done somethin' to me? Ain't you heard me good, woman? I said he screwed my old lady, and somebody with him put the meat to Payton's wife, too."

Sue Ellen said, "I d-don't believe that."

"You think I give a cowturd what you believe? There's the card with his name to it, the card I pulled out from under my old lady's naked ass in a motel bed. Stand up, Miss Texas."

She sat, fingers digging into the couch, then forced herself erect, eyes locked to his in dread fascination. Sue Ellen was numb on the outside, but beneath that unfeeling surface, tremor after tremor rocked her, stirred her blood, and she didn't know why.

"Start takin' it off," Luther ordered. "Ever' damned stitch of clothes."

"Listen," Pamela said. "There's a jeep outside. You guys better hightail it while you can."

"I hear it," Payton said. "Luther?"

"Move around down here and collect guns," Luther answered. "Always a passel of guns around a ranch house. Put 'em in a pile where can't nobody reach 'em. Get a pistol for yourself. I'll just wait for somebody to come through that there door."

"Luther, maybe we best—"

Luther chopped air with his pistol. "*No,* goddamnit! We come too far, been down too long. You try'n run out on me, you won't run far."

"Ah hell, Luther, you know I didn't mean—"

"Get them damned guns!"

Sue Ellen stood motionless, one hand lifted to the buttons of her blouse, her heart racing madly. Pamela wanted to yell a warning, but was stopped by the ominous muzzle of the pistol. Lucy shrank against the couch pillows, really afraid for the first time.

Flinging the door back, JR wobbled into the room with Ray's arm about his neck, with Ray leaning against him and keeping weight off the injured leg. Stepping behind them, Payton closed the door and locked it, then smiled expectantly at Luther.

"Hurt," JR panted, "Ray's leg—hurt—gimme a hand, stretch him out on the couch—"

"Floor'll do just fine," Luther announced and showed them the gun he held. "Lay him down quick."

"What the hell—" JR blustered, and Ray Krebs said, "Better do it, JR."

JR swung his eyes around the room, saw the women gathered, the men with guns. Then Luther said, "Go on, Miss Texas—get naked."

CHAPTER 33

"Money," JR said. "Not much in the house, but some jewelry—"

"After," Luther said, taking a left-handed drink from the whiskey bottle, his other fist holding the snub-nosed pistol steady. "After we get justice for you stickin' my old lady. You, cowboy—you the one screwed Mary Lou?"

Head and shoulders against an overstuffed chair, one hand squeezing down on his outstretched leg, Ray Krebs said, "Might be: didn't Wanda split the money with her?"

"You son of a bitch," Luther said, and stepped to slash the gun alongside Ray's head. Ray fell over onto his side and Lucy screamed, a keening of surprise and fear cut short when Luther looked at her.

"Wait a minute," JR said, "I can get you a lot more money—thousands of dollars."

Payton said, "Hear that, Luther?"

"You," Luther said to Sue Ellen, "keep right on peelin', baby."

Face gone mottled, JR said, "You raggedy-assed red-necks—you think you can get away with comin' in here and threatenin' *Ewing* women? Every Ranger in the state'll be on your tails the second you leave here. Wise up and take the money—ten thousand; ten thousand dollars—more'n you ever saw in your lives."

"Damn, Luther," Payton said. "Just think on that."

"High-priced ass," Luther grunted. "Our old ladies wasn't worth but a hundred apiece." He took another drink from the bottle. "Way I figure, it'll cost you that much *after* they been dicked, if'n you want to keep 'em good for it. You ever see a woman get a bottle rammed up her?"

JR lunged from his chair, arms spread wide as Payton yelled a warning. Viciously, Luther chopped twice with the gun barrel, making meaty noises against JR's head and driving his face into the carpet. One arm dropped across Ray's bad leg, and Ray stirred, groaned.

Sue Ellen had continued to move her hands, robot-like, staring straight ahead. She dropped her blouse, unhooked and stepped out of her skirt. In bra and half-slip, she stood for a moment, then reached behind her back to unhook her bra. Her breasts leaped out, their tips pinkly erectile.

"Sue Ellen," Pamela said, "please—"

She dropped the half-slip to puddle about her feet, lifted high heels one by one with a whispered song of nylon panty hose. Her eyes never left Luther's scowling face.

"Ain't that somethin'?" Payton husked.

"Yeah," Luther said. "C'mere, woman."

Obediently, jerkily, she obeyed him. He put down the whiskey bottle and played one hand over her breasts, rolling the nipples cruelly between thumb and forefinger. Sue Ellen caught her breath, but made no other sound. Her fingers toyed with the waistband of her panty hose.

Pamela said through a constricted, aching throat, "The money's better, you know. We—we'll double it: twenty thousand."

"Aw come on, Luther," Payton said. "That'll make you'n me *rich*. You so anxious for strange ass, you can have a go at Mary Lou. Damn—twenty thousand!"

"After," Luther growled, squeezing a breast until a tear rolled down Sue Ellen's cheek. Still, she didn't cry out. "You keep that short gun steady on these here others, Payton. You let somebody mess you up, and you might's well let 'em kill you, cause if'n they don't, I mean to put one right in your belly button. You got that, Payton?"

"Yeah," Payton said sullenly, "I got it, but I thought you was goin' to make their men watch—"

"Changed my mind, account of the way Miss Texas is actin' up. Goin' to take a while on her, so never you mind about the time. Way that gale's a-blowin' outside, won't nothin' nor nobody be movin' around till it stops."

Left arm around Sue Ellen's waist, Luther led her off into the library. She went quietly, her hips brushing his, her head up and the movements of her body lithe, sensuous, graceful.

Pamela said then, "You've got more sense than your partner. Let us go, and get all that money for yourself."

"Might," Payton said, sidling around with his big automatic as JR moaned against the carpet and Ray Krebs pawed at blurred eyes. "Might, exceptin' you all ain't got it here in cold cash. I ain't even figured out how Luther means to get it. And whatever you do, sassy lady—don't get him no more riled. I mean, Luther is one crazy scudder, and he's liable to burn down this whole house and everybody in it. Just do like he says and maybe we'll *all* get outa here with our hides on."

Reaching to take Lucy's hand, Pamela found it cold, and reassured the girl by squeezing. JR muttered and sat up, hand pressing the side of his cut head. Ray got propped erect again. Pamela thought that neither of them looked eager, or capable enough, to try anything on their guard. She concentrated on listening to the wind mourn around the house, to the rattle of strained windows and the occasional *pop!* of a torn-away tree branch. Pamela didn't want to hear any sounds from the library, and pulled Lucy close to tuck the girl's head into her shoulder.

Behind the closed door of the library, Sue Ellen stood breathless and throbbing. It was so unreal, dreamlike; it was something her good mama had feared for so long, ever since away back when Sue Ellen was winning her first beauty contests. *Don't ever get caught out by yourself, girl,* Mama always said. *I mean, you're so pretty and men are such low-down animals—and no good upstanding man will marry damaged goods.*

"I'm goin' to lay this gun close by," Luther said. "Don't you get no ideas about it."

Mutely, she shook her head, eyes big and staring, her nipples stretched so taut they ached. When her knees weakened, she went down to the carpet, looking up at him with her mouth open, watching him shuck out of overalls and dirty shirt. She saw the massive,

ugly thing all swollen, and smelled the grimy, feral
scent of his sweat as he pawed over her, pushed her
upon her back, and spread her thighs. Sue Ellen began
to shake violently, panting with each shudder that
rolled over her nude body.

"Never saw it like this afore, did you?" he said.
"Never got it put hard to you like this—"

She flinched at the pulsing of it, the alien spreading
as it sought, demanded entrance. There was no denying him, and she didn't want to—did—not—want—to.
Oh lord; so big and powerful, and his cruel hands,
strong fingers digging into her buttocks, his mouth
savage at her breasts. Grunting, hissing, pouring dirty
words over her, into her, he thrust and thrust, and
suddenly—impossibly, Sue Ellen found her body meeting his in wild abandon.

It all came boiling out of her then, every filthy word
saved back in her head, all the things she'd never
really allowed herself to think, much less say out loud.
And the attack her pelvis was making upon him, meeting his in slamming, gyrating madness. Lord—lord—
lord—what was this? Could this be Sue Ellen, who
always tightened up when her husband touched her?
Why—she raked the strange, hairy buttocks with fierce
nails and laughed when he slapped her mouth,
laughed at the flavor of her blood and as she called
him the names all over again.

And it began, deep down in some secret place, some
core hidden from herself; it began slowly, twisting itself over and around until it became a glowing vortex.
Sue Ellen struggled for breath, for some last vestige of
control, but everything slipped away from her, drawn
inexorably into the white-hot spinning. Gasping,
whirled helplessly in raging forces risen from some
dark maw, Sue Ellen arched her back, cried out, and
wrapped him into the long netting of her legs.

She exploded. She burned. She ripped into tiny,
blazing pieces that raced the stars and spiraled down
moonbeams. Oh God—was she dead?

No; a new spark shivered deep within her sensitized

flesh and Sue Ellen came alive, ravenously, boisterously, frantically, *alive*.

In the next room, JR said, "She's screamin'—my wife is screamin'. Oh you bastards, ain't no place far enough to hide you. We'll put a bounty on your heads, a hundred thousand apiece, and Mexico won't hold you; nobody you know won't turn you in. And it's worth the same money to any Ranger you try to escape from."

Watching Payton's gun hand, Pamela could see the man wince; his painted-on smile grew thinner. He said, "Might's well be hung for a goat as a sheep, then. Reckon ol' Luther's right; it just might be best to burn down this fancy house, with everybody left in it. Won't be no bounty on nobody's head that way."

Ray Krebs moved his leg, and Payton swung the pistol his way. "Set easy, cowboy. I'd as soon bust you wide open."

Pamela allowed herself to think of Miss Ellie, upstairs on her bed and drugged against pain. It was good she was out of it, because she couldn't help, and to hear, to see, what was happening down here might be too much for the old lady. And Bobby—she was thankful he was still in Dallas; that sudden, insane temper of his would send him leaping into a gun muzzle, and kill him.

JR, a great red-blue welt rising along his head, started to say something, to make more threats, but Pamela caught his eye and shook her head. The library door was opening and all faces turned to it. Luther came first, smirking wet-lipped, not wearing a shirt and buttoning his overalls one-handed. He left the library door open, and Pamela could see Sue Ellen in there, naked as the day she was born, lying spraddled out, her back to the living room, to her family.

"Hey now, Junior," Luther said. "Your old lady tells me you never been able to make her come. That right, Junior boy? Ought to thank me for screwin' her, account of she flat knows what it's all about now. You hear her in there, hollerin' and a-beggin' me for more?"

Her voice a whiplash, Pamela said, "No, JR! He *wants* you to jump him."

Luther motioned with his gun. "You picked you a woman? You can take her on in yonder with Junior's old lady; heated up like she is, she might join in."

Smiling, pale eyes flicking back and forth, Payton said, "You, sassy lady. You, Pamela. Time I'm done with you, old Luther'll be ready to go again, and he'll take care of yella-headed Lucy yonder."

Upstairs at the railing, Ellie Ewing braced her daddy's long-barreled Colt .45 against a post and centered the sights on the dark man's hairy chest. In a loud, clear voice she called out: "Put 'em down! Put the guns down, or I'll drop you!"

Sucking breath through his teeth, Luther looked up; Payton froze with his hand on Pamela's arm. Luther said, "Hell—ain't nothin' but a little ol' lady."

Ellie squeezed the old single-action's trigger and shot him. The heavy slug took Luther through the shoulder and jerked him around, slapped him spinning as if he'd been hit by a runaway car. The thunder and lightning, the rolling powder smoke of the ancient Colt filled the room. Luther staggered backward into the wall and his gun bounced away; he slid down the wall, mouth hung open and dripping.

"You!" Ellie snapped, and Payton threw away his automatic as if he'd somehow got hold of a live coal.

"Don't, lady! *Don't*, now—I ain't hurt nobody!"

Tasting the smoke and remembering its black bite, knowing for a few moments the flavor of other, younger times, Ellie said: "JR, pick up his gun. Pamela—get the other."

Pamela slid off the couch and scooped up Luther's pistol. Raw terror peered out of his eyes as she pointed it at him. He dug one hand into his shoulder wound, blood seeping through his clawed fingers. She called up to Miss Ellie: "They collected all the guns down here, piled them up. Shall I stand over them?"

Ellie came slowly down the stairs, the big pistol held steady in both hands, its hammer eared back. There was something regal about her, Pamela thought, a thing indomitable and eternal. She might have been climbing down from a covered wagon, or walking out to face some savage chief.

"Ah," JR said the automatic clenched in his fist. "Ah, boy—you were talkin' about burnin' us down—"

"Please, mister," Payton said through the sick smile, "I had to come along, account of Luther. He'da killed me if I didn't."

JR swung from him to where Luther sat on the floor. "Yeah, yeah—you red-neck bastard, oh *yeah*."

Ellie said, "If you mean to kill him, drag him outside to do it. He's ruined a carpet already. Lucy—get on in there and wrap something around Sue Ellen; the poor girl's in shock." She snapped at JR: "Well? You aim to stand there?"

He backed off, let the gun sag, rubbed at his battered head. "I—I can't, damnit. I just can't. I *want* to kill the bastard, but—"

The wind shook the house, tried to tear it from its foundations, and somewhere upstairs, a window broke. Ellie said, "Clean this up, JR."

He sank to the couch, held his head, "No, Ma."

She held the .45 on Payton. "Then get somethin' and tie them up. Let that one bleed, and maybe he'll do it for you. Is the phone out?"

"Yes, Miss Ellie," Pamela said.

Bobby's arms were aching, because even with power steering, he'd had to fight the big car back onto the road so many times. Once the highway was blocked by a camper smashed over onto its side, with its guts spilled out. Another time he and Jock had to wrestle a skinny cottonwood off the road, with the crazed wind tearing at them every second. Then a patrol car tried to stop them, but Bobby just kicked the Continental and threw it around the partial roadblock.

It was easy to slide off the road, easy to lose the

way in piled sand and debris, and he had to inch the car along, feeling out the road. If they piled up in a gulley, they had it. Nothing less than a wrecker would get the Continental out, and making it on foot was out of the question. With a whole lot of luck Bobby might, but not with Jock. So he coaxed the wind devils and prayed to stay on the road, and when they reached the ranch turnoff, he damned near cried with relief.

A rise in the ground shielded the car for a little while, and its headlights found an old pickup. "Somebody left it!" Bobby yelled. "Know whose it is?"

"Never saw it before," Jock yelled back. "Damned sand's gettin' in the car, with everything shut up. Can you see the house?"

"No lights; power must be out and nobody got to the generator yet."

"Give me a hand to the door. Damned wind's tryin' to snatch me off my feet."

They battled through the roaring, stinging wind, lanced now with sharply driven drops of rain. Jock pushed at the front door. "It's locked! Now what in hell—"

Pushing his face tightly to a small doorpane, Bobby peered inside. Then he turned and cupped his hand to his father's ear. "Wait right here. I'm goin' around back."

The kitchen door gave to his hand and he went in low, quick. All he'd seen was his mother holding a gun on a stranger. He didn't want to startle her, draw her attention, so he slipped down the hallway and came out behind the stranger at the door to the dining room. Two crouching, animal-flowing steps and Bobby was on the man from behind, left hand around his neck and cupping the chin, right hand slamming the head in the opposite direction, Bobby's knee taking him brutally in the spine.

At the study door, Lucy gave a little scream. Pamela could only go rigid in shock as JR looked dazed. Ellie

Ewing lowered her pistol. "Very neat, Bobby—but I already had him."

He let Payton fall, not knowing or caring if the man was dead or only unconscious. He looked at Luther against the wall, at the blood running, and said, "Let Dad in; he's at the front door."

Jock stood with boots wide apart, scarred old hands upon his hips, looking and listening to Ellie's concise report. He said then to his sons, "Get them out of here."

"Dad," JR said, "my head—"

"Goddamnit!" Jock roared. "Do like I said!"

Bending, flinging Payton's arm across his shoulder, Bobby lifted the unconscious man and carried him across the room, out the front door. Now holding Sam Southworth's old hogleg, Jock prodded Luther in the back. "Move it, cropper."

Shutting the door behind them, Ellie said, "Lucy, see to JR's head. Pamela, I expect you and me better go tend Sue Ellen."

"Yes," Pamela said, and: "Miss Ellie, where are they takin' them?"

"I'm not askin'," Ellie said.

Pamela moved along with her, into the library where Sue Ellen lay with glazed eyes and marks already turning blue on her nude body. "All right," Pamela said. "I understand."

CHAPTER 34

Ellie brought ice and towels, iodine, ammonia, and a rough know-how born from years of patching wounds on animals and men. She had two pistol-whipped men to care for, and didn't know how badly they were hurt. There was no calling a doctor and no sending for one—not until the wind died and roads were passable again.

Ray Krebs looked worse, so she treated him first. He moaned when she shifted his leg, but his eyes seemed clear enough. "No double vision?" she asked.

"No," he said quietly, like his mouth hurt him. "Don't think he cracked my head."

"Hold this ice to it," Ellie said. "Stay still. I can't feel any broken bone in your leg, either; more like it's badly wrenched. Reckon you were lucky, Ray."

"Yes'm," he said, "reckon I was."

She went to examine JR's head.

In the library, Sue Ellen shook off helping hands, but kept the Navajo blanket brought to cover her nakedness. "Get away from me," she said. "Just stay the hell away from me."

"You have every right to be upset," Pamela said. "God lord, such an animal—"

Sue Ellen swung to face them, her lipstick smeared, hair straggly and one side of her mouth swollen. "And you two sweet lil' things missed out. You didn't get raped; nobody threw you down and—and—"

Very pale, Lucy said, "I—I'm sorry—"

"*You,*" Sue Ellen glared, "flirtin' with the other one all the time. Is that what you wanted—to get spread out and mounted like a tethered mare?"

Wrapped in the blanket, Sue Ellen flung back the library door and hesitated in its arch for a long, trembling second. Then, red spots flaming her cheeks and her eyes fixed high upon the stairs, she stalked through the living room, glancing neither right nor left. JR's eyes flicked at her and away as he sat beneath his mother's hands.

With a sharp signal of her head, Ellie motioned the two girls to follow Sue Ellen. Then she said, "Can you stand up, boy?"

"Yeah; I—I'm just a little wobbly."

"Hold to me."

He stiffened. "Why you takin' me in there—where it happened?"

"Because," Ellie said, "we're goin' to talk family, and Ray Krebs ain't part of it."

"Ma, damnit—"

"Get on," she said harshly. "Get on in there, boy!"

When he was in a chair, head between his hands and staring at the floor, she stood listening to the wind curse around the house, heard the rattling of a loose tin section on a barn, the neighing of a spooked horse. She braced herself against the desk and used one foot to move Sue Ellen's half-slip and ripped panty hose out of sight under the desk.

Then she said, "Don't you *dare* blame your wife for what happened. Already, you're actin' like she's dirty."

He didn't look up. "She is; he did it to her and she'll never be the same, never be the woman I married."

"Who the hell are you, somethin' pure and special? You the best creature God ever waddled a gut into? Looks to me like you're not even much of a man."

"Why, Ma—"

"I'm not proud it has to be me, speakin' up to you, but it's been a long time neglected."

"Mother," JR said, sitting up straight, holding toweled ice to the side of his head, "you can't talk to me that way; nobody can."

Ellie's legs were shaky and her heart seemed to be at full gallop; her mouth was desert dry and she wanted a drink. But she needed to say this first. "It's your own fault Sue Ellen got raped. You hadn't been tomcattin' with somebody's wife, he wouldn't have come to pay you back. You've been lucky all your life, boy—lucky somebody hasn't blown your head clean off. And you set there, mean-mouthing your wife because she got *forced* into it, just once."

Shifting in the chair, mouth and eyes gone sulky and ugly, JR said, "I told you—but this ain't proper for a mother to be talkin' about—"

"Don't sull up at me," she snapped. "I'm more than

your mother and the woman's been actin' moon-blind over your failings all these years; I'm also a good, *big* chunk of Ewing Oil, and don't you forget it. I know you for what you are, JR—a mean man with a pencil, or makin' a shady deal, and throwin' around Ewing weight and money. But head-on to anybody, you're about as gutless as a drawn pullet. So make up to your wife; treat her kind and gentle, or by God, the only way you'll get into the Ewing Oil office is by appointment! Now hear me good."

Mouth working, JR heaved himself from the chair, heaved the toweled ice to the floor. "I'm your son."

"Can't deny it," she said. "I just ain't up to claimin' you right now."

He slammed the door behind him, and Ellie bent to pick up Sue Ellen's torn and discarded clothing. The girl wouldn't want to see any of this again; she'd put it in the fireplace and touch it off. The room seemed a mite chilly, anyhow. Kindling and starter wood were already laid, and seasoned oak chunks in the woodbox, so Ellie stuffed the clothing in, and flared a match to it.

Trash, she thought; white trash that Texas was full of, these days; if it wasn't Mexicans and blacks, it was poor white trash that didn't keep their place. In her early time, was a thing like this to happen out here, the criminals would hang from a cottonwood for days, as warning to others of their stripe, before some kind soul cut them down and buried them. But now—now when a man defended his home and womenfolk, seemed like the law got on the wrong side. Jock and Bobby were only doing what was right and natural, and they would say no more about it, to anybody. That also was as it ought to be.

She should have taken more of a hand with JR, less with Gary; Bobby grew up on his own just fine, and how was a mother to know when she was doing right, when wrong? Once they were full grown, it was too late to reach back and correct mistakes; you had to live with them as best you could. But there was no rule that said you couldn't try to keep them from getting worse.

Lucy paused outside Sue Ellen's door. "I guess you better handle her, Pamela. I—I just can't hack it right now. The same guy would have done it to me next. Oh wow."

"All right," Pamela said, "but see if you can give Miss Ellie a hand."

"Pam," Lucy said. "Jock and Bobby—what do you think they did with those men?"

"I don't want to know," Pamela said, "and neither do you. I don't even want to remember that any men came here during the storm."

"O-okay," Lucy said and backed against the rail while Pamela went into Sue Ellen's room without knocking. *Raped,* Lucy thought; would it hurt if a woman wasn't ready, if she didn't like it? She couldn't conceive of anybody not liking it, once the guy had it in. Even if he was all hairy and smelled bad, once it was in you could pretend it was Robert Redford or somebody and ball with him.

Still, the guys she'd had were those she picked. Ray Krebs kind of picked her, at first, thinking he was going to get himself an innocent little cherry. But Ray got fooled. Of course, it was different, balling a *man,* but she had the same grip on him, the same power she held over a panting boy.

She'd been missing a lot since Pamela came down on her; Ray keeping away, the kids at school not accepting her yet, especially since Roger got clobbered. But she could make up for the dry spell before long. Oh wow! Rape—and on Miss Texas herself, while JR sat in his chair and just ate himself up inside while it was going on, flashing all kinds of sex pictures in his head while his wife was getting screwed.

His wife . . . Lucy's stepmother . . . dear old Daddy sweating up a storm.

She didn't go downstairs, but into her own room where she flung herself across the bed. "Good," she hissed into her pillow. "Good for both you bastards."

In Sue Ellen's room, Pamela said, "Are you sure you want to be alone? You can talk to me, you know; you just haven't tried before."

Sitting on the edge of a double bed, blanket tightly protective of herself, Sue Ellen said, "Why should I talk to you? What do you want to know—what it felt like—how he put it to me—what he said?"

"You know better than that," Pamela said.

Sue Ellen curled her lips; inside their corner, she could still taste a faint echo of blood from the cut where he'd slapped her. "Oh yeah; I keep forgettin' how much experience you have. You already know all that stuff."

"All right, Sue Ellen," Pamela said. "I'll leave you alone."

As the door closed, Sue Ellen thought: a bath; she needed a bath. Even if the electricity was off, there should be enough water in the holding tank. She dropped the scratchy old blanket and her skin immediately felt more alive, able to breathe. Utterly naked and deriving a delicious satisfaction from it, she crossed to the full-length mirror and stood before it.

There were marks upon her thighs, and more upon her buttocks when she turned just so, and her breasts —her nipples ached and her pelvis remembered the wiry thrusting of his pubic hair, the thick strength of Luther himself, pounding, hammering. Bitch, he'd called her, hissing against her teeth and punctuating names with a wet tongue—bitch and cunt and one hell of a piece of ass.

JR never told her she was one hell of a piece of ass. The few times JR managed to do it with her had been rabbity and unsatisfying. But Luther—Sue Ellen admired her nude body in the mirror. Great tits, Luther said, and a pussy like a snapping turtle; like to drive any man crazy with them long legs and snapping turtle pussy, Luther said.

And she'd answered him back, called him all those dirty words forbidden by Mama, bit him and raked his

ass with her nails and sledged her crotch up at him
like the worst kind of whore. It was good, *good*, and
she almost cried when he pulled out of her, but he
calmed her by saying that Payton would screw her
next, and later on, Luther would come back for more.
But Miss Ellie had saved her from that. Saved her? Or
denied her? Sue Ellen knew that nobody would ever,
ever say another word about it, and she would go on
wondering.

Moving into the bathroom, she drew a full tub of
warm water and slid down into it, tingling at the way
water caressed her thighs, her belly. Every part of her
body seemed new and different now, as if she had been
asleep all her life and just come to. JR; that dirty,
son of a bitching bastard whoremonger JR; couldn't
do it with her, but chased off after trashy women.

What was Luther's wife like? Why did she go out
chipping when she had so much man at home? Was
it for money? Sue Ellen touched the tips of her soapy
breasts and shivered. It would be crazy, going into a
motel room with some strange man who was willing
to pay money, just to crawl on top of you. Because
your long legs and great tits and beautiful snapper
drove men out of their minds.

Downstairs, Ray Krebs cuddled a whiskey bottle
and listened to the wind. It sounded as if it was slack-
ing off, but then another gust would hit the house
like a giant hammer. Stock out on the range had to
fend for themselves at a time like this; there was no
safe place to put them, even if it had been possible to
round them up from a thousand or so grazing acres.

Roofing was being torn screeching from the barns,
and he hoped the horses were okay, and the young
stock JR had helped him get into the protective draw.
He took another drink and carefully shifted his leg.
Damn—ol' JR had come out of the library like a
turpentined bobcat and gone straight to the bar, Miss
Ellie staying in there alone. What the hell, having his
old lady dicked shouldn't tear a man up like that.

Look at Bobby Ewing; he didn't go around with his neck bowed all the time just because Ray had balled his wife long before Bobby knew her.

But Bobby didn't talk to him either, and if it wasn't for JR and Jock, he might be out on his hind pockets. Ray took another snort and found the pain in his leg easing considerably. That bastard had clubbed him pretty good with the gun, too, but that would heal quicker. It might have been better all around if *all* the women had been stuck by those croppers; then JR wouldn't feel put on by himself.

Jesus. The way Jock and Bobby hauled them out of the house. Ray wondered where they were taking them. They wouldn't do anything to the croppers— Jock would never let Bobby get blood on his hands. But Luther and Payton would be taken care of. Jock Ewing woud see to that. Ray took a drink to warm himself. *How* would they be taken care of? Ray took another drink, shrugged off his own curiosity.

One thing Ray Krebs knew for certain, and that was to keep his mouth shut about the entire incident, to pretend it never happened; and never to ask.

Taking a bottle of bourbon with him, JR wandered aimlessly about the house, into the deserted kitchen, back out to the foyer, looking at the stairs but not studying on climbing them. His head ached like the anvil of hell, and that was the only reason he didn't go with his father and Bobby. Not because he was scared or anything close. They didn't need him, anyway; two were enough to get the job done.

His mother still hadn't come out of the library, and Ray Krebs was sitting on the floor of the living room nursing a bottle. Damn—his ma had no right gettin' on him that way. How could he have foreseen that a couple of crazy bastards would come all the way to the ranch for some insane kind of revenge? It wasn't like he hadn't paid the dumb broads.

Sue Ellen—his ma telling him to be good to her, to act like she was still respected. Goddamn . . . how could he do that, knowing that she'd been pumped full of that mean bastard's semen? Oh shit, what if she had a baby from it? That might put the lie to his hinting around that Sue Ellen was barren, that being childless wasn't his fault. The truth was, he didn't mess with her much.

How could he mess with her *now*? It was different for women; everybody knew that. A man was supposed to hell around and sow his oats, and it was okay to plant them deep in a common woman's belly. But a wife had obligations and duty to home and family— at least a *decent* wife had, and Sue Ellen was always decent before now. Why the hell couldn't Pamela have been the one screwed; she was used to it from different guys.

Pamela would have liked to flee across to their own small house, to try and erase all vestiges of this brutal night. She wanted Bobby to hold her close and warm, to make her safe again. On the stairs, she clung to the railing as she'd hang onto herself. JR wasn't in the living room, nor was Miss Ellie; Ray Krebs was there, leg on a pillow, holding a bottle and grinning stupidly. Ray was drunk, but she figured he had a right to be.

She descended to him and couldn't help holding her arms across her breasts when she looked at the closed library door. Ray said, "Wanna drink?"

"I'll get one over here," Pamela said and headed for the bar. "Does your leg hurt? Your head?"

"Feelin' no pain," he chuckled. "Drunker'n seven hundred dollars on a Saturday night, or a tree fulla hooty owls. How come you ain't took to cover like everybody else?"

"I'm waiting for my husband," Pamela answered, and drank a stiff measure of bourbon. She had to chase it quick with water, her eyes running.

Ray said, "Just as glad wasn't you in yonder."

"Me too," Pamela said and watched her hand tremble. He might have killed her in there, the rapist. She didn't know if she could handle being forced, slapped around, clothing ripped off. An animal like that, he might have beaten her to death, or shot her. And if not, afterward how would she face Bobby with the stink of Luther's sweat upon her, his semen fouling her thighs? Even if it wasn't her fault, she might feel forever guilty.

Pamela began to understand how Sue Ellen felt, and knew a cold, implacable hatred for JR because he wasn't up there consoling his wife. Oil lamps flickered and the fire crackled; she smelled oak and kerosene and whiskey. It was possible she scented fear and hate, too. Miss Ellie—what a godsend she'd been with that pistol; so cool and determined, so deadly. Pamela poured a smaller drink and mixed it with cola. The wind wasn't yowling quite so loud now, its threat gone hissing and muttering off into the hills, like fading thunder.

She saw the bobbing flash of lights before hearing the jeep, and hurried to the door. Jock weaved in first, slapping dirt from his jacket with his hat, eyebrows and face smeared over with it.

"Bobby!" she said, protected within the circle of his arms. "Oh Bobby, I'm so glad you're back, so glad!"

He kissed her and she didn't mind the dust. "How's Sue Ellen?"

"Upstairs," she said. "She's doin' pretty good."

From the bar Jock Ewing said, "Ol' Ray's doin' all right, too. Lyin' there colder'n a wedge. Where's Miss Ellie?"

"In—in the library, I think," Pamela said. When he went inside, she looked quizzically at Bobby, knowing better than to ask.

"It's all right, baby," Bobby said, "nothin' like that will ever happen again. Dad's puttin' guards and alarms around the place, maybe even dogs. This made him realize that a wall of money is no protection at all."

She gave him a drink and he downed it. "Where's everybody else?"

"Looking into their own souls," she said.

CHAPTER 35

Hell of a note, Jock thought, when you had to kind of sidle in between guards and electric eyes and a bunch of other security arrangements. Time was when a man could ride the length of Muleshoe County with no more than a short gun in his hip pocket, and nobody with the brains God gave a billygoat would come up on a man's house without hollering, night or day.

Back then, Jock recalled, every ranch house had a pack of hound dogs, big and gaunt and a mite savage, and it was some hard to just walk up on a place without them raising a ruckus. Would be kind of good to have dogs around again, blueticks, maybe; he'd always been partial to blueticks or redbones. But what he'd get was more apt to be German shepherds or those crop-eared, slick dogs you couldn't trust all that much —Dobermans. Goddamned Krauts couldn't win any wars, so they turned out mean dogs to get even with the world.

Jock walked slowly around the stock pond nearest the house. His feet were cold and he stamped his boots occasionally. Wearing a heavy jacket and winter Stetson, gloved and long-johned and bundled from here to there, he felt all clumsy. And the wind still poked icy probes down his neck now and then. That big wind had been a bitch, all right; what it didn't blow down it uprooted or covered with sand. Eighteen head of cows lost and two weanling fillies; heap of damages to outbuildings and line shacks that weren't built to last, like the big house was. Sand ate streaks of paint off several of the cars, too, especially the Continental.

Looking off toward the house, Jock thought he'd
better get home. The Orloff investigation was done
with; they hadn't proved a thing on Ewing Oil, but
that didn't mean they'd stop looking, especially that
glory hound, Cliff Barnes. Chewing on a cold cigar,
Jock compared brother and sister and shook his head.
Pamela'd been tough and cool during that mess at the
house, near capable as Ellie herself. Had to admire the
girl for that, but damned if Jock would put up in any
way with her crusading brother.

As he neared the barn, he pondered some on Sue
Ellen. Since that night, she'd been kind of hid away
inside herself, only peeping out from time to time.
Didn't talk and carry on near as much, preened about
the same, but there was a difference about her that
nobody seemed able to get a handle on.

Well, it was done and behind them now. What JR
had to be waked up to was that old-oil–new-oil probe
that was coming on fast. Because Bobby had first mentioned it, JR had tended to let the thing slide. And
that investigation wasn't headed off easy, because the
FBI and U.S. Attorney General's office was running it.
The friends Ewing Oil had in Washington would
do all they could, but if things got hairy, they'd pull in
their necks like a loggerhead turtle in a thunderstorm.

Climbing onto the front porch, he worked mud off
his boots with the scraper, wiped them on the mat,
and went on inside. He felt the cold follow him in, reluctant to leave his bones. Here it was springtime, and
feeling like winter to him. Old, damnit, old; creaky
and short of breath and thinking more on the past
than the future. Did that come from being semi-
retired, from not having enough to do?

Damnit, he'd done everything he set out to accom-
plish: made Ewing Oil a power to be reckoned with,
piled up money that he would never live to spend,
and kept Ellie pretty happy, all things considered. He
had sons to carry on his name and business, and if he
had no grandsons yet, so be it. They'd come along.

Then why did he have to get out of the house and

stomp around, and have trouble sleeping, and food
not set easy on the stomach? Have to do something,
Jock thought; do more to keep the company straight,
fix it so JR and Bobby wouldn't take to feuding and
let business slide.

Up in the hayloft, Ray Krebs slid back on his belly
as Jock passed below. Damn, damn—if the old man
had caught him, if *anybody* caught him—but he had
no choice. He was in a vise, and all she had to do was
turn the handle to squeeze him flat. Ray wished she'd
waited, or never gotten the bug at all. It was cold up
here, though stacked bales of rich alfalfa blocked any
wind.

Under the blankets it could get warm enough, but
Ray figured he was old enough to have earned a soft
bed and no more sneaking around in haylofts. He
looked at his watch and pulled a blanket up around
his shoulders. Creeping around had its good points,
though; stolen goodies were always that much sweeter.

It had been a couple of months since those crazy
bastards had come busting into the big house to rape
and get even. Ray pulled the blanket closer, remembering how they'd been hauled out, one leaking plenty
of blood. Never heard from again.

Jesus—if anyone found Ray out, he wouldn't wait
around. He'd just split and hope nobody got on his
trail. More than one man had lost his head *and* his
ass over pussy, but Ray Krebs wasn't fixing to let it
happen to him. This Ewing bunch was something else.

And something else was coming up the ladder, moving catty and quiet. He ducked back into the bales
until he was certain it was her. Ray saw the cameo
profile when she turned her head, the flow of hair, and
watched the ripe, juicy body as it rose into sight.

"Ray?" she said softly, with that special tremulo a
woman's voice carries, when she's certain she's going to
make love, "Ray?"

"Right here, baby," he answered. "Right over here,
Sue Ellen."

Quickly, lithe and graceful, she came across the hay to the room he'd made for them. She looked heavier in a thick sweater and cord slacks, rubber-soled shoes; the cold pinked her cheeks and brightened her eyes, her mouth.

She kneeled before him, taking his face in her slender hands, chill hands with pointy little fingers. When she kissed him, her lips were flavored with winter, but warmed swiftly into the honeyed urgencies of spring. "I kind of hated to *make* you meet me here," Sue Ellen murmured, hot, spiced breath a frosty drifting about the sculptured loveliness of her face. "But I need a man, Ray—a *man* who knows somethin' about women."

His hands lightly upon her hips, Ray said, "Yeah, baby, I understand. Just so long as you know how dangerous this is for both of us. I mean, threatenin' to tell JR that I made a grab for you—"

"Just to have you love me, darlin'," she breathed, fingers sliding through his hair and tracing slow, exciting patterns on the nape of his neck. "I didn't know how else to go about it. There's a lot of things I don't know, Ray. Show me, darlin'—oh please, please show me."

What an armful she was under the blanket with him; what sinuous rolling of hips and eager flattening of wonderfully molded breasts. He had a tough time getting her clothes off, she was that anxious and wiggly, clamping her mouth to his and trying to beat his tongue flat with her own, teeth clashing, her breath gushing into his throat—wild, wild.

"Do it," Sue Ellen chanted, "do it, do it, do it!"

Into the cushioning of her breasts, against the column of her throat, low into the fluttering, quivering, and gentle mounding of her stomach, Ray said, "Easy, baby—you don't hurry it . . . easy, easy—there . . . oh yeah, pretty baby—you like that?"

"All the way down," she gasped. "Never—ahh—oh lord, all the way." Sue Ellen's hands were frantic at his head, tangling in his hair, strong.

"Damnit, now," he said, "I never done anything like—"

She fought him, cursed him, and he wanted so damned much to knock the hell out of this woman making such demands upon him. But he didn't dare mark her; he didn't dare even roll her ass out of his blankets.

One scream, and he was a dead man. Damnit, oh damnit. If he could, he'd kill her, twist off her damned head, tear out this heaving, rolling belly so insistently at him.

Maybe he could kill her and haul the body away, sink her in the stock pond with an old anvil. Maybe they'd think she ran away. Run away himself, beat the holy shit out of her and run, run before anybody found out.

Oh, damn!

Ellie brought Jock a cup of coffee and looked at the living-room clock. "They ought to be home soon, all of them. Jock—do you think we ought to tell the boys it's all right if they live in town. That stretch of highway gets more dangerous every year."

Taking the cup, he grunted his thanks and said, "Woman, you know that ain't what you want, and me neither. I reckon they can be inconvenienced to be home with their ma and pa. That's what the ranch always meant to you, a home place that's got its taproots sunk so far down in the ground that nothin' or nobody can ever tear 'em loose."

She went to the fireplace and put her back to it. "My daddy used to stand here every time he came into the room, summer or winter. It was a habit of his."

"Your daddy didn't give a damn for oilmen. It's a wonder he let me on the place."

Ellie moved away from the fireplace and stood at the big window, looking at where nightguard lamps were just flickering into false moonlight. "He'd have cared even less if he could know I let those leases go. I promised him on his deathbed that I wouldn't."

"Let 'em go to Digger Barnes," he said, peeling the wrapper off a cigar.

"It was better than losing the ranch to the bankers. Maybe Sam Southworth could have understood that."

"With Digger, you'd have lost it all."

She turned and came to his chair, lowered herself to the arm and put a hand on his shoulder. "I've always been beholden to Digger for failin'."

Jock lifted his gnarled hand to cover hers and she saw the age spots upon it, the interlacing of faded scars, but he would never be old to her. He said, "It's been good, Ellie. Maybe we could have done better with the younguns, but we was just about younguns ourselves. Did the best we knew how."

"I'm not complainin'," she said. "Never have."

"You ain't a complainin' kind of woman. Muleyheaded, but never one to holler calf rope."

"About to be muley now," she said. "I think it's long past time to make it up with Pamela's family."

"With Digger Barnes, runnin' off at the mouth for all these years on how I cheated him, stole from him? Make it up with Cliff Barnes, for tryin' his damnedest to put me and JR in jail?"

Turning her hand over, Ellie worked her fingers between his. "Cliff Barnes won't come if he's asked; it would spoil his image. But Willard—Digger—he's down on his luck, and he's Pamela's father. Never mind that you two were good partners for years before—before me."

"Damnit," Jock said, "you wasn't to fault, Ellie. I was about to split the blankets with him anyhow. He just never could get it through his head that we weren't supposed to spend up a new well and half of one not drilled yet. To Digger Barnes, money was just somethin' to be throwed away, not to be invested and made grow. For him, it was the findin' of oil and spendin' of money, not the keepin' and developing."

Ellie said, "I know, Jock; I know."

"I never interfered with the running of the ranch," he said, "nor told you how to do your house."

"It's worked out pretty good so far, me keepin' out of the oil business, too. So I'll make up my guest list for the spring barbecue, and you can make up yours, like always. And put out that cigar; you know what the doctor said."

"Go ahead on, then," Jock said testily. "Invite 'em, but don't expect me to do-si-do around 'em—*if* they show up."

She withdrew her hand and stroked his hair with it. "Pamela's about as strong-minded as anybody in this family, and she *is* part of *this* family. She'll bring her pa, if she has to drag him."

"Drag him," Jock mumbled, "drag *anybody* to a Ewing barbecue! Half the folks in Texas'd give their left—"

"Jock," Ellie warned.

"—left arms to even get an invite. Goddamn Barnes!"

JR drove a Mercedes today, one of the small fleet with "Ewing" license plates, because his Mustang was getting a new paint job. He worried while he drove. He worried alot lately—ever since that lousy cropper who'd taken Sue Ellen into the library and—and raped her. JR's stomach churned everytime he thought about that, and he thought about it several times a day. God knows it was bad enough having your wife despoiled, dirtied forever by a grunting, sweating redneck, but the rape had only been a start for troubles.

Never had he known his mother to be so angry, and at *him* more than the rapist, seemed like. Threatening to throw her block of stock around, even move him out as chairman of the board. So he had to choke back his feelings and be real nice to Sue Ellen, but goddamn!—he wanted to throw up every time he saw those bruises and scratches on her, and he just knew she was going to swell up with a baby that wasn't his.

He might have killed her then, JR thought as he flipped the untouchable Mercedes in and out of traffic lanes. Somehow, he would have killed the woman carrying a white-trash bastard.

A bodyguard was what he needed. If the old man could station guards around the house, he shouldn't begrudge JR having protection, too. But Jock and Bobby went around without one, and they'd look at him cross-eyed. Bobby was getting too damned close to the old man as it was.

With feeling, JR said "Shit!" and tooled the heavy car onto the off ramp. Everything was going haywire since the rape, and why the hell couldn't it have happened to Miss Smart-ass Pamela, or Lucy—no, not Lucy. Never Lucy.

It all came down to Sue Ellen. She acted strange, like she'd been turned into a different kind of woman, and one that JR didn't like. Not for a wife. And the way she came on, it was like she just didn't give a damn anymore. Not a week after what happened to her, she caught him coming out of the shower and reached down to grab his dingus—just like that. When he asked her was she crazy and tried to push her off, it just made her worse. Seemed like the rougher he got with her, the better Sue Ellen liked it.

Showing her ass and rubbing her own tits thataway, crawling all over him as if she was some low-down whore, even nipping at his belly with her teeth and moaning low in her throat. He had to throw her off and get the hell out of their room, because if she thought he was going to do it to her right after that cropper did, if she thought he wanted a wife of his to act like a cheap hooker, Sue Ellen Ewing was flat out of her mind.

Then, when he mentioned to his mother that maybe Sue Ellen ought to start seeing a shrink, Miss Ellie hadn't been a damned bit understanding. Something had to change, JR thought, and change pretty goddamned quick.

CHAPTER 36

Ellie felt younger. She'd uncovered a faded pair of her old Levi's and a flannel shirt. She wore comfortable boots and a ribbon in her hair. The Levi's snugged her up, tightened loose flesh, and seemed to buoy her as she walked across the grounds. She was heading for Bobby's house; she thought how it had been Gary's, and bit her lip. She tried not to think of him often, to wonder if he was alive and where.

It would be kinder, she thought, if sometimes people could be put down like crippled or terminally ill horses. And it was a pity human outlaws couldn't be moved along as bucking stock, taken to where their flaws could work for them. But damnit, people weren't horses, and the dam retained attachment for the foal, long after it was weaned. Ellie still didn't know what had sent Gary off his head and away from his home—whiskey, his wife, work he detested?

Still, he could have called, written, said *something*, even if it was I hate you all.

Pausing on the small porch, Ellie drew in the scents of spring—young grass, uncurling tree leaves, warm green brought upon a softly laughing wind. She loved spring and its fulfillment of renewal, life rising again from the cold grip of winter, a thousand deaths refuted, small and large. The air caressed her face, and for a moment, the raucous cry of a jay was musical.

Pamela invited her in when she knocked, and Ellie was glad; the girl was gone nearly all the time these days, doing volunteer work in Dallas, keeping busy, staying away from the ranch. Because of Sue Ellen's change? Harassment by Ray Krebs? Why? She'd done a wonderful job with Lucy, making the child stay neat and in school.

Pamela was in a loose robe, much too big for her. Bobby's, Ellie thought, and smiled at the memory of how long Jock had done without a robe of any kind, before she bought him one special for some birthday. And she'd done that mainly because she wanted to wear it when Jock was gone off somewhere, so she could wrap its rough warmth around her and know the lingering smell of him.

"Miss Ellie," Pamela said, "my, don't you look like a young ranch lady, off to do her chores. Would you like some coffee?"

"I'd love it," Ellie said. "You've done wonders with this old place, inside and out. I saw the crocus opening."

"Beautiful, aren't they? And brave," Pamela said. "They're the only flower I know that dares bloom in the snow."

Sitting at the little table, Ellie accepted a mug of coffee and sniffed its dark-smelling steam. "You've done all right, pushing through most of the ice you found around here." The girl was blooming, she thought, with a nostalgic tilt of he head, the certain suggestion of a twinkle in her dark eyes. Oh God, Ellie prayed, please don't let her start reciting lines from the *Rubiyat;* not this morning.

"I love Bobby," Pamela said evenly, joining her at the table and arranging the folds of the robe. "I have to make myself part of the family that loves him, too."

Tasting coffee, Ellie said, "You've just about succeeded. Those who don't accept you yet—at least, they respect you."

"Yes ma'm," Pamela said, "but I guess time will have to take care of the rest. I've gone about far as I mean to."

Ellie's eye defined a particular richness of throat and cheek, and way of sitting in the concealing robe. She said, "Child, you're pregnant."

Pamela sparkled, and there was no other word for it, Ellie decided, the inner glow that lighted Pamela's skin and danced within her eyes. "Yes," the girl said, "I guess I am. Does it really show?"

"Only to someone who knows how to look. I'm glad for you, truly, truly glad for you and Bobby and me—and especially for Jock Ewing. Have you told anyone yet?"

Pamela shook her head. "I've been saving it. Bobby might just suspect, because he's been teasing me about putting on weight. But nobody else, I'm sure. It's the main reason I've been keeping to myself so much, working with the Red Cross and what not. I don't guess I can hide it very much longer."

"No need to," Ellie said. "We'll combine the announcement with the ranch's annual spring barbecue—if you don't mind. Jock will snort and stomp around and act like it's his very own, and make a nuisance out of himself. Why, when I was carryin' JR—But never mind. Is it all right with you about the barbecue? We mean for you to ask your family, of course. That's why I came over this mornin', to tell you that."

Impulsively, Pamela reached across the table. "Why, that's wonderful, Miss Ellie! I'll do my best, and as for the party—sure; we can call it my Sticking Out Party."

It wasn't all that funny, but the two women laughed and laughed, still holding hands.

And far down the highway toward Austin, where there was little chance of her being recognized, Sue Ellen pulled her small Caddy into a walled-off motel lot that looked as if it had been designed to hide visiting cars from passing traffic.

The room was rented by the month, paid ahead so that she could keep a key and excite herself by running her fingers over its blunt metal and thinking, thinking with her eyes closed and maybe squeezing her thighs tightly together, rolling, then releasing them in a trick she'd learned. When she couldn't get to Ray and when JR wasn't home, she'd start out this way and wind up masturbating. Sometimes she did it when JR was home and snoring beside her. It sort of added a kick to feel him touching her skin, and build to a slow grinding orgasm by pretending he was Ray Krebs or someone else, anybody else.

He hadn't touched her since the rape. Oh, JR was icily polite when they were alone and attentively effusive before the family or in public, but she could see it in his eyes when he looked at her. He thought she was dirty, that he was too good for her now. The arrogant bastard, him with all his two-bit chippies and office whores. Oh, she'd gotten all the information out of Ray Krebs about their screwing around on business trips, swapping women and all that stuff.

Out of the car, she went quickly into the motel room, tingling with anticipation. What a change her entire life had undergone, for she was no longer a plastic dolly dressing and undressing and making herself pretty, only to sit and wait for nothing. Now she was powerful and commanding; Ray *had* to obey her summons or lose his job, if not his head.

How satisfying it was, to make him do whatever she wanted, her very own trained stud. He was sulky about it at first, but Ray always came through with that deep and punishing kind of loving that thrilled her, and if he meant it when he called her a vicious, conniving bitch, so much the better.

Cliff Barnes shuffled through a pile of papers, his office cluttered here as well as at home. He was on the trail of something interesting, because the same kind of pattern had begun appearing. Ewing Oil again, mixed up with Lone Star and Texas Independents, with a dozen other front companies, and everybody getting a slice of the pie as the consumers got screwed. They were plenty cute, moving a bill of lading from one outfit to another, a markup added each time, and probably the oil itself had never been budged.

There were plenty of slick little moves being made

by many outfits, but there was good old Ewing Oil, right in the middle again, selling old oil for new-oil prices. This time, Cliff thought, *this* time let old man Ewing try to wiggle off the hook by selling out an old friend as he'd done with Wild Bill Orloff. More than the state legislature was involved here. Cliff smiled and reached for the phone, hit a switch.

"Hello, baby—yes, get me the Department of Energy in Washington, then the Justice Department in Houston."

Leaving school, Lucy Ewing thought it wouldn't be so bad. She'd get this final semester behind her, and that was it. Did she want to go off to college, Texas, TCU, A&M? Not really, because she wasn't hunting a husband. Maybe she'd ask Grandpa to set her up in a boutique, or an art store, or something. Grandpa, not JR; she'd never come out and *ask* JR for anything, but one day she just might demand something from him. And wouldn't that shake him up, rattle the whole damned family right down to their toenails?

But she was saving up that special day, had been hoarding it close and gloating over it for years. When she turned *that* loose, Lucy wanted it to hurt like hell.

She sat on the bus, because Pamela was wise to Ray Krebs driving to school, and there was just no shucking Pam. Roger Hurley had stayed far away from her since he'd gotten clobbered at the disco that night, and maybe he'd passed word among the other guys, because they acted like Lucy had a bad case of something catching. And the male teachers were worse; since that little hassle with her counselor, they all made certain they never got left alone with her.

Not getting any was making Lucy a little edgy, kind of uptight, and she knew she'd soon have to figure some way to get Ray into the sack, or some other cowboy who could keep his mouth shut. She chuckled, and kids close by glanced nervously at her. Keep his mouth shut and his tallywhacker up, Lucy thought, and giggled again.

Pamela sat alone. Miss Ellie had gone. How quickly she'd noticed Pamela was pregnant, when the tummy didn't even show yet. Now Pamela would have to tell Bobby and see his reaction; he wanted a child, she was sure. At least, she thought he did.

Jock would be pleased, Miss Ellie said. Lucy was already there, but somehow not as close; a boy, Jock wanted a grandson, someone to carry on the name. His own kind of immortality, Pamela thought, although Ewing Oil was entity enough, a corporation that would outlast them all.

Unless it was uprooted by federal investigators, destroyed and the remnants of its very name flung to the winds. Then what would the newest Ewing inherit, what would be left for Jock's immortality?

JR came home early, swinging the Mustang into the long garage and making a mental note to tell the black driver-mechanic to check out its pinging, and have one of the houseboys wash and wax it. He was about up to his jawbones with the steady grind at the office, and Bobby's constant hassling about the investigation in Houston. When it started this way, JR would take care of it. What the hell did the kid want, to have him running back and forth to cover up each individual pile, like a cat with the squirts, hurrying to bury droplets of shit?

That's what other department heads were for, to take some of the heat. Bobby just kept pushing, though, as if he meant to personally run each and every facet of Ewing Oil. Damnit, there was no way one man could do all that. And there was no way the company could operate with *two* heads. Jesus—the old man couldn't see that, he must be getting senile. Every day, JR expected Jock Ewing to come booming down on baby brother like a herd of spooked whitefaces, but it never happened.

And since that blowup with his mother, JR felt his position was just a mite shaky. Nothing was going right; his bitchy wife kept rubbing it up to him, acting like the worst hustler in town. Instead of turning him on, it shut him off, and he couldn't raise a hard on a bet. Not that he wanted to screw Sue Ellen after what happened, but he had to admit that she was getting kind of interesting, like he was sleeping with a completely different woman.

Maybe they could get it on again, if he could just tell her what it took to get him up, make him randy. But thinking of his *wife* doing that—well, it wasn't something JR could accept yet. She didn't seem to be around all that much anymore. Mixed up with charity work and that crap Pamela got started in. Must be Pamela who put all those shameless ideas in her head, too. Let bad blood into the family, and it was like the Arab letting his camel put his head in the tent; pretty soon the Arab was out and the camel in. Same thing if you let a nigger move next door.

Walking into the house from the garage, JR had noticed that Sue Ellen's car wasn't in its slot. Good enough; he might get lucky and she wouldn't come home in time to nag him about where he was going. Hell, he didn't know yet, but Houston sure made for a good excuse. There wasn't much to do on the ranch now, either; maybe old Ray Krebs could come with him. JR grunted; he'd leave his business cards home this time. Only Ray would understand that a man just *had* to get his ashes hauled proper.

Nobody was in the living room or hall. JR punched the commo to Ray's quarters above the main stables. "Hey, ol' boy!" There was no answer, so he tried the barns and bunkhouse, where somebody told him no sir, haven't seen him most of the day—in a Mexican accent. Yeah, JR said, yeah, and climbed the stairs thinking he'd have to get hold of a call girl in Houston. They were safer, anyway; no red-neck bastard would pistol-whip a man for screwing a professional. Not and get away with it, anyhow.

The others didn't get away with it either. Bobby, with that deadly reptilian look to his eyes; the old

man's craggy face hard and unyielding; and JR—
nursing a busted head. What more did they want from
him? He had a business to run.

Bobby looked at the wall clock, then at Connie
Bullard, still working away at her typewriter. The
poor kid was overloaded now that she was handling
JR's work too. They had to get at least one more
secretary/receptionist. He told Connie: "Get hold of
the agency, see if you can find someone as efficient and
pretty as you are. And Connie—thanks for doing so
much, for helping me ferret out all the stuff JR keeps
trying to sweep under the rug."

Pink-cheeked, she looked up at him with big hazel
eyes, "Why, thank you, Bobby. I'm only doing my
job."

"And staying out of my brother's clutches, so far."

Her heart-shaped face went serious. "So far," she
agreed.

"Hey now; I was only kiddin'. I mean, if you get
involved with JR, that's your business. But if you
don't want to, you can be sure of your job here, because you're *my* secretary and a damned good one."

"Thanks again," she murmured. "Do you want me
to lock up?"

"If you like," Bobby said, and got his topcoat. Anything touchy was locked away, and he trusted this girl
anyhow. JR had trusted Julie, he remembered. But
what the hell—it was good to have that mess out in the
open and behind the company. Now, the one coming
up was something else. For weeks, he'd been trying to
find a way out for Ewing Oil, and succeeded in a few
instances. But to get anything done on the rest, he'd
have to go over JR's head, play the fink, and put the
hard facts before the old man. JR wouldn't like that.

"I'll be at home the early part of the evening," he
told Connie. "After that, I'll check in with the answering service myself. Have a good night."

It was good to be out of the gray, light-sprinkled
city, to speed away from buzzing stone beehives and

rediscover green grass, open spaces. The Mercedes purred along and Bobby felt like purring with it. There might be unpleasantness tonight when he by-passed JR, but until then it was a beautiful world.

Not, he thought, that he was any outdoorsy freak. One tour of the Nam had stopped all picnics and campouts forever. He would never go hunting, either; he knew exactly how the prey felt. Being hunted—it had happened to him often enough in the jungles.

But to hell with all that. He was a happy man on the way home to a beautiful and happy wife. Since the invasion of the house, his mother and father, and Lucy also, seemed to think a good deal more of Pamela. And less of JR? Possibly, but there were things some men could do and others couldn't. In the Nam, there'd been a sergeant who would just about go into coma at sight of a snake. The same guy would walk right into small-arms fire of an ambush and never lose his cool.

To each his own burden, but being scared of just about everything didn't say much for a man, not when others might depend upon him. Well, Bobby thought, it shouldn't happen again, not with the elaborate pre-cautions the old man was setting up around the ranch house proper. And if some bunch of strung-out terror-ists over here began imitating Italian and German kidnappers, it could be the whole family would need personal bodyguards.

Shake it all and kick back, he told himself; let some-body else worry. Tonight was happy time for Pamela and himself, a ride into Travis City, a flick, couple of beers, then home to beddy-bye that made him glad he was married, especially to a woman like Pamela.

CHAPTER 37

Bobby came bouncing around from in back of the house, oiled and warm in his sweatsuit, a three-mile jog behind him. Well, two miles, anyway. But it was the time of year when everything felt right, smelled right, made good sense, and he reveled in being out, moving around. Being chairbound had its disadvantages, but clean and early summer air cleared them away.

There before him spread the panorama of a to-be Ewing barbecue, and Bobby grinned as he thought that no military operation had ever been planned with as much detail—or as much confusion. Trucks stretched down the entrance drive as workmen unloaded and began to set up a dance floor, a bandstand, their hammers drumrolling a call to arms. There'd be another platoon out of sight around the garden, cleaning the pool and manicuring Miss Ellie's flowers.

A Sticking Out Party; Bobby laughed out of pure exuberance, out of this growing wonder he had helped create in his wife. Beautiful; damn, everything was beautiful, even though he knew his father would talk business and twist arms and call in favors from every political hack and lobbyist invited to the big bash. JR'd be working as hard trying to set up new connections, to grease any palm. It was always thus, at a Ewing barbecue, but this year the politicking would be more frantic.

At last, Jock Ewing was accepting the fact that the company was under attack, a more serious challenge that it had ever faced, even in its infancy. Bobby had heard all the old stories about how Aritex muscle men had gotten shot up in the middle of the street, how a stubborn, dangerous Jock Ewing had beaten off all attempts at big oil takeover. But this enemy couldn't be fought so openly; a defeat here would mean the end of Ewing Oil, maybe of Lone Star, and at least a wide swath would be cut through Texas Independents. This time, it wasn't the industry giants that would catch the flak, but the little outfits. And indictments wouldn't mean a slap on the fanny, a fine or two; some of these would be criminal, and somebody would do time.

"Oh damn," Jock Ewing said behind him, "you look like you been runnin' around in your long drawers. You oughta been around when we had to wear them things to keep warm."

"And what are you doin' hauling that case of whiskey, Dad? Here, let me give you a hand. You ought to be resting up for the big reunion."

Jock snorted. "I expect I got enough left to tote a case of my best bourbon, since I can't trust nobody else with it, and as for that so-called reunion—"

"Just try to act the civilized host. It won't break your back to be nice to my in-laws, this once."

Eyebrow lifted, Jock said, "Damned if you don't rear up on your hind legs a heap lately."

"Just practicin' to be a daddy," Bobby said. "Ain't that somethin'?"

Jock grinned. "Damned if it ain't, and I'll bet ol' Digger's chompin' at the bit. Don't know, though; he never paid a whole lot of attention to his own kids when they were little. Always runnin' off and leaving 'em."

"Different man," Bobby said. "If you'd been a wild-cat driller, how would you have worked it, stayed home and worked long distance?

"Know what one of the hammer-headedest things in the whole wide world is, boy? It's a young stud just comin' into his own and stompin' around the herd. Now, just you haul your struttin' somewheres else afore this case of whiskey gives me splints and spavins and a bad case of swayback too."

Bobby smiled after him, because the old man seemed in high spirits and willing to accept facing his ancient enemy, Digger Barnes. Then Bobby lost his grin, because he remembered that he'd have to corner his father, get him away from JR long enough to really explain the trouble the company was in.

In his son's apartment, Digger Barnes felt backed into a corner, felt like a drink. He also felt like a fool in his only suit, it smelling of mothballs and still kind of rumpled. It had been quite a spell since he wore it; drillers made do with jackets and jeans. He watched the kids swirl around Cliff's apartment and it was like he didn't know them, never really had. True enough where that gangly youngun was concerned, Jimmy Monahan; boy was supposed to be his nephew, or grandnephew by marriage.

"You got a drink, Cliff? Just a beer, maybe—somethin' to wet down an old man's throat. Come, fill the cup, for the bird of time has but a little way to flutter —or somethin' like that."

"Now, Daddy," Pamela said, "you can just hold off until you get to the barbecue, and I swear, if I see you gettin' smashed there, I mean to just haul you off. Eat somethin' and drink slowly, okay? Migod—where did you get that tie?"

She opened a closet and studied Cliff's ties on a rack. "Here's a nice blue job."

"My *best* silk?" Cliff hovered close by.

"Why don't *you* wear it to the party, then?"

"No way, and you know it. If anybody saw me hobnobbing with that man—"

"Daddy's going, and if there's any grudge to be carried, surely *he*—"

"He hates Jock Ewing's guts just as much as I do, more even. Dad's just going along with you so you'll get off his back about his grandkid. You're using that unborn baby as blackmail, Pammy."

"You're damned right I am—Cliffie. Anything to get those two stubborn old men together again. I want my baby to know both his grandpas."

Digger ran a finger inside his collar. "Can't he know 'em one at a time? I mean, I still hate that thievin' old bastard. Wasn't enough he robbed me blind, but he come within a froghair of killin' me with a wrench. Couldn't stand to me like a man, had to grab hold of a spanner."

"Daddy," Pamela said, "take off that awful tie and put on this one."

"He had a head on him, I'll give him that," Digger said. "Smart—he was always plenty smart, but he didn't have my nose for oil. I *found* the goddamned oil and he claimed it; I drilled and he peddled what came bubblin' up."

The Monahan boy said, "How did Mr.—how did Jock Ewing do you out of your part?"

"Partners—we were partners, one needin' the other, and I trusted him."

Cliff Barnes poured two shots of whiskey, and in spite of Pamela's warning frown, passed one to his father. "And Ewing stole your share."

"Wasn't all he stole," Digger mumbled. "I never said much before, but Ellie and me—well, Jock got her, too. Him and his money that she needed for the ranch."

Pamela stared. "You and—and Miss Ellie?"

"That so damned hard to believe?" Digger licked his lips and looked at his empty glass, but nobody moved to refill it. "She was straight as a saplin', with a great big laugh to her; sweet one minute, come at you with a buggy whip the next. Have I not in pitched battle heard . . . neighing steeds and trumpet clang . . . and do you tell me of a woman's tongue? . . . or somethin' like that. She had a temper, but there was such deep, rich honey to her—"

"Daddy," Cliff said, "stay here with me. Don't go out there today and let them humble you."

Pamela snapped at her brother, and Jimmy Monahan moved back a step. "Daddy's not goin' to be humiliated, and he's goin' to stay sober. If he hangs around with you, you'll let him get stoned, or help him do it."

Sitting down on the couch, Digger said slowly, "Must—must be somethin' to what they got, my little girl and Jock's boy. She picked him, Pamela did, and she ain't picked too many losers—besides me. And son, I gave her my word. That's about all I got that means anything now—except you-all, of course."

She came to kiss his cheek, to hold him. Eyes misting, she backed off and said to the Monahan boy, "Two hours, Jimmy, and drive carefully. If Dad had his license—"

"And didn't have to use my car," Cliff said.

Pamela said between her teeth, "Hang it up, sorehead. Daddy, Jimmy—see you at the barbecue."

"Along with every crooked politician in the state."

She said, "No running dogs of imperialism? Come on, Cliff, your dialogue's gettin' hackneyed."

Sue Ellen wandered among the tables, rearranging a flower here, a spray of fern there. She felt light and airy, almost as if she was on stage again, looking out into the mass of upturned and worshipping faces, hearing the bright thunder of applause come smashing down around her. The scent of flowers was heady, not as exciting as the musk of a man's sweat, but close, close. She had a smile for every workman who passed her, and delighted in seeing the light of need spring up in each man's eyes.

"Hi, Sue Ellen," Pamela said, crossing the newly installed dance floor. "My, the flowers are lovely; you have a special flair for picking and arrangin' them."

"Yes," Sue Ellen said, "don't I? Tell me somethin', will you? When you're pregnant, does that mean you stop doin' it?"

Catching her breath, Pamela said, "Not right away, not until the last couple of months, in fact."

"That's good. I feel sorry for any guy who gets cut off like that—or any woman."

Pamela looked at her, this young woman so beautiful and so changed of late. "I—I guess so. I'll get inside now and see what else needs to be done."

At the porch, she crossed paths with Lucy. The girl looked good, somehow more mature and calmer. Lucy said, "When's your daddy and cousin comin'?"

"How'd you know about Jimmy?"

Tossing her long, glittery hair, Lucy said, "Bobby told me. Said you were bringing somebody special for me."

"Wait a minute," Pamela said, "he didn't imply I was setting you up with Jimmy, did he?"

"Just said I might dig him. He's nineteen, right?"

"Wrong; next to you he's a baby. But I guess you have to start sometime—goin' with kids your own age, I mean."

"Sure you meant that," Lucy grinned. "What else? I'll go real easy on him, Auntie."

Pamela watched the girl skip down off the porch, and went in search of Miss Ellie. But when she found her, all Pamela could do was stand aside and watch the woman, thinking of what Digger had said, thinking that if some things had been different, Miss Ellie might have been her mother.

Sliding from sight, she went out through the bustling, terrific-smelling kitchen and crossed the backyard to her own home. Inside, she heard the shower going, opened that door, and yelled in that she was home.

"Great!" Bobby said. "I'll be out in a second, and you'll have to take me as is—wet and drippy."

"I'll take you any way I can get you," Pamela answered, "but what makes you think drippy is different?"

"Hah-hah!" he said, wiping at himself with a big fluffy towel as he came into the bedroom. Bobby smelled of soap and cleanliness. "You have insulted the great screwing Ewing, and now you must pay the penalty."

"Any time after *I* get a shower," she said, kissing him on his nose when he leaned over her. "Speaking of screwing Ewings—what's gotten into Sue Ellen? She's turning on every male that gets near her."

"Maybe JR's doing his homework."

"Uh-uh. He's home even less than he used to be. And I get these vibes from him; I think he actually hates her since the rape. Would you hate *me*, Bobby?"

"Hell, no! Why should I? Darling, I wouldn't, *couldn't*, hate you if you went out and balled on your own. I might take a few inches of skin off that beautiful butt, but I wouldn't hate you."

She put her arms around his neck, fretful that her expanded tummy didn't let her get quite close enough. "You're the best, Bobby—just the very best there is."

"I know, I know," he said, and patted her tummy. "Go take that shower, so I can prove it again."

Guests began arriving early in the evening. This time, Jock had outdone himself. An electric tram met the visitors, who had to park some distance away, and shuttled them to the house. Strings of yellow lights did double duty, casting a soft glow, and discouraging wandering moths and mosquitoes. Black and Mexican waiters moved among the guests with trays of drinks, and against the house, the orchestra stayed with soft background music for the moment.

Ray Krebs was dressed in his best, and making certain to stay out of range of any popping grease at the barbecue pit where a whole steer turned, basting slowly upon a massive iron spit. He wouldn't be here, but for this overseer's job, and the knowledge of that irked him. He was hired help, and never would cross that forbidden line into family—not unless he married into the Ewings. Not too bad an idea, he thought, nodding to his date as she sat waiting at a small table.

It didn't count that he was sticking it to Sue Ellen as often as she snapped her fingers, and that was pretty damned often. But what that woman made him do— he felt the bitter taste threaten to fill his mouth, and swallowed. It wouldn't be Sue Ellen, even if JR was to drop dead tomorrow. She'd gone out of her mind ever since that cropper put the meat to her. It was like she had an itch she'd never be able to scratch hard or long enough, but she was surer than hell going to keep trying.

He frowned and motioned to Raoul to baste the steer some more, and watched the Mex swab dark and bloody-looking sauce over the sizzling meat. It wasn't only him that Sue Ellen was balling; he knew of at least two ranch hands, and one of them a Mex, to boot. If there was any way out, he'd take it in a hurry, because Miss Hotass Texas was bound to get caught with her drawers down before long, and Ray Krebs didn't want to be the stud she got nailed with. He'd as soon stay a stud, not be turned into a gelding.

Jolene waved at him and he bobbed his head at her, took a good long drink of the mint julep he carried, then strolled slowly to her table. Where the tram was unloading, Miss Ellie played the gracious hostess, howdying every arrival and making them feel she'd been waiting just for them. Sue Ellen stood close by, nipples damned near exposed in a low-cut, gauzy dress, and JR all puffed up beside her. How'd old JR like it if he knew that his beautiful wife was going down on a common ranch foreman?

"Hey, girl," he said to Jolene, "let me get you another drink—well, I'll be damned! Looky yonder—if that ain't old man Barnes climbin' down from that electric choo-choo; *Digger Barnes.*"

"Who's he?" Jolene asked.

"Not much," Ray said, "only a Hatfield come visitin' the McCoys."

"Hatfield?" Jolene said, and Ray said, "Oh, shit—which is what's about to hit the fan, no matter how Pamela tries to keep everything cool."

Jolene rattled ice in her glass and said, "You're still tore up because your old flame got pregnant, right? Time to cut your own navel cord, boy. Pam's got clean away from you now."

"Yeah," he said morosely, "and if she somehow heals up this old sore between Digger and Jock, there's liable to be changes around here."

"And you one of 'em?" she asked.

"Not until I'm good and goddamned ready," Ray said. "You hear that, woman? Not until *I'm* ready to move on."

Pamela and Bobby moved across the grounds from their house, saying hi to folks they knew, stopping to speak with those one of them didn't. Looking over some heads, Bobby said, "There's your father. I'd better bust through this mob and stand by him, just in case."

"I'll go with you," Pamela said, but Lucy appeared at her elbow, in a dress all ruffles and lace, looking demure. Pamela said, "You look cute."

"Cute's not my first choice, but Grandma insisted— hey, where you goin', and where's that promised young dude?"

"Hang on," Pamela said, as she eased through swirls of people, saying yes, yes, how nice, but with her eyes ahead, focused upon Digger Barnes, just now saying hello to Miss Ellie.

CHAPTER 38

Lucy moved around the edges of the crowd, feeling a little stupid in this dress that was too young for her and not seeing any young people. All this hoopla about Pamela's baby. Lucy grinned; there'd have been a lot more if *she* was having the kid. Miss Ellie never questioned her charge account at the drugstore, so

long as it didn't go too high, so Lucy was still on the
pill, although she hadn't had much to protect against,
of late.

There was JR, standing tall and holding in his belly,
smirking and strutting with his arm around a good-
looking girl not more than a few years older than
Lucy. God, how she hated him for what he was and
what he'd done, but nothing she came up with had
bothered him even a little bit. She still wasn't there,
or worth only a "Hi, kid." What a two-faced fink. She
stood looking at him, watching the *accidental* play of
his hand over the young girl's hip, the inclination to
stray up along her rib cage and ease close to a conical
breast.

She walked straight to him, a phony smile hung on
her face, her eyes like cut and polished sapphires,
colorful but cold. "Hello there—Uncle JR."

"Hey, kid. Polite kid, ain't she, Susan? Lucy, this
here is Susan Stratford, new in the Dallas office. Ah—
I see my wife comin' across the yard yonder. Lucy,
honey, will you kind of guide Susan around for a
while? I'll find you again."

The woman was in some clinging thing that called
attention to every dip and curve; she had soft auburn
hair and an open face with violet eyes. Lucy said,
"Two to one Bobby Ewing didn't hire you."

Susan smiled, a double row of polished pearls.
"However did you know? JR hired me from a bunch
of girls the personnel manager sent up."

"Good ol' JR. Still has his eye, hasn't he?"

"I beg your pardon," Susan said, but Lucy was already gone, slipping through the crowd. Susan Stratford was left alone, holding an empty glass, smiling
her empty smile.

Digger Barnes and Jimmy Monahan alighted from
the tram. Digger grumbled, "Feel like a kid ridin' a
toy train. What the hell we have to do that for?
Couldn't walk up the road?" He looked at the crowd,
at so damned many people come to a party, and tried

to pick out Pamela or even Bobby Ewing, and failed to find either.

Fidgeting while folks pushed on by, Digger stood where he was until Jimmy nudged him forward. "Don't know about you, Unc," the boy said, "but I can smell that barbecue from here, and I'm some thirsty, too. Nobody's goin' to ask for my ID here."

Digger saw her then.

It had to be her; nobody else stood so straight and held her chin high like that. The hair—yellow lantern light couldn't bring back all its precious gold, but the hair was Ellie Southworth's. She'd changed, grown old, and that sent a quick spearhead of pain through him, a sense of being cheated of the laughing, flashing-eyed girl who lived in a treasured corner of his mind. Digger's fingertips lifted to his own face and traced the network of wrinkles there.

Over the heads of the crowd, between moving figures, her eyes found his, and there she was again—the young, lively girl of a thousand years ago. She was bright and beautiful, and he went to meet her, a runaway engine laboring in his chest.

They might have been alone on a misty hilltop set against sunrise, two people moving slowly together, hearing old music worn thin by being rubbed against the edges of swiftly passing years.

"Hello, Willard," she said.

Digger said, "Ellie."

"You look—"

"Tacky," he said. "Uncomfortable. But you—ah, you still hold the starshine captive, and shame the moon."

Her laugh was as he remembered, throaty but holding the silver pealing of far temple bells in it. "And you're still the poet, for which I thank you, Willard."

Ellie's hand was in his, small and capable, softer even than he recalled. Digger kept looking at her until the kid bumped his other arm and said something about going on to the barbecue and Digger said, "Yeah, yeah, go ahead."

"Let's take a walk," Ellie said. "Nobody can begrudge us a little time together."

"The rose arbor," Digger said. "I remember the rose arbor."

"Yes," Ellie said. "It's lasted as long as we have."

Pamela excused herself from a group when she saw Jimmy Monahan approaching. "Hi—where's Digger? Is he—all right?"

The boy pointed a thumb back over his shoulder. "Nervous as a jackrabbit at a bobcat convention, but sober. With some old lady that calls him Willard. Is that Digger's real name—Willard?"

Pamela's smile was at once tender and sad. "Yes, but nobody ever called him that, since I can remember. They're slicing meat over there, and the waiters have all kinds of soft drinks, too. If you see a pretty little blonde girl in a frilly dress, that's Lucy, the one I was telling you about."

Lucy saw the young guy coming and set herself in his way. This must be Pamela's cousin, because he was the youngest dude she'd seen here tonight. She made her smile sultry and struck her model's pose, one foot forward. He surprised her by not looking down, bypassing her for the barbecue tables.

"Damn," Lucy said, "is the clown blind?"

Back in the kitchen, the black cook peeked out a window. "Sam," she said, "this herd is drinkin' more'n last year. Good thing you got them Mexes to pop corks and bust seals for you. Me, I got to chop up this other bowl of salad while you rests."

In a lower voice, she said, "You see Mister Jock settin' out there, crochety as an old hen? Already on his third cigar."

Sam said, "Millie—that's account of Digger Barnes is here. And what you talkin' about—Mexes? Them's *Hispanics*, woman."

"His-my foots," Millie said. "Who Digger Barnes?"

"That's right, you ain't been here all that long. He

the man liked to of married Miss Ellie first; bad blood
atween him and Mister Jock, and not all over her—
money, too. Bad mix, women and money."

"How you know?" Millie said. "You ain't never had
both at the same time. Now haul this salad out yonder
and give a hand to your *His*-my-foot-*spanics* before
they gets the idea house niggers thinks they better'n
yardboys. Play hell with race relations."

Sam laughed. "Mister Jock and Digger Barnes butt
heads, be playin' hell *amongst* relations."

Sue Ellen Ewing knew a lot of men were staring at
her as she leaned prettily upon the bar and admired
lantern reflections in her glass of bubbly. Older men
stopped and chatted with her, because they weren't
supposed to be in any danger. They didn't realize how
she was checking them out, filing the healthy-looking
ones for future reference. Sue Ellen smiled and nodded,
making a wager with herself that she could make the
oldest man's thing stand up. She glanced at the corner
of the house, where Jock leaned alone, sullenly drinking. Even his, she thought, and the very idea made her
laugh aloud.

A younger man brushed against her thigh, and she
gave somebody's husband a lingering, inviting look
from beneath heavily mascara-ed lashes, showed him
a lifting of firm melons that his wife couldn't match.
But they were all so many cowards, fearful of Jock
and JR, scared silly to stay too long with her, to whisper a proposition.

And everybody pretending to be enthralled with
Pamela. Big deal, carrying a little volleyball under her
dress. She didn't show all that much yet, and had the
nerve to call this barbecue her Sticking Out Party.
Good lord, how old Jock had lapped up the announcement, strutting around like he'd done the job himself.
Already talking about his grandson, so damned sure
it would be a boy and the heir to Ewing Oil.

Shit—if JR Ewing carried more than a couple of
peanuts between his legs, *she* could have given old

Jock a grandson a long time ago. But JR, the stupid bastard; *he* didn't see that he was losing out to Bobby more every day, losing out to Pamela and her unborn brat.

Her mother's fault, she thought bitterly, and took a fresh glass of champagne; all that stay-a-virgin crap, all that fidelity bullshit. If it wasn't for all that early programing, Sue Ellen Ewing could have read the omens and got herself knocked up by a lover—by Ray Krebs or one of the others—and who'd know the baby wasn't JR's?

Slick JR, sly JR—hiring on another pretty woman as secretary. She wondered what made Julie put him down and quit. This Susan would do the same probably, because if any of them ever got serious about JR, or demanded that lasting relationship, she could kiss ass. *No* woman was fixing to move Sue Ellen Ewing from her place.

Putting down an empty glass, she picked up a full one and rolled her hips enticingly as she moved in on her husband where he was playing up to a couple of state representatives. "JR?"

"Yes, honey?"

"If these darlin' gentlemen can spare you for just one little bitty minute—"

"Gentlemen," JR said and clamped her elbow too hard as he walked her away. "You're half-smashed; what the hell's wrong with you?"

"History, baby; history is wrong with me. Not the Alamo, but maybe Waterloo. Seems like they let ol' Napoleon run around for a while after Waterloo, but they chopped off his balls later, anyhow."

He shook her. "Don't you talk like that! Actin' so damned trashy—"

Pulling her arm away she said, "*You* better start actin' halfway smart! If Pamela has that *boy* your daddy wants so bad, guess who's goin' to be sittin' in the catbird seat at Ewing Oil? You're already losin' out to Bobby in the company."

JR wanted to knock her down. He said, "What do

you know about anything—except lipstick and powder and hair dye?"

"I know Bobby is cuttin' you out with the old man. How much attention have you paid to that Houston investigation? Bobby's brought it all to the old man. What have you done to protect Ewing Oil and your own dumb ass? Don't you realize the government can lock you up? I'm so pretty I'm supposed to be stupid, but what's *your* goddamned excuse?"

"Sue Ellen," he said, tight-voiced, "I swear I'll slap your dirty mouth if you keep on like that."

She braced hands upon her hips and stuck out her chin. "Like hell you will; you don't have the guts. So go screw yourself, turkey—*fuck you!*"

He was standing with his mouth open, helpless as if a mule had just belly-kicked him when Sue Ellen wheeled and left him to head directly for the bar again.

Under the rose arbor that hung the air like a scented mantle about them, Ellie and Digger Barnes sat in warm semidarkness, seeming to touch each other without actually doing so. Music reached them as was their due, one of the songs that had been theirs. The babble of voices might have been quickwet shouts made by a springtime freshet laughing over rocks, for they were miles from anyone else.

"It wasn't only the girl," Ellie said. "With you, I realized that sometimes there would be other women."

"Not because I wanted them," Digger said. "Not even because I needed them."

"I know, Willard. But you runnin' off to hide when you failed, when you brought in a duster—that wasn't the kind of man I could tie to. My daddy was a fighter, and I broke a promise made to him on his deathbed to give you those leases. Wait—" she said, as he started to protest, "—if not you, I'd have had to sell them to somebody else. My daddy didn't realize how desperate it all was, how I *had* to go back on my word to him or lose the whole place to the bank."

Out of their sight, the orchestra picked up a waltz, slow and classic. Digger pulled in a deep breath of roses and said, "So you married Jock Ewing, after I failed you. Of all the times for my luck to go wrong—"

She sat quietly and he thought Ellie's own special scent would shame the roses. He said, "I never seemed to have any luck since. Oh, a few little strikes, but more losers than winners. It was like I lost interest."

Ellie said then, "Jock wanted to marry me and had the money to back the ranch. I could have made a worse bargain. The *land*, Willard; it's somethin' you never understood. Generations of Southworths are buried here, and I mean to be the next. Our blood and sweat, our joys and sorrows—they're part of this land, and the land is part of us. That's what you didn't understand, that I had to have a man to stay here with me. You would never have done that, Willard."

"No," he said softly, "reckon I wouldn't. I still get the itch sometimes, only now it's all too late and too far away. Jock—he been good to you?"

"It's a good marriage, always has been. We pull in different directions sometimes, but it's good."

The roses smelled dusty now and the music dragged slow and mournful. "Well then," Digger said.

"You—we—have a beautiful daughter, Willard, and she'll give us beautiful grandchildren."

"Christ," Digger said, "Pamela should have really been ours, but damn—oh damn."

She put her hand upon his, unerring in the near dark. "I think about you; always have, always will. You were my first love, and it's not many women who can look back on a poet, too."

Digger swallowed and the roses smelled of ashes. How the hell could they do that?

"Best we be gettin' back," Ellie said. "We're not too old for gossip, I expect."

At a barbecue table, Lucy Ewing sat down next to Jimmy Monahan. "Hi, I'm Lucy."

He wiped his mouth. "Pretty blonde in a frilly dress."

"Oh, you noticed."

"I was told. Pamela said you were around somewhere."

Lucy took a couple of bites from her piled-high plate. "Didn't see you dancin'."

"With any of *those* old ladies?"

"After we eat, we could get it on."

Jimmy chewed thoughtfully. "Shake up all the little old ladies and little old men. Better just stay cool tonight."

Lucy kept checking him out; he was tall and good-looking and sort of laid back. He was older than the kids at school, too. "You in college? You got anything going with a girl?"

After a sip of beer, he looked at her. "Yes and no. Yes to school, no to anything meaningful with a lady."

Lucy made a face. "A *lady*? I wonder if you've ever balled a *girl*. You dig girls, don't you? I mean, you're not gay?"

"Are you?"

Lucy's eyes snapped wide and she stuttered, then discovered he was laughing at her. "Oh hell," she said, and joined in the laugh.

At another table, all the way down at the end, Ray Krebs poked at his plate and Jolene said, "Hey now; we're settin' with the white folks, so act like it."

"Sorry," he said. "You see ol' Jock climb up on the bandstand and holler it out for everybody to hear? Like no woman in the world ever had a baby before."

She drank some beer. "None of your old flames ever had one?"

"All right, so it got to me."

Jolene refilled their glasses from a pitcher. "I can get to you, too. So don't tell me no sad stories, cowboy."

Back at the bar, Sue Ellen was holding court, and

this time some sharp-eyed wives stood with their men, nudging each other and vacuuming in every word to repeat later. Sue Ellen was drunk; everytime she waved her champagne glass, she spilled some. Then she drank some, and when the glass was empty, reached for a filled one.

"Know I shouldn't have got on his back; works hard, my JR. *My* JR—hah! Anybody's JR *but* mine. Damnit—a wife's got needs, too. Right, ladies? Right? I admit it. Look at me, ladies—your husbands sure as hell are. I look good because I work at it, diet and exercise and I haven't gained one pound of fab—flab since I was Miss Texas. But you old bats wouldn't know about bein' Miss Anything, would you?"

"Come on, Joe," a woman said. "This is too much."

"Yay!" Sue Ellen said behind them, waving her glass. "That's the answer, baby. I'm just too much— too much for sneaky ol' JR or anybody else. You hear that? *Anybody* else. You don't b'lieve me, just ask ol' —ask ol' lover boy over there—oops! But that'd be tellin', wouldn't it?"

Then she gasped in pure shock as a black waiter stumbled and grabbed uselessly at tumbling drinks. Icy liquids sprayed down Sue Ellen's front and the waiter stood helpless, mumbling apologies.

"Goddamn you," she said. "Gimme that towel, you clumsy bastard." Dabbing at her ruined dress, she said sweetly then: "You all *will* excuse me? I'll be back to regale you with torrid tales of the Ewings, soon's I change my dress."

"Sorry again, ma'm," said Sam.

In the kitchen, Millie raged at him. "Damned if'n you ain't the beatinest nigger—what you do that for? One of them drunk honkies coulda busted you good, and wasn't no cause of your'n to keep her from sayin' who she's layin'."

"Cause for Mister Jock," Sam said. "He always treated us good. Maybe she'll pass out, time she gets upstairs."

"Sam, Sam," Millie said, "you'd been right to home, saying' Marster and shufflin' and eatin' watermelons."

"Don't run off at the mouth to me, woman," he said. "Right's right, and got no color to it."

CHAPTER 39

Standing not exactly between them, but close enough to separate them, Ellie said, "Jock, we have a new guest and an old friend."

Across a gulf of many years, a chasm littered by brittle shards of hate, the two men looked at each other.

Ellie said, "Remember, you share a bond now: Pamela's baby."

"Boy," Jock said, looking into Digger's eyes. "A boy, bigod."

"Damned right," Digger said, "for the first one."

"Shows you ain't lost all your good sense," Jock said.

And Digger said, "Shows you mighta picked up some good sense along the way."

"You want a drink, make a toast to the grandson?"

"On the wagon, damnit. Promised Pam to stay sober. I'll take a Coke or somethin'. It ain't like bustin' champagne on a ship's bow. Pam's got to do the launchin' all by herself."

"Well, hell," Jock said. "You swear off eatin', too? I make up that barbecue sauce myself."

"Guess I'll try it out," Digger said.

They had gone as far as they would for now, Ellie knew, and didn't crowd them by insisting they shake hands. Instead, she came between them and took an arm of each. "I'm hungry myself," she said, "and no woman here will have two such handsome escorts."

It wasn't easy for Ellie to make small talk, but she rattled on—about the ranch, how Pamela was redoing a room in the little house for the baby's nursery, the new crop of foals—anything to keep it going. They were served and found a reasonably clean area at one of the tables. She kept an eye on Jock, sensing that he was nowhere near sober as he appeared.

Jock said, "Don't know about you, Digger, but I been ready for this youngun a long time. JR kind of disappointed me and Gary—well, Gary's kid ain't quite the same."

"I never thought on it much," Digger said.

Licking at his fingers, Jock put down a gnawed rib and poured a drink from one of several bottles on the table. "Sure you ain't havin' any? Well, here's to the boy, anyhow. That kid's goin' to have everything, and I mean everything."

Fiddling with his glass of cola, Digger said, "No sense spoilin' him, right off."

"Time somebody around here got spoiled. Lucy— she's a little pampered and doin' all right." He poured another drink.

Ellie said, "Your sauce is great, Jock. Aren't you hungry?"

"Can't get the kid a Shetland; mean little bastards, Shetlands. A P.O.A., maybe; then when he outgrows one of them pint-sized Appys, a *good* horse. Might keep him away from Hondas, but if a Honda's what he wants—"

Digger said, "No, goddamnit!"

Blinking at him, Jock said, "No, what?"

"No, you're not goin' to take it all. Not twice."

Ellie said, "Now, Willard—"

And Digger said, "My daughter in your house; my woman. All stuck together with my money. You ain't goin' to jump claim on my grandson, too, and I don't give a damn if his name *is* Ewing!"

Jock tossed back his drink. "Whine and cry—that's what you're good at. Besides tellin' damned lies."

"Lies—*lies?*"

"About how I robbed you, swindled you out of millions. Every barfly in Dallas and Muleshoe County knows the story by now. Well, it's all bullshit, and you damned well know it. Millions—hell! When you and me split up, you got every damned dime comin' to you and then some. You never looked beyond tonight's drunk and tonight's woman, and you pissed away more money than I was able to save."

"How about that big strike—" Digger was standing now, backed away from his chair. People nearby had stopped talking to watch and listen.

"*My* strike, *my* investment, *my* money. You show me a paper with your name on it, and I'll pay you off everything that field brought in, plus interest for all these years."

Digger was shaking. "We was partners, didn't need any papers—"

"We were partners *before* that strike," Jock said, also rising to his feet. "When I paid you off, that was it for you. Steal, hell! If I'd wanted your money all I had to do was watch you get drunk and take it all away playin' poker. That's what other hustlers did."

"You—you lie, goddamnit," Digger said. "Everybody knows—"

"Con yourself," Jock said coldly, "because you've told that lie so long you believe it now. Gives you an excuse for failure. Digger Barnes, you never needed an alibi for failin'—you been a loser all your life, and every day you live you just go on provin' it."

Ellie said in the stretched silence, "Jock, there was no need to go so far."

Lip curling, Jock poured yet another drink. He saw Bobby and Pamela's stricken faces on the edge of the crowd, and saluted them with his glass. "Why not, Ellie? Everybody's heard *his* side of the story so long, it's time they got to hear mine."

He drank and with a quick, powerful slash, broke

the glass on the edge of the table and scattered the pieces. "Here's to truth." Then Jock Ewing walked away.

Pamela put one hand over her slightly swollen belly and glared around at the interested spectators. They melted back and away, and she said to Bobby, "I can't stand this. I won't."

Going to Digger, she said, "You all right, Daddy?"

"Sure, why not? Since I'm such a welcome guest here, I'd just as soon have me a drink, yessir—a big ol' drink. Like the man said—I wonder what the vintner buys, half so precious as that he sells. Or somethin' like that."

"No, Daddy," Pamela said. "Please don't drink—"

Bobby took her arm. "It's his choice, darlin'. It's always *his* choice."

Ellie said, with a catch in her voice, "Willard, oh Willard."

"Don't recall anybody by that name, ma'm," he said, and drank hugely. "Ain't nobody here but us Diggers."

Turning into the circle of Bobby's arms, Pamela said, "He—he destroyed him, in front of Miss Ellie and everybody else, just cruelly and totally destroyed my daddy. He d-didn't *have* to, Bobby."

He stroked her back, her hair. "I know."

Into his chest she said, "I can't stay here; I won't stay here and see his gloating face over and over again."

"All right," Bobby said, looking at Digger Barnes, at the paleness of his mother. "Okay, baby, we'll move out tonight."

Ellie said, "Don't tell Jock tonight. He's drinkin' too much, and you'll only make it worse." She watched Digger stride off into the crowd, carrying a bottle. "*He'll* make it worse, too. He always did."

"You're not blamin' us for moving out?" Bobby asked.

"You're a man and woman grown," Ellie answered. "Maybe I tried to hold you all too close. It's the land, Bobby; the land won't let go its own."

He nodded at her and started Pamela away from the mob, walked her toward their small house hidden behind the row of trees. It meant a lot to his mother, to have her brood around her, to try and bind them to the land as she was tied. It hadn't worked with his brother Gary, and if the Southworth land would claim Bobby Ewing, it would have to wait a long time.

Pamela stopped. "Listen. Oh God, it's Daddy singin' 'The Yellow Rose of Texas.' He'll be dancin', too—all by himself. Makin' a bigger fool of himself, a clown for them all to laugh at."

"It didn't take him long to get a bag on," Bobby said.

"He hasn't had a drink for a while, and when he's had a dry spell, the first ones hit him hard and quick. But he won't seem any drunker all night—until he passes out."

"Want me to scoop him up, take him back to Dallas with us?"

She shook her head and brushed at blurred eyes. "N-no, but thanks. He may try to fight you. I can usually make him listen. Why don't you pack whatever we might need right away. I'll find Jimmy Monahan and have him drive Daddy back, put him to bed." Then, more softly: "Is it so wrong to not love your father sometimes?"

"Not wrong," he answered. "It doesn't come automatically."

Digger was cutting up, the hub of a circle of laughing people who urged him on. He sang and danced, and stopped to recite solemn poetry, punctuating every line with a drink from his bottle. Pamela just couldn't force herself to break through the crowd and make yet another scene. Jimmy, she thought; she would first find Jimmy and have him ready to guide Digger to the car. Maybe her father would be too drunk to argue by then.

She found a chair, stood upon it to look over the crowd, but didn't see Lucy and Jimmy. The stables, she thought; Lucy might be showing off her horsemanship, trying to impress Jimmy. Climbing down with a little grunt, she headed for the barn, for the stables wing.

In the hayloft, Lucy said, "You got it all together, lover? You look decent and true blue and young Joe College?"

"Yeah," Jimmy answered, "but you've got hay in your hair and your dress is buttoned wrong."

"Damn," she said, "take care of my hair while I— Pamela's passin' down there, and she's sure to check up here. Wonder how come she's lookin' for us?"

Brushing at her bright hair, Jimmy said, "Maybe it's not us, and we can get it on again."

She grinned at him. "For Mister Cool, you sure get turned on."

"You could turn on Dallas and Fort Worth, and still have enough left over to light up Waco."

"Thanks," Lucy said. "Now try lookin' dumb and innocent. Pamela—oh, Pamela! Are you searching for us?"

Looking up, Pamela said, "For Jimmy."

Winking over her shoulder at him, Lucy said, "He's hidin' up here somewhere. Can you *believe* hide and seek? Come on up and help me."

"I can't," Pamela said, "and he's got to carry Digger home."

"It may take me a while, huntin' by myself. I mean, you give *some* boys a little ol' beer, and they freak right out."

"All right," Pamela said, not sensing the put-on because she was tired and angry and, most of all, sad. She had only a little trouble climbing the ladder to the loft.

Lucy said, "You didn't really believe hide and seek?"

"Jimmy," Pamela said, "this isn't so damned funny. I need you."

Miffed, Lucy said, "You should have been here a little while back. Ray Krebs and Jolene were gettin' it on, right down there in the empty stall. You do remember Ray?"

"Don't act bitchy," Pamela said, patting a handkerchief to her sweaty forehead as her tummy grew a busy little wave inside. "I don't give a damn what you guys were doin' up here. I just need Jimmy now. Get him into the car, Jimmy; Digger ought to be on the verge of passing out. Please drive him home and tuck him in."

"Sure," Jimmy said, contrite. "Later, Lucy."

"Not too much later, huh?"

"No way," he said, vanishing down the ladder.

Lucy said, "Want me to help you down, or something? You don't look too good."

"Just a dizzy spell. I'll be okay. You go ahead."

"You sure?"

"Just a little rest," Pamela said.

The small arena lay below and left of the stables, floodlights on because Sue Ellen Ewing was putting on a show of her own. High heels veed under the stirrups, slinky gown blowing back over her rounded knees, Sue Ellen was cantering a horse around and around.

At the far fence, Bobby pulled up the Mercedes and jumped out. "Sue Ellen, you damned fool! If you get a foot hung—"

"Who'll care? Stand back, Bobby—all you other folks—I'm about to do the first striptease from the back of a horse. You reckon Lady Godiva undressed *before* she got on her horse?"

Elbowing his way through a small, drunken group at the fence, JR said angrily, "What's this? Woman, what the *hell* are you—"

Sue Ellen pulled up the horse and almost lost her balance. She said, "Well, now—at least you admit I'm a woman."

"Why didn't you stop her?" JR said, noticing Bobby across the arena. "And the rest of you—get on out of here!"

"Meant to," Bobby said, "but she was lopin' that horse pretty good and I might have spooked him."

Sue Ellen laughed. "You'd have got a good look at some real legs, little brother; and I'm not wearin' panties, so you'd have seen a whole lot more—"

"Shut up, Sue Ellen!" JR snapped. "You've always been a *good* woman, not like—"

"Like who?" She swayed in the saddle and the horse did a jittery side pass. JR and Bobby both ducked through the rails and came to her. JR said, "Like Bobby's old lady, damnit! You're not that kind."

"Help her down," Bobby said, and took the reins to lead the horse to the fence and tether him there. When he walked back to the center of the ring, JR was shaking Sue Ellen and saying something into her face.

Bobby said, "My wife; what kind is she, JR?"

"You know," JR said. "Everybody knows."

Bobby nodded, and pivoted off his right heel and the ball of his left foot to drop a left hook into his brother's belly. Sue Ellen yelped as JR went wheezing down, then struggled back to his feet, holding his belly. Bobby chopped a short right hand to the head, and JR went down again.

Sue Ellen said, "Don't—don't kill him."

"It's an idea," Bobby said.

"Just let the son of a bitch sit there," Sue Ellen said. "If you'll help me to the house, I'll get out of everybody's hair, go to bed." She held out her hand and Bobby took it; they left without looking back.

JR struggled up and brushed at his pants, his jacket sleeves. His belly ached, but nothing like the side of his head. Goddamn—who'd figure Bobby to hit that hard? JR teetered, caught himself, and made it to a horse trough where he splashed water on his face. He felt some better when he left the horse for one of the hands to unsaddle, and walked around the stables.

There was a shaft of light from some car pulling out early, and he looked up to see her sitting in the hayloft window, the woman who turned his brother against him, who was about to give the old man a grandchild.

What was Lucy, then—some nothing to be forgotten? Jock would marry her off to some red-neck rancher and that would be it. If there was to be a rightful heir in this damned family, *Lucy* was it.

From where she sat, could Pamela have seen what happened in the arena? Something else to gossip about to his mother, another way to point up Bobby's strength and JR's weakness to his father.

Going into the stables, he walked down the alleyway and climbed the ladder into the hayloft. She was still looking out the window, forgotten floodlights from the arena dimly lighting that end of the loft. He said, "I always go too far."

Pamela flinched and turned around. "Oh, JR, you startled me."

"What I said was, I always go too far. Did you see what he did to me?"

"I—I didn't see anything." She started around him, but he moved to block her way. "Please," she said.

"Bobby knocked me down, twice."

"Because you always go too far?" The smell of whiskey hung heavily around JR, and she felt queasy again.

"Because of you."

She edged around him, stood near the ladder. "We're movin' out tonight, so there's less chance of it happening again."

JR touched his tender cheekbone and found a small cut. "You can't move out; it'll kill my mother; it'll split the family."

"Don't lay that trip on me," Pamela said, and reached for the ladder. "You, Jock, Sue Ellen—you're all a mess that's too late for cleanin' up."

JR snatched her wrist. "Damnit, I said—"

She didn't have time to scream. The fall was so quick and surprising, and the ground jumped up to slap her into blackness.

The living room was heavy with anticipation, with dread, and to even whisper in it seemed sacrilege. Jock leaned close to Ellie on the couch and said, "I got Doc Watkins and his nurse here quick as I could; motorcycle escort and all. It was quicker'n takin' her in to the hospital, and Doc Watkins is good; you know he's good."

"Yes," Ellie said. "You did all you could; now we wait." She reached over and gave Sue Ellen's thigh a vicious pinch. "Wake up! Drunk or not, you're goin' to be awake until we find out how bad Pamela's hurt."

Head lolling upon her neck, Sue Ellen wobbled up to lean against a window frame and stare out into the night. On the lawn, across the empty dance floor, servants were cleaning up debris. The yellow lanterns seemed out of place now.

Bobby Ewing came downstairs, moving slow and stiff; there was the look about his eyes and a thinned mouth.

JR said, "Dad—don't let him near me."

"She lost the baby," Bobby said, walking toward his brother.

Ellie stood between them, hands against Bobby's chest. "Bobby, don't! Don't make it worse than it is."

He stopped, but stared over her head at JR. "She went into the loft because of two crazy kids. What were *you* doin' there?"

Ashen, looking sick, JR said, "I was drunk; I—I felt bad, I thought I could patch things up. I swear, Bobby. Don't look at me that way, damn you—*don't*"

"The baby's gone," Bobby said in a monotone. "The doctor won't be sure if she can have another, not for some time."

Unexpectedly, Sue Ellen said from the window, "Stop it! JR wouldn't deliberately push her—"

"JR would do any damned thing," Bobby said, "to anybody. But not for much longer. I'm givin' you a break, big brother; I won't kill you until Pam tells me exactly what happened. But if it was how I think— you'd better start runnin' now. A good head start would give you a little better chance."

Ellie said, "Bobby Ewing, in my house—Cain and Abel—"

And Jock said, "There'll be no talk of killin'—"

The doctor came downstairs, and Bobby whipped around to him. Watkins said, "She's out of danger. Wouldn't hurt to move her to the hospital tomorrow, just in case. I'm leaving my nurse with her."

"Can I see her, Doctor? Is she conscious?"

Watkins nodded. "Good strong girl. Go ahead, but don't give her any more problems, and let her get some rest."

Up the stairs three at a time, Bobby darted into the bedroom. She lay in the bed, hair spread over a pillow, wan and drawn. He dropped to his knees beside the bed and gently took her hand.

She whispered, "I don't know why, but I feel like a-apologizing."

"It wasn't you, wasn't your fault. It's these—these damned vultures. You're goin' to the hospital in the mornin', and after that, we shake the dust of this hoodoo ranch off our feet."

From the doorway, Ellie said, "Please don't. It's been hard on both of you, but almost as hard on us. We weren't ready for any of it—Willard Barnes's daughter in the family—such a change in Bobby. Then the rape did awful things to Sue Ellen, and maybe to JR."

"JR," Bobby said.

"Whatever else he is, he's your brother," Ellie said. "If you kill him, you kill a part of yourself—and a part of me."

Pamela said, *"Kill* him, Bobby?"

"Yes," he said. "Yes, yes."

"It looks rich here," Ellie said, "and it is. But it wasn't this way all the time. I worked my tail off, stayed in the saddle till I fell off the damned horse, got calluses and rope burns and snakebite. My daddy did it before me, and his daddy before him. This land is *family* land, and if I don't keep my family together on it, all that work, those other generations—they were all for nothin'. Pamela, I need your help. Please help me."

Back straight and chin held high, Ellie Southworth Ewing walked from the room and closed the door.

Bobby said, "Did he shove you?"

Moistening her lips, Pamela said, "No. It—it was an accident."

"You—you still want to stay here? I mean, don't let my mother's speech get to you. Your daddy was cut up in little hurtin' chunks, and now our baby—"

"We'll have another," Pamela whispered, and drew his head over to her breasts. "No accidents next time, Bobby. I promise." Her words trailed off and her breathing grew deeper, slower.

Across the yard, Sue Ellen held to JR's arm as they stood in the door of the guest house. She said, "Did you push her?"

"No," JR said, conscious of the pistol's weight in his back pocket. "Hell no."

"But you're not sorry about the baby," Sue Ellen said. "And neither am I."

Before he followed his wife into the guest house, JR turned and looked up at the bedroom window. He saw a shadow in it, and moved back to duck in the door.

Upstairs in the big house, back to his sleeping wife, Bobby Ewing looked down for a while, then up and out, up and across the vastness of rolling lands he could not see in the night, but which he knew were there.

Which he would always know lay there.

Dell Bestsellers

STORMY SURRENDER

by Janette Radcliffe

author of *The Heart Awakens*
and *Hidden Fires*

Betrothed against her will, Lady Barbara
Grandison sailed from England to join the
fiance she loathed. When her ship was captured by an American vessel, Lady Barbara
was taken prisoner by the ship's fearless
captain Trent. The long days and storm-swept
nights at sea turned into a fiery love affair and
her dreaded enemy became her heart's desire.
From worlds apart they became prisoners of
destiny, captives of desire.

Dell $2.25

At your local bookstore or use this handy coupon for ordering:

★ ★ ★ ★ ★ ★ ★ ★ ★ ★ ★ ★ ★ ★ ★ ★ ★ ★ ★

A NOVEL
by Stirling Silliphant

★ ★ ★ ★ ★ ★ ★ ★ ★ ★ ★ ★ ★ ★ ★ ★ ★ ★ ★

In December of 1941, the Hawaiian island of Oahu seemed as close to Eden as any place, until the massive military destruction in the tropical paradise shook the world! PEARL focuses on six people who are permanently scarred by the event: a U.S. Army colonel and his wife; a woman obstetrician and an Army captain; and a Japanese-American girl and a young Navy flier. It is a novel of shattered lives, dreams and innocence, in one of the most crushing events in U.S. history—the bombing of Pearl Harbor!

Now a Spectacular ABC-TV movie!

A Dell Book • $2.50

No spirit was wilder,
No passion greater
In vengeance or
in love

Tarifa

by *Elizabeth Tebbets Taylor*

She was a beguiling child, a bewitching temptress.
Many men worshipped her, many loved her,
some even tried to tame her. But only one man
could possess her. Bart Kinkaid, a daring sea
captain saw past her dark desires to the burning
within. Like ships in a tempest-tossed sea, their
love soared beyond the boundaries of time itself.

A Dell Book $2.50

THE ODDS

the sizzling novel of a 20th century tycoon

by Eddie Constantine, author of <u>The God Player</u>

In 1939, in Nazi-run France, the penniless young son of a village whore began his odyssey of ambition . . .

Within a decade, Charles de Belmont was one of the richest financiers in the world. He'd loved the most beautiful, the choicest women. And controlled the most powerful—and dangerous—men.

He'd learned to play THE ODDS.

Dell $2.25